MW00577363

Crossroads of Darkover

Darkover® Anthology 18

Edited by

Deborah J. Ross

The Marion Zimmer Bradley Literary Works Trust
PO Box 193473
San Francisco, CA 94119
www.mzbworks.com

Cover design by Dave Smeds

ISBN-13: 978-1-938185- 52-6
ISBN-10: 1-938185-52-8

Dedication

To the memory of André Pereira (1988-2016)
loyal friend of Darkover

From the obituary written by his sister, uncorrected:

Andre always loved so much to read. He had so many books that sometimes his shelf wasn't enough. His favorite author, among a lot he read, was Marion Zimmer Bradley, and he owned a very rare collection of her books. As his reading of every books in Portuguese had ended, he started to read in English. He dominated the language easy, since a kid and that's why he translated freely for the Portuguese some books which only exist in English, for this way provide in the internet for those who cannot read in English. Yes, André was generous, not only in this, but in everything in his life.

Contents

Introduction

By Deborah J. Ross

Crossroads...the intersection of two paths...can be a harmonious joining or a disastrous collision. Crossroads can also mean a turning point, an event or decision that changes our lives forever. Darkover has from its inception been a place where paths intersect and cultures meet, where characters are transformed, and where choices cannot be undone. The contributors to this volume responded to the concept with an extraordinary and diverse array of interpretations. Some are perfectly in keeping with previous adventures on the world of the Bloody Sun, but others highlight contemporary concerns.

Besides being a consummate storyteller, Marion Zimmer Bradley had the ability to give voice to the issues of the day before their time. In publishing, that meant sensing what people would be concerned about no less than one to two years before it hit the headlines. The first Darkover novel, *The Planet Savers* (1958) centered on the political manipulation and sabotage of a planet's ecology. *The Heritage of Hastur*, which depicted a sympathetic, heroic gay protagonist, was published in 1975, a time when the gay rights movement had not yet gathered momentum. Likewise, her exploration of the roles, freedoms, and restrictions placed on women, *The Shattered Chain*, came out in 1976, the following year. Likewise, the authors of *Crossroads of Darkover* have not hesitated to tackle controversial themes. I am continually amazed and heartened how the imaginations of these gifted writers keep Darkover alive and relevant.

At this point in composing the Introduction to *Crossroads of Darkover*, I found myself drawn into listing the various stories that demonstrated the concept of "variations on a theme." I began with two examples of fields that Marion never delved into but which have contemporary relevance:

One author used her own expertise in physical anthropology, including investigating genocide, to create a protagonist who is a forensics expert. Another story featured a sociologist with particular interest in women's cultures.

With every anthology I've edited, I've seen a "meeting of minds." Certain themes recur perennially, but I also find a happy coincidence of unusual elements. For example, the telepathic, gender-fluid chieri appeal to many writers, and the Renunciates (Free Amazons or Comhi-Letzii), Dry Towns, and Towers have seen many adventures. This anthology is no exception, but this time the Ya-men, hardly ever mentioned before, make an appearance not once but twice.

As the anthology came together, a process in which it often seemed to have a mind of its own, patterns emerged that went beyond common themes. "The hunt for dead things" described several stories, the forensic scientist's analysis mentioned above, the search of ruins by a very different protagonist, basically a grave-robber, and the *laran*-Gifted heroine in a third tale. Another story echoed the theme of uncovering things perhaps better left hidden, only from the perspective of those who desperately wished to keep them secret.

As I continued writing in this vein, I realized that my descriptions were rapidly devolving into a listing of stories with little information about them except that they demonstrated a concept. Since I presumed the reader had not actually read these stories yet, my comments would likely have little to no meaning. When I am a panelist at a science fiction or fantasy convention, one thing I particularly loathe is an author holding forth on his or her *unpublished* work, as if all of us should be intimately familiar with it. This introduction is not precisely the same thing, but as I realized how uneasy I was becoming with the direction it took, I determined not to do the same thing to my own readers. Hence, the discerning reader will notice that I have not identified the stories referenced and that the list is woefully incomplete. I hope it is an amusing process figuring out (and anticipating!) which ones I meant—and the many I have left out will furnish delightful surprises.

As with previous anthologies, these stories span an enormous time period of Darkover's history, from the early settlements and origins of legend to the "modern" world, a part of a star-spanning family. Some are humorous, some tragic, some romantic, others gritty, but each is a gem in its own right, complete in itself yet adding to the richness that is Darkover.

Deborah J. Ross

The Short, Inglorious War

by Rebecca Fox

One of the sources of misunderstanding, not to mention outright culture clash, between Darkover and the Terrans is the Compact, a principle of honor that forbids all weapons that do not bring the person wielding them into equal risk. Swords are exempt, for instance, but distance weapons are banned. The Compact came about at the end of the Ages of Chaos (*The Fall of Neskaya, Zandru's Forge, A Flame in Hali*) in response to the horrors of *laran* weapons like clingfire and distance spells (see *Stormqueen* and its sequel, *Thunderlord*, for examples). The Terrans, not knowing this history, assumed the "primitive" people of Darkover were superstitious about technology. The firestorm arising from the Sharra matrix, which engulfed and destroyed the spaceport at Caer Donn, should have disabused them of this notion and demonstrated that the Compact was designed to eliminate weapons of mass destruction created by mental powers. The following tale illustrates how quickly humans forget, and how resourceful the Darkovans are at preserving their most dangerous secrets.

Rebecca (Becky) Fox is a Kentuckian by happy accident and an Arizonan by birth. She has sold short stories to a number of anthologies, and someday—if she can stop being distracted by horses, wild birds, Walt Disney World, and the Internet for long enough—she may actually finish a novel. In her "other life", she's a field biologist and an associate professor of biology at a private four-year college, and enjoys pointing out to her students that the dinosaurs are in fact alive and well and eating at your bird feeder. Becky shares her life with three parrots, a Jack Russell terrier who makes no secret whatsoever of being an evil genius in a dog suit, and a big goofy gray thoroughbred gelding who was once the world's worst racehorse.

On the last day of the last ten-day work period of the quarter, Jameson MacRorie came back from lunch twenty minutes early. Even though he'd already filed all of his required reports that morning, he couldn't seem to shake the nagging feeling that there was something he still needed to do.

When MacRorie came through the automatic doors leading into the wing occupied by the Office of Cultural Reconciliation and all who sailed in it, he stopped short and stood there for long enough that the doors buzzed at him to move. Every light in the office was blazing at full strength. After the dim light outside, it made his eyes water.

He'd expected to find CR dark and quiet like it always was during the lunch hour, except for perhaps a light in Miralys's office. Miralys often brought her lunch and ate it at her desk; she said the food in the commissary was too bland and too *Terranan* for her tastes. MacRorie had always rather suspected that she also had no desire to waste her break engaging in the absurd and sometimes exhausting rituals of Terran small talk. He couldn't really fault her there.

The office wasn't quiet, either.

"If you don't leave my office in the next fifteen seconds, I am calling Security. I don't give a damn—as you *Terranan* say—*who* you say you are." Miralys was practically spitting with fury. In the nearly-vacant space, her voice carried easily. After five years of working side by side with Miralys, MacRorie had no trouble picturing the look on her face. If her visitor had any sense at all, she or he would start running now.

"Young woman, you will know your place!" The man's voice nearly froze MacRorie where he stood. "I will not be spoken to that way by a *native* who has no business in this office!" It was a voice MacRorie had come halfway across the galaxy to Cottman IV, better known to its inhabitants as Darkover, in hopes of never hearing again.

"My *place*, as you so quaintly refer to it, is right here. Though if you'd like to discuss this matter with the Interim Legate personally, I'd be delighted to call her and interrupt her afternoon meal."

Sure enough, MacRorie came around the corner to find a man's bulk barricading the door to Miralys's office cubie. Even from behind, even with the other man wearing a trim civilian suit instead of a Spaceforce uniform, MacRorie had no trouble at all recognizing the intruder: Colonel Jeremiah Ostrom. MacRorie was also positive that Ostrom knew perfectly well that for an unaccompanied man to transgress a Darkovan woman's private space like this was a violation akin to casually slapping Miralys on the behind. Ostrom always did his reading. He'd always told MacRorie that it paid to know a culture's weak points.

MacRorie was almost tempted to let matters continue on to their natural conclusion. It would have served Ostrom right for Miralys to slap him and turn him over to the MPs. But friends didn't leave friends to face a snake like Ostrom alone.

So MacRorie cleared his throat. "Colonel Ostrom? Sir? I didn't expect to see you here. What brings you all the way out to Cottman IV?" Over Ostrom's shoulder Miralys shot MacRorie a look of naked gratitude.

Ostrom turned with a thunderous look that suggested he knew that he'd just been thwarted in his attack on Miralys, but composed his face into a pleasant smile almost instantly. "Well, if it isn't Jamie MacRorie. Been a long time, son. Since Mupenuru, I think. Your secretary here said you were still at lunch."

MacRorie clenched his teeth so hard Ostrom probably heard it. He counted to ten in Standard and then in *cahuenga* before he spoke. "Miralys isn't my secretary, sir. She's a cultural consultant to the Interim Legate, as I'm sure she's already told you. Has master's degrees in history and interstellar relations from the university on Vainwal. But it sounds like you were here looking for me, anyway. Care for a smoke in the courtyard? More privacy out there."

Ostrom frowned ferociously, but he gestured for MacRorie to lead the way outside.

"I don't exactly love that you've got a native so intimately wrapped up in Legation affairs," Ostrom grumbled as he lit a cigarette and handed the lighter back to MacRorie. "I don't care what degrees she has." Ostrom looked as if he missed the days when the Office of Cultural Reconciliation was mostly just another front for Terran Intelligence.

MacRorie shrugged. "Wasn't my decision; she's been here longer than I have, and she reports directly to Interim Legate Bell. Besides, it's not like Cultural Reconciliation handles anything sensitive. Most of the stuff we're interested in, the Darkovans know better than we do anyway. Sir."

"Guess I'd better get used to it." Ostrom didn't sound particularly resigned. "Given that six months ago I let them talk me out of retirement and into a five-year tour as a special consultant to the Sector Chief of Cultural Reconciliation. See this end of the galaxy, use my experience with Spaceforce to do some good. That sort of thing. You know how it is."

MacRorie fixed his attention firmly on the looming monstrosity that was Aisling Reinol's sculpture of Mother Terra bringing the light of civilization to her lost colonies while he tried to get his expression under control. *Hiring this asshole as a consultant to the Crows is like putting a wolf in charge of the sheepdogs. Christ.* When he was pretty sure he could get the words out without sounding insubordinate, MacRorie said, "So what is it I can do for you, sir?"

"Nothing much, really. Did you know that in all these years the Terran Empire's been on Cottman IV, no one in CR has ever put together a full digest on what your natives call their 'Ages of Chaos'?"

"You're looking for something." The words came out flat and bitter. "I told Director Caldwell flat-out when he reassigned me that I wouldn't be involved in anything like Mupenuru ever again."

"Relax, son. It's just a report. Most of my brief is focused on plugging administrative holes—you probably know better than I do that Cultural Reconciliation has been understaffed and underfunded for decades. Besides, the CR folks assigned to Cottman IV have never exactly been top-shelf, and they've had a distressing habit of going native on us. But I know you, MacRorie. You're a loyal son of Terra, and you've got a hell of a knack for seeing the things no one else does."

"Like the pure unobtainium in the Holy of Holies in the Temple of the Sun on Mupenuru." MacRorie kept his voice even with an effort. "That was just a report, too." Ostrom's pretty speech would have been a lot more reassuring if MacRorie hadn't known from personal experience that the man lied as easily as he drew breath.

"And your report had nothing at all to do with what happened. Spaceforce put down an uprising led by extremists in the Solar Priesthood that threatened the democratically elected government of Mupenuru. I know you've felt guilty all these years, MacRorie, but I assure you the timing was purely coincidental." Ostrom's expression was fatherly, sympathetic. Once upon a time, back when he was innocent and stupid, MacRorie might have believed it was genuine.

An uprising our people incited so that you'd have an excuse to send in the troops and level the Temple. I know. I was there for the whole goddamned thing. "There's nothing the Terran Empire wants on Darkover."

Ostrom clapped him on the shoulder. "Well then, son, you've got no reason to worry about writing me my report. I'll see you next month."

"You're troubled," Miralys said, sitting down at the reader beside MacRorie's in the Archives. She had a little basket full of records cubes, probably research she was doing for the Interim Legate. There was no one else in the reading room, but MacRorie supposed it was a public enough area that being alone with him here didn't violate her Darkovan sensibilities. "You have been since *Mestre* Ostrom left."

"It's nothing important. Just thinking about some things that happened a long time before I came here." Since his conversation with Ostrom, MacRorie hadn't been able to shake the image of troop carriers descending on the Holy City on Mupenuru. When he slept, he could hear the hum and sizzle of heavy beam weapons and the thump of energy mortars.

"Jamie, if he's asked you to do something that's against your conscience, you know it's within your rights under Empire law to refuse." Her gray eyes were solemn and full of concern.

He shook his head. "It's nothing like that. All he wants is a report. Checking CR's math on some things."

Miralys was silent for a moment while she slid one of the

cubes into the reader and tapped out a series of search queries on her keyboard. When she spoke again, her words sounded absent-minded, but he had the oddest sense that her entire attention was focused on him. "My foster father says that you should never ignore a bad feeling in your—what's the word in Standard?—oh yes, *guts*. If you ever want to talk about it, you know where to find me."

A bad feeling in my guts. Yeah, that just about covers it. MacRorie leaned back in his chair and sighed.

MacRorie's report went together slowly, and after two solid weeks of twelve-hour days in the Archives he was beginning to see why no one had ever bothered to compile a definitive account of the Ages of Chaos. What Cultural Reconciliation knew about that time period was probably more folklore than fact anyway; most of Darkovan history was transmitted orally and the events Ostrom wanted to know about were more than a thousand years old; Hell, even *Terran* history that ancient wasn't entirely trustworthy.

Or at least MacRorie devoutly hoped it was more folklore than fact. Some of the things he found in the fragmentary records gave him chills. Clingfire. Bonewater dust. Lungrot plague. Targeted lightning strikes. Destruction on a scale that made his head swim. If any of those things actually existed, it would be like a treasure trove for Ostrom and his friends. The only thing that let MacRorie fall asleep at night was the fact that all of the planetary survey data he was assembling as part of his report suggested that if any of that stuff had ever existed, it didn't now. And based on the so-called 'matrix mechanics' he'd seen in the Trade City surrounding the Terran Legation—who made their living telling fortunes, demonstrating minor telepathy to astonished tourists, and bending the odd spoon—the dreadful psychic gifts in those stories had to be pure fancy. Ancient myths aside, nothing MacRorie had seen here on Darkover was anything CR hadn't seen on a round dozen other First Expansion worlds.

Even so, most nights MacRorie woke sweating from dreams where he could only stand by helplessly as forms in the heavy armor of Spaceforce ground troops cut down scores of

Mupenuran civilians with beam weapons.

Sometimes the Mupenurans in his dreams wore Darkovan clothes.

It felt somehow appropriate that it was pouring icy rain on the day Ostrom came back. Even all the lights in the Legation building, tuned to the bright yellow of Mother Terra's sun, couldn't make the day feel less dreary. It seemed to get even darker when Miralys peeked around the doorframe of MacRorie's office to warn him that she'd seen Ostrom in the hall.

"Guess it's time to go and face my fate." MacRorie heaved himself resignedly to his feet, gave Miralys what he hoped was a reassuring smile (it felt more like a fear grimace), and headed off to find Ostrom. The sooner he got this little *auto-da-fé* over with, the happier he'd be.

Behind him, Miralys's spoke so softly he almost didn't catch her words. *Oh, Jamie. What is your Terranan phrase? Keep your eyes on your own back? I don't trust* Mestre *Ostrom.*

"It's 'watch your back'," he corrected absently over his shoulder." And don't worry. I don't trust him, either."

If he'd actually turned around, MacRorie would have seen her look of stunned surprise.

"It's a bang-up report as usual, son—wish everyone was even half as thorough as you—but for one thing." Ostrom stabbed at the map projector controls with a thick forefinger and the map of the continent shifted dizzily until the view settled on the region surrounding Lake Hali. There wasn't much to see there beyond some hazy aerial views of the countryside taken by the Terran expedition that had first rediscovered the settlement on Cottman IV. Ostrom's finger hovered accusingly over the blurry image of Lake Hali. "Why's there so little data here?"

MacRorie sighed. He'd known from the beginning that this was going to come up, though he'd also hoped it wouldn't. "That's the *rhu fead*. It's where the lords of the Comyn bury their dead. It's sacrosanct. We don't go there. Even Darkovan commoners don't go there. Ask Miralys if you don't believe me."

"Oh, I'm sure she'd back the party line about the place. *They* always do. I thought you of all people would have learned over the years that impassable sacred sites make awfully convenient hiding places."

"What I've learned over the years is that most of the time a sacred place is just a sacred place. Lake Hali's a little weird—it's actually a giant cloud in a canyon—but the *rhu fead* is just a mausoleum. Nothing in there but bones. I'd stake my career on it." *If the Darkovans had a cache of advanced weapons stashed somewhere, do you really think us greedy* Terranan *would still be here?*

"Then why not order a drone overflight just to be sure?"

"With respect, sir, the Empire signed a treaty with the Hasturs—that's the ruling family of the Comyn, as I'm sure you know—when we relocated the Legation from Port Chicago to Thendara. We promised to respect the boundaries of their holy sites. And that includes taking unmanned images." MacRorie suppressed an irritated sigh. *Not that something like that matters one hill of beans to the Empire when there's a hundred kilos of pure unobtainium adorning the Holy of Holies.*

"Get a damned satellite scan, then. If the natives are as cow-and-plow as they want us to believe, how the hell are they going to know we're taking pictures from orbit unless some idiot goes and tells them?" Ostrom's glare suggested that it wouldn't go well for MacRorie if he decided to be that idiot.

'Just a report,' my ass. MacRorie took a deep breath, remembering Miralys's words about being asked to do something against his conscience. He willed himself not to shout, and mostly succeeded. "If I can be frank, sir, no way in hell. You asked for a report. You have it. I've done everything legal within my power to get you the information you want. But if you want to break a decades-old treaty with a world we're trying to bring into the Empire just because you're not a hundred percent satisfied with my work, you can take it up with Interim Legate Bell yourself. I don't want anything to do with it."

"MacRorie." He could hear the warning in Ostrom's voice

and ignored it.

"I'm within my rights to refuse an illegal order, and you know it. Sir. Now may I be dismissed?"

When MacRorie emerged from the conference room on the heels of Ostrom's door-slamming exit, he found Miralys standing in the hall with an armful of flimsies. She shot him an inquiring look, and for a moment he almost told her what had just happened. But what would that accomplish, other than making her worry? "Guess Colonel Ostrom was hoping that report would be more interesting," he said lightly instead. "Hopefully we've seen the last of him for awhile." He felt like he'd just lied to her.

"Avarra grant." Miralys offered him a tiny smile, but it didn't reach her eyes. "It would be nice if we'd seen the last of him *forever.*"

"Your lips to God's ear, as we *Terranan* like to say. At least assuming his replacement wouldn't be even worse than he is." *And that I haven't just gotten my ass dishonorably discharged after that meeting.*

But ten days passed with no demands that MacRorie report to the Interim Legate and no orders reassigning him to duties somewhere even more isolated and less habitable than Cottman IV. Then three weeks passed, and then two months. Finally, MacRorie stopped waiting for the other shoe to drop and went back to his life (such as it was).

Every so often MacRorie wondered whether or not Ostrom had gotten his satellite scans. He told himself it didn't matter and he didn't care, which would have been a lot easier to believe if he'd ever stopped having bad dreams about Mupenuru and Miralys had ever stopped looking so worried.

When he asked her what was the matter, she told him it was nothing he needed to trouble himself over. He tried his best to believe her. And then the *Ursula* came back on her monthly turn-and-turn-about run between the Outer Arm and Inner Colonies.

Tony George, Assistant Quartermaster on the *Ursula* and a good friend from the bad old days, was waiting at their usual table in the back corner of the Commercial Lounge. He looked up from whatever electric blue concoction he was working his way through and waved. "Jamie. How's business out here at the ass end of the universe?"

"Same as always. I still don't understand how you drink that garbage. You must enjoy abusing your liver and your taste buds both." MacRorie slid into the booth opposite and ordered a beer from the dispenser.

"This is top shelf compared to the stuff we've got on board. Goes down easy. You're just spoiled, man. And I bet you still don't have those fifty credits you lost on that ballgame either, do you?"

MacRorie shrugged an apology. "I'll make it up to you next month with interest."

"That's what he always says," Tony said to the air.

"And yet you still make bets with me. But what about you? What's new in the spacing lanes?"

"Same old stuff. Business sucks. No one wants to spend any damn money while that mess with the Telos colonies is going on. Everyone's worried they're gonna be next."

"Look on the bright side," Jamie said bracingly. "You could be doing the Eta Tau run. At least no one's shooting at anyone out at this end of your route."

"Yet." Tony raised his eyebrows and MacRorie felt his stomach sink. "You know me, Jamie. I'm not one to go sticking my nose where it ain't wanted, but y'all sure have some interesting cargo scheduled to drop at Port Chicago in the morning. What's your boss man Ostrom doing here with sixteen men and ladies in cheap civvies traveling on sketchy business visas with a load of crates they don't want anyone taking a close look at?"

MacRorie swore softly. "Special Forces."

"You know it, man. Y'all aren't up to anything that's going to wreck our business out here, are you?"

"I'll have to get back to you on that." MacRorie downed the rest of his beer in one swallow and ordered another.

The next day MacRorie pleaded illness and called out of work. It wasn't that much of a stretch; his sleep had been so full of nightmares that his eyes were gritty and aching and he might as well not have slept at all.

Besides, there was no way he could walk into CR and face Miralys knowing what he knew. But warning her would be even worse. The *rhu fead* couldn't have more than a sketchy honor guard. Darkover's population was tiny and places like that didn't tend to need much more than their reputation to keep the nosy at bay. So long as no one knew Ostrom and his soldiers were coming, there would likely be no more than a couple of dozen casualties. It would be a diplomatic incident, nothing more. After Mupenuru, MacRorie knew all too well what happened when a bunch of civilians armed with target weapons and garden tools showed up to guard their holy site against Spaceforce's elite.

At 1500, he opened a bottle of the local rotgut, swallowed a fistful of pills, and drank until the room swam before his eyes. Maybe this way he wouldn't dream, and when he opened his eyes again the whole goddamned affair would be over.

No such luck. Sometime around 2300 hours, MacRorie woke in a sweat with a throbbing head and his mouth full of cotton, thinking—of all the damned things—of the Compact that bound the lords of the Comyn. The Compact by which every *Terranan* on Cottman IV who wanted to leave the bounds of the Spaceport and the Legation had to swear to abide.

The Compact forbade the use of any weapon that could kill at a distance, and it predated the Empire's arrival on Darkover by at least a thousand years. Given the horror and disgust with which Darkovans universally regarded Terran energy weapons, MacRorie had always been pretty sure the Compact wasn't talking about crossbows.

People don't make laws banning things they don't have.

The thought had MacRorie out of bed and yanking a shirt over his head before he was even really aware of what he was doing.

MacRorie knew Miralys lived in Legation housing when she was working, but until just now he'd never bothered to find out precisely where. For an unaccompanied man to visit a

Darkovan woman's private domicile was an unforgivable insult to the woman's honor. It was something MacRorie would never have countenanced except in an emergency like this.

Miralys's flat was on the second floor of a charming little apartment block set back from the road in a tidy garden and painted to resemble native buildings. If MacRorie had been in less of a hurry, he might have paused to appreciate her taste. Instead, he charged up the steps and banged on her door, praying to whatever gods happened to be listening that he'd wake her before he woke her neighbors and someone called Security.

To his surprise, she came to the door almost immediately. She was fully dressed, in sturdy boots and outdoor gear of native manufacture. Her expression was grim. She looked, he would think later, like she'd been expecting him. Like she'd been expecting all of this.

He barreled through the door before she had a chance to stop him. "Miralys, this is important. What does the Comyn keep in the *rhu fead*?"

"Why Jamie, as you well know, it's where the lords of the Comyn bury their dead." She said it in a faux-cheerful singsong. Her gray eyes were steely.

MacRorie took a deep breath. "There's something I need to tell you." As soon as the words were out, he had the uncomfortable sense of having taken some irrevocable step.

"Ostrom."

"Yes, and a platoon of Special Forces. And I have no idea in hell what we're going to do about it."

The utter futility of his errand suddenly struck him like a blow to the sternum. Lake Hali and the *rhu fead* were nearly thirty klicks away. He had no idea what Ostrom's timeline might be; for all MacRorie knew the guards at the *rhu fead* were already dead and the raid in progress. And even if he and Miralys did manage to liberate a flier from the Legation motor pool and get there first, it would be him, her, and maybe a couple of blaster pistols against Ostrom and sixteen soldiers in armor with heavy weapons.

For a long uncomfortable moment Miralys seemed to weigh him with her eyes. When she finally spoke, the words weren't at all what he'd been expecting. "You'd better come with me. I think we're going to need your help."

All MacRorie could do was gape at her like the idiot *Terranan* he apparently was while she crossed the room to rummage in a carved wooden chest. Finally, she thrust a bundle of fabric and fur into his hands. When he shook it out, he discovered it was some kind of coat. Probably hers, judging by the color and the elaborate floral embroidery.

Miralys gave him an exasperated look. "Put it on. It won't fit, but it's better than nothing. I know you *Terranan* are prone to freezing to death in perfectly fine spring weather. And hurry up. We don't have a lot of time to catch up with the others."

While MacRorie was still trying to parse what had just happened, Miralys led him out of the Legation compound through a largely-unmonitored service entrance he would never have figured she knew. From there, they picked their way through the Trade City, and into the narrow dark alleyways of the Old City of Thendara itself.

Miralys stopped once for about thirty seconds, closing her eyes as if concentrating fiercely, and then grabbed his wrist and dragged him on again.

By the time they stopped, somewhere on the outskirts of Thendara, MacRorie was so hopelessly turned around that he couldn't have found his way back to the Legation if he'd wanted to. He just stood there for a moment with his eyes closed, catching his breath, and when he finally lifted his head to look around, he felt like someone had just punched him hard in the gut.

Wherever the hell this place was, it was unmistakably some kind of private airfield. A little knot of people in Darkovan dress—cloaks, knee-high leather boots, the whole bit, plus a tall woman robed head to toe in red—was standing by a pair of lightweight aircars of a type MacRorie had never seen before.

The sight was so completely incongruous that all he could do was laugh helplessly. How in Mother Terra's name had no one on the Terran side ever noticed a *very well lit private airfield* practically in the shadow of the Legation? *Jesus. What else have we missed? Is this the real reason the Comyn don't want a damned thing to do with us?*

Miralys glanced over at him, and he got the distinct sense that if the situation were less dire, she'd be giggling at his discomfiture. *For an Intelligence man, you're sure not very smart, are you?* It was like that moment in the hallway at the Legation what seemed like a million years ago now: a whisper just at the edge of his hearing. MacRorie opened his mouth to protest that he was an information analyst, not a spy, (and why the hell was he telling her this, anyway?), realized she hadn't actually said anything out loud, and shut it again. This time she did grin at him slyly. But before he could even begin to parse what had just happened, one of the men broke away from the party by the aircars and came towards him and Miralys.

The stranger was a tall, erect older gentleman with long silver hair gathered tidily in a ponytail. As the man got closer, MacRorie could see that he wore a blue cloak fastened with a silver clasp in the form of a stylized tree. He seemed somehow familiar. "Da," Miralys said with a warm smile, holding out her hands. The man took them, smiling back.

"My foster father, *Dom* Felix." Miralys said by way of introduction "Da, this is Jameson MacRorie from the Legation. He's the one I told you about."

Miralys's foster father was Dom *Felix?* The man who had advised the Hasturs for at least two generations? Jesus Christ. MacRorie suddenly felt like a particularly stupid country bumpkin standing there shivering in Miralys's coat, which barely fastened over his midsection and whose sleeves only barely came down past his elbows. He devoutly hoped that his feelings didn't show on his face and that he didn't look as stupid as he felt. "Sir. It's a pleasure." MacRorie extended his hand, only to snatch it back, remembering that the CR précis on the Comyn said that they preferred to avoid touching strangers.

Dom Felix favored him with faint smile and a solemn half-bow, and that was when the enormity of the choice he'd made the moment he decided to go to Miralys's apartment finally settled on MacRorie. Treason. This was treason against the

Terran Empire. A violation of every last word of the oaths he'd taken when he graduated from the Academy.

Dom Felix's sharp eyes, which were a startling shade of amber, caught MacRorie's and held them. "It is never wrong to act to prevent the loss of innocent lives," he said firmly, and MacRorie knew that somehow the older man had heard his thoughts. There had always been rumors that the Comyn could read minds, but until just now MacRorie had never really believed them. "And for your courageous action we thank you. Miralys, *chiya*, ordinarily I'd disapprove of you coming alone with a man who is not kin to you, but you were right to bring him. If we are able to use your Gift to bring him into the circle, I think we will prevail."

"You're planning to *fight* them?" MacRorie's mouth felt suddenly dry. Counting him and Miralys they were ten altogether, and most of their merry little band looked to be somewhere around *Dom* Felix's age. Except for the woman in red, that was. On second glance she didn't look as though she was even out of her teens.

Earthforce heavy weapons would slice through those flimsy little aircars like they were paper.

"Of course we're going to fight them," said Miralys. "They can't be allowed to enter the *rhu fead*. But we're going to fight them *our* way, Jamie. You'll see." Her smile was all confidence, but MacRorie could see the terror in her eyes.

For the journey to the *rhu fead* the group split up, five to each little aircar. "It'll be cramped," Miralys said, "but we don't have far to go. And Jamie—for everyone's safety, please be careful not to touch our pilot while the aircar is moving." Miralys went up front with the pilot, a grizzled old veteran who called himself Gareth. MacRorie knelt uncomfortably in the back, sandwiched between *Dom* Felix and a stocky man with red hair gone mostly gray who'd given his name as Rhodri.

MacRorie could only stare in dazed fascination as Gareth apparently directed their aircraft with little movements of his hands. Certainly there were no visible controls, other than a couple of small knobs and a handful of indicator dials. Watching Gareth too closely made MacRorie oddly dizzy. He thought of the matrix mechanics in Trade City, bending spoons and reshaping glass. *Is this another application of their matrix technology? If it is, what the hell else can these people do?* He supposed he was about to find out.

They landed on the grounds of the *rhu fead* under cover of darkness. By now MacRorie was cold clear through and had lost all sense of time. It might be six hours or six minutes until dawn. For a giddy moment he wondered if this might all be a dream born of pills and alcohol, but then he barked his shin painfully on something he hadn't seen in the dark and stumbled.

The grounds were quiet and still; no one came to meet them. The shrine itself was a shadowy bulk looming over them, more sensed than seen. MacRorie shivered, but not from cold. "We've sent the guards away," *Dom* Felix said in answer to MacRorie's unspoken question. "Your 'Special Forces' will be here soon."

"Great," MacRorie muttered. "Terrific." It didn't seem tactful to ask *Dom* Felix how he knew. MacRorie wasn't sure he wanted to know anyway.

"You're wondering how we can possibly fight the soldiers," Miralys said from behind him. "You told Colonel Ostrom there was nothing to find on Darkover. We're going to show him that you were right."

"But—" There *was* something to find here. Even if MacRorie's gut hadn't been screaming at him all night, Miralys and *Dom* Felix had as much as said so.

Dom Felix's voice was kind. "With your memories, *Mestre* MacRorie, we can weave them a dream that they will believe in their hearts to have been real. A dream wherein they will find that they have just made a terrible mistake."

Almost involuntarily, MacRorie remembered the scores of Mupenuran civilians, armed only with personal blasters, farming implements, and rocks, who had tried to barricade the doors of the Temple of the Sun. Terran soldiers had cut them down in mere minutes like so much grass.

The funeral pyres in the Holy City had burned for two solid weeks after the troop carriers had finally lifted into space again.

"Yes," *Dom* Felix said.

MacRorie shook off the memory's spell with an effort. "But how are you going to get *my* memories into *their* heads?"

"A very long time ago, most of us—save Miralys, and Viviana, our Keeper, who are both far too young—were part of the working Circle at Tramontana Tower." It sounded like a tangent to MacRorie, but somehow he knew it wasn't. MacRorie supposed Viviana was the girl in red. *Dom* Felix's voice was soft. For a moment he sounded old and tired. "Once we did far more difficult things than what we will attempt tonight."

"What do I need to do?" MacRorie heard his own voice shake and swallowed hard. What good were seven old men, two women, MacRorie, and a bad dream going to be against a platoon of Special Forces?

"Only relax and don't fight the rapport," *Dom* Felix said. "Miralys has the Ridenow Gift. She will take care of bringing you into the circle."

"If we're very lucky and the gods are very kind," Miralys murmured, so softly that MacRorie was pretty sure it was meant for his ears alone. Without thinking, MacRorie reached out and squeezed her hand. She didn't pull away.

After that, there were several minutes of what struck MacRorie as incomprehensible babble.

"Eduin will monitor."

"Miralys, I must count on you to keep our *Terranan* from accidentally disrupting the energon flows."

And then *Dom* Felix said, "If we are to do this thing, we must do it now." He was right: in the distance, MacRorie could hear the muffled thump of the engine of a Terran heavy atmospheric flier.

The rapport was far beyond anything for which MacRorie's previous experiences could possibly have prepared him. He wasn't sure precisely what he'd expected, but this searing, soul-baring intimacy wasn't it. He'd felt Miralys gathering him up, for want of a better term, and then there was a moment of disorientation and something like agony (he thought he might have screamed aloud and felt a wash of embarrassment), and then MacRorie could *feel* every member of the circle.

Dom Felix, cool and silver and resolute and somehow almost alien; Rhodri, sharp like the edge of a knife and vibrating with impatience; Miralys, who underneath her uncertainty was as solid and steadfast as a pillar of granite. The others, who moments before MacRorie had known only as names and faces half-seen in the dimness, he suddenly knew better than he knew his dearest friends. And there was Viviana, the Keeper, holding them in sure hands and weaving them together like the threads of a tapestry. The analogy, MacRorie thought, had come from Miralys's mind.

MacRorie wasn't sure if this was the most wonderful or the most terrifying experience of his entire life. And if it was like this for him, a blind *Terranan*, what must it be like for the Comyn?

Not so blind as all that. No wonder Miralys told me you have a reputation for having good instincts. Dom Felix's mental 'voice' was full of amusement and something like delight. *This will teach me to be so certain that I know all of what is to come. Perhaps there is hope for you Terranan yet.*

The roar of a military aircraft landing put an end to whatever else *Dom* Felix might have said. It was time.

Afterward, MacRorie could never find adequate words to explain what happened after the troop carrier landed. He saw seventeen figures, all in heavy armor and carrying beam rifles and particle cannons, descend the troop carrier's ramp. The figure wearing the commandant's insignia must be Ostrom.

Distance weapons here? *How* dare *they?* Miralys's 'voice' in the rapport was full of cold fury, and Viviana's anger, sharpened to a point that MacRorie thought might actually kill given the power behind it, echoed hers.

Easy, easy. Striking them down will only bring scores more Terranan to take their place. That was *Dom* Felix. *The work we do tonight may be less satisfying, but it will give us a much more lasting solution.* And then *Dom* Felix did something—MacRorie could feel the power of it roll through the circle like an ocean wave—and the soldiers simply froze where they stood and didn't move again.

Jamie. Miralys was gentle and regretful. *It's time. I'm sorry.*

MacRorie's vision seemed to double. He could see the soldiers standing there motionless, but the sight was somehow overlaid with the dream *Dom* Felix and Viviana and Rhodri and the others wove from the memories of Mupenuru that Miralys drew from his mind.

Darkovan figures, scores of them, seemed to materialize in the night air. Men and women, Comyn and commoner. Some of them carried torches and scythes and rakes, others axes and shields and swords. Some wore armor, others only homespun tunics and breeches. They arranged themselves in ranks, standing between the soldiers and the *rhu fead.* At first the figures were insubstantial like ghosts or clouds of mist, but within a few breaths it was as though one of MacRorie's nightmares had taken on flesh and bone.

One of the figures called a challenge to the soldiers. It spoke with Rhodri's voice.

MacRorie knew that none of this was real, that it was only a dream, and yet he still wanted to shout for the Darkovans to run. They were no match for the Terrans. They had to know that. Some small part of him that was still aware of his body could feel tears running unchecked down his face.

The Terran soldiers moved, or rather to MacRorie's doubled vision, ghosts of the soldiers, still in armor, seemed to rise from their motionless bodies, gradually becoming more and more solid. Most of the soldiers raised their weapons, though three of them looked at the crowd of civilians and hesitated. The figure of Ostrom gestured peremptorily.

MacRorie wanted nothing more than to look away, to break the circle, to *run.* He knew it was dishonorable, cowardly. But he knew how this ended, and after Mupenuru he couldn't bear to face it. He struggled to turn away, but between them Viviana and Miralys held him fast.

The Darkovans could not stand against Terran heavy weapons. Most of them fell right where they stood, looks of surprise and terror on their faces. A man with flaming red hair and a heavily-embroidered green cloak managed to get close enough to Ostrom to strike at him with a sword. Ostrom, his strength augmented by his armor's servos, knocked the green-cloaked man aside with casual ease. From the way the man had fallen, MacRorie knew his neck was broken.

Unimpeded, the dream-soldiers proceeded up the broad steps and into the *rhu fead*. Somehow, even though the figures were out of sight, MacRorie could nonetheless see what Ostrom and the soldiers saw in the dream *Dom* Felix and the others gave them.

The doors of the *rhu fead* gave onto a vast mausoleum; rank upon rank of Comyn dead, a record of bones and ashes and personal relics spanning a thousand years and more. But no weapons. No treasures born of a technology unknown to the Terran empire. Search as they might, Ostrom and his people found nothing but generation upon generation of the dead.

And as the first rays of dawn touched the *rhu fead*, the ghostly figures of the soldiers returned to their living bodies, and the armored bodies began to move. Some of them removed their helmets. MacRorie could see the horror of what they'd just done written deep into their faces.

Eventually the ramp folded back into the belly of the troop carrier, and the troop carrier lifted into the deep purple of the early morning sky with a muted roar.

MacRorie seemed to slam back into his body like a stone falling from orbit. Shivering and weeping, he stumbled to his knees in the chilly, dew-soaked grass and lost what little was in his stomach. Someone shoved something sticky and sweet into his hand and told him to eat it.

From somewhere in the distance, Miralys said, "Oh gods, Jamie. I'm sorry. I'm so sorry." He could hear the tears in her voice. Then, mercifully, MacRorie passed out.

They were all several days recovering in an inn in the town of Hali, not far from the *rhu fead*. Apparently the use of psychic powers—what Miralys and *Dom* Felix and the others called *laran*—severely depleted one's physical resources. MacRorie, who had come into the circle untrained and unprepared, was the last of them all to rise from his bed. (Much later, Miralys would tell MacRorie apologetically that three monitors and two healers had labored for a night and a day over his dangerously exhausted body.)

Finally, MacRorie felt human enough to risk leaving his bed and descending the stairs into the inn's common room. It was a cozy space with a crackling fire and bulky, well-upholstered furniture. MacRorie sank into a deep chair and decided he never wanted to get up again. A serving girl brought him a mug of some local beer. It tasted surprisingly good. He sipped it, feeling somehow lighter than he had in all the years following Mupenuru.

Eventually, Miralys and *Dom* Felix appeared. They both looked much more chipper than MacRorie felt, though MacRorie was pretty sure he saw new lines in *Dom* Felix's face. Miralys grinned at him, irrepressible as always.

"We have it on good authority that the Hastur has been to see the Interim Legate *personally.*" She sounded positively gleeful. "He's demanded an immediate meeting with the Sector Governor to discuss the desecration of our most sacred place, and to demand that whoever led such an atrocity be disciplined appropriately."

MacRorie couldn't find it in himself to regret Ostrom's undoubtedly imminent termination. 'Deniability' was a watchword in Terran Intelligence, as he well knew.

"Meanwhile, we backward Darkovans have been busy burying our dead." *Dom* Felix had an undeniable twinkle in his eye. "Caradoc Aillard broke his neck in a riding accident near Hali on the day of the raid. He never liked you *Terranan* meddling in our affairs anyway, and he had a wretched sense of humor. I somehow doubt he'd object to having been used as a prop in our little drama."

MacRorie remembered the green-cloaked man who'd fallen at Ostrom's hand in the dream, and *Dom* Felix smiled and nodded.

If he hadn't spent so much time in what he supposed was telepathic rapport with Miralys and *Dom* Felix and the others, the exchange would have made MacRorie deeply uneasy. But MacRorie knew, with the certainty with which he knew his own name, that Miralys had not spent her time at the Legation reading all of their most secret thoughts. In fact, the telepaths among the Comyn spent a great deal of time and effort *not* to know what others were thinking. (Given some of the things MacRorie considered in the privacy of his own mind, he really couldn't blame them.)

"But what about the sensor logs from the soldiers' armor and the troop carrier?"

Dom Felix shrugged innocently. "*Terranan* ships have always had sensor problems in the vicinity of Lake Hali. It's something about our geology, I think, but I have very little understanding of your *Terranan* science."

MacRorie laughed and shook his head appreciatively, and after a few minutes, he gave up and asked the question that had been on his mind since he'd come to his senses in his bedroom at the inn: "What's really in the *rhu fead?*"

"Terrible weapons that to our shame once nearly destroyed our world. Someday I will tell you the story of how Lake Hali came to be transformed into mist." *Dom* Felix sounded very old and very tired. "But thanks in part to you, *Mestre* MacRorie, those weapons will not be used to destroy any others."

"You could have gotten rid of us *Terranan* at any point," MacRorie said finally, thinking of those weapons and remembering the power he'd felt in the rapport with the others. "Why haven't you?"

"We need each other, *Mestre* MacRorie." *Dom* Felix said. "My people are not what they once were. Nor, I think, are yours. But if we can survive one another, perhaps one day we can forge a new future for all of us ... together."

MacRorie wasn't sure what to say to that. *Dom* Felix's voice echoed in memory: *Perhaps there is hope for you* Terranan *yet.* Was this what atonement felt like?

It suddenly struck MacRorie how long he must have been away from the office, and he wasn't sure what to do about it. Was the Interim Legate looking for him?

Miralys met his eyes, and then she looked away, out the window. Finally, she said, "Jamie, we can change your memory the way we changed the soldiers'. You can go back to work at the Legation like none of this ever happened. All you'll remember is going into the Trade City for a drink and being struck over the head and robbed."

"By ill-mannered *Terranan*, of course," *Dom* Felix said with a hint of a smile, and MacRorie couldn't help but chuckle.

And for just a moment, going back to his old life sounded almost appealing. Mother Terra knew, it was the simplest and least confusing option. But MacRorie had slept soundly through the night every night since he'd awakened here in the inn. "No," he finally said. "What happened at the *rhu fead* was the first unambiguously good thing I've done in a lot of years. I think I'd like to remember it." And maybe he could finally lay the ghosts of Mupenuru to rest, even if it meant having no idea what in hell he was going to do next.

Smiling shyly, Miralys covered MacRorie's hand with her own. *Dom* Felix put a hand on MacRorie's shoulder.

"Whatever it is, we'll figure it out together," Miralys said. "You're one of us now."

Behind him, MacRorie could feel *Dom* Felix smile. "Welcome to Darkover, Jamie MacRorie."

A Study of Sixes

by Gabrielle Harbowy

Many Darkovans, particularly those of the aristocratic Comyn, have six fingers, a visible demonstration of their *chieri* heritage. There's a lovely exchange in *Stormqueen* in which Cassandra, who is six-fingered, explains how it helps her to play the *rryl*, a Darkovan lap harp. The following story explores being six-fingered from another perspective.

Gabrielle Harbowy is a writer and award-nominated editor of fantasy and science fiction. Her published novels include *Hellmaw: Of the Essence*, (Runner-up, Science Fiction category, San Francisco Book Festival) and *Gears of Faith*. Her short fiction has been a finalist for the Parsec award, and has appeared in such anthologies as *Beast Within: 2*, *Metastasis*, *Cthulhurotica*, and others. She's edited books for Pyr, Circlet, and Dragon Moon Press, as well as co-editor of the award-nominated *When the Hero Comes Home* anthology series with Ed Greenwood.

There had to be a way to wrap a face-scarf that didn't make the mist of your breath catch in your own eyelashes, but if there was, Tristan hadn't found it yet. He wondered if his briefings had covered it, perhaps in one of the sessions when he'd been busy daydreaming about going offworld instead of paying attention, or whether freezing your eyes shut with the moisture of your own breath was just one of those rite of passage things that all new arrivals had to solve for themselves.

"Warm enough?" Corin, his guide, asked beside him.

Tristan measured the question for sarcasm, almost disappointed to find it absent. He considered a few neutral-sounding platitudes—he didn't want to make a fuss—but you couldn't lie to a telepath. That much from his briefings, at least, he remembered.

"Yes." His eyes stuck shut and he strained his lids one at a time to pull them open again. Swiping a snowy glove across his face would only make things worse. He had already learned that the fun way.

Colin laughed. "You'll get used to it. Just a little farther."

"My kingdom for a monorail," Tristan muttered, softening the complaint with a muffled laugh of his own.

"You didn't come all this way just to *not* experience our world," Colin chided, matching Tristan's playfulness. "Does Terra not get cold?"

"Not like this. Not where I've lived, at least." Tristan scrunched his left-hand fingers in, withdrawing them from their individual sleeves to gather in the palm of his glove. They huddled together in a fist to share warmth. But they had none to share, so it didn't help. The outer edges of his hands twinged painfully. "Where did you say we were going?"

They passed through the outer gate of the spaceport and into the ring-city—where the merchants brave enough to meet the Terrans and trade with them saw a lucrative business. Tristan considered stopping to replace his more temperate "cold weather" gear with some of the native garb on display. It looked like home-spun wool. Back on Terra, there was a premium on artisan goods. Here, they were the default. He wondered at the constitution of the merchants standing around outside in this weather. The spaceport was new enough that the ring-city was still somewhat makeshift.

He could barely feel his fingers. They weren't even aching anymore, and he knew that was bad.

"Hold up," he said to his guide, and doubled back to a glove-seller's stall, physiology making the decision for him. He plucked a pair seemingly at random and passed the merchant a too-large coin and a grateful nod. Protests in a foreign tongue followed him as he jogged back to Colin. He'd forgotten to tell the guy to keep the change.

"He says you took—" Colin started, then shook his head. "Well, it's too late now. Come on, there's our carriage."

And it was. An actual carriage. Old fashioned and drawn by real horses. For a moment Tristan wondered if he should regret having bought gloves just to go immediately into warmth, but only for a moment. The carriage blocked the worst of the wind, but it wasn't heated. He was glad of the gloves after all, and resolved to make warmer socks his next purchase.

The driver clucked to the horses and they started off. Tristan peeled off his useless Terran gloves and rubbed his hands, then slid them into the new pair, wriggling his fingers into their soft woolen spaces. They felt awkward, like he had them on the wrong hands or something. His thumbs were in the thumb sleeves. His pinkies, however, were in sleeves far too long for them. And one more finger hole lay empty on each hand.

Colin was watching him, from the opposite bench. Their knees almost touched as the carriage jolted along. "Genetic variation. Some Darkovans have six fingers per hand."

"What do you call that? Do you have a name for it?"

Colin shook his head, like he hadn't understood the question.

My accent can't be that bad, Tristan thought. He tried again. "On Terra we call it polydactyly. It's not common in humans, but it's a desirable trait in housecats."

"We don't call it anything. It doesn't affect anything, so why should we?"

"Huh." Tristan sat back and thought a little. "Doesn't that come from a specific bloodline? From interbreeding with the..."

"The Chieri, yes."

"But it's not 'Chieri-touched' or 'Chieri-blooded' or anything like that?"

"Of course not. That would be redundant. Some status-obsessed Darkovans consider it a mark of status, but it's just another variation, like the color of our hair or eyes. We know where the trait comes from. Brown-eyed is brown-eyed. It doesn't need another word." He tilted his head, as if looking at Tristan another way would make his questions more sensible. "Why does this pique your curiosity so?"

You couldn't lie to a telepath, but you could reframe a genuine truth to divert them.

"Back home on Terra, this would be a source of discrimination. It would limit who got status, or who would be favored for a job, or who a person could love, or pair with. That it doesn't matter here...I think that's what makes it most interesting."

He had clearly lost Colin a sentence or two back. The young man had a certain naïve nature that Tristan wasn't sure he'd ever seen on anyone older than fourteen or so. He still thought the world was a good and fair place. Well, it wasn't Tristan's job to convince him otherwise.

It was his job to catalog this finger thing, but in a field sociologist way, with curiosity and without raising much of a fuss. If all the Darkovans were as blasé about it as Colin here, this wasn't going to be easy. He changed course. "So, what's the deal with last names? Only the royalty have them, or something?"

Colin thought for a moment. "Basically. Important families have family names. No one else needs them."

"Isn't there any resentment about that?"

"I'm not sure what you mean. It helps us identify our betters."

Tristan tried not to wince. *Betters*? "They've got you snowed good, don't they, kid?"

That innocent blink-blink again. "We're quite used to snow here."

Tristan sighed. "Never mind."

~ooo~

"To your first day among the natives." Chelle lifted her glass in a toast. Tristan answered her with side eye, but mustered enough good grace to touch his glass to hers. He downed the mulled wine, grateful for its heat.

Chelle—Dr. Michelle Lansing—was his superior, but had broken herself of the formality of surnames and titles in her time among the Darkovans.

"Frustrating lot that they are," Tristan grumbled.

Chelle laughed. "I'll drink to that, too. Remember, it's only your first day, and they're slow to trust."

"I *wish* trust was the issue. Trust just means time, and time isn't going anywhere."

"Well, if not trust, then what?"

"Fingeredness doesn't seem to matter to anyone. It isn't a source of discrimination like it would have been back home. When a thing makes no difference, it doesn't even get its own word. As far as I've been able to figure out, the word for six-fingered person is just 'person.'" Which was commendable, really, even if it wasn't helpful.

He could hear the rise of frustration in his voice and fought to temper it. It wasn't Chelle's fault the locals were stubborn or had different priorities than his own. If they hadn't been different, he wouldn't be out here studying them; if they hadn't been stubborn, they wouldn't have survived long enough to be studied.

"It's got to matter to someone," she said. Tristan huffed at the obviousness of her statement. "Someone *aside* from you," Chelle amended.

"Possibly a musicians guild, if this place even has such a thing. Or the glovemakers. It's got to matter to the glovemakers."

Chelle pushed her chair back and got up, patting Tristan on the shoulder as she passed him. "Looks like we know what you're doing tomorrow."

Tristan grumbled again, just on principle.

~ooo~

Leatherworkers had trade shops here, because of course they did; meanwhile, the royals or nobles or whatever they called them had their own retinue of artisans on call, because of course *they* did.

There were other people studying and cataloging the boring things like nobility and customs. Tristan's focus was on the hands and just the hands. The rest of it, well, that was all represented by blanks in his reports that he could fill in later to make it look like he cared about Comyn and Houses and *laran* and crystal matrixes and all that. He could see his publication in his mind's eye. In *Journal of Xenobiology*, maybe, or *Journal of Abnormal Physiology*, since Darkovans were technically still human. Maybe some publication that focused on hybridization would pick it up, since humans weren't supposed to be able to crossbreed with any other species in the first place, but that wasn't his concern. Let them. His name would piggy-back across the field, added as co-author on paper after paper. He'd be the groundbreaker, the expert. Let them nod to him in all the research to follow.

Tristan stepped out of a shop and pulled his new cloak tightly around him. It was warmer today. "Warm enough to snow," was what one of the merchants had said, and it had struck him oddly that weather could get so cold that snow, the poster child of cold weather, would refuse to stick a toe out of its nice cozy cloud.

He spotted a few flurries drifting above the ring-city and caught himself thinking about that nice mulled wine.

The next shop was his goal, though he'd stopped in at all of them. There were two reasons for this: outfitting himself for the weather was the main and obvious one, but also he didn't want to give away his special interest in human polydactyly. As part of the slowness to trust that Chelle had mentioned, Darkovans didn't like to be studied blatantly. They were more receptive to open and general curiosity, especially about things that didn't mean much to them; if they couldn't be made to understand the Terran fascination about something, they couldn't see the point of expounding at length about it. The fact that extra-fingeredness didn't even have its own word was the definitive sign that Darkovans didn't think they had anything to say about the matter.

Tristan rubbed his hands together. They ached all the time now, making him feel like an old man who could forecast the weather by the pains in his bones. The next shop was the glovemaker whose wares he'd overpaid for yesterday. Someone different was minding the shop today—a son, perhaps, or a brother—so that made things less awkward, though the young man of course recognized his own wares on Tristan's hands.

"Oh, you bought those from us. You like?" His Common was pretty good for a Darkovan, the result of much interaction.

"I like very much. In my haste, though, I seem to have picked up the wrong kind." He wiggled his fingers, highlighting the empty finger sleeve that buoyed along with the rest of his hand.

The guy laughed. "Oh, sorry about that. Did you want to trade?"

"I kind of like it," Tristan quipped with a sly grin. "Gives me a place to hide my house key." Armoring himself against the blank look he expected to see in response, he turned his attention to his hands and carefully peeled off one glove, then the other, flexing his fingers. They looked shriveled and dry; dehydrated like meat, almost, from the constant cold. His old wounds throbbed.

He handed the gloves back over, a little sorry to see them go. "So, how do you know how many of each kind to make? Do you have a general idea of how much demand there is, or...?"

The glovemaker shrugged. He put the gloves off to the side and picked a new pair, handing them over. "It's a business thing like any other. You have your sizes and styles, and when one sells you replace it. When a lot sell, you replace with a lot."

The new gloves were a much better fit, and more stylish as well. Soft suede on the outside, lined with a thick layer of spongy wool.

"Sure. Say, do you know if there are any music concerts coming up? My department head, she's a big fan. I told her I'd ask while I was in town today."

It wasn't like these places had flyers on the walls, or a network with a calendar of events he could download.

"Public concerts? Not that I know of. But I do make gloves for Meridian Leynier-Alton. He's one of our better-known *rryl* players. He takes private performances all the time. You could hire him. Or invite him over for a cup of *jaco* and a lesson."

"Perfect. Thank you so much."

Tristan's path was now suddenly clear. Which was to say, now he knew his next step would be finding out what, or who, a *rryl* was.

He hadn't been lying about his supervisor being a music fan—you never could tell who was a telepath just by looking at them, so not lying to Darkovans was just good practice—so he headed back to the Terran compound, where he found Chelle at her desk, and asked her. If she didn't know, the database would.

"It's a harp. Kind of," Chelle said. "It's got a pretty sound.

Here..."

She tapped a few keys and pulled up an entry, with a 3-D drawing and a few paragraphs, and a sound file attached. Stringed music flowed from the tinny speaker until Tristan—politely—asked for it to stop.

"Don't suppose you've got that Meridian guy's address in there?"

"Meridian Leynier-Alton? He's something of a local legend. Teaches lessons out of his home. I'll get you a map if you get me an autograph."

~ooo~

If Tristan had cared, he would have noticed that Alton was the last name of the ruling family, and would not have been surprised to find that the musician's residence was practically on the palace grounds. Equipped in his new and warmer clothing, the chill was almost tolerable. A few stray flakes still drifted down from the gray sky, and chatter around the city was that they would be joining together into a proper storm by morning.

Meridian was in residence, and most receptive to a visitor, even if that visitor was only the friend of a fan and not an actual fan himself. He wove a half-true story about how he was hoping to schedule a series of lessons and a chat; if Chelle would be impressed by an autograph, she'd be doubly impressed that he'd actually tried to pick up the instrument. The subtext was that he wanted, in a non-collegial way, to impress her. The truth below that was that Meridian was a striking man, and perhaps what Tristan really wanted was to impress *him*. He let all that be as plain as he could without speaking a word of it, but the musician was either *laran*-talented or just generally perceptive to such advances.

The six-fingered *rryl* player accepted him as his student and got up to fetch his instrument. He was tall and long-limbed, yet somehow didn't seem at all ungainly about it. The Chieri blood, Tristan knew, although no one referred to Meridian as such. No one called him a six-fingered man. Just a man, a musician, a tutor.

When he came back, he set the *rryl* in Tristan's arms and positioned his hands just so. He wore thin indoor gloves, as

Tristan knew *laran*-talented people often did, and in comparison to Tristan, Meridian's six long fingers filled out his gloves perfectly.

"Is there be much of a difference in technique, between..." Tristan started, and let the question hang. He wanted to seem shy about asking. The fact that he suddenly *was* shy about asking helped tremendously.

"Numbers of fingers?" Meridian asked archly. "Not really. An extra finger helps the beginner, but at similar proficiency, our playing would be indistinguishable by sound."

"There's no difference in the music written by composers with...?"

"Of course not. Why would there be?"

Tristan swallowed. Meridian lingered behind him, and his cologne was making it hard to think. "On Terra, there would."

Meridian pulled back. "Well. Be grateful you're not on Terra anymore, then," he said, and that seemed to be the end of that.

"But—"

"Tristan," Meridian said firmly. "I'm sorry that your world places more importance on extending your maps than on extending your minds, but if you want to get along here, that's a thing you're going to have to get over. Is there no one with six fingers on Terra?"

"It's a desirable trait in cats," Tristan answered, but it was weak even to his own ears.

Meridian came up behind him again, touching his wrists and then his hands. Ungloved. He ran his thumbs lightly over Tristan's scars. "But not in Terrans," he guessed gently.

Tristan hung his head, waiting out the flush of his cheeks. "Not in Terrans."

Meridian drew his fingertips back to Tristan's elbows and lifted gently, guiding him to his feet.

"In that case, welcome home."

A Plague of Aunts

by Jane M. H. Bigelow

Interactions between Terrans and Darkovans do not always go smoothly, as exemplified in Rebecca Fox's "The Short, Inglorious War" and other stories in this volume. Opportunities for misunderstandings abound, and those frictions escalate all too readily. On the other hand, when romantic chemistry clicks in, combined with uncommonly good common sense, the results can be delightful if hilarious. The love story of Duvin and Ginevra follows this principle. When you add a passel of relatives into the mix, fun and feathers fly!

Jane M. H. Bigelow had her first professional publication in *Free Amazons of Darkover*. Since then, she has published a fantasy novel, *Talisman*, as well as short stories and short nonfiction on such topics as gardening in Ancient Egypt. Her short story, "The Golden Ruse" appeared in *Luxor: Gods, Grit and Glory.* She is currently working on a mystery set in 17th century France. Jane is a retired reference librarian, a job which encouraged her to go on being curious about everything and exposed her to a rich variety of people. She lives in Denver, CO with her husband and two spoiled cats.

The messenger from the spaceport caught up with me yet again just as I reached the street where Ginevra's house stands. Five tall, narrow houses share the street, which is shaped like a whisky bottle. I'd found it with only one wrong turn this time in spite of the fog.

Ginevra would be there by now, back from the family estate up in the Venza Hills. Pretty place, but I still don't see why people say the countryside's relaxing. Everyone there seemed to be working dashed hard all the time, and the birds set up a racket long before it's even properly light. It had only taken

Ginevra five days to persuade her brother, Alastair, to escort her to Thendara after I had to come back here. No, really, I did have to. Uncle needed a signature for the investments.

That had gone all right, hadn't it? He'd sent me a message back saying, "Done." I'd just sent one follow-up message to Aunt Amelia, describing Ginevra and her family in more detail. Yet here I was with several more messages. Amazing how seldom anyone pays interstellar rates to tell you good news—but there wasn't anything I could do about whatever it was, now was there? And it had started to rain.

The porter opened the door while I was raising my hand to knock. Martin, their majordomo and runner of all household matters, took my cloak away so that it could drip without making the entryway all slick. I slogged up to the parlor on the first floor still clutching the messages. Time enough for them once I'd said hello to my beloved.

Ginevra sat at a narrow table in front of the room's largest window, her red-blonde curls fizzing out from a big wooden clasp. The copper inlay along its edges glinted in the firelight. The room always looks warm with its wooden paneling and embroidered cushions on the chairs. Right now it felt wonderful. Ginevra had shed a couple of layers of wool; her sleeve fell back as she tossed a paper into the fire. She has such delicate wrists. She also has excellent aim—it landed in the very center and flamed up before I could see what it was.

"Oh, ah, sorry!" I stepped backwards through the doorway and knocked my stack of message scrips from my hand. Ginevra's maid sprang up to get them. "No, really, I'd rather—" I tried, but she'd already gathered them and handed them back. Marja seems to have decided that since her lady has unaccountably decided to marry me, she'd better take care of me. Kind of her, but it makes me feel like a small child with a nursemaid.

Ginevra smiled. "I'm not throwing things at *you*, beloved."

"Good thing. I'll have to make sure I never make you that angry. But, Ginevra, what—"

"What are all those messages?"

"Don't know yet. You know, it would save ever so much shoe leather if you'd just allow message alerts."

"What a horrible idea! It's bad enough that some of the inns have them."

"Those are loudspeakers, love, and I'll admit they're intrusive. Message alerts—"

"What would all the messengers do if we didn't need them anymore?" Ginevra smiled at me. Good question, that. "Now, all those messages?"

I hauled a chair over to the other end of the table. "Aunt Amelia, Aunt Amelia, Aunt Amelia, oh look! This one's from Uncle Albert. Aunt Amelia, and more Aunt Amelia." I shuffled through to find the first one.

"Duvin, who r ths ppl? Pls resp."

Then, "Why no ans prev msg?"

A day later, she'd sent, "No mentn any db??"

And later that same day, "Not heard of. Evn yr uncle's xotic gds frds. Blst u boy ans!" What? Oh, the foreign trade lads. I have never managed to convince Aunt Amelia that under modern communications schemes, it's just as cheap to put in a whole word and much easier to read. A groan escaped me.

"Duvin?"

"Half a mo. Let me read Uncle's."

It said, "Duvin, my boy, please answer your aunt before she breaks us with interstellar message fees."

"Duvin?" Ginevra came over and touched my shoulder. "What's wrong with your aunt?" There was a furrow between her nearly-invisible eyebrows.

"Nothing really." I reached over to smooth the furrow; she moved away.

"Duvin. You groaned."

"She's all right. She's just never been off Herschel V, and she doesn't understand so many things, like how long it takes to get a message out and back."

"Oh? I daresay that does happen, when people aren't galactic travelers. It must make it hard to communicate with them."

Bit frosty there. "I didn't mean criticism of you, Ginevra! You pick things up right away."

"Thank you for your kind opinion."

I hadn't meant any insult, but I guessed it was best to stop digging now. The hole was deep enough. "She's a smart lady, really. She just doesn't listen. It's as if this sheet of glass goes up between her and whoever she's arguing with." I had a brilliant thought. "That's one thing I love about you—you do listen."

That went well, but I simply had to blather on. "Now, why are you throwing papers into the fire?"

"Oh, it was just a piece of foolishness."

Ginevra's a perfectly awful liar. Her face goes absolutely still, and she looks off to one side. She's excellent at being stubborn, though. I decided—yes, it really was *my* decision—to change the subject. We did get some actual wedding planning done, if you can count discarding three different schemes.

Then I had a brilliant idea. I do get them sometimes, and I treasure every one. "Ginevra," I began, and then hesitated. Maybe it wasn't so brilliant. I suspected planning it would take the skills of an invading general. Not that I know any invading generals, but we had to read history in school.

"Yes, Duvin? Hello? Duvin?" She put her head to one side and gave me the puzzled shepherd look.

"Why don't we just move this whole thing off Darkover completely? No," I could see she was about to object, "Not to Herschel V. You'd love Thetis! It's beautiful, flowers everywhere, and warm oceans with gentle waves to swim in. Have you ever been swimming? I could teach you. It would be easy for you, what with you being so graceful already."

"Thank you, Duvin, but are you trying to fool a poor little Protected World girl? Swim in an ocean?" She gave me a measuring sort of look.

"No, it's absolutely true! You can ask anybody. And they do discounts for groups, so we could get your family out there, and we wouldn't have to worry about your ways or my ways. We could just do it."

"That does sound beautiful. I just...What is it, Marja?"

"*Damisela*, there's a messenger again."

From guess who? This one was priority. Can't think why, as it didn't say anything different than the last lot. All these dashes across to the Terran HQ were getting me fearfully fit. "Think about Thetis, please?"

"I will."

For once, the line at the Messages Department at Terran HQ was short. One thing about all these repetitive messages: answering them was dead easy. "I'm fine. They have their own money and don't need mine. I am not going full assimilation." Be a damn sight easier if I were.

"Is there any way I can, ah, expedite this?"

"No, I'm sorry." The tech hadn't even looked at me.

"I mean, I don't at all mind paying higher rates. And you lot must be getting tired of sending messengers after me."

"The laws of physics don't care." He stopped, cleared his throat, and added, "Sorry. I would if I could."

I'd like to know why nobody invokes the laws of physics for good things. Why can't the laws of physics compel aunts to read messages all the way through? Still, "Ah well, can't argue with the laws of physics, can we? Would you have an explanation of that I could ship off to my Aunt Amelia?"

He called one up, and even explained it to me. It all made perfectly good sense to me when he said it. That sort of thing always reminds me of when a bird goes by overhead, and you hear it, and you know it's probably a bird or something like it, same eco-niche, you know—but it's all gone so fast, and it *might* have been a meat-eating gliderbeast. If you want to know how it works, I suggest you look up "Interstellar Communications for the Non-Physicist," Terran Federation Publications 56.93.1. Just don't ask me to explain it.

I sent it off, attached to a message explaining that there are no computers on Darkover outside of the Terran Zone and maybe some mapping planes. I told her she should at least meet Ginevra before she judged her. Two more messages from Aunt Amelia came in while I sent mine. "Could you possibly just hold any more of these?"

Yes, there was a form for that. Whew.

Ginevra comes with me to my dancing lessons, which is awfully sweet of her, given that she already knows all of this and could probably teach the class. It does give us an excuse to dance together.

It's a good thing that the dance studio's uphill of her house. It means it's downhill back. That gives me time to catch my breath before we do the stairs to the parlor. Alastair passed us on the stairs, giving me a welcoming buffet on the shoulder as he loped on up to his study. Ginevra assures me they're meant as a welcome, and she's an honest woman.

She'd a letter waiting for her. To guess by the dirt and thumb prints on the outside, it had come a long way, yet she set it aside.

"Don't you want to open that? I don't mind."

Ginevra went over to the window. "No, thank you." Crisp and clear as a language lesson. That's never a good sign, but I pressed on.

"But, you put up with my going through all of my daft aunt's messages. It doesn't seem right—"

She popped the seal off the letter so briskly that it shattered into several pieces, all of which went flying. "Since you insist. It's from my Aunt Bruna, and I think I know what she says." She'd read about half of it when her hands started to shake. "I am not a brood mare!"

Well, no. She certainly wasn't. I didn't understand, though. It seemed like shouting, "I am not a manufacturing plant!" or "I am not a mangel-wurzel!"

She held the letter out to me, then snatched it back as I frowned over the rounded Darkovan script. "Here. Aunt Bruna writes, 'Shouldn't you consider your duty to bear Gifted children? If you must desert Dalereuth Tower, then at least marry a Comyn of known abilities. Your own ability is slight but steady; matched with—oh!"

No one had lit the fire yet. She began ripping the letter into shreds, saying a few words I still hadn't managed to get translated. Alastair claims he doesn't know them either. Women's curses, he says. It was good, thick paper, none of your Federation flimsies here, and she'd only torn up about half of it when a very young servant girl ran into the room. She dipped a quick curtsey. "Would it please you, *damisela,* to have me light the fire?"

Alastair thundered into the room, looking alarmed. After one look at his sister, he went silently to a chair in a dark corner.

Ginevra ignored the girl and continued her human shredder routine. I was feeling dashed chilly myself, so I said, "Yes, please," and the child set about it. Only when Ginevra had reduced the letter to a pile of very small pieces did she call for *jaco*.

"Aunt Bruna was always so encouraging when I was new to *laran* work, and earlier, when Mama died so soon after Father, she was the only one who didn't say stupid things to Alastair and me. But now she just doesn't listen!"

I nodded. "My Aunt Amelia doesn't listen, either. But here's a thought: you could have Martin hold all your aunt's messages for you. I've done that with Aunt Amelia's, I mean, I'm having the communications techs hold them, not Martin, of course. I just get a batch of them now and then," Mostly then, I must admit, "And skim through them all at once. Much easier on the nerves."

Ginevra was so happy that she hugged me, brother or no brother. "What a good idea!"

Alastair coughed.

"Oh, dear," said Ginevra, "The chimney needs cleaning again."

It really would be much simpler if I just went full assimilation. From what I can tell, if you want to do that you just find a friendly Darkovan family, Comyn if you can manage it, change the spelling of your name, and disappear into the mountains. Terran HQ forgets about you. I wished they'd forget about me, but no such luck. They kept wanting a reason for my staying on, and after they'd hustled me out of Thendara one time to keep me away from Ginevra, I wasn't about to plead young love. Maybe I could get hired on with Istvan MacAndra, my guide when I first got here, as a tourist guide. At least I have some skills for that; can't really see myself raising chervines.

After that day's bother, I couldn't face collecting messages from home. I set off across town again, enjoying a rare sunny day. Half of Thendara must have been doing the same. Shopkeepers along the way had hauled out racks and tables of goods. Should I buy Ginevra that hair clasp with the green sparkly bits? I decided to risk it.

Even the long Darkovan day was starting to dim by the time I got to the house. Ginevra and Marja had set up in the parlor again, with Marja stitching away at something dark green next to the front window. Ginevra sat very still in the half-light beyond Marja, holding something in her hand. I peered into the dimness. Was she all right? She'd gone even paler than she usually is, and—she was crying!

Marja thrust her needle securely into her work. "No, don't interrupt her!" She popped up to stand between Ginevra and me. Would she ever believe I'm not a barbarian? And while I may not be the brightest light in the harbor, I'm not entirely stupid.

I waved her back. "All right, all right," I whispered. "But will you please tell me what's going on?"

Ginevra messed about a bit with whatever she held and let it drop back into her blouse. "It's all right, Marja. I'm done."

Oh, dash it. I didn't want to add to her troubles, but I surely did want to know what was going on. I rather thought she'd been using her starstone, and she didn't do that often. "Ginevra?"

"It's all right, I said."

"No, it isn't."

She glared at me. I thought of three more things to say and rejected all of them. The silence stretched on. Well, she hadn't thrown anything.

"Ginevra? You were crying."

"It's—oh, very well, it's not all right. But it isn't really tragic, either. My cousin at Dalereuth Tower is not in sympathy with me, and it makes me sad."

"*Domna* Bruna again?"

She sniffed. "It isn't as easy to, to not-listen as it is to have messages held."

"I can believe that." Sometimes I wish I could do telepathy. Right now I was glad I couldn't.

It had been a good evening, all told. Ginevra's friends are beginning to get used to me; one even remembered that I'm not from Terra, though she couldn't recall where I *am* from. I faced the usual questions as to what I do. Mostly, I told them, I fill out forms to stay on Darkover. That got more of a laugh than it probably deserved.

We trooped up the stairs like an uphill parade, Martin the majordomo, Ginevra, then me, then Alastair. The fire was banked, and a small lantern gave the only light. Three steps into the room, Ginevra stopped so suddenly that I trod on her heels, and Alastair trod on mine. There followed a brisk exchange of *Oh, sorry, no, not your fault*, and *Oh-are-you injured?* questions. Too bad I'd lost the courtesy contest at the foot of the stairs. When a man who's a head taller and 20 kilos heavier, all of it muscle, and wearing traditional Darkovan boots made, I think, of the hide of some poor beast that died of old age and hard living—where was I? Ah. When he treads on one's heel, the heel loses. I was just wagging my foot around a bit to make sure nothing was broken, when Ginevra spoke.

"Aunt Bruna." I don't think Aunt Bruna could hear her say, "Why?"

The fabled Aunt Bruna turned out to be a tallish woman with red roan hair, braided tightly back into a lumpish mass at the back of her neck. Ginevra took a deep breath and shoved some curls back behind her ears, and began to make hostessy noises about refreshments and such. Martin dashed around lighting candles before quietly disappearing down the stairs.

Aunt Bruna talked right over her. "Since you wouldn't answer me by mind or by pen, I've had to travel from Dalereuth to get some answers. Is this the *Terranan*?" She looked at me the way our steward looks at a horse that has probably got spavins. "Ginevra, he's shorter than you are!"

I straightened up, as if that would make a difference. Then Ginevra laughed, and I didn't care.

"Our steps match when we dance," she said.

"Hmph. It won't all be dancing, my girl!"

This was getting annoying. I mean to say, I quite recognize that senior ladies have a right to express themselves pretty freely, at least there's never been any arguing that with Aunt Amelia, but I wasn't a horse, with or without spavins. I could talk.

Ginevra went on as though her aunt hadn't spoken. "And

Duvin is my affianced husband, not some footman on approval."

Oh, were footmen supposed to be tall here, too? Curious.

"He faced down Alastair over bared steel for my sake!"

"But wouldn't take up a sword to defend himself," muttered Alastair from his corner by the door.

I should think not. I haven't the least idea how to use a sword, and I don't wish to learn.

One corner of the *leronis's* mouth moved. "Very romantic," she noted. "And this paragon's name is?"

Alastair stepped forward. "*Domna* Bruna Syrtis-Ridenow, may I present Duvin Wrothesley, of the Pelham Plains of Herschel V." That's the estate, not that I spend much time there. New London is much more amusing.

I bowed. Useful trick, bowing; nobody seems to mind much if you don't actually say anything, which is good. Moments before, I'd wished passionately for a chance to talk. Now I couldn't think of a thing to say except the usual. "It's an honor to meet you, *Domna* Bruna. Ginevra has spoken of you often."

"Ah, good, you do speak *casta*. Since I've had not information save rumors, young lady,"

I could feel Ginevra stiffen.

"I've had to come all this way to see for myself, and leave Dalereuth Tower short-handed. More short-handed, I should say, since *you*," she paused to glare at Ginevra, who blushed all the way down her neck, "have deserted us. And speaking of one's life work, just what do you do, *Mestre* Wrothesley?"

Ah. Well. "Nothing much," probably wasn't an acceptable answer. I've used "exist beautifully" from time to time, but this very serious lady didn't look as if she'd be amused. My "fill out forms" line didn't seem good either. It's so bally difficult to talk with serious people. Maybe that's where Alastair got his grim outlook—no, wait, aunt, not mother, it couldn't be. And it certainly wasn't the moment to let everyone know I'd been traveling to forget about Emma.

Someone cleared his throat. Martin had oiled in quietly as fog. Made me think of Fensey. How I miss the old IPA!

"I'm sorry to interrupt, but we have guests." Martin really did look sorry, too; usually he's got about as much expression as my uncle's butlerbot. He stood in the doorway, pretty well filling it, in fact. Was whoever it was right behind him?

Alastair seized the chance to dilute the effect of Aunt Bruna. Must stop calling her that. She isn't my aunt, at least not yet, and if I keep thinking it I'll say it. "Show them up, Martin." Risky, that. What if they were somebody like that daft friend of Ginevra's who asks the most embarrassing questions? Still, any interruption was welcome. Martin stood aside.

Or maybe not this interruption. In walked—or should the word be, staggered—Aunt Amelia and Uncle Albert. They both looked dazed; even in first class a trip of that length messes about with your body's own rhythms. Besides, I could still remember my own first sight of Darkover. I stood there with my mouth hanging open, a one-man traffic hazard, and I've seen a few planets.

We blinked at each other for a bit, they taking in my Darkovan wool and leather and I taking in their sleek ship stretchies. Aunt Amelia's hair was even shorter than when I'd left. Uncle Albert was rather colorful, with a red face from the stairs and blue fingers from wearing an elegant-but-thin jacket of Andleran fleece.

Uncle Albert was trying to look around the room without staring; Aunt Amelia didn't try to pretend. There is a line of chervines carved all around the room, each one with its foreleg tangled up in the back leg of the one in front. Until now I always thought it looked like a bit silly. Wouldn't they trip each other? Now Martin disappeared fast enough to set the candles flickering in the breeze; the chervines looked as if they were moving.

I didn't get to muse on that for long. Behind my dear old relatives stood a message runner whom I knew all too well. Couldn't think of his name, of course, I'm dead awful with names, but I'd seen him many times, generally with their messages.

"Ah, *Mestre* Wrothesley is here!" he cried joyfully. "He will know what you need, I'm sure." He turned to go, but not without giving Uncle Albert time to offer a tip.

"Ah...Duvin, m'boy" muttered Uncle, when the messenger

held out his hand rather than offering a swiper.

"Did you get coinage yet?" His blank look answered that. I handed over a few coins, and the messenger left.

Well, that explained how they'd found the house. But why were they here? "Is everything all right at home?"

"Everything at home is just fine," said Uncle Albert. "But Duvin, my boy, we're more than a bit worried about you. You won't deny you're a susceptible fellow," He paused, thanks be to whatever deities were listening, and I mouthed, "Not now" at him. Ginevra knows she's not my first love ever, but I haven't exactly burdened her with all the cast of characters over the years since I started to notice girls. It's all rather embarrassing. How could I have been so wrong so many times?

"You've lingered here weeks longer than expected *and* cut communication." Uncle Albert smiled. I'm sure it was supposed to be reassuring. "We mean no disrespect to the young lady,"

I could hear at least two people sniff, and someone said, "Hmph."

"But we are worried. It's all so sudden!"

Alastair understands a bit of Standard, like most Darkovans who spend much time in Thendara. "Sudden. Yes, it is very sudden."

What to do, what to do? Alastair was clearly working up a longer statement. "Ouch!"

Ginevra moved past me, murmuring apologies for her clumsiness in stepping on my foot. "Please," she said in careful Standard, "Do have seats and I will send for food and drink."

Aunt Amelia sat in the nearest chair, a spindly thing that creaked enough to worry me. It held. Near her, Uncle Albert dropped into a cushioned number that I happened to know was Alastair's favorite.

The fire flared and sank; Aunt Amelia sneezed. I handed her my handkerchief; she tidied up a bit, started to wad it up, and then shrieked, "Oh, Duvin! Why did you hand me *this* for my nose?" She addressed the room at large, "He never did have any sense. This lovely work, hand-sewn, possibly," she held an unused portion up to the light of a nearby candle, "Yes, quite possibly hand-woven, Duvin, how could you? This is a treasure."

Ginevra sent me an impatient look.

"I'm sorry," I told her.

Then, to the relatives, "Just wait a mo, I have to introduce you "

Then, in *casta* to the Darkovan side of the room: "Sorry for standing here like a stuffed frog,"

Ginevra laughed. Alastair didn't.

"This is my aunt, Amelia Wrothesley, and my uncle, Albert Wrothesley. Forgive me, *vai leronis, Dom* Alastair and *Damisela* Ginevra, I'll use Terran Standard for a moment."

I waved at Alastair, who seemed to have swallowed a fly. "Aunt, Uncle, this is *Dom* Alastair Ridenow-Leynier, Ginevra's brother and the lord of this house. This lady," bowing to Aunt Bruna, "Is *Domna* Bruna Syrtis-Ridenow a *leronis*, a highly trained telepath, and *Dom* Alastair and *Damisela* Ginevra's aunt."

"Saving the best for last," and I repeated that in *casta*, "This is *Damisela* Ginevra Ridenow-Leynier, my affianced bride."

Ginevra smiled her beautiful smile. "Duvin, please, I don't think my Standard is up to this yet. Please tell her that I am glad that she likes the handkerchief. The cloth is from our own estates. I myself made it, but indeed it is to be used."

She probably could have said all that herself; she's a quick learner. She's a little self-conscious about her accent, though I think it's beautiful—quite musical. It *was* rather nice to have something straightforward to do. I translated.

"Translate this, Duvin," directed Aunt Amelia. "Tell her I wish I spoke her language, and compliment her on using ours to greet us. Then say, 'We apologize for inconveniencing you by landing on your doorstep with no warning. However, when our nephew neglected to meet us at the spaceport—"

Wait a minute! "What—how—"

"We had no choice but to try, with the aid of a random employee who seemed far more—"

I hauled in a great lungful of air, choked briefly on the wood smoke in the room, and managed to make myself heard.

"How was I supposed to know to meet you?"

"We both sent messages, Duvin. Surely even on this backwards planet you do get messages?"

Solid stone houses do not dance the gavotte. I was certain of that. Why did this one seem to be whirling and jumping? I'd meant to pick up messages often, truly I had. But we'd been busy trying to create a ceremony that would combine Darkovan traditions and mine, without giving me a bunch of rights I bloody well didn't want or leaving Ginevra unprotected. Just now and then we managed to slip out and wander around Thendara together. Sometimes we didn't even have to take Marja with us.

"Duvin!" That was Aunt Amelia. "Did you or did you not get our message? Can't these people even deliver a simple message?"

Aunt Amelia rides to hounds, and in moments of stress the vocal training shows. Most people use a synth to get the volume needed to boss a gang of hounds, but traditionalists do it unaided.

"It isn't their fault," I said.

"Hmph."

Curious, how much she sounded like Ginevra's Aunt Bruna. That aunt sent my aunt an approving look, even though she surely didn't understand what Aunt Amelia had asked me.

"I was having my messages held—"

"Oh, Duvin!" Aunt Amelia sounded much as she had when I put sliced beets all round on the tablecloth at our Fall Festival party. I still think they looked quite festive. It was worth being denied dessert to get past her, just once. She usually caught on to my plans about the time I'd got them worked out myself.

Now Uncle Albert chimed in. "Duvin, my boy, you know better than that. Here's your aunt and I, dashing halfway across the galaxy to find out what's going on. I've had to leave the business in charge of a subordinate I don't completely trust."

He never did.

"And you're not even bothering to pick up your messages?"

Aunt Bruna said, in Standard, "*Mestre* and *Mestra*

Wrothesley, please accept my condolences for having a young family member who is as ungrateful and uncooperative as my own."

She spoke Standard. She had understood every word, with no rude listening in to strangers' thoughts required. It needed only that.

Domna Bruna gave me a look that could have sliced the hardest cheese on Herschel V. "Yes, I speak Terran Standard. It is an ugly language, but essential if one is to do research into the deep history of the non-causative sciences." You could have called her expression a smile, I suppose. "For people who do not believe in such things, the *Terranan* have published a remarkable number of studies. Your folk legends are also intriguing, especially in the case of the more remote lands of Terra."

"Yes, Aunt Bruna," Ginevra said quickly. "That's all true." She got one dirty look for that, and several grateful ones.

"Sir?" That was Martin. I hadn't even noticed when he came in. Odd, how much he's like Fensey. Still doesn't seem quite right to treat a human being as an appliance, but he seems happy. Or he does when he's not dealing with this much confusion. He went on, "How many bedchambers shall I have prepared?"

"Yes, I'd like to know, also," commented Alastair in his driest, *I-will-be-calm* voice. "Are we to have the pleasure of your relatives' company?"

Oh, ah. I wondered if it would be polite to ask if they even had room enough for my relatives. I'd never seen the house above this level. I mean to say, why would I? But even Darkovans wouldn't offer if they hadn't room, would they?

"We can," said Ginevra quietly.

"Thanks awfully for the invitation," which I strongly suspected, no telepathy required, they didn't want accepted. "They may have arranged for a room."

I asked. They hadn't. "The young man at the intake tried to make us waste time with that, but I refused," said Aunt Amelia.

I felt pity for the young man, whoever he was. "They've invited you to stay here."

Behind me, I could hear Martin murmur, "*Vai dom*, I'll need to send the boy for more candles if they do stay."

"But I'd better warn you that the conditions are, well, luxurious in some ways but...not what you're used to in others. I'm staying at a little place just on the Terran Zone side of the line—it isn't done here to have the engaged couple stay under the same roof." In fact, if I'd understood correctly, it could mean that the couple already were married in the eyes of the community, and we had agreed to wait a little. Alastair thought we ought to wait until I'd experienced at least one Darkovan winter; Ginevra and I disagreed.

Ginevra suddenly jumped as if someone had prodded her in the ribs. She blushed, and said, "But the refreshments! You will surely stay long enough for that."

Uncle Albert wrecked his digestion years ago at business luncheons. He opened his mouth to speak.

There's nothing wrong with Aunt Amelia's digestion, and she enjoys her food. She looked sternly at Uncle Albert. "Some refreshment would be delightful."

He sank back into his chair. He was as pale now as he'd been red before.

Alastair looked at him with a worried frown, and beckoned to Ginevra. She was looking at her aunt, so it didn't do him any good.

Sending my uncle into a major attack of dyspepsia wasn't going to help our cause. He's too polite to turn down the party-giver's prize dish even if it's lobster and fiery chilies torte. I do not jest. Unfortunately, he also hates having a fuss made over his poor digestion.

Someone must have signaled to the kitchen staff already. A little maid trotted in, bending at the wrists a bit under a load of tea, teacups, wine and goblets, a basket of nut bread, and two cheeses. I took it from her before I remembered that one isn't supposed to do that sort of thing here. Alastair and *Domna* Bruna glared at me, but the maid looked grateful.

I was trying to figure out a discrete way to tell Ginevra that she'd better not spring anything too adventurous on our merry little throng when Aunt Amelia spoke up.

"Why, thank you, *domna leronis,*" she said. Oh well, at

least all the words were respectful. "That would be perfect! Poor Albert overworks himself, always has, and his digestion suffers dreadfully for it."

Now I was really worried. No one had said anything. This kind of scattiness wasn't like her, and she's never been a manipulator. If she wants something she just says so. "Aunt Amelia? Are you feeling quite the thing?"

"Of course I am! Why should showing elementary politeness for someone's kind concern mean that I'm unwell? This lady told your friend that she should order up some plain roast chicken, which will be just the thing for Albert."

Aunt Bruna's head snapped around like a hunting dog's when it hears the foxbot. "My dear, I didn't speak aloud. I suggested to Ginevra that she might include some roast chicken in the repast since your husband suffers from dyspepsia—forgive me if I intrude, but he was thinking of it too strongly for me to ignore. You heard my thoughts."

I can't remember ever seeing Aunt Amelia speechless before. Uncle Albert said, "Did I talk about it out loud? I do talk to myself sometimes. Bad habit, I know, but I do. Perhaps this lady," he nodded to *Domna* Bruna, "does too?"

"No," she said. And then, to Aunt Amelia, "You can't have had any training in using *laran*, not on a *Terranan* world. Oh, my dear, all those years! You must be a strong-minded woman."

Aunt Amelia laughed a little. "Well, I know my own mind—or I thought I did. You believe that I have this *laran*?" She sounded dubious.

I started to explain about *laran*, but Aunt Amelia cut me off. "I know what *laran* means, Duvin. We had that whole interminable trip to read up on," she paused for a moment, "Darkover." She turned to Aunt Bruna. "If I understand correctly, and I believe I do—" She shot me an auntly look, and I closed my mouth. Can't even think what I meant to say, but it seemed as though I ought to say something. Evidently not.

"If I understand, you are saying that I heard your, hm, thought conversation with Lady Ginevra? It seems unlikely. Don't you Darkovans hold that it is limited to people of Comyn descent?"

"We have come to doubt that in recent years. *Laran* is more complex than we had thought, and more widely present. A genetic component is undeniable." She shot an auntly look at Ginevra, who said nothing.

Aunt Bruna continued, "As to your hearing our thoughts, yes, I do say so. Did anyone else in this room hear me suggest plain roasted chicken? Anyone except Ginevra, of course."

Well, I certainly hadn't. Alastair shrugged. "I heard my sister's answer." Uncle Albert said nothing more.

Aunt Amelia had *laran*? The most prosaic woman I'd ever known...and the one who always seemed to know what I was up to. I looked over at Ginevra; she wasn't looking at me a bit. They were all looking at my aunt.

Maybe Ginevra and I could slip out of the room and find the Darkovan equivalent of a Justice of the Peace. Or the next flight to Thetis. Or a J.P. and then a flight to Thetis. I started edging towards her.

Aunt Amelia wrung her hands. Don't believe I've ever seen someone do that before, but I don't know what else to call it. "I'm sorry! I didn't mean to eavesdrop."

Aunt Bruna smiled. "*Domna,* you have a very proper concern. No harm was done."

Uncle Albert levered himself more upright in his chair. "Amelia? Do you really think you have this? Wouldn't you have known before now?"

"It isn't a disease," protested Ginevra. Her aunt gave another one of those looks, and Ginevra subsided.

"Hmm" Aunt Amelia said. She'd a faraway look in her eye. "Fancying that one had special powers wasn't exactly encouraged at school," she said. "The head teacher once threatened to ban all fantasy novels if we didn't stop our foolishness. I hadn't thought of that kerfuffle in, oh, many years." She reached over to grasp Uncle Albert's hand.

He looked a good bit more cheerful. "Well, it would explain a lot. No wonder you always knew what I was really thinking!" He turned to *Domna* Bruna. "Dashed awkward when she'd asked me if I liked her new outfit."

"Yes, it can work like that," she agreed. One corner of her mouth moved again, just a little.

Aunt Amelia said softly, for her, "And it explains Grandmother MacLeod. She claimed she saw the future, sometimes." She took a hasty gulp of tea from the nearest cup, mine, as it happened. "I won't start doing that, will I? She was not a happy woman."

"It's hard to say without testing you, and I think that we'd best allow you to get some rest before that happens. Hm. Gifts do skip a generation sometimes. Ginevra, how are the rooms coming along?"

"Aunt Bruna, they haven't even said they wish to stay here yet."

"Nonsense. They must stay, now. How else can we get this wedding planned in reasonable time and offer *Domna* Wrothesley at least a little of the training she needs? Besides, it's much too late to send someone off into the night."

When had it gone completely dark? No one had come to close the shutters, and I could see that two of the moons had risen.

Domna Bruna switched to Standard. "I've never worked with a mature adult before, *domna*, but we could at least begin. You may well wish to spend some time in a Tower, but—"

"What?" cried my aunt and uncle in unison.

"No, dear, that won't be possible," said Aunt Amelia. "I've my own concerns back home. Besides which, I've managed so far in my life. One problem, I gather from my shipboard reading, is ignoring chatter. I already know how to do that." Didn't she just!

Is there some common gene in all aunts? *Domna* Bruna continued speaking as if no one had spoken. "Really, Alastair."

He'd been standing quietly in a corner. Now he jumped as if she'd stuck him with one of Marja's precious needles.

"You seem to have done nothing to expedite this wedding."

That clearly stung. Never thought I'd feel sorry for Alastair. "Probably because I didn't want to expedite it, Aunt Bruna. And neither did you until just now."

She didn't blink. "It's a poor mind that won't change when circumstances do so."

"Yes, exactly," said Aunt Amelia.

I slid over to Ginevra and murmured, “Did we just win?”
“I think so.”

Quevrailleth's Sister

by Leslie Fish

Darkover is home not only to the descendants of a Lost Colony ship (*Darkover Landfall*) but a number of sentient nonhuman races. None is more intriguing and has more wide appeal than the *chieri*. An ancient race of graceful, gender-fluid forest dwellers, they once traveled the stars but now have returned to the planet of their origin. Marion Zimmer Bradley included *chieri* characters in *The World Wreckers*, highlighting both their loneliness as a people on the brink of extinction, their emotional sensitivity, and their telepathic powers. To this, Leslie Fish brings an appealing young heroine caught in an oppressive culture and longing for the same depth of connection.

Leslie learned to sing and to read at a very young age, playing guitar at sixteen, and writing the first of hundreds of songs shortly thereafter, including settings of Rudyard Kipling's poetry and the "all-time most notorious" Star Trek filksong ever written: "Banned From Argo." She's recorded a number of albums and composed songs, both alone and collaborative, on albums from every major filk label. She was elected to the Filk Hall Of Fame as one of the first inductees. In college, she majored in English and minoring in psychology, protest and politics, joined the Industrial Workers of the World, and did psychology counseling for veterans. Her other jobs included railroad yard clerk, go-go dancer, and social worker. She currently lives in Arizona with her husband Rasty and a variable number of cats which she breeds for intelligence.

It was night cycle on G Deck, so only the dull-orange floor lights were lit, and the normally crowded and noisy space now sounded of nothing but the breathing of a hundred sleeping steerage passengers. Elena, curled up on her cot against the rear bulkhead, was awake—but that, she guessed, wouldn't last long. The fever had a firm grip on her again, and soon enough it would drag her back down into a sea of dreams and then to deep and silent darkness.

Perhaps this time it would hold her there, and she would never rise up to consciousness again.

And who would care, really?

As the fourth daughter of Omar Manborg (whose clan rated no higher than G Deck), with her unlovely face and endless health problems and most unfeminine mind, she was nothing but a liability. Even when the *Nasser* reached its goal and the proper settlement began, she couldn't be sold for so much as the price of her passage—as Mother never tired of telling her.

Why not leave me home, then? she remembered asking Mother, thinking that as an orphan on the streets of the abandoned Purist enclave she could walk into the city proper and be taken up by the orphanage. There, at least, she'd be allowed to go back to school...

Her arms tightened unconsciously around her treasure: the sack that held her other dress, wrapped around her one book, *The Encyclopedic Dictionary of Science.* She'd just gotten into the Bs on that day when her brothers had dragged her out of school and hauled her home, given her barely time to pack, and then harried her onto the transport that carried her and the rest of the clan and most of the population of New Stockholm off to the spaceport and onto the ship. She still studied her treasure whenever she could; she'd been halfway through the Cs when her latest "non-contagious unspecified ailment" had left her feverish and forgotten on her cot against the rear bulkhead.

Memory supplied the only answer to her question that she'd ever gotten from Mother: the usual slap and screech and rant about Family Honor, and how not one drop of their precious blood would be left behind for the Faithless to contaminate with their filthy culture.

Now, as then, that made no logical sense. Any microscope she had ever looked in showed that her blood—in fact, the blood of any other Pure—was no different from the blood of any Faithless. It certainly wasn't affected by culture, anyway. At least, not unless one counted larger numbers of foreign microbes found in the blood of the Pure, which technically made them more filthy than the Faithless.

There was no point mentioning this to Mother, of course. There wasn't time, and anyway it would only garner the usual result, a slap/screech/rant about how Elena was much too literal-minded for a proper female, and couldn't understand the deeper meaning of things, and this was the result of sending girls to school in the first place, and thank Nameless that the Pure were escaping at last from this Faithless world. No, Elena would have to reason out the answer by herself.

The problem was that contemplating this conundrum sank her deeper into her own mind, down to the level of dreams...

The lone structure rearing up out of the smooth lawn resembled a single huge pale-blue crystal, rising taller than the trees to a sharp peak that caught the last rays of the sinking sun in a flare of blood-red. Quevraillleth paused in mid-step, struck by the image of a blood-tipped fang, and shivered in the growing chill.

Oh, go on, child, nagged kir mother's-sib behind kim. *You'll grow no warmer waiting.*

...Or braver, Quevrailleth admitted, and forced kirself to move forward.

A few steps more and the disturbing peak passed out of sight. The blue crystalline wall filled all kir vision, until a *chieri*-sized section ahead of kim melted away like mist, revealing a blue-walled corridor and exuding a feeling of warmth and welcome.

Larshkenye is anxious to see you. Mother's-sib chuckled audibly, a charming atavism. *The usual mood from that door is grim determination.*

Quevrailleth stepped quickly into the corridor, feeling the door close behind kim, knowing that the walls of the crystal tower would cut off any further contact between them. They both knew perfectly well that the only reason the venerable scholar Larshkenye had called upon such a child as Quevrailleth was the sheer amount of kir power, not anything to do with affection or even respect for kir studies. *If only I had been talented at music, or conversing with beasts, or sensing the presence of minerals, or anything else!* ke mourned—and then deliberately put the thought aside. If ke was here to be used, then so be it.

Larshkenye was waiting, and so was the fate of all their kind.

A slightly-impatient sense of welcome led down the corridor, where *kyrri* servitors scurried back and forth, then up a ramp, then to the left. Quevrailleth dutifully went that way.

Larshkenye sat on one of two large cushions in the center of the main chamber, dressed only in a soft grey robe, holding a truly enormous starstone, staring at a section of the glass-smooth wall. Long-robed *chieri* adepts, members of Larshkenye's working circle, studied the walls and spared Quevrailleth hardly a glance. Ke went to the second cushion and sat down, waiting to be noticed—then realizing that ke had already been noticed, and scanned and evaluated.

Presently the ancient *chieri* turned to look at Quevrailleth, and the walls revealed themselves as screens. The one where Larshkenye had been staring was a map, Quevrailleth realized; a map of a portion of the Overworld.

I've found one, Larshkenye announced without preamble. *A compatible mind, within reach, and...* Ke turned quickly to look at the screen again, *...just gone into receptive mode.*

Ke reached out and gripped Quevrailleth's hand with urgent force. At once Quevrailleth felt the contact, the direction, and the feel of the target mind.

Can you lock on? Larshkenye asked.

With kir other hand, Quevrailleth reached under kir robe for kir starstone.

Elena dreamed, and knew she was dreaming. She could feel her body baking with fever-heat, and her mind couldn't seem to stay focused on any thought. She struggled to keep thinking, stay aware, not slip off into directionless images—such as that one there, of an ancient elf sitting in a softly-glowing blue room. No, she must hold on to herself, lest she go down into the darkness from which rising came never. No, if no one else cared, she did. *I haven't even finished the Cs yet!* She remembered. *That's too unfair! I want to finish the whole book!*

And then someone else was there with her, another elf, likewise in a long robe, but much younger, feeling...puzzled. The elf seemed to struggle with words, thinking in complex images and feelings rather than simple precise thoughts, but clearly wanted to ask her something.

What is...'book'? the young elf finally managed.

And that was so silly that Elena just had to laugh. Distantly she felt her arms pulling tight on the sack that held her treasure. She pictured it vividly in her mind: the construct of plastic binding and sheets, printed with words and pictures and diagrams. *The world's wisdom, speaking in silence,* she tried to explain. *I've only just begun to learn from it...* A sudden surge of fury shook her. *I must not die until I've read every last word!*

The young elf and the older one gave the impression of trading glances of alarm, determination and reassurance. The younger turned back to her and said/felt/projected: *Not die. Gain knowledge. Agree! Me, too!*

Elena laughed silently again, charmed by this marvelous dream-companion. She had never had a dream like this, never even imagined a mind like this guileless young elf's. She got the distinct feeling that the elf was very young, really, and not much respected by its—his? her?—elders. A kindred spirit, indeed. *Me, too! Me, too!*

There was a timeless pause, and Elena got the impression that the older elf was placing a hand on the younger one's back, in warning perhaps, or bracing, or anchoring in some fashion. The young elf moved closer, both slender hands outstretched, shyly asking: *May I touch/know/draw closer?*

Elena hesitated, automatically tightening her grasp on her treasure. A maiden, as Mother so often told her, did not allow such intimacy from strangers, or even casual friends, and certainly not if they were male. But this elf, she decided, did not act like any man or boy she'd ever met, and was probably not a thief either. Cautiously, Elena nodded agreement, but added, *Only on the shoulders, mind.*

The elf (girl?) looked briefly bewildered, then carefully

moved closer and settled her hands as softly as feathers on what felt like Elena's shoulders—first lightly, then somehow deeper...

It was as if they were kissing—nervously watched by a sympathetic elderly nanny—best friends who had known each other forever, and knew each other's secrets and sorrows. Quevrailleth—what a beautiful name—was the child of an immeasurably wealthy and ancient clan/tribe/people whose children were few and whose land/world was cold and diminishing in some fashion. Her people treasured knowledge, and desperately sought for more in hope of saving themselves; they eagerly taught/trained/schooled all their children, never even thinking of the difference between males and females! They had immense knowledge of this bizarre craft of speaking mind-to-mind, of understanding living things and of changing matter and energy by mind-craft/magic alone... And yet, there were profound gaps in their understanding. They seemed to lack a kind of precision, the rudiments of science that even a girl of 12 from an admittedly-poor clan—like Elena—knew without effort.

They could not even read! They didn't even have the concept of it.

I could teach you! Elena enthused, grateful that she had something to offer to her friend. *And I could read to you from my book...it has pictures...diagrams...*

And then her attention was snagged by the memory of a diagram: "atom", atomic structure, how the particles and their relationship resembled a solar system with its sun and planets...like the new planet the Pure were going to...

On that thought she slipped into the darkness of sleep.

Quevrailleth pulled kimself up to wakefulness with the echo of Larshkenye's urgent summons still ringing from the walls. Ke was lying sprawled on the cushion, bone-tired, ravenously hungry, frantically thirsty, and kir head beginning to throb with the threat of a massive headache. Larshkenye's servitors were fluttering about, and one of them had just set down a nearby tray laden with food, drink, and a choice of curative potions. The water in the goblet was still sloshing, and that seemed the most enchanting sight in the world.

Nonetheless, ke ignored it to look at Larshkenye, who was hovering at kir side radiating concern. *Did you get all that?* ke asked urgently. *The knowledge...*

All of it, Larshkenye confirmed, staring at kim. *Those savages, sailing the physical void in metal ships...*

The tower's servitors discreetly hurried away.

...And so much like us. Quevrailleth promptly seized and gulped down the water, then the *kirian* tincture, then the sweetcakes, scarcely pausing for breath. Ke began to slow down over the fruit-rolls, enough to ask: *How soon can we re-contact?*

You saw as well as I, Larshkenye replied, still watching. *A few hours, at least. The alien child...is fevered, and will need much rest.*

She will not die?! Quevrailleth paused in mid-bite to ask.

Not in the next few hours, surely. But what of you, Child? How fare you?

Slightly surprised/amused/annoyed by the triviality of that question, Quevrailleth fed kimself the last of the fruit-roll with one hand while rubbing kir forehead with the other. *The headache is fading,* ke considered. *I could use some more water.*

Larshkenye took the goblet, got up and went to a large urn that Quevrailleth hadn't noticed before, used it to refill the goblet, and returned. *Reports of your power and focus have not been exaggerated,* ke noted.

I'm so grateful for that! Quevrailleth replied, with not a trace of irony. *That mind... Her skills, her memories, the knowledge in her 'treasure'—we need that mind!*

And yours, Larshkenye stated decisively. *You must rest now, at least as long as that...child. We'll need you strong and fresh when we contact...her again. Have you finished? Then sleep now.*

That was not a request, Quevrailleth knew. Ke duly finished the last of the food and drink, slid the tray aside and stretched out on the cushion, distantly noting that Larshkenye had moved away to study one of the screens in closer detail.

Even as ke recited to kimself the formulaic poem that

automatically guided kim down the levels into sleep, Quevrailleth considered that Larshkenye appeared to be oddly nonplussed by the revelations of that alien child. Well, no surprise there: such amazing similarities to *chieri*-kind, and such astounding differences! How could such a flower have arisen in that unbelievably savage culture? And what was it like to be born into a fixed gender, long before the age of fertility, and remain in it for life? Ke couldn't imagine it.

Pondering that thought, Quevrailleth slid into sleep.

Elena awoke to the bustle and noise of day-cycle, desperately thirsty, famished, needing to empty her bladder, and feeling miserably weak—but no longer fever-hot. Apparently her fever had broken in the night, as had so often happened before. Only the memory of that strange dream still lingered.

But was that truly a dream?

It had been so vivid, so clear—and filled with ideas she could never have imagined for herself. The proof of reality, she remembered from school, was that it could surprise you. So...

Could there truly be a race of elves, somewhere in space, who had great powers of mind-magic and thought nothing of whether a child was male or female? Could it really be true?

Elena pondered that as she pulled herself off her cot—carefully clutching her sack—and tottered up the row to find one of her female relatives to accompany her to the hygiene unit, and then the food and water dispensary, which took a long time. She was near to bursting by the time she finally got to one of the toilets, and Aunt Sara grumbled at having to make a second trip because Elena had wakened late.

Outside the food dispensary a boy made a grab for her.

Two others distracted her aunt, who slapped and screamed but was of no help whatever to Elena. The onlookers, all men, snickered at the spectacle but made no move to interfere. Elena wriggled like a snake in the boy's grip, bit the hand that he had clapped over her mouth which made him snatch it away quickly, and yelled: "Manborg! Omar Manborg! You're being robbed!"

That made the bystanders straighten up and pay attention. Someone passed on the shout, and there were sounds of running feet. Worried now, the boy loosened his grip just enough for Elena to get a double-handed grip on her sack and swing it over her shoulder with all her strength. The corner of the bag, and the thick book inside it, connected with his temple. He went down to his knees, howling, and Elena swung again. This time she hit him in the ear, and his yells redoubled.

The crowd abruptly split apart and fat Uncle Rasheed lumbered into the gap, bellowing questions. The other two boys spun away from Aunt Sara and darted off into the crowd, which closed seamlessly behind them and did its best to look innocent. Aunt Sara gabbled incoherent explanations and pointed to Elena, who was still pummeling the crouching boy. Uncle Rasheed, drawing his own conclusions, grabbed Elena by the elbow and pulled her away, demanding to know what she thought she was doing, attacking a young man of the respectable Vandannik clan.

"He tried to steal me!" Elena shouted at the top of her lungs.

The boy took the opportunity to struggle to his feet and stagger away. The crowd let him pass, but only with much hooting and laughter at him for being bested by a girl.

Uncle Rasheed rocked from foot to foot in indecision, while Aunt Sara calmed down enough to speak clearly and loudly confirmed Elena's story. It was plain that Uncle didn't want to get involved in a debt of honor with a more powerful family, but the alternative, Elena knew, was for him to drag both females back to the Manborg enclave in the sleeping area and throw the problem in Father's lap.

"I've had nothing to eat or drink yet," Elena managed to shout so that Uncle Rasheed couldn't ignore it. "And I'm perishing from thirst!"

Relieved at seeing a third option, Rasheed shoved Aunt Sara at Elena and ordered, "Feed the girl, then."

Elena didn't wait for her aunt to reach her, but clutched her bag close and hurried up to the dispensary bar. With her aunt flanking her and Uncle Rasheed making a show of standing guard, Elena collected a bowl of thick stew and a tall canister of cold sweet tea, tottered to the nearest table, and drained them as fast as she could.

She could sense the urgency, even if her aunt and uncle didn't; the story of the Vondannik boy's disastrous attempt to steal a Manborg girl would be spreading like a grass-fire through G deck, and just whose family honor would demand satisfaction was a tangled question indeed. Bad enough that it would provide juicy gossip for the whole deck; worse that it might end with Father using the opportunity to sell her to the more prestigious Vandannik clan for as good a price as he could get, without even waiting for the ship to land and the settlement to set up. She shuddered at the thought. No, best to get back to the Manborg enclave as quickly as possible, with Aunt Sara and Uncle Rasheed as reliable witnesses to give their own accounts.

Her belly hurt from its speeded filling, but she pushed away from the table, clutched her sack close, and pulled herself to her feet. Her aunt and uncle promptly took her by an arm apiece—she was utterly grateful for that much support—and hurried her back to the dormitory zone.

Once there, they dumped her unceremoniously back on her cot and waded into the debate already in progress. Yes, the argument was going much as expected; Papa was practically wallowing in his self-righteous outrage, howling about the Family Honor and what the Vondanniks owed for such a vile insult. Uncle Rasheed happily added the juicy details of the attempted theft. Aunt Sara piously added notations about "the girl's" modesty and decorum. The Vondannik emissary could only counter with deprecating comments about how plain and sickly "the girl" was, and how "unwomanly" for actually fighting with a boy. That gave Mother the perfect opening to complain about how weak and unfit the Vondannik boy was, that a mere sickly girl could fight him off, and if she was such a poor prize, then why had the boy tried to steal her in the first place?

It was obvious that now they were haggling over prices.

Elena lay down, curled around her treasure-bag and bellyache, and tried to shut out everything. Seen from any angle, her future looked miserable. She would be sold, either tomorrow or within the year, possibly even to that disgusting Vondannik boy, with all that implied. She would never see the inside of a school again. Her learning would be cut off. Her mind would subsist like a potted plant, its only food and water provided in scant morsels, controlled by those who begrudged its existence.

Oh, if only I could run away and live with the elves!

...And that brought up another thought.

At least I can speak to them again.

She closed her eyes and did her best to remember how she had felt that last time—down in the fever-depths, dreaming but aware—and called silently into the blankness.

Quevrailleth, best friend, elf-friend, are you there? Quevrailleth, are you there? Are you there?

This time Quevrailleth sat in the middle of a circle of cushions, with Larshkenye facing kim and a full circle of a dozen adepts surrounding. Ke was impressed at the number, and what this implied about the importance of the contact with that alien child.

The map on the screen had both expanded and tightened its focus, centering on a particular light. Ke could feel Larshkenye probing, strengthening the connection to that light/location/mind, but Quevrailleth didn't really need that. Ke knew the way to that mind, and in fact could feel the child reaching for kim even now.

Yes, ke answered, *I'm here! Draw near, touch...*

Contact came in a rush, as if Elena were desperately throwing herself into kir arms, clinging tight and bursting into tears, a fountain of woe. Quevrailleth braced kirself against the onslaught of emotion, supporting and consoling...

...And caught a flash of alarm from the assembled circle, particularly from Larshkenye: *Don't go too deep! Don't let the alien overshadow—*

Ke realized that the full circle had been assembled not to assist in the quest but to shield/anchor kim.

Against this pathetic child?! How much a fool/weakling do you think I am? ke blazed back at them, carefully shielding the thought from Elena.

There was a sense of embarrassed withdrawal, smoothed over with the standard studious calm, but Quevrailleth caught the underlying attitude anyway. Yes, Larshkenye had thought of kim only as a talented but inexperienced youth, had not even bothered to see how much ke had studied and practiced, or what kir strengths were, but only meant to use kir power as a thoughtless/obedient amplifier. *Undervalued! Like Elena.*

Ke favored Larshkenye with a brief stab of chill disgust, and turned kir full attention back to the alien child, comforting and probing. *There, there, my little friend,* ke soothed. *Have no fear. I'll protect you. Whatever is the matter?*

I will be sold, soon! Elena displayed the whole wretched image, innocently unshielded, holding back nothing. *My mind will wither!*

The complete picture was appalling. Quevrailleth—almost spitefully—took care to display it all to the attentive circle. Ke felt them wince.

—And caught from Larshkenye a flicker of fear: *Beware contamination!*

From this innocent? Quevrailleth let all the rest of the circle see it.

There was another general feel of embarrassment, this time not centered on Elena. Quevrailleth shamelessly exploited it. *Find a solution, then,* ke demanded. *Save this child!*

Even as the challenge flickered around the circle, raising questions and analyses, some of it bled over to Elena, making her raise her head in wild hope.

Oh please, my best friend, my elf sister, can I come and live with you?

There was shocked silence all around the circle. Into it Quevrailleth threw, like a rock into a pool: *Why not?*

Ke could feel an incoherent tide of arguments rising, especially Larshkenye's pet fear of "contamination," and cast kir counterarguments like more stones, hard and fast. *I know the technique—*

The shocked reaction to that showed Quevrailleth that none of them had bothered to examine kir own studies, to learn what ke knew. No, they had thought of nothing but kir power, and nothing more. Ke pushed away kir annoyance, and pressed on.

We have the assembled power, and the tools. At worst, we

can seal the tower so that no 'contamination' spreads. Think what we could learn from her: body and mind—and 'book'. This is the best opportunity we've had in centuries, and you know it. And it is the rightful thing to do.

Wordless opinions flowed about the circle, agreeing to one or another of Quevrailleth's points, until only Larshkenye held out—past caring how shamefully cowardly ke looked—a lone beacon of fear.

Against that, Quevrailleth threw kir last stone.

Call it 'contamination' if you will, but I shall not abandon this child. If you will not bring her here, then send me to her!

Even as the dismayed reactions rose, Quevrailleth planned tactics. Once on Elena's 'ship,' ke could create a shielding illusion; ke could assume the appearance of any of those overlooked females, or even males, or pass invisible among them. Ke could protect Elena, learn from the minds of the whole horde, and transmit back all that ke learned. Ke could even learn to control the 'ship', or at least the minds of those who steered it...

No, no! Larshkenye wailed almost audibly. *You are young, strong, potentially fertile— We cannot afford to lose you!*

Lose me, or gain her, Quevrailleth held firm. *Those are the choices you have.*

There was a long breathless pause, and in the end it was Larshkenye who gave way. *Bring her then,* ke sighed, defeated.

The images in the screens flickered and shifted. The adepts of the circle stirred and settled, and began to raise and focus the power needed. Starstones began to glow.

Quevrailleth turned kir full attention back to Elena. *Yes*, ke promised, *You shall come live with us. We will bring you with our 'magic,' but it may be a hard passage. Hold tight to me.*

Elena shivered in a joy as vast as the sea, broken only by one question: *And my book?*

Quevrailleth felt kimself smiling. *Yes, certainly, hold tight to your book.*

Elena did, wrapping her body close around the sack and clutching it with one fist while the other arm reached out blindly to a form she could almost feel.

There was a flare of immense power...

On G Deck, Mother and Aunt Sara almost swaggered down the aisle between the cramped cots, down to the end of the row, by the rear bulkhead. Mother, her speech all prepared, began making the announcement before they reached the last cot.

"Rejoice, rejoice, oh daughter of the Pure. Your future is assured! You have been purchased by the House of Vondannik for..."

She trailed off, seeing that the cot was empty, before she could reach the gem of her speech: the price. It was more than enough to compensate the House of Manborg for the girl's ship-passage, and now Mother had no fitting audience for her announcement.

"Elena?" she snapped in annoyance, looking about. "Oh, where has that stupid girl gotten off to?"

"She was rushed in her meal," Aunt Sara considered. "Perhaps she's found some woman to accompany her back to the food dispensary, or maybe the hygiene unit..."

They searched G Deck until nightfall, finding no sign of Elena, and were obliged to report the disappearance to Omar and all the assembled Manborg clan.

That set off more speculations as to who had stolen the chit, and from what deck, and just who owed what to whom for their insulted Family Honor—which lasted all the rest of the voyage to Phi Coronis IV. There the case was soon forgotten in the efforts of settlement, though resentment remained between the House of Manborg and the House of Vondannik for generations afterward.

Quevrailleth wakened slowly, sprawled on the pillow as before, but much weaker this time and with a much worse headache. Someone familiar — ah, Larshkenye no less—lifted kir head and poured a large dose of *kirian* between kir lips. In a few seconds the headache subsided to distant drumbeats, to be replaced with a raging thirst. Larshkenye promptly supplied a goblet full of cool water. When the thirst was satisfied a ferocious hunger took its place, but Quevrailleth ignored it and pulled kir heavy eyelids open.

The first thing ke saw was a *kyrri* servitor trotting about the chamber, dutifully pumping a small spray-bottle full of air-purifier. A knot of robed *chieri* adepts, the remains of the circle, were crowded around a large cushion by the near wall, and others were peering at the diagrams on various screens.

"Elena?" Quevrailleth croaked, and then realized that ke had spoken aloud. How curious!

Larshkenye snatched kir hands away as if they'd been burned. *I warned you about contamination!* ke projected.

What, because I used the girl's form of communication? Quevrailleth sneered, pulling kirself back upright. *It's a useful skill. Tell me, did the girl arrive safely?*

Larshkenye only pointed to the cluster of adepts. *Intact,* ke admitted, *and her treasure too. Unconscious yet, but unharmed.*

Quevrailleth managed to roll to kir knees, noticing that kir body felt strange. *And did you find any plague or toxins upon her?* ke continued. *And how long have we been asleep?*

Some six hours, Larshkenye admitted, fidgeting with the hem of kir robe. *That was a mighty working that you performed. And no, the creature carries no plagues nor poisons that could affect any of us. It appears that her sickliness was only the product of an allergy to a food-plant common on her home-world. Shocking that none of her kin even thought to look for it.*

Then why are you still so afraid? Quevrailleth snapped, torn between frantic hunger and an urgent need to see to Elena.

Larshkenye slapped the floor in exasperation. *Because there is more than one form of contamination! Look at yourself! Look at how you have changed through contact with that alien creature!*

Puzzled, Quevrailleth pulled out kir starstone and did a quick scan of kir body.

Yes, there were notable changes. What were those zones of elevated heat, rapid growth, fierce alteration of internal organs? There was something familiar about those changes, something like... *Elena, just 12 years old.*

Slowly, Quevrailleth realized what ke was seeing. *No wonder I'm so hungry,* ke thought, stunned. *No wonder...*

You are in Season, changing, Larshkenye accused. *And not just from the kirian you've consumed, nor from pollen-laden wind...*

Quevrailleth remembered carefully keeping out of those winds, for nearly a century now. Perhaps it was time.

...Nor from close-bonding with any of our own. You are becoming female, purely from deep contact with that alien creature—who is female herself. You cannot possibly breed with her, and there is no one of us in male phase within normal calling-distance. How could this happen?! Contamination!

Imprinting, Quevrailleth corrected, thinking fast. *She is passing into adult female phase herself, and shall remain there lifelong. Yes, we must study her further.*

Larshkenye winced mentally, but said nothing.

Without such 'contamination,' we are dying, Quevrailleth concluded. *Can we but gain the knowledge her people have...*

Then hunger reasserted itself. Ke sent a wordless message to a servitor, who quickly brought a laden tray, and addressed kimself to the food. Eating like a forest fire not only eased the raging hunger, but gave kim time to think. *No, not 'ke' or 'kim' for an unforeseeable future, but 'she,' 'hers,' 'her.'* Quevraillath played with the unfamiliar words, understanding that they would always have somewhat different meanings to Elena and...herself. *But we did the right thing!*

Elena became aware that she was breathing wonderfully cool, clean air. She couldn't remember breathing air that felt, smelled, and tasted so good. Just breathing it drove away the headache she could feel lurking in the back of her skull. Oh, it was lovely just to lie here...on something much softer than her cot...and breathe, breathe...

But another thought intruded. *My treasure! Where...?* She flailed about with hands that felt too heavy, too clumsy, but encountered the familiar cloth of her sack.

Yes, said a familiar voice, but not in her ears. *You have it, and you are here. You are safe with us.*

Elena pulled another deep breath of lovely cool air and dragged her sluggish eyes open. The first thing she saw was the unmistakable face of Quevrailleth, the silver-eyed young elf, who was her best friend in all the universe. Behind that face was the soft blue wall and ceiling of the elf-castle, and there were glimpses of other elves nearby. And there was that feeling of being scanned, seen, studied down to the cells again. Yes, it was no dream; she was really here.

For an instant she thought of her family—Mother, and Father, all her brothers, her remaining sisters who hadn't yet been sold away, Uncle Rasheed and Aunt Sara, and all the enclave of the Pure whom she would surely never see again — and forgot them without a second thought.

Oh, my friend! she thought, her heart pounding with joy so that she thought it might burst. *My elf-friend, my sister, let us never be parted again!* Her arms were still too heavy to lift, but she thought a kiss at Quevrailleth.

Sister, indeed, Quevrailleth thought, holding fast against that sheer onslaught of happiness that made the others back away in amazement. *I think you have very much to teach us.*

Yes, Elena agreed. She forced her sluggish hands to pull open the sack, dig through the folds of cloth, and draw out her treasure. *Here it is.* The book was old and battered, but still intact. She accepted Quevrailleth's help in raising her head and spreading the treasure open on her lap. The other elves were drawing near again, fascinated. Elena remembered that she'd been somewhere in the Cs, and fumbled among the pages. Her eyes fell upon a word she understood but hadn't truly read yet.

"Cell...(noun)...the basic unit of life..."

Elena felt the elves reading her as she read the words, and felt their amazement at the precision and detail. She moved her eyes further, to the diagram, and felt their attention tighten. They were far more attentive students than her classmates had been.

And there Elena had a revelation of her future. No, she would never be kept from school again. Much as she could learn from the elves, they had still more to learn from her—a lifetime's worth, and more. She would be student and teacher both.

She would *be* the school.

Indeed, thought Quevrailleth, casting a thoughtful look at the others. *I would not call this 'contamination.'*

Larshkenye only sighed and turned away.

The Cobbler to His Last

by Rosemary and India Edghill

Darkover, with its ancient Terran roots and unusual social evolution, presents as a perfect setting for "a stranger arrives, bringing his or her tortured past or expectations or prejudices..." Competence in one arena does not, as we all know, translate well from one planet to another, particularly when any of the many Darkovan cultures is involved. The presumption of superiority can prove as perilous as it is foolish, as this tale demonstrates.

New York Times best-selling writer Rosemary Edghill (aka eluki bes shahar) has been telling tales for over 35 years. She's written not just science fiction and fantasy novels, but also romance, mystery, steampunk, comic book tie-ins, young adult urban fantasies, and technothrillers. In addition to working as an editor, anthologist, book designer, illustrator, and reviewer, she's known for her collaborations with such notables as Marion Zimmer Bradley, Andre Norton, and Mercedes Lackey. Rosemary lives in the Pacific Northwest with "far too few" Cavalier King Charles Spaniels.

India Edghill would like to say that she was raised by wolves in the exotic Indian jungle before being sent to an elegant boarding school in Graustark, from which she was kidnapped to live, live, *live* with either Mame Dennis or Doctor Who. But alas, while India would like to say this, it's quite, quite untrue. Instead, she's the prize-winning author of novels set (mostly) in the Ancient Middle East, and of fantasy and science fiction short stories. Almost fifty years of research and writing has given India masses of totally irrelevant information upon almost any subject you care to name. India lives in the beautiful Willamette Valley, along with a quite amazing number of Cavaliers.

The chandler to his wax and the woodsman to his ax:

let every man stick to his trade.
—Proverb of the Kilghard Hills

"My advice is to forget any notion of even *trying* to work here," Dr. Hamilton said. "I don't think the reports the Colonial Service has archived with New Alexandria—that you say you've read—could possibly give you an accurate picture of what trying to do research here is like."

Grace glanced toward her husband. Valor was regarding Romald Hamilton with an expression of sympathetic interest that had, as she knew, little connection with whatever thoughts might fill his mind. The two of them had been ordered to report directly here the moment they arrived on Cottman IV.

"We understand your concerns, but I assure you, neither of us is an armchair anthropologist," Valor said. "We wouldn't have come if all our permissions weren't in place. We've studied all the material on Dark—er, on *Cottman IV*—that the Service has placed in the University archives on Coronis IX, and we're more than willing to 'print any liability wavers you want."

"You have to remember that—for us—research on Cottman IV is a once in a lifetime opportunity," Grace added, to soothe Hamilton's apparently frayed nerves. Their field of study was the social evolution of isolated colonies. Grace's specialty was systemic female oppression, Valor's the emergence of foundation myths. Most of the cultures they'd studied—Sapphire, Vainwal, Riverwild, Twilight, Xanadu, Wolf—had long since been brought into the Imperial fold, and the story of their disunited years existed only in historical records.

But "Darkover" was different.

A living, breathing splinter culture, re-contacted less than a decade ago! We can learn so much here!

"It's a once in a lifetime opportunity to *vanish*," Dr. Hamilton said flatly. "I don't think the archives could possibly give you an accurate picture of what trying to do research here is like. This is a Class D world. Without Comyn permission, Terrans can't leave Thendara at all. I can't warn you about what to expect outside of Thendara because I have very little idea of what's out there—and no way to protect you."

"Which is one of the reasons we're here," Val said. "Your Legation will benefit directly from our fieldwork under a new program being run jointly by the University of New Alexandria and the Department of Colonial Affairs."

Grace continued, "The idea is, Val and I go and do our jobs, New Alexandria pays the way—and DCA and Spaceforce reap the rewards in raw data and analysis."

"Assuming you actually get back to file your reports," Dr. Hamilton said bluntly. "I appreciate your qualifications—and we could certainly use the data—but I don't think either of you understands exactly how...well...*uncivilized* this place is. The locals routinely, eat, wear, and exploit animals, just to begin with, and personal honor still revolves around the Code Duello. It's perfectly all right to kill someone here—so long as you've filed a formal *Intent to Murder,* of course."

"You're having no success in changing their social patterns?" Grace asked.

"We are having precisely no luck in doing *anything* with the natives," Dr. Hamilton said with exasperated relish. "Including convincing them they're a Lost Colony. We've showed them the proof, and they simply reject it. Usually, when you show people at the cow-and-plow level that there are faster and easier ways to get things done, they embrace the idea immediately and start looking around for items they can use to open up a trade relationship."

"But not here?"

"Not here," Dr. Hamilton said bitterly. "Most of the locals won't even come into the Zone." He looked as if he might want to go on, but stopped himself. "So the Service can't guarantee your safety, doctors. Not outside the Terran Zone."

"But I'd understood that the native rulers were...." Grace paused, not sure how to phrase it tactfully.

"Civilized?" Dr. Hamilton said. "Oh yes. The Comyn are certainly civilized—if you want to call it that. In fact, they think *we're* the barbarians. The worst that would probably happen to either of you here in Thendara is getting accosted by the City Watch and escorted back to the Zone. But if you manage to leave the city...well, more than half the Terrans who leave

Thendara never come back. And we never find any trace of them, either."

"I suppose that such a harsh environment would be dangerous for the inexperienced," Grace said, "but we're here to study people, not mountains or weather."

"I see I can't stop you," Dr. Hamilton said, smiling ruefully. "But I did have to try. And since I have failed to convince you of the fruitlessness of your intentions—" Dr. Hamilton did not look especially upset by that fact, "—I'll do what I can to help you. Take a couple of days to look around the Zone and the city, and I'll see if I can get you an audience with *Dom* Istvan."

"He's the head of the local, ah, divine warlords and their ruling council?" Grace asked.

Hamilton was nodding. "I haven't heard that phrase before, but I'd say it's apt. Their personal prestige has declined over the past few centuries, but the Comyn Council is still how things get done here, at least for us poor Terrans. You'll need Lord Hastur's permission to leave Thendara, and having his approval can smooth your way amazingly. Take it from one who knows."

With that, Dr. Hamilton released them to their accommodations, and promised to round up the Diplomatic and Cultural staff so Grace and Valor could pick their brains.

As with many far-flung frontier posts, any new arrival was an excuse for a party.

Although it took a week (a period which, on Darkover, was ten days long) before Lord Hastur summoned the two offworld scholars to Comyn Castle, Grace and Valor were far from idle. They'd been sleep-taught two of the main languages on the trip here, and used the immersion method to polish their understanding and pronunciation (and fill in the inevitable gaps). They bought local clothes, ate in local cookshops, walked the streets beneath the oddly-eldritch light of the Bloody Sun, and breathed the sharp, cool air. Each day the difference between their portside hostel—with its Terran-standard light levels, temperature, humidity—and Darkover—wild, anarchic Darkover—seemed greater than before.

Comyn Castle sat on a crag from which it could glower down on Trade City, Terran Zone, and Spaceport alike. It housed the City Guard, the Comyn Council, Lord Hastur, King Stephen (a man whom no Terran had ever seen), and several hundred more residents, not counting the army of servants who lived in Comyn Castle year-round so that it would always be ready for use.

Not that people are likely to come flying down from the Hellers on a whim, if the pictures I've seen of Thendara in winter are anything to go by. I'd say nobody could survive in that kind of environment, but people are capable of the most amazing things. And it's probable that Four wasn't colonized intentionally; I know Andi Norton is doing what should be the definitive search through First Expansion databases, so....

Grace's musings were cut short as Doevid, their driver and one of the handful of Darkovans willing to work in the Trade City, brought the pony cart to a halt. About six hundred yards ahead, the street ended abruptly in a stone wall whose enormous wooden doors stood open. Wisps of straw littered the cobblestones, and the air was redolent with the smell of horse. Apparently Comyn Castle had its stables in the basement.

"I go no further, *Mestre* Valor." Doevid gestured at a line of inlaid pale stone that bisected the street. "What lies beyond this is the business of the Comyn, not of poor fools like me."

Valor did his best to convince Doevid that he'd been hired to take them to the entrance of Comyn Castle—and not merely to abandon them in the road—but Doevid was firm in his refusal to cross the line. Grace didn't know how long the contest between the Irresistible Force and the Unmovable Object would have continued if not for the intervention of one of the castle's inhabitants.

"Pardon me, *mestre,* but are you and your good lady perhaps the *Terranan* visitors whom Lord Hastur is expecting?"

The speaker was young—though precise ages were hard to calculate in places where people grew up without proper medical attention—and had hair of the brightest red Grace had ever seen. He wore a green and black tabard over tunic and trews, and the baldric belting the heavy wool cloth into place held both sword and dagger.

"We are," Valor said cautiously.

The boy smiled radiantly. "Then I am come in a good hour!" he said. "Surely the Commander of the Guard will excuse me if I am on Hastur business. Come with me—I can bring you to Lord Hastur by a way much quicker than walking around half the escarpment."

Valor glanced at Grace, who shrugged. *Why not?* She hauled her Darkovan skirts out of her way as Valor helped her negotiate the dismount from the cart. The young Guardsman looked tactfully elsewhere.

Another young man, dressed like the first (Was it a uniform? What did it mean?), came hurrying out of the stable area. "Lord Lorill! You know you must—" Catching sight of the visitors, he fell abruptly silent.

"Lord Hastur expects these *Terranan* visitors," young Lord Lorill announced proudly. "I shall escort them."

Valor and Grace followed him across the roadway and through the wide wooden doorway. Heads swiveled and eyes stared as they walked directly into the main stableyard; a few of the curious horses whuffled hopefully. Grace regarded the beasts with doubtful interest. She'd watched Darkovans steering their mounts through the Thendaran streets. It still seemed exploitive, not to mention a precarious method of transport—

"Father is receiving his visitors in the Cloud Chamber today, and I think he'd agree that it would be most uncivil to make you traverse ten staircases and the whole width of the castle."

Lord Lorill escorted them to an ordinary looking wooden door. He slid it back, and Grace saw that it led into a small room. He gestured for them to precede him inside, then stepped over the threshold and slid the door shut again.

As Grace attempted to frame some questions in answer to that—Lorill was the son of the Regent? What was he doing in the stables?—the box began smoothly to rise.

It was an elevator.

There was an elevator in Comyn Castle.

Where are the controls? What is the mechanism? The power source? Why didn't Dr. Hamilton mention something about this atypical technology? She glanced at Val as she struggled to keep the indignation from showing in her face, and caught a glimmer of amusement in his eyes.

"Your pardon if I have disturbed you, *Mestre* Valor and *Mestra* Grace," Lorill said smoothly. "I had been given to understand that the *Terranan* have many machines in their dwelling-places."

"Indeed we do," she said neutrally. "I am pleased to find that your people and mine are not so different as I had expected."

The elevator stopped, the door slid back, and they stepped out into a carpeted hallway. The walls were paneled with exotic woods and lined with trophies—swords, spears, shields, full suits of armor—and hung with banners and tapestries.

By the time they reached their destination, Grace was thoroughly lost. Whoever had designed this place had meant it to be a labyrinth. "I thought Darkover was supposed to be peaceful," she said.

"And so it is, *mestra*," Lorill said, stopping outside a pair of ornate doors inlaid with one of the numerous native clan symbols, "for its people have fought like banshees since the time of Varzil the Good to make it so." He smiled at her engagingly as he pushed open the door.

The chamber in which Dom Istvan of Hastur chose to receive them was well-lit and inviting, for whatever burned in several tall alabaster cylinders gave forth a bright white light, and there was also a small fire laid in the substantial fireplace. The walls were hung with heavy velvet curtains that stood as a backdrop for more trophies, and in front of them was placed a large and ornate chair in which sat the Comyn Lord.

Istvan Hastur looked more than old enough to have sired someone Lorill's age; his red hair—long enough to catch back at the nape of his neck—was sprinkled with white, and his face was seamed by both wrinkles and scars. Behind him stood two people: one, a man of middle years, wearing both sword and dagger on a baldric bearing the Hastur device—*Probably the ceremonial officer designated as a "paxman,"* Grace thought—and the other, a slender and anonymous figure wearing a red cloak, its hood pulled so far forward that none of the wearer's features could be seen.

"The *Terranan* scholars, *vai dom,*" Lorill said, bowing deeply.

"So I see," Dom Istvan said. "You may return to your duties, Cadet."

Lorill bowed again, and stepped backward through the doorway, closing the door again.

"Sit, sit," Dom Istvan said, waving them toward the low-backed bench opposite him. "I will send for refreshment, and you may repeat what your Dr. Hamilton has already told me." He raised his hand, and a boy—surely the child could be no more than eight!—rose from his seat at the back of the room and disappeared behind the hangings.

"If he's already told you," Grace said boldly, "why bore yourself with our repetition, Lord Hastur?"

Her guess about his character was right: the Comyn lord smiled at her. "Why, to see if each of you tell the same tale, *nikhya.*"

The diminutive seemed harmless enough—it was the *casta* word for "daughter"—but there were almost certainly some local implications that she wasn't aware of. Beside her, she felt Val shift, and knew he'd caught that sense of subtext as well. *Daughter—oh, I think I see. To the great Lord Hastur, I am a mere child. Subtle.*

"My wife would hardly lie to your lordship when we have come seeking your favor," Val said—and was it her imagination, or had Val placed extra stress on the words *"my wife"?*

"Your *casta* is excellent," Dom Istvan said, "but of your courtesy, perhaps we will continue in Terran, for I have few opportunities to practice your tongue."

"Of course," Val said smoothly, switching languages. He explained their plans—he would work in Thendara, and Grace would travel to interview as many women as possible during their stay.

Lord Hastur regarded him silently for a moment before

looking at Grace. "And you mean to force your wife to travel without you, while you pursue your own interests elsewhere?" he asked.

"We have agreed upon this course of action together," Grace said firmly. She reflected that if she had come to Darkover to study systemic female oppression, she was getting experience of it firsthand. "We can spend only a little time here, and we wish to see everything we can. With your permission, of course, Lord Hastur."

"Yes, yes, with my permission. Nothing in all the land may be done save with Lord Hastur's permission," Dom Istvan said crossly. His paxman turned his head aside and smothered a cough; apparently the statement was a joke. "Very well," he said briskly. "But if you truly wish to permit your wife to engage in this folly, *Mestre* Valor, at least ensure she is properly protected. I will tell you plainly: if you do not provide escort for *Mestra* Grace, neither of you will leave Thendara."

Valor glanced at Grace, who smiled and shrugged, very slightly. Valor said, "Yes, of course. What do you suggest, Lord Hastur?"

"That you hire the *Comhi-Letzii* as her escort. They will keep your lady safe, or die in the attempt to do so—nor will she be exposed to insult while she travels with them. I will have a message sent to the Guildhouse here, so its mistress will know to expect you."

Grace nudged Valor, who asked, "How much is this apt to cost, Lord Hastur?"

For the first time in the entire interview, Lord Hastur seemed surprised, but the expression vanished almost instantly. "I'm sure you will find the Guildmistress willing to negotiate a reasonable fee."

"It's a good thing New Alexandria's funding this," Val muttered, so low Grace could barely hear him. When Lord Hastur rose to his feet she thought for an instant that they'd been overheard, but he had risen in response to the woman who entered the chamber. She was tall, slender, and her head was crowned by masses of gleaming copper-red hair. Grace and Valor stood, belatedly, as the woman crossed the room to stand beside Lord Hastur's chair.

"My wife, *Domna* Marcella Isabetta Ridenow-Hastur. My dear, these are Valor Moore and his wife, Grace, the *Terranan* I spoke of. Dare I guess why you've honored us with your presence?"

"You know very well." Domna Marcella smiled at her husband. She turned and held her hands out to Grace. "I've come to steal you for a few hours. All the women in the castle wish to meet you."

What a wonderful chance! Grace thought.

"Curious little cats," Istvan Hastur said indulgently. "Well, run along and amuse yourselves, then. I am certain we can find something to entertain *Mestre* Valor in your absence."

Grace smiled back and said, "It is an honor. Val, I'll get myself home later."

"Of course, she will be properly escorted," Lord Hastur said instantly.

"So *that's* all right," Grace murmured. Valor rolled his eyes at her—making sure Dom Istvan couldn't see his face.

The Comyn woman—the Comynara—had left her attendants out in the hall—a dozen women and, oddly, a couple of (male) armed guards. *(Surely nobody is expecting armed assault here in the castle?)* They swept Grace along as they ascended in another of those astonishing elevators, this one larger than the last. It rose up and its doors opened into a large semi-circular room, its curved wall set with tall, narrow windows. Grace looked out at a view that ranged from the far mountains to a rather unromantic view of the new spaceport.

Ah, so they were in one of the castle towers, and this was a "solar." A warm, well-lit gathering room in which women could do such repetitive tasks as weaving among company. Tedium assuaged by talk, a common social motif. Grace noted that, just as she noted the women's floor-length skirts; such over-long clothing on upper-class females in a dimorphic culture proclaimed "I don't need to work."

Grace took careful mental notes. Not all the women's skirts pooled on the floor; the younger the girl, the shorter her skirt. The littlest girls' skirts came only to mid-calf. And many of the adult women wore garments that covered them just to the ankle. Servants, Grace tentatively identified them. In cultures like this, the line between servant and mistress was often blurred, but servant or mistress, everyone in the solar, from *Domna* Marcella down to the smallest girl, had long hair, and almost all of that hair glinted some shade of red. The little girls' hair fell loose about their shoulders or was plaited into a loose single braid. Adult women wore their hair styled in braids or in intricately-coiled chignons, and wore hair clasps in the shape of butterflies. The delicate butterflies contrasted oddly with the daggers at the women's waists.

Domna Marcella seated herself on a high-backed chair, and gestured Grace to a similar chair. "Will you sit with us, and take some refreshment?"

Grace knew a cue when she heard one. "It will give me great pleasure to do so, and I thank you for your hospitality."

Once Grace was seated, Marcella offered her some sort of tea and a plate of small sugary cakes. The solar was now full of women and girls all gazing at Grace. The adults stood quietly; the young girls giggled and peered at her from behind their fingers. Nervous or excited at seeing a stranger, Grace decided. While the little girls didn't wear the butterfly clasps, butterflies were embroidered on the cuffs of their long sleeves. The pretty winged insect dominated Darkovan female decorative motifs; Grace looked forward to finding out why.

"How pretty," she said to the girls, pointing at the bright embroidery. "Do you like butterflies, then?"

More giggling, and the girl with the reddest hair said, "We all like butterflies, *Mestra* Grace. Don't you?"

Grace sensed she was missing something. "Well, they're very pretty. What do they mean?"

"I'll have my first butterfly clasp soon," the girl said, which didn't really answer Grace's question. "I'll be thirteen, next week and old enough to wear a hair-clasp and to marry—"

Married at thirteen? Grace took a deep breath, and managed to smile. "And that is what you want? To marry?"

The girl stared at her. "Of course! Don't *you* want to marry?"

Grace explained that she *was* married. "See? This is my wedding ring."

"Then why are you traveling to the Kilghard Hills? Why is your husband making you do that?" The question seemed to be asked in all innocence, but at that point one of the older ladies spoke up.

"So you wish to marry, do you, *damisela?"* the lady asked. She spoke in a soft, pleasant voice, but the girl seemed to wilt, merely nodding silently. "Then I advise you to mind your manners, or you'll be lucky if a Dry Towner kidnaps you. Now go back to your governess. Perhaps, *Mestra* Grace," she said, seizing the conversation ruthlessly, "you would tell us of your journey here. Is it true you came all the way from Terra?"

"Not from Terra itself, though I have been there," Grace said. "I began my journey on a planet called Coronis IX—"

As she spoke, the women took up their tasks again; even *Domna* Marcella took up a piece of embroidery from the basket sitting beside her chair. Grace could hear the hiss and clack of the loom, and the soft susurrant buzz of a spinning wheel. Rather to her surprise, the solar, despite its odd half-circle shape, had excellent acoustics. Unfortunately, that meant Grace heard even whispers with clarity. *"Her husband sends her out to ride the trails? Is he mad?" "He's a* Terranan. *He's mad." "Look! You can see the nape of her neck!"* That speaker sounded truly shocked; Grace made a note to review the cultural taboos again before she rode out of Thendara on her research trip.

"What others will you speak with now that you have come all this way?" *Domna* Marcella asked.

"As many as will speak with me. As many as wish to," Grace answered. "And naturally, I wish to speak with the indigenous inhabitants as well." The peoples called, variously, Catmen, Trailmen, Ya-men. *Always "men", of course. Why not use "folk" instead? Catfolk. Trailfolk.* The Darkover "nonhumans" were undoubtedly no more than small, splintered-off, and inbred groups of colonists who had evolved unique subcultures through isolation. She didn't get any further, because all the women, *Domna* Marcella among them, simply laughed.

"I wish you joy of that, *Terranan* researcher!" *Domna*

Marcella smiled, and inclined her head, and after a few more questions, Grace knew herself politely dismissed.

She thanked her hostess and followed the servant *Domna* Marcella had summoned, walking as slowly as she could without being obvious about it. She hoped to overhear any unwary words the Comyn women might be tempted to speak before she was out of earshot.

In fact, no particular discretion was needed, for Grace might as well have been out of sight even before she exited the solar door—although clearly she wasn't out of mind.

"Well, I had heard *Terranan* women were all fools, but *really—*"

"How in the name of the Blessed Cassilda does the poor woman think she's going even to *meet* a Catman, let alone talk to one? Who wants to meet a Catman anyway?"

"She is going alone? Seriously? She'll never come back."

"Perhaps that's what her husband wants?"

Grace reminded herself that she'd deliberately hung back to eavesdrop; she could hardly complain now that she didn't like what she overheard.

"Her situation is not as bad as it could be," *Domna* Marcella said, "for her husband is hiring Renunciates to escort and guard her. Still, I would not care to attempt such a trip myself."

"Who would, save someone mad as a *Terranan*?"

"Are all *Terranan* mad?" One of the little girls, her voice keen with interest. "That lady didn't seem mad."

"Well, perhaps not quite *all* of them are mad," *Domna* Marcella reassured her, and then the servant beckoned to her, and Grace reluctantly continued on her way.

"So Istvan Hastur sent you, did he?" Guildmother Annelys n'ha Bethenyi sat across the desk from Grace and regarded her steadily. The woman's hair was cut as short as Grace's own, and unlike the flowing garments worn by women of the Comyn, she wore a plain tunic, a sturdy leather vest, and a pair of sensible wool trousers that looked warmer and more practical than Grace's skirts. "You're that *Terranan* woman who has the notion she can ride from the Thendara to the Sea of Dalereuth and...back again."

"Is it so strange to you, that your culture should be worth studying, Guildmother?" Grace sighed. Rumor, faster than starships, had once again outstripped her. "Though I'm learning it may not be as easy as I'd been given to expect. I thought Lord Hastur's name would open more doors."

"It opened this one," the Guildmother pointed out. "And if you will hear advice, *mestra*—"

"Call me Grace." Grace found the endless honorifics so common in conversation here tiring. "And yes, please advise me."

"Then give up this notion. It isn't at all safe."

That's exactly what Istvan Hastur said! Grace shook her head. "I can't. This is my profession, Guildmother. I—I have said I will do it."

There was a long pause as Annelys studied her. Grace wondered what she was looking for, and what she saw. Finally Annelys said: "Then I suppose you must do it, or at least try. Very well, you may hire escorts from the *Comhi-Letzii*, if any are willing to be hired once they have heard your plans. Come back tomorrow, and we will discuss the journey with you."

Relieved, Grace thanked the Guildmother. She'd been starting to wonder if even these "Renunciates" would be willing to accompany her.

"So long as you understand that and that we cannot work miracles, you should be satisfied. And so long as you employ us, we will do our best to keep you—" Annelys hesitated, as if choosing just the right word.

"Comfortable?" Grace ventured.

"Alive," Annelys said.

By the end of her second day on the road, Grace had almost resigned herself to the misery of horseback riding and the guilt of animal exploitation. At least the horses didn't seem to mind being ridden, which helped ease Grace's conscience. Or perhaps the animals simply enjoyed traveling in a herd. Any Renunciate whose route lay anywhere along their path had elected to travel with them (For safety? Or was it something mandated by their quasi-religious vows?), and all of them brought a horse (or two), not to mention pack animals....

In short, anybody who didn't notice Grace's party coming from a good distance away was clearly not paying attention.

Despite this area being noted on the TE maps as "comparatively heavily settled," it would be at least four more days before they reached Armida (where, Grace had been reminded many times, there was no guarantee anyone would be willing to speak to her). Since it would silly to waste the travel time, Grace decided there was no real reason, academically speaking, that she shouldn't interview her two Renunciate guides.

Shallia n'ha Sherna and Melane n'ha Devra patiently answered Grace's questions about the so-called "Free Amazons"—a name Grace intended to study more closely when she had a chance. Grace questioned cautiously, knowing just enough to realize that the all-female guild/caste was barely tolerated by the male-dominated societies of Darkover, and hence those *in* that semi-permitted group were apt to be wary when questioned by an outsider. But apparently, judging by Shallia's tart comments to Melane when she either didn't think Grace was listening, or didn't care, the Free Amazons merely thought Grace was crazy.

"Half mad and all *Terranan*," Shallia said. "Ah, well—I'm sure she means well enough—"

"You're sure of no such thing." Melane sounded bored; as if she'd heard this all before.

"*—and* her money's good. And just maybe we can bring the little idiot back alive, assuming she wants to come. Her husband sounds dreadful—being a free woman's all very well, but—"

"But only if you're actually free," Melane finished. "Our current employer isn't a free woman. Too bad she doesn't know it."

Now what in the name of Harmony did Melane mean by that?

For the first time in her life, Grace wasn't sure she wanted to know the answer to a question.

They were not, as it turned out, going to Armida itself, as

apparently Armida was a manor house belonging to the Comyn. Instead they were going to an establishment several rungs lower on the social ladder, a farm belonging to a friend of Melane's.

Fields surrounded the holding, although the forest lurked around its edges as if striving to take back the land humans had stolen from its border. The buildings clearly proclaimed "solid farming community." A gate barred the way into the yard around the biggest house—a substantial dwelling of log walls and heavy beam eaves carved with images of fruit and flowers. A youngster stood by the gate and pulled it wide as Grace and her escort rode up. The child's clothing made it impossible for Grace to determine whether it was a boy or a girl. Thick trousers covered the child's legs, and a double layer of warm wool tunic protected everything from the neck to the knees.

After carefully dismounting, Grace walked up steps to a covered porch. At the top a woman about her own age waited. Her clothing resembled the child's, but a flaring orange skirt was belted around her waist over the tunic and pants. Long braids wrapped about her head like a coronet, and a yellow shawl draped over her broad shoulders. For the first time, Grace envied the heavy local garments. *It's the skirt, it lets in too much cold air; I need trousers—*

"Welcome," she said. "You must be the star-woman we were told to expect. I'm Charis. We've all been waiting for you, so I hope you're hungry and thirsty!"

"Of course!" Grace answered. She'd known they were expected, but what she hadn't been expecting was to be thrown a party—and to find that every woman for miles around had come. She supposed the women had very little to entertain them, and had eagerly clutched at this opportunity to socialize.

She also learned that it was a good thing she wasn't here to interview the men as well as the women, because she wasn't going to meet any men. The men, Charis informed her, had so little to do they had all been packed off to help Lord Alton move the sheep to summer pasture, after which they would head north for firewatch duty. "We certainly don't want them loafing around here! Now come along, Grace, so the Mothers can talk to you."

"All the mothers, or just some of them?" Grace asked, and Charis stared at her. Of course the conversation was taking place in *casta*, but Grace had thought herself fluent in the language by now.

"The *Mothers*. The—" Charis struggled for a moment, then said, "—they who give us bread."

Grace nodded, and after she had been introduced to the Mothers (and spent some time answering their questions, something she was becoming used to by now), she realized the explanation was simple. The Mothers were the clan matriarchs, the women who administered the women's work on the farms. The Mothers also ensured that children were cared for, the sick were tended, and that young women were properly mated.

"They will find a good man for you, never fear," Charis assured Grace, as she led her away from the gathering-within-a-gathering and toward the yard between main croft and the largest barn.

Grace looked around hopefully, but neither of her Renunciate guides was in sight. "I think there's been a misunderstanding," she said carefully. "I already have a husband, but his work took him elsewhere." Grace held out her left hand, letting Charis see the wedding ring.

"Well, of course you don't want him underfoot all the time—bad enough in deep winter—but do mean your man went somewhere and *you* came *here?* From Thendara? By yourself?" Charis sounded scandalized.

"Yes," said Grace firmly. "I did."

"Then the Mothers *definitely* will find you a better man," Charis said, equally firmly.

Grace had to admit the party in the croft-yard presented a pleasant, friendly sight—so long as she ignored the animal carcass roasting over the open fire. Long tables covered with platters of food had been set around the edges of the yard. A great deal of it seemed to be breadstuffs and cakes, and very little vegetables or fruit. In fact, most of the fruit seemed to have been used to create the drinks; Grace's first sip of what smelled like apricot nectar made her cough. Liquid fire on the tongue, biting sharp.

"Well, that must keep you warm when it snows!" Grace managed to say when she could breathe again, and Charis beamed. But after that, Grace merely pretended to sip at the various liquors pressed upon her, and at that, she found herself faintly dizzy.

Although perhaps she should blame the dizziness on trying to do her job while countering well-meaning attempts to find her a husband. No matter how many times Grace explained she *was* married, that fact was waved aside. If a husband didn't take proper care of his wife, she had every right to demand a man who would.

Grace's last muddled thought just before she fell asleep was that the women of Darkover had some rights after all. Just...not very many of them.

The next morning, Grace decided—after her head stopped pounding—that "when on Darkover, wear even warmer Darkovan clothing" might be the smartest move. Trousers under the skirt seemed to work for the local women, so she'd try it. She'd have to borrow a set from her Free Amazon escort, but she doubted they'd mind; all of them seemed very worried about her well-being, after all.

Grace rummaged through the packs, dragged on another layer of long underwear, and then pulled out a pair of the trousers her escort wore. They seemed long enough, felt thick and comfortable, and Grace thought they'd do far better than the skirts she'd acquired in Thendara. Fortunately, they weren't made of animal skins....

"Domna Grace, what in the name of Sharra's Fire are you *doing?"* Shallia sounded absolutely appalled, and Grace, startled, clutched the trousers to her chest.

"I'm so sorry," she said, "but it's so cold here, and I was hoping to borrow a pair of your trousers—"

"And become a Renunciate?"

"Oh, no, just wear—"

"Our clothing? Claim our rights without understanding or giving anything in return?"

"Of course she doesn't understand." Melane walked into the room and gathered the trousers out of Grace's hands. "*Terranan* Grace, if you put on our clothing, you must become in truth what you think merely to play at. You must take the Oath, and spend a year in a Guildhouse learning our ways. Is that truly what you want to do?"

Grace took a deep breath, and reminded herself that field research never went effortlessly. "No. All I wanted to do was wear more useful clothing. Warmer."

Shallia still looked appalled, but Melane's expression softened. "We would welcome you, of course. But let us see if we can find something warmer for you that will not mean you must renounce the life you are accustomed to."

"You'd be better off with us," Shallia muttered.

"Thank you," said Grace. "And of course I'd be very interested in reading your Oath and studying your customs."

"I think a divided petticoat, and a divided skirt, would keep you warmer," Melane said. "I'm sure our hostess could stitch them up for you before we leave here. And fur-lined boots—"

"No," Grace said. There were limits; she'd ride an animal, so long as it permitted that, but wear one? *Absolutely not.*

For the next several weeks, Grace and her escort rode through the High Hills, stopping at any sign of a smallholding to speak with the inhabitants. Grace became heartily sick of hearing the words "I'm only a woman," for even though the women ran the steadings—leaving their husbands and older sons free for other work—each woman swore to Grace that of course the farm was "her man's land."

I can't believe people live like this! But they know nothing else, poor things. They need to learn there's a better way. And they can't do that on a Class D world!

Since Grace had insisted she must visit the Dry Towns, Guildmother Annelys had arranged for her and her escort to join a trading caravan led by Lord Kazel Ridenow. Lord Kazel was distantly related to Lord Akram, who apparently ran the Dry Town city Daillon, which would help Grace gain access to the Dry Town women. The Lord of Daillon's great-grandmother had been a *Comynara*, which would help even more.

Once they'd joined Lord Kazel's caravan, Grace's escort kept to itself. After her first—and only—attempt to interview the women traveling with the trading party, so did Grace.

Once they rode through Daillon's gates, Lord Kazel (and two armsmen) led Grace's party—Melane and Shallia had brought four more of Grace's guards with them—Linea, Neyrissa, Ruana, and Vanda—through a maze of narrow streets lined with large, square, featureless dwellings until they reached a massive gate set in long windowless walls. Grace waited, with Shallia and Melane at her back, as Lord Kazel dismounted and spoke earnestly to the men guarding it. Finally—and apparently with deep reluctance—the guards sent a messenger to Lord Akram.

Grace continued to wait, not at all discomfited. One of the classic tactics of establishing social dominance was to make someone wait; whoever waited, lost. Here, in his own city, at his own gate, of course the Lord of Daillon won. But at last the guards returned, the gates opened, and Grace finally rode into the private world of the Dry Towns.

"I only hope it's this easy to ride back out," Grace heard Melane tell Shallia in a low voice.

Architecture told one a great deal about a society, and Daillon's was no exception. Grace wasn't surprised, once the gates had closed behind them, to find herself in a rather nice courtyard. She and the others handed over their horses to male servants who refused even to glance at the women. The armsmen remained there; Lord Kazel was escorted elsewhere, then Grace and her six Amazons were led through still more corridors until they reached a set of beautifully-carved doors. A heavy chain hung beside one, while an equally-impressive lock dangled from the other lintel.

"*If Akram gives you what you wish, do not expect to meet with him,*" Guildmother Annelys had said, all the way back in Thendara. "*His* kihar *would be far too badly damaged if he were to speak with a woman as an equal.*"

Grace took a deep breath and walked through the doors into the Dry Towns women's world. It was an honor, a privilege, an experience almost impossible to achieve. *Just keep reminding yourself of that. This will be unique. And no man at all could* ever *replicate this research!*

She listened to her own thoughts with surprise. She would never have thought this way before she'd come here. Men and women were equals—nearly interchangeable in their duties and capabilities. Everyone knew that.

With an effort, she focused her mind on the present.

The Dry Town women's quarters struck her as deliberately claustrophobic, a labyrinth of tiny chambers. Finally, Grace climbed a set of stairs leading upward through a stairwell whose tiles portrayed a night sky.

At the top, she stepped out onto a rooftop. The Dry Town women sat upon piled cushions at the far end of the one area in all the women's world open to the sky. Before her sat half a dozen women whose ages ranged from perhaps mid-teens to a matriarch who must have been—Grace adjusted her assessment to account for the inferior nutrition and health maintenance of these women—and decided the oldest was probably barely sixty or seventy.

The Dry Town women wore the most elaborate clothing Grace had seen on Darkover: layers and layers of deep vivid skirts, heavily embroidered vests, close-fitting bodices with sleeves that ended shortly below the elbow. Below that, they wore bracelets, wide bands of precious metal. *"No woman is free in the Dry Towns,"* Shallia had said, and now Grace saw why. Jeweled chains ran from one bracelet to the other through a ring on the belt each woman wore, binding their hands.

Before she could stare too long, Grace was beckoned over to the women. Her escort—in the courtyard Grace had thought the veiled person was a woman, but the clothing was slightly different from that of the women she saw here, and there were no chains upon the wrists—a eunuch, Grace thought—quickly named the women. Ysaba—the eldest—was Lord Akram's mother; the youngest—Hayilla—was his newest wife. Apparently Dry Town women didn't rate even the most perfunctory honorific. The rest were either wives or concubines; Grace knew both words—at least in *casta*—but context was all. She did not wish to venture a guess as to what either meant here.

She lowered herself to the place apparently reserved for her. The six Free Amazons stood watchfully against the wall, as near to Grace as they could get.

"So," Ysaba said, "you are a *Terranan* lady?"

"Yes." Grace didn't bother to correct the Darkovan term. Now, to tactfully introduce the subject of her visit—

"Why are you here?"

Grace blinked; usually it took far longer to get to the actual reason for her presence. "Because I—I am a student of people. I study how they live. I hoped—"

"To study us as if you were a man?" Ysaba glared at Grace. "Of course his lordship, the ruler of our days, my son, has permitted this, so of course we must also permit it."

"Thank you," Grace said. "I—"

"But first, you will answer *my* questions," Ysaba announced. "And of course drink *jaco* with us." She gestured at an astonishingly elaborate assortment of cups and brewing pots spread across the crimson carpet at their feet. "Now, why has your husband forced you to do this?"

"Perhaps I'm not married," Grace suggested, and heard gasps and giggles from her hostesses.

"And perhaps I am Sharra In Chains. Now come, tell us!"

In the face of such sweeping disbelief, Grace suddenly realized the women didn't really care why she had come; to them, she must seem a lifeline to the outside world. Of course they wanted to hear her story. "Well, my husband's work and mine are not often together," Grace began, and saw bafflement on every face watching her. "His duty led him elsewhere, but I wanted very much to come here."

"But the danger?" The question came, timidly, from Hayilla. "Does a husband let a wife run into danger?"

"Use your head, Newest Daughter-in-law," Ysaba said. "That is why she comes escorted by the Women-Who-Pretend-They-Are-Men. Well, *Terranan* Grace, it is time for you to make a most important choice: which spice to drop into your *jaco.*"

All the other women giggled; Grace got the distinct impression she was not the first visitor to listen to this particular welcome joke.

"It would be a great kindness if you would choose for me," Grace said, which apparently pleased the old woman, who nodded ceremoniously. It seemed to be some sort of signal, for a dozen or so female servants—*Lower-status clothing; same style, simplified; less expensive fabric; simpler, and longer, chains*—and a flurry of little girls bright as butterflies came up the staircase and onto the rooftop. *(No boys,* Grace decided tentatively. *Raised elsewhere? Or doesn't Akram have any sons?)*

All the women regarded her with both interest and a deep suspicion. Was she really married? Yes, she was—she wore a wedding ring to prove it. Everyone stared at the plain gold band she wore on her ring finger.

"*That?* Is your husband so very poor?"

"Does he not honor you?"

"Why do you have to do this for him?"

"Are you truly married?"

"Once I am married, *I* will wear chains," one of the girls—she could not be more than ten—said happily. "What is a little ring good for? How can you be properly married without chains? Why didn't your husband give you chains? *My* husband will give me chains of copper and gold, and a lock set with jewels, and—"

"And if you do not learn better manners, you'll wind up chainless and wandering the streets and sold to the Comyn!" her mother said firmly. "Now apologize to the poor *Terranan* lady."

"Oh, that's not necessary—" Grace began, but the little girl got to her feet to stand in front of Grace. "I am sorry, *Terranan* lady, and I'm sure your husband will give you chains if you ask him to."

Grace opened her mouth, and couldn't think of a thing to say.

She'd hoped to listen far more than she talked, but constantly found herself being led into answering questions instead. The Dry Town women would only exchange the tales of their own lives for the tale of hers. So Grace sat patiently (if a bit stiffly) as day turned to evening and doled out information about her own life, and keenly noted every word given in return.

Food was brought, and the drinkers switched from jaco to tea. As the conversation continued, Grace kept reminding herself to remain dispassionate and detached. But it was hard to remain professional while listening to a little girl who couldn't be more than ten chirp happily that she was going to be married *next week*.

"But you're very young to be married?" Grace suggested, and the little girl stopped and jumped up and down, chanting,

"I *know!* I'm younger than *any* girl in the clan who's *ever* gotten married *before!*"

"But aren't you very young to be a married woman?"

A smiling woman stepped forward to swirl her veil around the little girl, who hugged her excitedly. "Yes, and we are all very proud of my Lenary. Of course, such a worry, too, for she will be far away. But who better to teach her the duties of a wife than her husband's mother?"

Would the mother-in-law be happy to take on raising another woman's daughter? This question caused general laughter. "Oh, in this case, she will be delighted, for she is my own milk-sister." There was no danger, apparently, that Lenary would be rushed. That was what the woman said, "Lenary will not be rushed." A few more answers made it extremely clear precisely what Lenary would not be rushed into, and Grace worked very hard to keep her face smooth and her expression pleasant.

By the time she had herself under control, others were vying for Grace's attention. She ought to raise the question of returning tomorrow—her plans involved returning to the Free Amazon encampment each night and commuting to Lord Akram's palace to interview the women—but there never seemed to be a proper moment to introduce the topic. Forty days—a Darkovan month—would barely be enough time to sketch an outline of female Dry Town culture, but it was as much as she could spare, and she'd hoped to use this initial meeting to set up a framework for her interviews.

But, she now realized, Ysaba didn't have the power to approve or forbid *anything*.

Perhaps Lord Kazam will be willing to negotiate with Lord Akram for me. As Grace thought it, she realized she was heartily sick of ridiculous honorifics and elaborate arrangements of go-betweens.

At long, long last Ysaba rose to her feet. For a long moment, she gazed upon Grace, then she nodded. "You have entertained us well, *Terranan* Grace. You are welcome in my son's home. Now it is late, and surely you must be weary."

"I need to—" *I need to leave now, but I will return tomorrow.* Grace stood up, nearly fell right back down again—her knees were astoundingly stiff and sore—and then managed to straighten up under her own power.

Ysaba waved her hand as if dismissing everyone on the roof and then walked to the stairwell, followed by Lord Akram's wives and daughters. For all their impractical ornamented clothing, the Dry Towns women could move quite fast; before Grace could speak, the rooftop was deserted save for the presence of a single servant.

"Do we just...leave?" Grace whispered.

Shallia winced slightly. "Not without Akram to order the guards to open the gates, *Terranan.* Do *you* wish to be the one who awakens him?"

Melane put a hand on Shallia's arm. "Grace is clearly meant to sleep here tonight. And I think your devoted bodyguards should sleep within your bedchamber, not outside its door."

The following morning, Grace rose early. She hoped that today she could manage to broach the subject of returning to the encampment; she suspected that if she could not, her Amazon guides might simply abandon her here.

She went in search of Ysaba, but found she was still abed. In fact, nobody was awake but Grace, her Amazon guard, and the servants—all of whom seemed delighted to talk. After several hours Hayilla, Lord Akram's newest wife, swooped in to claim her time. Grace would have been naïve indeed to miss the undercurrents here—Hayilla was jockeying for a rise in status, while Ysaba was doing everything possible to maintain her own supremacy *"—but I am sure I shall be the first to gift Lord Akram with a son, and then..."*

And then, a few decades from now, that son would be lord of Daillon, and Hayilla would be where Ysaba was now. It was tragic, Grace thought—so much energy spent to gain such a worthless prize! She didn't say so, of course. Researchers did not share their opinions with their subjects. In fact, as she framed her next question, Grace felt entirely virtuous.

"If I may ask—please remember I don't know your ways, but—would it be permitted for me to try on your chains?" Nothing gave the true feeling of another culture like wearing its clothing and...well, Grace supposed she'd have to call the Dry Town chains "accessories."

Hayilla smiled enigmatically and reached out to touch her wrist. "Of course you wish to feel like a real woman. Come with me."

Hayilla led Grace into a small room that seemed almost like a jewel box; there she clapped her hands and her chains chimed softly. A servant entered, and began removing Grace's clothes. She decided not to object; the only way she would understand the restrictions of the Dry Town garments was to wear them.

At least nobody is demanding I go off and live in a Guildhouse for a year...

At last Hayilla turned Grace to look into a narrow mirror. "See how much prettier you look in proper clothing?" Hayilla asked. "It's a pity about your hair, but it will grow," she added consolingly.

The belt was tight, the bodice form-fitting, and the sleeves set in so that she couldn't lift her arms higher than her bustline, but... Grace had to admit the luminous spidersilk did flatter her. "Yes, it is pretty. But—"

"But something is missing, yes. Hold out your hands." Hayilla clicked wide copper bracelets around Grace's wrists, then clasped a chain onto the left bracelet and ran it through the ring on the wide belt and clipped the chain's end onto the right bracelet.

"There. Now you are a proper woman." Hayilla smiled as Grace stared into the mirror.

In a horrible fashion, the chains were...lovely. The copper gleamed; the chains flowed and glinted as she moved her hands. But then she reached out, and her left hand pressed against the belt, and she could move her right hand only far enough to reach her face.

"Isn't that better?" Hayilla asked, as Grace tried not to panic.

"Lovely," Grace said. "But—" What to say that would make Hayilla understand Grace could not wear these? *Oh, of course.* "They are lovely, Hayilla, and I thank you—but my husband would not like me to wear this."

Hayilla took Grace's hands and pressed them gently. "Of course, Grace. I understand. Trust me."

Despite everything she could do, Grace was unable to explain to anyone that she must be let to come and go as she wished from Lord Akram's house. She would have been utterly panic-stricken if Shailla and Melane hadn't been able to send the other four Amazons back to the camp. Surely that was a good omen for Grace's freedom? *Perhaps I can speak to Ysaba about this tonight. Even if she has no power, she must certainly have influence...*

But at dinner that evening, Ysaba and the other women seemed determined to press wine upon her. Grace could feel Shailla and Melane's disapproval, and she managed to pour most of it down the back cushions, but she still felt terribly drowsy. *It's the heat and the travel. I'll just rest my eyes for a moment. No one will care...*

And apparently her hostesses thought she was asleep, because they promptly began discussing Grace in shatteringly frank and unflattering terms.

"She should let her hair grow. No one will ever take her for a man, however much she tries to act like one."

"Do you believe *she* believes this tale of writing down what we tell her? To *study?* What man wants to study about women?"

"And all the questions she asks! She will ask *anything!*"

Grace had a sudden nagging feeling that all the women she had seen on her travels had said almost exactly the same things about her after she left. *Mad...rude...tactless... clearly her husband doesn't want her...* She wanted to defend Val, but she felt herself drifting as the women's talk washed over her, until Hayilla's outraged protest yanked her back toward wakefulness: "Her with us? Say you jest!"

"No jest—remember, she too is a woman," Ysaba snapped. "And she clearly needs our protection—"

They all think that, Grace realized muzzily. *Every woman I've met on Darkover has wanted to help me. But they're the ones who need help, not I...*

"Truly, mother?" The sound of a male voice nearly made Grace sit bolt upright. She caught herself just in time. *It must be Lord Akram; no other man would dare come here. But why?*

She opened her eyes the merest slit, just to see. All the women were on their feet save for Ysaba, who still sat. Lord Akram touched his mother's chains, then glanced toward Grace. "This one? She's old, and I just spent far too much on this useless one—" Akram chucked Hayilla under her chin and Hayilla smiled— "And Lord Hastur might object. He sent her, after all."

"A gift," Ysaba said instantly. "How could it be otherwise?"

Grace drew breath to object, and Melane pinched her arm hard. *What has given Lord Akram the idea I'm a present? I'm not, and I'm certainly not staying in his harem!*

"Well, if I must keep her, I must," Akram said with a sigh. "Do you really think she will bear sons?"

"Why not? Say your prayers and do your duty, and be rewarded."

Lord Akram didn't seem to think this was enough guarantee, but he also didn't seem inclined to argue with his mother. "As you say, One-Who-Created-Me. Tell those who came with her to leave my house now."

Before Ysaba could speak, Melane bowed. "Of your courtesy, it is night, and dark. Permit us to leave at dawn, and we will be satisfied with your hospitality."

What about protecting me? They can't just leave me here! Grace remembered Dr. Hamilton's words when she had first arrived: "*More than half the Terrans who leave Thendara never come back.*"

She closed her eyes tightly as she listened to Lord Akram's retreating footsteps. It was a long time before she dared open them again.

It was dark, and a hand pressed over her mouth. As she tried to fight, a voice hissed "shush" in her ear. Grace nodded, and Shallia took her hand away from Grace's mouth.

"We have risked much so that you may have a choice," Melane said. "Will you come away, or will you stay?"

"Please don't leave me here!" The desperate entreaty Grace heard in her own voice shamed her. "I— I—"

Melane hugged her quickly. "We will not leave you, *Terranan* Grace, my word on it. Now keep silence, and do as we say."

The two *Comhi-Letzii* were already armed and dressed. Grace cast about for her traveling clothes, but they were gone. She would have to make her escape in the clothes Hayilla had dressed her in. Shallia produced long heavy veils and helped Grace and Melane wrap themselves in them before pulling on a pair of voluminous trousers over her own pants and wrapping her head and torso in a more abbreviated form of the same veil—a eunuch's dress.

"Now follow," Shallia whispered.

And walk relaxed, because any woman fully veiled and moving about the household at night has a man-sanctioned right to be where she is. And—

"And whatever you do, don't speak." Melane told her softly.

Grace flinched. *I understand the Dry Town women better now.* Tears prickled in her eyes, and she couldn't tell whether they were caused by rage or terror. *Just let me get out of here, and I swear I will never,* never... But even Grace didn't know who she prayed to and what she promised. Maybe that was part of the problem.

At the main gate, Shallia in her eunuch's guise explained to the guards that Lord Akram had ordered these—a careless gesture toward her veiled companions—to Lord Jaelat's. The guards simply opened the gate, and the little party walked out of Lord Akram's compound as if they had every right to. And they kept walking, because—

"I'm not risking my freedom just to get the horses," Melane said grimly. "As soon as we get to the camp, we'll have horses enough. And then we're going straight back to Thendara."

Grace did not argue.

The Legation would expect a copy of her work notes before she and Val left Darkover. Grace had clung to that duty as if it were a lifeline through all the days between Daillon and Thendara, waiting for them moment she would be able to enter her findings into the database. It meant she didn't have to think about Melane's acid comments when she'd learned Grace had tried on Dry Town clothes. Or Shailla's scorn. Or the fear and contempt of the other Amazons.

"You told them you wanted to stay, you Terranan *fool! You risked all our lives to play at dressing-up! Stay in the Terran Zone from now on, unless you like the feel of metal on your wrists!"*

Grace hesitated, staring at the blank screen. Had she actually risked kidnapping and enslavement in Daillon? She wasn't sure. And so, no matter how happy she'd been to see Thendara and Val, she'd left a lot of things out of the recounting of her adventures. But her report deserved to be filled with facts, if not conclusions.

What would I say? That I've learned that women on Darkover are second-class citizens at best, and at worst...

"You aren't free, either, mestra. *Remember that,"* Melane said when she bid Grace farewell at the Thendara Guildhouse.

...at worst, are regarded as livestock.

That wasn't either pretty or properly academic. She'd certainly have to dress it up a bit more for a formal paper. But it would do for now. And perhaps someday the work she'd done here would help the Darkovan women emancipate themselves from their brutal heritage.

Only you didn't meet a single woman on all your travels who thought she was oppressed. And every single one of them—even Melane, even Ysaba—felt sorry for you! They wanted to help...

What had they seen that she hadn't? Grace was used to turning the lens of her discernment outward, upon the cultures and the people she studied. She'd never imagined such scrutiny being turned on her.

What did they see that I don't?

"Grace? Darling?" Val poked his head into her borrowed work-cubicle and frowned. "Are you still working on that report? You've been at it for hours. Aren't you tired?"

Of course I'm working—it's my job! And why should I be tired? For the first time in their relationship, Grace wondered what Val actually meant by those seemingly innocuous words. *Does he think I'm weak?*

For some reason, Melane's whispered words echoed in Grace's ears. *"Whatever you do, don't speak."* Or rather, speak carefully, because however sympathetic Valor might be, he could not possibly understand.

No man could.

"Oh, no," Grace said, and made herself smile. "No, darling, I'm fine. I'm perfectly fine."

What did all those Darkovan women see when they looked at me?

"Why wouldn't I be?"

Were they right?

Night of Masks

by Diana L. Paxson

An old proverb says, "Get three Darkovans together and they hold a dance." Midsummer, Midwinter, birthdays and harvests, there is no lack of occasion. On a world as bleak as Darkover, merriment provides a welcome respite from the demands of a harsh climate, rugged mountain ranges, few mineral resources, and unending labor. But beneath every festival lie darker forces and deeper truths, truths that can often be revealed only by the masks they wear.

Diana L. Paxson is the author of twenty-nine novels, including the books that continue Marion Zimmer Bradley's Avalon series. She has also written eighty-six short stories, including appearances in most of Marion's Darkover anthologies. She is currently working on a novel about the first century German seeress, Veleda.

The piece of leather thinned beneath my fingers as I drew it from the dish in which it had been soaking. I gave it a shake to dislodge the extra moisture, then molded it carefully over the cheek of the carven head that was the foundation for the mask. Once all the layers had been glued and tooled and painted, this one would be a half-mask for a catman, black tufted ears laid flat and green glass eyes fiercely staring.

Midwinter had passed, and with it the hours spent stitching gloves for holiday giving. Most of the year that was how I helped support the household where I and my two lovers lived, but during the dark days between Midwinter and Avarra's Night I could set my imagination free making masks for the festival. The Night of Masks was a new custom to Thendara, brought by folk from Aldaran and popularized by Terrans looking for excitement on New Year's Eve. Between

Terran pressure for Darkover to join the Federation and King Rinaldo's attempt to turn us all into *cristoforos*, it had been a difficult winter. People were eager to forget their fears at a festival. I shivered despite the warmth of the room, recognizing that during the past few months, there had hardly been a moment when at some level I too had not been afraid.

There was a clink as Ramona lifted the lid from the pan where she was simmering chunks of rabbit-horn and began to add slurry to turn the broth into a sauce. I took an appreciative breath. She had turned up on our doorstep a month ago. I guessed her to be in her forties, though we had not asked. She was taller than either of my lovers, round-bodied in a loose blouse and several petticoats that added bulk to her hips. When we were all here, the house was crowded, but Ramona had been a chef in Thendara's most expensive inn, and she produced astonishing meals from the limited ingredients we could afford. She smiled as Adriana, still combing out the dark, silky hair she had tied under a kerchief for her work at the tavern, came out of the bedroom

"When will Kiera return?" she asked in a deep voice. "If I leave the pot on the flame much longer it will dry out."

I glanced out the window, where the sky glowed rose as the red sun went down.

"She should be on her way," I answered, feeling the pulse of warmth that a thought of either of my two lovers always roused. "Leave the pot on the stove...and pitch your voice higher."

Kiera and Adriana both had employment that took them out during the day. Except when we took our goods to market, Ramona and I both worked at home, I making gloves, and Ramona baking spiced pastries, so I had had a better change to know her. Newly sensitized by modeling the masks, I noted the strong jaw and betraying neck structure of a person who had come to maturity as a man. My lovers and I had been trying to teach Ramona more womanly mannerisms, a reverse of the training sessions at the Guildhouse in which women learned to speak and move with the freedom of a male.

"If 'tis ruined, I trust you will take the blame!" Ramona half-sang.

I picked another piece of leather from the dish and pressed it into place on the other side of the form. On the shelf behind me stood masks in various stages of completion—a Trailman, a Dry Town warrior, and a Keeper, her face hidden by a crimson veil. Above them rested the Lord of Light and the lovely face of Evanda that always reminded me of Adriana. Beside them was a head representing Avarra. I had carved it long ago, but I had never dared to actually make the mask.

From the cross-beam hung my masterwork, a banshee whose fierce beak was set with bits of red foil so that it seemed to glow. No one had purchased it, but it made a good advertisement for my skills. The only persona for which I had never made a mask was the Free Amazon. The right to that identity had been bought with too much pain.

The lamp flame bent as the outer door opened and a burst of chill air wafted through the room. A flicker of deeper awareness confirmed my recognition at the familiar sounds of Kiera stamping snow from her boots and hanging cloak and jacket in the mudroom to dry.

Tall and leanly muscled, with the ginger hair that betrayed her Comyn heritage, Kiera paired well with Adriana's willowy grace. Then the two of them were beside me, limbs strong and slim entwining my own round curves. As bodies touched minds melded, and my world was complete once more.

As we parted I saw that Ramona had turned her back, gaze fixed on the bubbling sauce. I could feel her longing, but the woman tried her best not to intrude on our privacy. Did she even know she was broadcasting her feelings? Men were rarely taught that sensitivity.

"And what is today's word from the neighborhood?" asked Adriana. As tensions elsewhere took up the limited resources of the City Guard, Kiera had volunteered to organize volunteers for local security. In addition to the self-defense all Free Amazons were required to learn, she had trained as a warrior and worked as a caravan guard. Adriana had lived on the streets. Of our trio I was the only one who had always been protected. I looked at Ramona, wondering how *she* had dealt with losing the safety of her previous life as a Darkovan male.

"The usual—" Kiera responded with a snort. "Derision,

diversion, and despair..."

It was as good a way as any to describe the mood of the city since Lord Regis had so unexpectedly surrendered his authority to his long-lost brother and Rinaldo Hastur had claimed the title of King. The steady appearance of unexpected (and often inexplicable) pronouncements from Comyn Castle had provided plenty of opportunities for humor. Their effect on the increasingly tense relationship between Darkover and the Terran Federation remained to be seen.

"Cassi, you had best make sales while you can! They say that the king's *cristoforo* priests want him to forbid the festival—" She poured herself a mug of *jaco* from the pot on the back of the stove and sat down.

Ramona dished fluffy piles of millet onto our plates and covered them with a generous dollop of rabbit-horn in brown sauce while I set out bread and sheep-cheese.

"On my way home I met Caitrin," said Kiera when our first hunger was sated. I paused in the act of spreading the soft cheese, catching the hint of anxiety in her tone.

"Is she well?" asked Adriana. Caitrin was Kiera's oath-mother, and she and her free-mate, Stelle, had become mothers to all three of us.

"Oh, *she* is fine...but someone at Thendara House is stirring up all the old talk about men trying to infiltrate the Free Amazons."

I shivered, remembering. When we were at Nevarsin I had seen the charter that gave the *Comhi-Letzii* the right to live free of male control. But the history of the Order of Renunciates chronicled men's attempts to take back that freedom, most recently during the Yellow Plague three years ago.

Adriana's face had gone white. "I thought they had accepted me!"

"They do!" Kiera reached out to clasp her hand. "The talk wasn't about you—just that we are an abomination living here..."

"It is because you took me in," Ramona said gruffly.

I used to think I had been brave to join the Free Amazons instead of accepting the protection of a husband. I had not known I was a lover of women, but I had already realized I had no interest in men. Renunciates had the protection of an entire Sisterhood. For me, this had been the easy way.

Perhaps I should not be surprised that Ramona had chosen this moment to break with her past. In these disturbed times, all identities were in question.

“But how would they know?” asked Adriana.

“What business is it of theirs anyway?” I added.

“They accept the three of us,” Kiera said slowly, “but maybe they think that adding someone else will challenge their authority.”

I glanced up at the monk-masks glowering from the shelves on the wall. “That’s not the only authority that needs challenging.”

~ooo~

The next morning I took Kiera’s advice and packed up a basket of masks to take to the Terran Trade sector’s marketplace. On one side the square was walled by the spaceport terminal, its gray walls stark against a sky heavy with cloud. For weeks Thendara’s weather had wavered between snow, sleet, and hard frost, as if reflecting the uncertainty of the town. Opposite, the four stories of the Sky Harbor Hotel rose with a kind of defiant gaiety. The square itself was filled with booths selling cheap Terran items to Darkovans and overpriced Darkovan crafts to tourists, half of which were stamped “Made in Vainwal”.

For a moment I wished myself back in Nevarsin. It would have been colder, but there, monks and townsfolk and Free Amazons played their roles without duplicity.

I set up the tripod and began to hang the masks from the hooks. The air was brisk, but there was no wind, and the masks glowed bravely in the pale light of noon.

My first customer was a Terran, a tall boy with the pale complexion of those who spend most of their lives in space and the tinny accent of someone who has learned his *cahuenga* from a machine. Apparently most of his knowledge of Darkover came from stories written by people who had never been here, so I was not surprised when he chose the mask of a Dry Town warrior with beads sewn into his flaxen dreadlocks and a ferocious grin.

"Will you wear the mask at the festival?" I asked, dropping the coins into my pouch.

"I will," he grinned. "I already have the costume."

"If you carry a sword, it had best be a real one," I said thoughtfully. "It would be better if you carried no weapon at all."

"But why?" Clearly this did not fit his fantasies.

"This mask will change your face, but it would take more art than mine to change your identity. On Darkover, if you wear a sword, people assume you know how to use it. Men who are drinking are easily insulted, and the Night of Masks will be a wild one. Be careful."

I waited, wondering if he would decide he didn't want the mask after all, but he was a Terran, and I only a native woman. After a moment he grinned again, paid me, and carried his trophy away through the crowd.

The Terran who came late in the afternoon was of a different order, an old Darkover hand who wore a well-worn sheepskin vest over his uniform and whose Hellers accent reminded me of Adriana. He had reached first for the furred mask of a Trailman, whistling a greeting and smiling as if it brought back memories. Then he noticed the tonsured *cristoforo* monk on the lowest peg, where I could cover it quickly if any real monks appeared. His eyes lit in amusement at the molded features, which were set in a sanctimonious leer copied from the monk who preached at the corner of the square.

"When I was a lad on Terra we had parades where men would wear masks that mocked our leaders. I mind there was a one that went about my town with just such a face, tellin' us what we were doin' wrong."

I laughed. "I don't expect to sell it, but it did my heart good to show the man for what he is!" Perhaps I should have made a mask in the image of Brother Gabriel, a true holy man whom we had known at Nevarsin. Would wearing it transform one of the king's *cristoforos*?

"You show the truth, *mestra,* but maybe you should hide that one away. The mood in the town is ugly," the Terran replied, taking the Trailman mask and paying me more than I had asked.

I was packing up when someone called my name. The red sun had dipped behind the spaceport and the clouds were releasing the first flutters of snow. Turning, I saw Stelle, her round face framed by the white wimple of a healer, with Caitrin, tall, with graying blonde hair and a lean build like her oath-daughter Kiera, a half-step behind. By the time we had finished exchanging hugs and greetings I had invited them home to dinner.

We were already on our way when I began to wonder how Ramona would feel about having two more people to feed. It was later still when I remembered what Kiera had told us about talk in the Guildhouse and wondered how Caitrin and Stelle would react to Ramona.

The opening door released a rich aroma of simmering stew.

"That smells wonderful!" I exclaimed, shaking the snow from my cloak and hanging it on a peg.

Ramona's face lit. "You are lucky it is not ruined! We have been waiting for you!" Her strong features grew rigid as the others followed me into the room.

"Ramona, here are Stelle and Caitrin, come to join us at dinner," I said brightly. "Can you use your magic to stretch the stew? We bought cheese-breads at the market to add to the menu, so no one will starve!"

Kiera jumped up to give her oath-mother a welcoming hug. Caitrin's grey eyes widened as she saw Ramona, but her gaze was neutral as Kiera pulled out a chair for her to sit down. Stelle, whose face could always mask her feelings, wore a benign smile.

For a few moments the clink of spoons against pottery was the only sound.

"*What* is in this?" exclaimed Stelle presently. She had already half-emptied her bowl.

"Chervine stew with white-root and onion and some mountain herbs," Ramona said stiffly.

"I thought so!" Caitrin looked up. "I ate it once at a banquet held by the Trail-Guides' Guild at the Inn of the Four Moons."

The Inn was famous throughout the Federation, a place to impress prospective customers or give off-worlders a taste of Darkovan culture without having to leave the comfort of the Terran Zone.

She took another bite. "The chef was called Ramon MacCrae."

Ramona took a deep breath. "It is true. That was my name."

Recognizing the courage it took to make that statement, I felt an inner chill. The passion of youth had impelled Adriana to her transformation, but Ramona had endured half a lifetime imprisoned in a body that did not match her soul.

The stew congealed in my belly. I looked back at Stelle. "You didn't encounter me at the market just by chance."

"No," Stelle sighed. "Mother Doria sent us because of the talk against your household here."

"Ungrateful bitches!" Kiera exclaimed. "When half of them owe their lives to Adriana's blood in their veins." We all fell silent, remembering the terrible days two years before when Adriana had given her own transformed blood to protect the Renunciates of Thendara House from the Yellow Plague.

"They do not insult Adriana," said Caitrin. "If you had moved into Thendara House when you returned from Nevarsin there would have been no problem. Some are saying you three should be cast out of the Renunciates for harboring Ramona. Mother Doria summons you to a hearing at Thendara House tomorrow eve."

The murmur of women's voices ceased as we filed into the Guildhouse common room. It could have been any evening from the decade since I had taken my oath as a Free Amazon. As I sat down next to Stelle and Caitrin I adjusted my weight to keep the couch from creaking, as I had so many times before. Kiera took her place beside me. A deep breath brought me the scent of tripe stew. Thendara House had not changed, but my neck was tensing even as the rest of my body tried to relax into the familiarity.

I looked around the circle. The waves of hostility coming from some of the women were a miasma of the spirit, as palpable as the aroma of the stew.

"I have called you here," said Mother Doria, "Because it is our tradition to bring conflict into the open where everyone can speak her piece rather than leaving it to fester in the dark. Kiera and Cassilde, you no longer live under this roof, but you are still daughters of this house and bound by our laws. A complaint has been made against you because you have extended the protection of the Renunciates to a man."

"In body," I answered, "but Ramona has a woman's soul."

Yllana snorted. "On Vainwal they have doctors—I don't call them healers—who alter people's bodies. They say folk take on new sexes as readily as putting on one of Cassi's masks! If he wants to look like a woman, let him go off-world."

"Might as well accept Federation status and be done with it if we allow such a thing!" said Gwennis.

"We have to fight to preserve our ways!" echoed her lover, Janetta.

"Like the people in the old days, who rioted when King Varzil signed the Charter that guarantees our right to live free?" I asked.

"There are still men who would like to go back to those 'old days'..." murmured Stelle, looking at the gouge in the door made when Dermot Sandoval's men came searching for Caitrin.

"Is not our purpose to make this a world where custom will not rule how people live?" Kiera said then.

"Yes, yes, Darkover *can* change, but it must be on our own terms, in our own time, and in our own way," Mother Doria replied.

Over the mantel hung a moth-eaten needlepoint tapestry of the Lake of Hali. It had been there since the time of Margali n'ha Ysabet and her freemate, Jaelle n'ha Melora, who had left the Guildhouse to join Damon Ridenow's household at Armida and become part of what was called the "Forbidden Tower." They had changed the ancient system that required a Keeper to remain a virgin, but the daughter Jaelle bore to Damon Ridenow was torn to pieces by an angry mob. For the Free Amazons to change would someone have to die?

"This is not the time of King Varzil. The situation on

Darkover is very delicate just now. The king's *cristoforos* already think we are an abomination—if it is believed that we accept men, even a man in a gown, they will call us whores," Lassandra said then.

"Worse than that—it could invalidate the Charter!" said another woman.

"Go back to Nevarsin," said someone else. "They accepted Adriana, maybe they will accept him as well!"

"Let him become a monk! They are already *emmasca* in those gowns!"

"Ramona is not asking to take oath as a Renunciate." Kiera tried to stem the flow, but now everyone was talking at once.

"*You* are Free Amazons. Outsiders will assume he is one, too."

"By living with you he claims the Charter's protections."

"You must cast him out!" Cora's shrill cut through the babble.

I closed my eyes, fighting the waves of hatred and sick fear. These were my sisters! It had not occurred to me that I should shield myself against them.

The meeting ended shortly thereafter. I could only be grateful that Mother Doria, having allowed everyone to have their say, was willing to see if this battering by public opinion would persuade us to fall into line without the need for a formal judgment.

"Merciful Avarra!" said Kiera as we started home. "I would rather fight a banshee than go through an evening like that again." It was not a description, but a prayer.

"Merciful Avarra indeed!" agreed Stelle, who had been called out to one of her pregnant ladies and asked for our escort. "I cannot say that all those women who are baying for Ramona's blood are entirely wrong. Adriana's transformation was a miracle of the gods, but Ramona has received no such blessing. Between the Terrans and our own extremists it has been a long time since one could call Thendara peaceful, but I have never known times like those we face today, when every Ya-man with a grudge feels free to come out of his hole. It is not a good time to push the boundaries."

I looked at her in alarm. I had counted on Stelle, at least, to support us. Was I still a Renunciate if Thendara House was no longer home? Or had 'Free Amazon' become no more than a mask I wore?

When we had left Stelle with her patient we turned back up the hill toward home. I took Kiera's arm, but I needed the strength of her spirit more than her support on the icy road. The words of the Amazon oath were echoing in my memory.

"From this moment, I swear to obey all the laws of the Guild of Renunciates, and any lawful command of my oath-mother, and the Guild members...and if I prove false to my oath, then I shall submit myself to the Guild-mothers for such discipline as they shall choose."

"What if they cast us out?" I asked. The fire in the stove had been lit, but I was still huddled into my shawl.

When we returned from Thendara House, Ramona and Adriana had been waiting. Telling them what had been said did not take long. We were still arguing about how to respond.

"I will leave tomorrow." Ramona's strong-features had set into a mask of pain.

"No!" Kiera exclaimed.

Ramona shook her head. "You three are oathed to each other—you owe nothing to me."

"I suppose," said Kiera, "it's the principle of the thing. This is the same war the Sisters of the Sword were fighting when they joined with the priestesses of Avarra and won the Charter."

"They say that the world goes as it will, not as we would have it," Adriana scowled. "But if the first Renunciates accepted that, Thendara House would not exist. If *we* accepted that, none of us would be here today." She gestured around the little room. Smiling or scowling, from the shelves the masks on their forms looked down.

Ramona smiled sadly. "Perhaps, but I am not worth jeopardizing your safety."

"Stay here!" exclaimed Adriana, but she had never lived at Thendara House. How could she understand how it would hurt to lose it?

"We will find a way," said Kiera, but she had always been a

fighter. One by one they turned to look at me.

"I don't want you to go," I said helplessly, "but I am afraid."

"At least wait until after the festival," Kiera said quickly. "Even Gwennis and Janetta will not expect us to put you out until the city has settled down."

That night sleep was long in coming. We had ended our discussion without decision, but I sensed that my lovers were leaving the choice to me. When I did drowse, dark figures with the faces of my masks haunted my dreams.

I woke to the delectable scent of spice-muffins wafting from the other room. Kiera and Adriana were both already gone. When I emerged from the bedroom Ramona was taking a tray of muffins from the oven. Silently she set two on my plate and a cup of hot *jaco* by my hand. It had gotten colder during the night, and ice was forming around the window-panes.

"Thank you," I muttered, reviving a little as the hot liquid went down.

The chair she had pulled out creaked as she sat across from me, her face grim. "It is I who thank *you*. You have already given me much, even if you cannot let me stay. They are brave, but you are wise to fear."

"You were a man, with all the privileges *we* had to fight to win!" I burst out then. "Why change?"

"It was easier than being at war with myself." She sighed. "You have always been comfortable in your skin, is it not so? What if you were forced to wear one of those masks you have on the shelf up there and could not let it go?"

"You have to be free to choose..." I said slowly.

"Just so. I choose these clothes—" she lifted a fold of her wool skirt, "to show who I really am."

I understood, but Ramona was a woman in a male body without the *chieri* heritage that had enabled Adriana to transform her flesh to match the soul within.

"But it is not enough," she went on. "Cassilde, there is magic in your fingers. Make a mask that will show me as I wish to be."

"Yes," I breathed, feeling the flush of warmth that had

always heralded inspiration. *This* I could do.

The sun had set, but the light of many torches lit the low clouds. From somewhere down the hill came a muted mutter of many voices and the vibration, sensed as much as heard, of a deep-toned drum. It sounded as if half the population of Thendara had taken to the streets. The other half, I supposed, were inside their houses with barred doors.

But our household had absorbed the holiday spirit along with a jug of wine Adriana had brought home from the tavern. Adriana had swathed herself in the red draperies worn by Keepers in earlier times. Kiera wore the head of a stag-pony with branching horns. I had chosen the catman mask, and was now regretting I had not provided the costume with a tail. But all of us fell silent as Ramona tied her mask on. There had been no time to carve a new foundation, so I had used the block for Avarra as a base. The goddess was said to have a kindness for Free Amazons, so perhaps She would not mind.

I had made sketches of Ramona's face before I set to work, but after staring at the mask for three days I could no longer tell if it resembled her. And in any case, the face was only a part of a costume—one never knew what a mask would really look like until it was put on.

"Look!" Kiera turned Ramona toward our little mirror.

The mask did not, I realized with some relief, show the fierce majesty of Avarra, though the shape of the face was the same. What we saw reflected was the face of a mature woman, serene, focused, secure in her power.

For a moment, Ramona did not move. Then she straightened and took a step, head turning to watch the image move. Another step, and her posture shifted as if to balance the weight of hip and breasts, and once more. And this time, we *saw* her body alter, though her physical substance had not changed.

"Is this how you see me?" her voice came slightly softened through the lips of the mask.

"This is who you *are!*" Kiera grinned.

Ramona turned to face us, her eyes glittering through the slits in the mask. "If someone asks who I am dressed as, what shall I say?"

"Tell them you are a queen," Adriana replied, draping a spangled veil over Ramona's brown hair, "for surely you are claiming your sovereignty."

From the road outside came a burst of laughter as a group of revelers went by. We snatched up our cloaks and ran out to join them.

A piper from the Hellers was perched at the base of a statue in the Terran market square. Adriana was dancing, her shape wavering between that of the lad she had been when she learned those steps and the lissome young woman she was now. Terran beer and Darkovan ale had been flowing freely. My own feet were tapping, and I did not resist when she pulled me into the dance.

Weighted by my own fears I had not realized how much I needed this night of revelry. And I was not the only one. When I paused for breath, I sensed an undercurrent of desperation beneath the gaiety. At first I had laughed when I sighted masks I had made among the revelers, but as the night wore on I thought I glimpsed figures not of my making swelling the crowd. At midnight everyone would unmask. I told myself my vision was addled by the wine, and drank again.

The celebration had spilled over the borders of the Terran zone long ago. The settling clouds were becoming an icy fog that curdled in the alleys and set spheres of brightness around the torches. Somehow Ramona and I had gotten separated from the others. When I glimpsed the Crowned Chervine on a tavern sign I realized we had nearly retraced our steps to home.

I was about to suggest that since we were so close we might as well take refuge there when a new sound rose above the din—singing, no, a dissonant chanting—punctuated by a dull clangor of bells.

As if they had precipitated from the fog, around the corner a trio of *cristoforo* monks appeared, flanked by a dozen men in imitations of their garb, and a dozen of the City Guards. *I never made those masks!* was my first thought. Then I realized their faces were bare.

"Banish the abominations!" they cried. "Away with the masks that hide men's souls!" Then the chant began once more:

"Lord of Worlds, remove our sin,

"Let the cleansing now begin!"

As the monks advanced, the guards formed a line and began to drive the crowd back down the hill. Someone screamed, and the laughter of the crowd turned to a roar of rage. I heard the shiver of breaking glass. More light flared as someone set a bin of trash aglow.

I clung to Ramona's solid strength as people struggled around me. I was fighting for breath, fighting to focus, all the fears that had haunted me given a terrible reality.

Men surged forward and the line was broken, but the monks were upon us, features more fanatically contorted than I had ever dared to show them in a mask. As the surge of the crowd ripped me away from Ramona's side, I turned and ran.

Unwilled, my feet found the path to our house. I slammed the door behind me. *I should go back, I can't go back! I should....*the inner battle raged. I clung to the kitchen table, shaking in every limb.

Torchlight gleamed through the little window, setting a spark of crimson on the shelf aglow. As the light grew I recognized the monstrous shape of the banshee.

Masks! I'll give you a mask! Certainty bloomed with a force that banished fear. I tore off the half-mask of the catman and lifted down the massive head of Darkover's most terrible predator. The hood of my cloak provided some padding as I settled the heavy construction into place, buckled the straps, and hooked on the rod that would let me clack the hinged lower beak against the upper.

The roof of the tavern was burning. In the ruddy light I could see Ramona's tall figure in the center of a surging crowd, Kiera and Adriana by her side.

"Spawn of darkness, what whore's face do you hide!" One of the followers leaped forward and grabbed Ramona's mask.

Merciful Avarra! They will go mad when they see she is a man! but it was the fanatic who fell back, eyes widening as the mask jerked free. It was Avarra Herself whose face blazed through Ramona's features, eyes aflame, brows bent in holy wrath. I had given Ramona the face Avarra wore for blessing. I was seeing her other face now.

"You have called for cleansing!" Her deep voice cried. "Let it begin!" She pointed toward me—no, it was toward the banshee.

The energy that had impelled me this far became a rush of power that drove my identity to the edge of awareness. From my throat came a screech that shocked through the thick air as my lifting arms spread the cloak like mighty wings. I was aware of screams, of gaily-clad shapes giving way before me. The tumult faded as people ran.

When I could think again my sight was dazzled by blue fire. As my knees began to buckle, the weight of the mask was lifted. Someone caught me, I blinked, and the world began to come into focus once more.

Kiera was standing before me, the starstone she always wore on a chain beneath her shirt unwrapped and gripped tightly in her hand. Adriana stood behind her, the banshee mask held at arms' length. It was Ramona, I realized then, who was holding me. Feeling me stir, she set me on a bench that had somehow survived the fray. In the light of the flames that still flickered on one of the tavern's walls I saw that we were alone.

Kiera bent over me. "Are you alright?"

"I will be..." I whispered. I felt emptied of everything, including fear.

"What should I do with the mask?" Adriana asked.

"The Guard will be looking for it," said Kiera. She glanced back at me and I nodded. "Throw it on the fire."

"This, too," said Ramona, holding out the mask the fanatic had torn away.

"But don't you need—" I began, then looked at her again. Ramona's features were not as perfect as those of the mask, but her serene expression was the same.

I got to my feet and held out my hand.

"Let's go home."

The Song of Star Girl

by Marella Sands

Marella Sands spends far too much of her time thinking about what needs to be in her author bios. This time, she's pretty sure it involves rabbits, kabobs, palm trees, and campfires, but not necessarily in that order. Currently, she is: working on a novel of alternate history; producing novellas for her Angels' Share series; shopping around a novella-length Thai ghost story; and producing short stories. This is her fourth sale to the Darkover anthologies and she has also sold a story to *Lace and Blade 4*. For this particular tale, she was contemplating the *Ballad of Hastur and Cassilda* (which dates back to at least the Ages of Chaos) and thought that it must have had historical roots in actual Romeo and Juliet style tragedies deep in Darkover's past.

The contemporary form of the *Ballad of Hastur and Cassilda* comprises an origin story for the Comyn families of the Seven Domains, said to be descended from Hastur, son of the god Aldones, who loved two sisters, Cassilda and Camilla. Jealous Alar attacked Cassilda and Hastur with a magical sword, "meant to banish, not to slay," but instead sent Camilla, who had taken her sister's place in Hastur's arms that night, into the realm of shadows.

Alann shouted in triumph the moment he saw the blue stone shining at the bottom of the pool. He'd been searching the bog for days to find this one thing: a magical blue stone that could amplify psy power. Because it could interact with a human mind, only the person who would eventually wield it should touch it with bare skin. Alann pulled a rag out of his pocket, and though he was trembling with excitement, he reached down gently, slid the rag through the pink sedges, and grasped the stone firmly.

The bog near Mariposa was odd and treacherous, full of soft soil and strange bubbling pools that smelled of creatures that had fallen in and rotted away ages ago. But if you knew just where to step, and came in the late spring when the snowmelt from the distant mountains had carried silt and stones from higher elevations, you could find all kinds of interesting things. And the rarest and best of all was now in his hand.

Alann backed out of the pool gradually, careful not to step away from his intended path. No one was sure what permeated this bog, or what made up the weird mists that seeped from it on sunny days, and so all but Alann avoided it.

The mists swirled around him, carrying the scents of things best left undisturbed. Alann liked the mists; sometimes they showed him visions, and sometimes he lost hours of his life while the tendrils entwined between his fingers. The best time of the year was right before winter set in, when the bog had been gifted with the summer warmth for several months. That was when visions were the strangest and strongest. Alann could spend days here, forgetting to eat or sleep, just breathing the foggy air.

But not today. Today, he had found his prize. It would be a gift for Callie, the girl he had admired for almost all of his eighteen years.

Callie and her sister Lori shared a mother but not a father. Through their mother, they were descended from the first child to be born on this world, the woman Lori was named for. People of that line were often tall, willowy, with pale hair and eyes. Lori looked like that, but Callie did not. Callie looked like her father; brown-haired and brown-eyed, and was, to Alann, the most beautiful woman he had ever seen. He had watched her as long as he could remember, and had memorized the features of her face almost before he could walk.

Once free of the bog, he sat down to put on his shoes and look once more at the stone. It glowed almost purple in the morning light.

"What do you have there?" asked a deep male voice.

Alann looked up, startled that anyone was within miles of this place.

The stranger was dressed for travel with sturdy boots, a jacket, and a rucksack. His blond hair hung in waves to his shoulders and his blue eyes stared at Alann with a mixture of amusement and curiosity.

"Nothing," said Alann. "It's nothing."

"Well, it looks like one of those magic stones people are always going on about," said the other man. "I thought they were found in the mountains."

"They are," said Alann.

The other man stared at Alann a few moments, but Alann didn't elaborate.

"I'm Rafe di Asturien," the man said. He nodded politely. "I was headed toward the settlement of Mariposa but apparently got a bit lost. I don't suppose you could point me in the right direction."

"Why are you going there?" Alann jammed the rag containing the stone in his pocket. He would look at it again when he got home and wrapped it in a nice cloth to give to Callie.

The other man shrugged and looked a little lost. The expression made him seem even younger than Alann, though Alann judged they were probably nearly the same age. "New Skye is feeling a bit crowded to me these days. I'd like to homestead where there's more open land and the mountains aren't looming over you all the time. I'd heard that Mariposa was doing well, but could use new blood, so I thought I'd come."

Alann just stared.

"So," said Rafe, "can you point me toward Mariposa? Or, better yet, are you going there? Can you show me the way?"

Alann had no desire to lead this handsome man to Mariposa, where new men were always celebrated. Women were always looking for bed partners who weren't closely related; therefore, every young woman would find him interesting, and his rugged good looks would only add to his success with them, and detract from Alann ever finding a woman for himself.

But, he had no good reason to refuse, especially since Rafe could just follow him to Mariposa. He said, "Come," and headed across the field of waving pink and green grasses.

Rafe clapped him on the shoulder. "Thank you. What's your name?"

"Alann."

"Don't talk a lot, do you, Alann?"

Alann shrugged.

"This is a beautiful place. What's its name?"

"I don't think it has one. No one comes here except me."

"And now me," said Rafe. "Well, even if I don't come back, it was worth seeing once."

Alann's vision flickered for a moment and he saw the place as if through a cloudy lens, full of low-lying clouds and odd animals swimming in the fantastic landscape. He blinked and the vision was gone. Sometimes, he saw glimpses of what he believed to be the future, because sometimes they came true, like the time he had seen the way Tirza's baby would look at its naming, and the exact time the blizzard would hit Mariposa last winter.

He sensed this vision was from a distant future, so he put it aside. He would prefer to know more immediate things, like how much Callie would appreciate his gift. He could imagine the light dancing in her eyes and the brilliant smile she might have, and his heart leaped a little just thinking about it.

Ever since they were old enough, Alann had been trying to gain Callie's love. He brought her presents; he ran errands for her; he was gracious and solicitous at all community gatherings. And she was friendly in return, but so far, she had never chosen him to share her bed.

As far as he knew, she had never chosen anyone, which was a well-known source of consternation to her mother. "You know every woman should do her part to increase the size of our population," she would say, and Callie would only laugh. "Mother, I'll do my part when I find the right man."

Every time he heard Callie say that, Alann's knees wobbled. He was right man if only he could get her to see him.

Rafe didn't quiz Alann any more, which Alann was grateful for. They walked to Mariposa in the noontime light and arrived just as people were putting away the remains of their midday meal.

Lori spotted the visitor first. "Alann, who have you brought with you?" She laughed and held out her hands to Rafe, who took them and bowed over them. Her pale eyes and hair glistened in the bright light of noon; Rafe seemed as taken with her beauty as almost everyone was. Alann might prefer Callie's looks, but Lori had been judged more beautiful by the community. And if Rafe were smitten with Lori, he might not even look at Callie.

"My name is Rafe di Asturien," Rafe said before Alann could answer the question. "I'm from New Skye, and looking for somewhere to homestead."

Others began approaching. Liam Aldaran nodded to the newcomer. "Welcome. There's plenty of land here, especially on the east side of the lake, toward the bog. Few want to set up farms there because of the oddity of the land."

"Not *in* the bog," said Rafe slowly. "That wouldn't make good farmland."

"No, no," said Liam with a chuckle. "The bog is farther east. Sometimes the mists get close enough that you can see them from the shores of the lake, but they never get so close they'd be in bed with you."

Rafe smiled. "I'm not afraid of a bit of mist."

"Then feel free to look around, but first, stay with us a few days and meet everyone." Liam gave his own daughter, Moriana, a significant glance, and she blushed. She already had one child, but he was weaned now and everyone was waiting to see who might father her second.

Lori looked at Rafe coyly. "Alann can show you some good spots where a house would be protected from the worst of the winter storms. I'd love to come when you go to explore the area and pick a location."

Rafe smiled even more broadly. "That sounds lovely."

Callie stepped forward, her dark hair and eyes as captivating as always. "I'll come with you."

Alann's heart twisted against his lungs and he felt light-headed for a moment.

Liam gestured to Rafe. "That's for the future. For today, come, place your belongings in the common lodge, and then join us for a meal. I'm sure there's enough leftovers to feed you something. Welcome to Mariposa."

Rafe followed Liam toward the building where the community gathered for dances and storytelling, as well as where they put visitors. Lori and Callie, along with several of the settlement's other young women, followed along behind.

Alann seethed and went back to his mother's house. His chores waited. He would have to give the stone to Callie later.

The next few days were a trial for Alann. Even his mother was taken with the new arrival. She prattled on about how Rafe di Asturien had helped a woman repair the roof that had been damaged over the winter. Rafe di Asturien had built a ramp so Lori's grandmother could get into her house with her bad knees. Rafe di Asturien had practically woven the stars into a crown and set it right on his awful blond head.

At least he had Callie. Alann hung around her house and did chores for her as usual, wondering how best to present his gift. Just handing her a stone didn't seem a grand enough gesture, especially considering how rare the blue stones were.

In the evening, he sat on the steps of the house where Callie lived with her mother, two younger brothers, and Lori, and ate the bits of bread, meat, and fruit he had brought with him to see him through the day. The sun glowed a fiery red as it lowered itself toward the western horizon.

Should he carve a box and place the stone inside? Find a way to incorporate it into a piece of jewelry? Set it in a metal frame and turn it into a work of art?

No one knew much about the stones, only that they brought out or enhanced psy powers in some people. To other people, they invoked headaches and nausea. Callie had never displayed much in the way of special powers, even though most people expected to have at least limited telepathic ability by the time they reached adulthood. A few had gifts like Alann, where they could glimpse the future or predict the weather. But if Callie could do any of that, she had not said.

This stone could be the thing that prompted her mind to develop her powers. Who knew, perhaps she could be as strong as some of the people of New Skye were rumored to be. Here in Mariposa, no one was particularly gifted, but some of the families in New Skye had, if rumor were correct, very powerful gifts. So powerful they were difficult to control. Some, it was said, had even died of them.

He wouldn't want Callie to die! But maybe she'd want to have a little power of her own. And she'd be grateful that Alann was the one who had given her the opportunity.

He was basking in the thought when Callie came out of the house and sat down on the stairs next to him.

"Mother made more stew than we could eat. Would you like some?" She held out a bowl to him.

Despite the fact that he had already eaten, Alann was suddenly ravenous. Anything from Callie's hand was a gift that could not be denied. He took the bowl and sipped the stew. It was much more flavorful than the stews his own mother made.

"Mother wanted to thank you for bringing the spices back from the bog. You always find the best, and they're never moldy or wilted."

"I'm glad she uses them," he said. While his mother trusted in his ability to navigate the bog safely, she wouldn't eat the plants he found there.

"You could come with me sometime and I'd show you what could be picked," he said. "There are lots of little pretty flowers there, down close to the ground. When you're walking by, you don't see them. You have to look closely. But they're the prettier for all that."

She laughed softly. "I don't want to go to the bog! Two years ago you were in a trance for a day after you breathed too much smoke, or fog, or whatever that stuff is. And then you told stories about flying animals, and lakes made of clouds, and people able to lift metals out of the core of the planet with their minds alone. You should stop going there yourself, or you'll go back to raving, and this time never stop."

"The mists help me see what's true and what's not," he said, which was as close as he could come to explaining things in words. "Someday, there will be a lake of clouds instead of a bog. Someday, our people will be strong enough to forge great weapons with their minds, aided by the blue stones."

Callie shuddered. "Don't talk about weapons like they're good things. I hope that never comes true."

This was his opportunity. "But the stones help people all the time. Power is nothing without someone to wield it. What if you had a stone of your own? Maybe then you'd be able to find metal in the core of the planet yourself. Or communicate your thoughts to others. Or see the future."

"I don't want to do any of those things," she said firmly. She flipped her brown hair over her shoulder. "If anything, I'd want to know more about the weather. I'd like to be better prepared in winter before we get hit with the big storms. Or to know when conditions are right for a prairie fire."

That was Callie. Always practical.

"I would like that, too," he said. "Weather predicting would always be useful in Mariposa."

"Or anywhere," she said. "Sometimes, I'd like to walk away from here and go somewhere else. New settlements are being founded all the time. I think I'd like to go to the southwest. They say there's a dry land there that's near the sea. It might be a challenge to grow crops there, but wouldn't it exciting to go where everything is so different?"

"I'd go there with you," he said. "I'd go anywhere with you."

Callie patted him on the knee. "I know you would. I couldn't found a town by myself, anyway. I'd need friends to go with me."

Alann's heart was as light as it had been in tendays.

"Rafe says there's plenty of people in New Skye who want to leave. We could find more people to come with us."

Alann's heart froze for a moment, before he realized she meant to leave Rafe behind, homesteading here on the shores of Lake Mariposa, and go to a distant land with Alann. Even if other people came along, he would be with her on a grand adventure.

Alann finished the stew and returned the bowl. "Just give the word, and I'll be ready to travel with you to the dry lands of the southwest."

"What are you two talking about so seriously out there?" asked a voice out of the darkening evening. Rafe di Asturien. He waved goodbye to someone; in the dim light, Alann thought he recognized Moriana.

"Traveling," said Callie.

"Travel is good for the soul," said Rafe. "You should do it sometime. But go farther than New Skye."

"I want to go to the southwest. Do you know anyone who's been there?"

Rafe frowned and ran a hand through his hair. "No, I don't think so. I haven't heard much about that land."

"Would you ever go there?" asked Callie.

Alann's heart nearly stopped. He'd already said *he* would go!

"But Mariposa is now my settlement. Why would I leave?"

Callie said nothing, but her face reflected her thoughts clearly. *You'd come to be with me.*

Rafe gave a shallow bow. "Tomorrow I head out to look for my homesteading site. I assume the two of you will still be coming? Especially you, Alann, since you're my guide."

"Of course," said Callie in a sad small voice.

"Yes," said Alann.

"Good. I will see you in the morning." Rafe walked off into the deepening gloom.

Alann sat in silence with Callie for several minutes. "The southwest is still there. We can go, and see the ocean. They say there's so much salt in the water, you can't drink it."

Callie gave him an absentminded smile. "It's a nice dream."

"Sometimes, dreams come true."

Callie's smile faltered and she shrugged. "Sometimes." She took a deep breath. "Sing me something, Alann."

That was the one thing he had always been able to do for her: sing to her when she was sad. His grandmother had taught him the songs of her childhood, and they had been a comfort to him, and to Callie, as long as he could remember.

He sang *The Tale of Snow Girl and the Flower*, a slow song that had never failed to lighten Callie's heart. In the song, a girl made of snow could only become a real girl and have the man she loved if she completed the task set for her by her grandmother: find a special flower on the distant mountain peak, pluck it, and bring it back before it wilted.

Alann's grandmother had taught him two versions of the song: in the one he sang to Callie, the girl brought the flower home, and gained the love of the handsome Royven, and had many children and grandchildren and lived a long, happy life with the people she loved. The final refrain was the one Alann always sang so softly only Callie could hear him.

She walked in sunlight, bright and clear,
Head held high, no room for fear.
And the crimson leaves around the shore,
Rejoiced to see her evermore.
In sunlight, finally, she turned her face
To life and love, and each precious place.
Clouds dropped blessings ever after
To hear Snow Girl's eternal laughter.

In the other version, the girl was named Star Girl. His grandmother had said that instead of being made of snow, she had come from the heavens where it was eternally cold. In this version, the girl was supposed to retrieve a metal object that predicted weather from the high slopes of a mountain, but the object broke in her hand and fell into a chasm. The grandmother pronounced the girl cursed to remain a girl of the cold heavens, doomed to never know the warmth of male companionship. The girl threw herself into the chasm and perished. Royven's love went to another girl, the grandmother died, and by the next midsummer, no one remembered Star Girl at all.

She walked in sunlight, bright and clear
Yet bent her head near chasm drear.
And the crimson leaves around the shore
Dimmed in twilight evermore.
From sunlight, ever, she turned her face
From life, and love, and each precious place.
The clouds wept salty tears ever after
In the absence of dear Star Girl's laughter.

Alann kept that version to himself.

When he was finished with the song, Callie sighed, got up, and went back into the house.

Alann went to bed but did not sleep well. His dreams were full of visions of blue stones, lakes of mist, and the dark head of Callie turned away from him, toward a horizon where a blond man stood. Then a burning pain overtook everything. He awoke in a cold sweat.

The mood of the dream was slow to depart. Alann dragged himself out of bed, even though he felt shaky and weak. But this was no day to be sick, especially from nothing worse than a bad dream. He dressed and equipped himself with enough food and water for the day. Annoyingly, his mother packed extra food in a satchel for "our new guest," as if everyone in Mariposa weren't already trying to buy Rafe's good will with food and drink.

Alann stepped outside to see the others had already gathered in the common area. Callie was laughing, probably at something Rafe had said.

Hate blossomed in Alann's chest. Rafe could have any woman: he did not have to pursue Callie. But here she was, laughing and standing so close to him their shoulders touched.

"Ready?" asked Lori.

Alann jumped. He hadn't seen her walk up next to him in the morning half-light.

"Sure."

Lori saw the direction of his gaze and patted Alann on the shoulder. "The newness will wear off eventually, or we'll get another visitor who will distract everyone from him. Don't worry." Her smile was condescending and somewhat sad.

Alann flushed, embarrassed that he had been so obvious about his thoughts. He stuffed his anger down further into his heart and lifted his head. "Never mind," he said. "Let's have a good day."

Lori beamed at that, no doubt pleased with herself for talking him out of a dark mood. Or maybe just for saving herself from having to put up with his foul mood all day on their trek. Alann didn't care, just so long as he didn't draw her attention again. He had to think about what to do with his stone, and when it would be best to give it to Callie.

Maybe he shouldn't give it to her as it was. Perhaps he should fashion it into a magnificent gift, one that would win

Callie's heart instantly. That was all he needed to do to get Callie to look away from Rafe and at Alann instead.

Rafe gestured toward Alann. "Come, lead us, friend! You know the area." He smiled brightly and both the women smiled at him in return.

Alann ducked his head and nodded. "Follow me."

"Tell us about New Skye," said Callie.

Rafe chuckled and the women followed suit. "It's like Mariposa, I suppose," he said. "But more people. There's not much farmland left near the main settlement, which is why many people are leaving for other places. Some want to head toward the mountains, like the followers of Valentine. I don't see the appeal of high places, though. I wanted to see the broad plains and walk in the sea of grass. And then, when I get here, I find pink grass and bubbling pools! I had no idea it was so strange here."

"Only the bog is strange," said Callie.

"No one goes there," said Lori with a chill in her voice. "A child ran into the bog two years ago and was swallowed up. Only Alann goes in and out without care." It had been her cousin's youngest who had died that day, and Lori hated to talk about it. Alann was surprised she had even brought it up.

Alann decided they weren't leaving him out of the conversation. "I take a great deal of care," he said. "You have to watch where you put your feet. And don't breathe too deeply of the mists. They can give you visions and bad dreams."

"Then we'll stay away," said Rafe. "Clearly, you lost someone you loved in the bog, so there's no need to risk either ourselves or the temptation to dwell on bad memories."

Lori let out a little sigh.

"But we were talking about you," said Callie. "What's your family like?"

"Like most," he said. "My mother bore eight children to four upstanding men of the community, but she usually lived with my father, Tomas di Asturien. I was the third child. My brothers have all moved to other settlements, and my sisters have started their own families, except for the youngest. She's only eight. I decided this year was the year I would set out on my own and be like my brothers. Mikal's two years younger than me and he already has a farm and a child!"

"How old are you?" asked Lori.

"Twenty. But what about you? I am betting that Alann here is related to Liam Aldaran as they could almost be twins, but what about the two of you? I know you live with your mother, but I haven't heard any comments about a man in the house."

Alann clenched his fists. It could well be that Liam was his father but his mother refused to say who had sired any of her children. Alann's two siblings who had survived childhood had parted ways with their mother years ago and were long gone to homestead somewhere else, leaving Alann at home with a bitter woman who refused to say why she was unhappy, or who made any attempt to change.

"My father is Orvus, who was at the singing the other night," said Lori. "Callie's father died in a winter storm a few years back."

"Ah. I'm sorry for your loss, dear Callie. But Orvus—was he the man who played the lap harp so beautifully?"

"Yes, him," said Callie. "He was always willing to play for us when we were sick as children or when we had headaches as adolescents."

Alann listened to the other three prattle on as the conversation turned to crops, babies, and homesteading. No one asked him any questions, so he set their path in silence. He was headed toward the low-lying scrubby hills that bordered the eastern shore of Lake Mariposa. Though the hills were not steep, the soil was loose and rocky enough that their feet slipped occasionally.

"I don't want to farm *this*!" said Rafe with a laugh.

"Of course not," said Alann. "But from the top, you can see more of the plains than from below."

"That makes sense. Lead on, good fellow."

From the top, the view was amazing. To the west and south was the lake. To the north and indicated by a haze of smoke from the morning cooking fires, was Mariposa. To the east lay the flat grassy landscape, which stretched away from the mountains into the thin purple line of the distant horizon.

Rafe took a deep breath. "Beautiful. But where will I build my house?"

Alann pointed to the south and east. "There's a hollow in that direction. It'll shield a house from the worst of the winter weather, but also catch the summer sunsets and breezes."

"Isn't that too close to the bog?" asked Callie. She stepped closer to Rafe and he put an arm around her shoulders as if to protect her from the threat.

Alann gritted his teeth and did his best to sound polite. "I've never seen the mists go that far to the south. When the wind is just right, they might come between Mariposa and the homestead, but in that event, one *could* walk around the lake. Or wait until the wind changes."

"I don't mind walking. After all, I walked from New Skye to Mariposa," said Rafe lightly; Lori and Callie beamed at him. "And I have enough patience to wait out the weather if need be. It sounds like a grand location."

"Should we go there now?" asked Callie. "I'd love to see it."

Alann's mood grew darker. He had offered to show Callie the hidden spot on several occasions, but he'd abandoned the attempt when she'd made it clear she wasn't getting near the bog she feared. It seemed she felt differently if Rafe di Asturien might be involved in the adventure.

"I don't think so," said Rafe. He shot Alann a look Alann could not interpret. "I'd rather eat lunch here where I can see the lovely view." His gaze had settled on Lori, though, not the horizon.

Callie noticed and her smile faltered slightly. Alann's heart lifted.

Lori laid out a small blanket and the four of them put out the food they had brought. Rafe told funny stories about his grandmother chasing a chervine through New Skye and falling in the mud while the chervine jumped up on a rooftop and escaped both pursuer and mud. After that came a succession of stories that had the women laughing and even Alann found himself joining in on occasion. His hatred for Rafe dimmed a bit.

When they had finished eating, Rafe settled back in the grass. "This is the life! A homestead to start, new friends to eat with, and laugh with, and perhaps...other things." He let his voice die away and held a hand out to Lori, who took it and blushed mightily.

"Nothing in New Skye can compare to the loveliness in Mariposa," he said, and he kissed Lori's hand.

Callie's face fell. Rafe noticed and held out his other hand to her. "My apologies. I did not mean to seem to say that there was only one beauty here."

Callie took his hand, but she kept her eyes on her lap and did not smile.

"Well," said Rafe after a few moments, "perhaps we should start back. I can't start building a house today, but soon."

"Perhaps the day after tomorrow?" asked Lori. "I think several of the men would be free that day and could help you lay out the foundations and walk the edges of your steading."

"And in the meantime, perhaps there will be chervines you can chase," said Alann.

That made Rafe laugh. Lori looked at Alann and smiled in her serene way. But Callie still would not meet anyone's eyes.

The walk back to Mariposa was much different that the walk out. Lori and Rafe walked on ahead, hand in hand, speaking low enough that Alann could not hear.

Callie dropped back, and Alann stayed with her.

"Her beauty always attracts the men. They never see me," said Callie.

"I see you," said Alann. "I always have."

Callie did not seem to hear. "Mother says I shouldn't worry about it. That we are all supposed to have children by many men, so there's no reason I can't have a man that Lori had first. I suppose that's true. It's important for the gene pool—we hear it from the cradle. It's just that, someday, I wish a man would see *me* first."

Alann stopped and took Callie's hand. She looked up in surprise.

"I see you," said Alann clearly. "I always have. You are the most beautiful woman in Mariposa. I will go with you to the southwest. I would go with you across the ocean. I would go with you anywhere."

Callie looked stunned. Alann's heart lifted with hope. Now she could see his devotion! His thoughts tripped ahead to how happy they would be together, as soon as she accepted him and loved him as he loved her.

"But," said Callie at last, in a tone that stung him to the core. "You're a sweet boy, and you'd be a darling traveling companion. I'd trust you to find us food, and you're strong and patient and kind. But you're like a little brother to me. How could we be together like that?"

"I'm not your brother." He stepped closer and put a hand on her shoulder. His heart beat against his ribs so wildly he thought it might rip itself free from his chest entirely. This was his chance! "Love me. Ask me to go with you across the continent. Only ask, and I will come."

"I..." Callie looked at the backs of Rafe and Lori, who had not noticed their companions were no longer just behind them. They saw only each other. "I don't know. I'll...I'll have to think about it."

"Love me," said Alann again. The thought that she would not look at him lanced him in the heart, swept through his bones, and burned at the end of every nerve. She could not reject him, not after all this time.

Callie shrugged his hand off her shoulder and would not meet his eyes. "I said I'd think about it."

Alann thought about the stone in his pocket; the writhing and misery in his soul demanded that he present it to her. That would be the catalyst she needed to see him as a lover rather than a brother. Maybe he should give it to her right now.

But no. He needed to think of a way to make the presentation special. To make it something that would cement her heart to him forever. Rafe wasn't the only one who could be patient.

They walked the rest of the way back to the settlement in silence. The gloom that lay over Alann's head seemed to encompass Callie, but it was clear Rafe and Lori were oblivious.

After a few days of rain, the sun rose to meet a glorious red and purple sky. Alann's weather sense told him the settlement was in for at least a tenday of beautiful weather. He let Liam Aldaran know, and the community rejoiced. With good weather, the Midsummer feast would be the best Mariposa had seen in several years.

The only thing marring it would be the attendance of Rafe di Asturien. Alann kept that feeling close and avoided those in the community he knew were the most adept at picking up stray thoughts.

The day before Midsummer, Alann got up, ate some stew, and walked outside to finish his work in decorating the common ground. Flowers had been spread around, vines and twigs had been woven into strings of garland that graced the entire area, and tables had been set out in preparation for tomorrow's feast. Everything was nearly ready. Alann was supposed to decorate the area where the musicians would play.

His mother left the house with him, a smile on her face for the first time in tendays. Few things made her smile, and Alann was glad to see her looking forward to something.

"This will be a Midsummer to remember," she said, as she surveyed the festive décor. "I've never seen so many flowers!"

"It's been a good year," said Alann. "Everything is green and blooming at just the right time."

His mother moved off to deliver her vegetables to the area where the women would be cooking much of the meal. The few cookpots and spits the community had that were large enough to prepare more than just a small family meal were shared by all. Alann might foresee a time when metal was not quite so rare, but that time was far in the future. For today, what few metal tools Mariposa had must be cared for and used as wisely as possible.

Alann had just begun to weave a rope of garland when he heard a laugh. It sounded like Callie. He glanced up.

Callie stood arm-in-arm with Rafe in the shadow of the common lodge where Rafe was still sleeping until he had finished his house. She lifted her face to his and he leaned down to kiss her.

Alann's heart stopped, as if ice water had squeezed frozen it solid. Callie and Rafe!

Rafe looked over and saw who was staring at them. He said something in a low voice to Callie and moved away. Callie waved gaily after him without noticing Alann.

"Stop staring at them," said his mother.

Alann turned around. His mother stood watching Callie with a hard look. "She'll learn soon enough you can't trust a man. They'll have their fun and then where are they when the babe comes?"

"It's important for women to have children by at least several men," said Alann automatically.

"I know. The gene pool. I say, let the damn gene pool worry about itself," said his mother. "You're a good boy. When you find someone, you'll take care of her properly."

"You know I will, Mother."

"If you want Callie, my son, you'll have to be patient, and let her get this tryst out of her system. She needs to learn that you can't depend on a pretty face to bring you food in the winter."

"Like Liam Aldaran?" he asked, shocked by his own audacity. Alann had not asked about his own father's identity for years.

"You know I'll never tell who sired my children," said his mother. Her good mood vanished. "The wretched men who left me pregnant and moved on to other conquests do not deserve names. My mother said her grandmother told her of a time when men were more faithful. When they stayed and had many children by the same woman and they all lived together. But no one does that anymore. At least some men stay, even if their women are pregnant by others. That seems difficult for many to do, though." Her face darkened.

"Maybe we can go back to the old ways," said Alann.

"I don't think so," said his mother. "You can't go back. Now, women have lots of children by lots of men and all men are supposed to take care of them all. But they don't."

Alann forbore to mention that his mother was the only woman in the settlement who seemed to be avoided by nearly everyone. Men came by Lori and Callie's house to help out and bring food. Liam Aldaran and Ysabet had lived together for twenty years even though they both had other lovers. Somehow, his mother had managed to cut herself off from everyone, just like Alann's older siblings had cut themselves off.

Alann was going to be different. He was going to have Callie, and they would live in the old ways. Surely that was why she hadn't taken multiple lovers yet. She was just waiting for "the right man," as she had insisted to her mother. Alann only had to make her see that he was that man.

"Do you know what I heard from that di Asturien boy the other day?" his mother asked with some anger. "That someone was advancing the idea of stud books! So we could breed people like animals. Shameful!"

Alann's mind filled with a dim vision of the future. Yes, there would be stud books, and registries, and breeding programs. They would bring nearly unlimited power to a select few, and madness to many. Alann's heart froze at the horrors he could dimly perceive, and was thankful he could not see the fullness of the future.

But he could sense enough. The dim future twisted through his thoughts, each path leading to an even more awful result. War. Insanity. Death. The despair of thousands of souls caught up in fire and choking dust. It would come. Not tomorrow, or even in a generation, but it would come.

Alann felt like he were choking himself. Choking on his dread of the future. He couldn't bear it. He had to get away. Now.

He ran toward the bog, toward the only place that felt like home, and the only place where he knew no one would follow, or find, him.

Despair weighed him down and it took him much of the morning, and part of the afternoon, to get to the bog. Alann was weary, thirsty, and hungry by the time he arrived. It had been foolish to leave Mariposa without supplies, but it was too late now to go back. Hunger, thirst, and tiredness were passing things, and not important. He just needed to be in the bog.

Alann walked carefully along paths he knew well until he reached what he considered his special place. It was a tussock of pink grasses where many of the small flowers he had told Callie about grew. The mists from the surrounding pools sometimes covered the entire tussock so that he could breathe them in for hours while lying on the higher ground.

Once Alann settled onto the grass, he was able to take deep breaths and relax. The mists enfolded him and lifted him up. Here, he was the person he was supposed to be. Here, he was more intimately at home than anywhere else he'd ever been.

Dimly, he was aware of the march of the sun overhead and the turning of the planet beneath him. Yet even as his awareness reached out to encompass the natural world, he couldn't shake his anger at Callie's interest in Rafe.

Rafe had to know of Alann's interest, or else why retreat when he saw Alann looking his way when he was with Callie? Wasn't it enough for him that Moriana and Lori and every other eligible young woman in Mariposa was willing to share his bed?

Why pursue Callie as well?

Perhaps a better question was, why would Callie pursue Rafe, when Alann was right there? Or was that the problem: Alann had always been there. He had always been available to do chores for her, and sing for her, and help her in any way he could. She must think he would always be around when she needed him, and that he would always do just what she wanted him to do, while she bedded other men, without taking his feelings into account.

She didn't deserve the stone he had found for her!

Alann reached into his pocket to throw the stone back in the bog, but it had come out of the rag. His hand closed around its bare hard surface.

His mind exploded in a fury of blue sparks that seared his thoughts and reached into the core of his being. Behind the sparks flowed the mists of the bog, as if they could exist both within the bog and within his mind.

Alann screamed and drew his hand out of his pocket, but it was too late. The stone would not be denied. The powers that had manifested so occasionally burst into full being. All at once, Alann sensed the distant shifts of weather that would bring Mariposa rain within a tenday. He felt the energy of dead and decaying things trapped under the peat of the bog, waiting for a future day when they could burst forth and create a lake of mists and clouds, where strange creatures would swim and where people such as himself could walk the lakebed without harm.

Other glimpses of the future came to him. Great towers staffed with dozens of people, all pooling their powers to travel from one place to another instantaneously, to create deadly weapons of dust and fire, and to control their own bodies in ways no one had yet dreamed of. Men and women shackled together by copper bracelets, proclaiming their lifelong fidelity. People driven mad by the powers bred into their lines: powers to see the future, or force one's mind into another's, or to communicate with animals. Kings and wars and death. The future was full of fire and torment, and it would come from the blue stones, and the people who wielded them.

Alann writhed on the grass and did his best to push those images out of his mind. He focused on the one thing that could ground him: Callie, and his love for her. But his mind now had the stone to use and he was able to reach out to her mind and find her, locate her from afar. His mind reeled when he realized she was with Rafe and Lori, and that they were in Rafe's half-built steading. Even from this distance, his mind was strong enough to sense the heat of their passion, and the fulfillment of their joint desire.

Despair ripped through his mind and he screamed. He would have thrown the stone away but his hand had spasmed around it and he could not let it go. He could not turn aside his sight or control his visions.

He stumbled through the bog, knowing somehow where to step, and where to avoid stepping. He could go to them. He would find Callie, and they would leave this place together. She might have had Rafe tonight, but she would have Alann for the rest of her life.

Nothing could stop him. Callie could follow her dream to go to the southwest dry lands and he would go with her. They would homestead and raise children and live long, happy lives without Lori or Rafe or Moriana or anyone else!

He strode across the grassy plain and brought the mist with him. It cozened his mind, caressed his hands, and danced around his head like the crowns he saw on the future kings of the land.

It did not take him long to reach the steading of Rafe di

Asturien. Inside, Rafe lay on a makeshift bed on the ground, one arm around Lori, the other around Callie.

Alann held up a fist. It looked strange and black, burned like meat left too long on a fire, but he couldn't focus on that right now.

Rafe pulled his arms away from the women and held up his empty hands to Alann. "My friend, nothing has happened here against anyone's will."

"It's against mine," Alann said, his voice low and rumbling. "Callie and I want to leave this place. She wants to see the dry lands. She wants to see the ocean! I'll see those things with her."

Alann launched himself toward the makeshift bed. Rafe managed to push Lori aside with his left hand while holding up his right to defend himself.

Rafe shouted, "Get out!"

Alann wasn't sure if Rafe were speaking to the women, or to him, but what did it matter? He wasn't leaving until Rafe was dead. He swung his fist at Rafe.

Callie caught his hand in her own. "No!" she screamed.

The blackness in his hand swept over Callie, along with a blue light that was blinding in its intensity. Alann closed his eyes as the mind of Callie awoke and drew on its own power. Her thoughts burst in upon Alann, forcing his own thoughts aside.

What is this? What's happening? Callie's terror was palpable.

Alann wanted to reach out to her, but her power was too strong. It surged through his mind, stinging and burning wherever it went. In those thoughts, Alann could see himself as Callie saw him: sweet, but a bit of a buffoon; faithful, but weak-minded and needing to be led; patient, but dull. She hadn't meant it when she said she saw him as a little brother; she saw him as little more than a pet. Something that followed you around because it was helpless to do anything else, and which you endured because it would be unkind to do otherwise.

She would never have left the settlement with him in tow. She would never have taken him for a lover.

Instead, after so many years of laughing off would-be suitors, she had taken *this* man, this stranger, as her mate. Memories of what she and Rafe had just done tumbled through Alann's mind, puncturing what hope he had left, driving his despair that much more deeply into his soul.

Callie was aware of her intrusion into his mind; he realized that now. But as powerless as he was to stop her, she was powerless to control her new-found talent.

No no no! she screamed into the wintry void that had overtaken Alann. *Let me go!*

But there was no one to help her. Alann's mind leached away, driven to the corners of sanity by the force of her power. Callie's panicked mind continued to slam into his, slicing it into pieces, throwing around the remains like a dog with a meal too big to swallow in one gulp.

Now Alann could not tell who was screaming, him or Callie. Or both. It was all one, the two of them trapped in agony and confusion and a terrible burning.

Suddenly, the link was broken. Alann fell backward and lay on the bare dirt floor of the half-built shelter.

"Callie!" shouted Lori. "Callie, no!"

"Alann, what did you do?" screamed Rafe.

Alann lay, paralyzed, on the floor. The mists continued to swirl around him, offering him forgetfulness, even death. But his mind was frozen, ripped to shreds. He could no longer choose a path, not even one that led to a peaceful end.

"He killed her!"

"No," said Rafe, his voice still loud with anger, but now also thick with sorrow. "The stone did that—see how burned his hand is where he touched it! Several people in New Skye have died just so. It's not his fault."

"It is!" said Lori. Her voice was filled with such misery Alann could barely recognize it. "My sister is dead—he should pay for her death!"

"He has paid. Without the stone affecting his mind, we could have talked," said Rafe. It seemed as though Rafe were sobbing, but that couldn't be so, could it? "Now she's dead, and his mind is probably destroyed. I need to go to Mariposa, and tell Liam Aldaran what has happened, and get some men to come for the body, and to carry Alann back to the settlement. He will need to be cared for until his mind recovers, or he dies of his injuries."

There was the sound of bustling activity, and weeping, and after the passage of time, the raucous sounds of many people talking at once. Then came the bumping of being carried back to Mariposa. But Alann had no time or attention to spare for that and let his awareness of the outside world slide away. In the mists in his mind, as if on the shore of another world, he saw Callie in the distance, where fog swirled around her ankles and caught at her wrists. He called to her, but the mists moved rapidly to hide her from him.

So he sang of Snow Girl, but this time he sang the old version, the story of Star Girl and her mysterious metal object, and of her true home in the distant frozen heavens.

The mists parted. Callie turned her smiling face to him, and held out her hand.

The Raptor Matrix

by Evey Brett

Of all the sentient nonhuman races on Darkover, perhaps none is more mysterious and least depicted than the Ya-men. They were mentioned in *Winds of Darkover* and *The World Wreckers*, but never explicitly depicted, thereby becoming prime material for anthology contributors to "fill in the gaps." In addition to this mysterious race, this story involves the Ridenow Gift of empathy, particularly with nonhuman races.

After being ordered (or perhaps coerced) to move to southern Arizona by her Lipizzan mare, Carrma, Evey Brett developed a fondness for the local creepy-crawlies such as snakes, scorpions, tarantulas and Gila monsters, not to mention the coyotes, buzzards and hawks that frequent the area. Some of those critters (and/or Carrma) have influenced a number of Evey's stories, including one in *Masques of Darkover* and several in Lethe Press anthologies. When not feeding carrots to her equine mistress, Evey can be found shuffling papers for the city or reading submission stories for *The Magazine of Fantasy and Science Fiction*.

Three swords swung at him: one parried left, one thrust, and the last swung at his legs.

Pick one, Domenic told himself. *Quick!*

He ducked. The flat of the blade smacked his shoulder, sending him tumbling into the dirt.

Wrong one. Again.

Around him, the other cadets snickered. Domenic's opponent faced old Di Asturien, the arms-master, hands raised as if saying, *I don't know what to do with him.*

"All right, you lot, back to pairs. On the double!" Di Asturien said. "Except you, Cadet Ridenow." He extended a hand to help Domenic up. Domenic accepted, shamed by his poor performance.

When the other cadets were out of earshot, the Arms-master asked, "Could you not *see* that sword coming at you, lad?"

Domenic rubbed his upper arm, too embarrassed to answer. He *had* seen the sword. Problem was, there'd been three of them, and he hadn't known which was the true one.

"Is it your eyes? Do you have trouble seeing?"

Domenic shook his head. "My vision is fine. It's..." *Don't ask. Please don't ask.*

But Di Asturien let out a long, understanding sigh. "I've been watching you these past few weeks. It's *laran*, isn't it? What's troubling you?"

The old man was so kind, so understanding that Domenic couldn't bring himself to lie. "I...*see* things. Possibilities. Only a few seconds, maybe a day ahead, but..."

"But just enough to confuse the hell out of you. I don't recall your father mentioning that in his letter."

Because he didn't want to let everyone know what a failure I am as a Ridenow. "Perhaps he wished me to be treated like the other cadets, without preconception as to my abilities."

"Perhaps." Di Asturien sounded skeptical. "I think it's time we had a chat with the Cadet-Master. Come along, lad."

The meeting did not go well. While sympathetic, the Cadet-Master still had his rules to follow. "It just happens, sometimes. *Laran* gets in the way. I wish I could keep you, Cadet Ridenow, but you'd be a liability rather than an asset. You'll be better off in your father's household. I'm sure he'll be able to find a place for you."

Of course he'd think that. He hadn't been there when Domenic and his father, Lord Serrais, had gone riding to inspect their lands. Domenic had gotten a premonition that his father's gelding was about to step into a burrow, panic and break its leg. So he'd yanked on the bridle, hoping to avert the disaster—and the gelding had spooked, thrown Lord Serrais from the saddle, and let out a terrible scream as it caught its leg in the gnarled root of a tree.

"But I was trying to stop it," he'd told his father, sobbing, after the gelding's misery had ended.

"You damn fool of a boy. I ought to have you whipped for losing me my best horse and nearly breaking my neck. Were you *trying* to get me killed?"

"No, Father, I never meant—"

And he knew that his undoing was not so much making a mistake. A simple mistake could be forgiven.

It was in causing his father a great deal of pain, which was anathema to any telepath, especially a Ridenow who was especially strong in empathy. His father's look of pure anguish and disappointment—neither of which Dominic had the *laran* to feel—had nonetheless stung for days.

"I'll write a letter to your father," the Cadet-Master was saying. "I'll explain what happened and that it wasn't your fault. Perhaps some time with a *leronis*—"

"Please don't send me home. I'm...not wanted."

Di Asturien gave him a pitying smile. "I'm sorry lad, but there's no place in the corps for a cadet who's a danger to himself and everyone around him. Go home. I'm sure you'll find your place. I'll bring your letter by the time you've finished packing."

True to his word, the Arms-master met him, letter in hand, just as Domenic was securing his last saddlebag. "Good luck, lad," was all he said before he returned to his duties.

"You're my only saving grace," he told his mare, patting her affectionately on the neck. She snorted and nosed at his pockets. Chuckling, he withdrew the apple and let her nibble on it, happy to please one creature, at least. *She* liked him, to the point that none of the usual Ridenow tactics used by the rest of his family to bond with animals had worked. He always liked to say that Honey had been named for her yellow coat, not her temperament, since the mare would let no one else ride her. She'd earned a number of epithets, the least of which was, "Stubborn beast!"

No, he couldn't go home. Better to face a winter in the Hellers, which would certainly be warmer than his father's icy distance.

So he set out from the barracks, having no particular destination in mind. Honor told him he should go home and face his father's disappointment and deal with whatever consequences might arise, but when he looked down the paths of his possible futures, turning down the road leading to Serrais always ended badly.

It wasn't long before he was out of the city and onto a dirt road leading west. For the most part he was alone, save for the occasional rider or wagon bearing trade goods, which left him more than enough time to ponder his situation. His father hadn't bothered with a *leronis* when Domenic had come of age and had a bout of threshold sickness. "I've seen worse," he'd said, and left Domenic to sweat through the rest. When it was over, his father had tested him for the family Gift of empathy. When it had been negative, Lord Serrais's potent unhappiness had left Domenic sick for the rest of the night.

Of course, when his younger brother, Gavin, who'd already shown signs of the Ridenow Gift, had lain thrashing, their father spared no expense to send for a *leronis* as fast as possible. Domenic had watched her tend to his brother, doing his best to stuff down his jealousy. When Gavin at last lay safely asleep, Domenic dared to approach their visitor. "*Domna*? I was wondering if..."

The *leronis*, possessing a bit of empathy herself, didn't need him to finish. They went to one of the studies, where she unwrapped her matrix stone and used it to look deep inside him.

For a long time, he sat there, waiting, hoping she would be able to tell him that even if he didn't have the Ridenow Gift that he would have one that would still allow him to be of use to his father.

But that didn't happen. He knew, before she told him, what the answer would be. Out of a half dozen futures, none gave him the answer he craved.

"I'm sorry," she told him, utterly sincere. "But you don't have the Ridenow Gift, not even the potential for it, and your precognition isn't strong enough to warrant training at a Tower."

He'd cried when frustration finally got the better of him.

The *leronis*, stricken, gave him what comfort she could, which was little enough. It just proved his father right: he was useless. Too confused by possibilities to fight, unable to deeply bond with an animal, and lacking the empathic Gift entirely.

"Perhaps your sons..." she began, but that was no help, either. How could he provide any sort of future for his sons when he had none himself? Gavin, bearing the gift, would inherit the domain, leaving Dominic...where?

Nowhere, which accounted for his destination now. After a day's ride, he'd made it to the foothills of the Hellers. The terrain was far different than the plains he'd grown up on, and he welcomed the change of scenery. Honey walked steadily onward, minding her footing on the rocky ground.

Help me.

Domenic startled. The words were so faint he was sure he must have misheard.

Please.

The word wasn't a verbal cry, but mental. It was his *laran* playing tricks again, he was sure of it. The one Gift he'd never possessed had been telepathy. Even the *leronis* had confirmed it when she'd examined him.

Over here, you young fool.

The world blurred and split into three different futures and gave him only an instant to glimpse what each of them held. One led mundanely up the path through the mountains. One led down a more precarious trail where even Honey had trouble with the footing. In the third, there was something—no, some*one*—

The world snapped back into *now*. Domenic spun the mare around, trying to make sense of what he'd seen. If he chose poorly—

Stop dithering and help me. I'm down here!

The words came with a tug so sharp that he kneed the mare down the slope before he'd even thought about what he was doing. He leaned back to counterbalance Honey's descent, clinging hard to the saddle as she slipped and slid until they reached the bottom. Stones clattered around them, and a cloud of dirt momentarily obscured his vision.

Domenic dismounted. Honey snorted and sneezed from

the dust, and he patted her neck in sympathy. Looking around, he saw nothing but a pile of rocks, and what seemed to be a boot, attached to a leg, which was attached to—

Rushing over, Dominic found a man only a few years older than himself lying on his stomach beneath the stones. The man grinned weakly. "It's about time. I thought I'd be stuck here forever."

Or until the carrion-birds came, Domenic thought, and soon discovered the problem. The man's left arm was trapped beneath a particularly large rock, one which would be impossible to move in his current position.

And however Domenic moved that rock, he was probably going to cause more pain. "What's your name?"

"Aran Lindir."

"I'm Domenic." He left off his surname, not wanting to evoke the usual expectations that came with it. He inspected the rock's position. The tips of Aran's fingers were still pink rather than blue, meaning there wasn't enough pressure to cut off circulation. By some lucky chance, his arm was saved from being crushed by being trapped by two smaller but sturdier stones that kept him from pulling free.

Domenic circled the large rock, judging the best angle to lift from. His *laran* was of little help, showing him half-dozen possibilities that included dropping the rock and breaking Aran's arm or wedging so that it became immobile. He did his best to ignore them and trust his own judgment. "How did you end up here?"

"The damn horse spooked and tossed me down the slope. By now it's probably run off to some town or another."

"I didn't see any stray horses on the road." He squatted on the far side of the rock, sought a good grip, and prayed to whatever gods might be listening that he didn't mess this up. "I'm going to lift, now. Get ready to move."

Aran braced himself. Domenic took a deep breath and hauled the rock upward. Aran snatched his arm away and let out a cry of pain. The rock slipped from Domenic's fingers, landing with a terrible *crunch* on the other stones.

"Thank goodness that's over." Aran struggled to roll over and sit up, groaning with each effort. Domenic helped him, and for once he was glad he wasn't an empath, otherwise he'd be privy to the man's every ache and discomfort.

A little of his color returned, and he drank greedily from the water flask Domenic offered. Now that Domenic had a chance to look, he found Aran handsome, even with dirt in his tousled red hair.

Then he cringed, ashamed of such thoughts so near a strong telepath, especially with what he was about to say next. "I need to take off your shirt so I can get a better look at you. Does anything hurt besides your arm?"

"Everything," Aran confessed, "though I think it's mostly bruises and stiff muscles from lying there so long."

Domenic did his best to avoid skin-to-skin contact when he removed the man's shirt, which was dirty and torn, and was surprised to see not one but two leather pouches for holding a matrix stone. The oddity was soon forgotten as he noted the livid red and black bruises covering Aran's chest and arms. More worrisome was the large gash on his left arm. It bled sluggishly, and the surrounding tissue was red and inflamed. The rock had done some damage after all.

At least Domenic had managed to stay in the Cadet Corps long enough to learn how to care for injuries and wounds without using *laran*. He did what he could, cleaning the dirt from the ugly wound and binding it with bandages from his pack. Aran's shirt wasn't fit to wear, but it would work for a sling. Domenic was glad that he'd packed a larger shirt meant for him to grow into, and this he dug out of his bags and gave to Aran.

"Thank you," Aran said when he was clean and presentable. "I really thought I'd die out here."

"It's a good thing you were able to reach me."

"I must have an Alton in the family line somewhere. I have a knack for making myself heard to anyone with the telepathic Gift, latent or not. You were the first mind I'd sensed in over a day."

So Aran already knew Domenic was no telepath. It left him feeling a bit gutted. "Were you on your way somewhere?"

"I'm on my way to speak with Lord Serrais."

Domenic stiffened. Of all the Domains in Darkover...

"What? Did I say something wrong?"

Only everything. His hope at being useful away from home evaporated. Rude as it was to pry, he couldn't help asking, "What is your business there?"

"It's a private matter of some urgency. Why?" He narrowed his eyes. "What's your full name?"

This he couldn't evade, and was sorry for it. "Domenic Ridenow, son of Estevan Ridenow, Lord Serrais."

"I'd say I'd found the perfect guide, but something tells me you weren't on your way home."

"I wasn't, but I will take you." Honor bound him to aid a man in need. It was clear Aran wouldn't be able to make it far on his own, weak and exhausted as he was. After all, Domenic wouldn't necessarily have to speak to his father, just drop Aran off and leave again.

Honey had wandered out of sight but returned at Domenic's whistle. He grabbed the mare's bridle and looked her straight in the eye. "You will carry him. And you will be gentle."

She jerked, and her stubbornness rose.

"You *will*."

She snorted, then licked and chewed, her sign of assent. He owed her, though. At their next stop, he'd be sure to buy her a whole basket of apples.

Her ears went back the moment Aran started to mount, but she stayed rock-steady throughout the awkward fumbling.

"Good girl," he said, stroking her head. "Ready?" he called up to his companion, who'd gone a shade paler.

"On to Serrais."

As they headed carefully up the slope, Domenic couldn't help but wish he were going anywhere but home.

That night they camped in a clearing off the main road. Domenic made stew with bits of dried meat and a rabbit-horn he'd managed to snare along the way. Aran leaned wearily against a tree, banished there after his fumbling attempt to help with dinner nearly caused the boiling pot to tip over. He kept an eye on Domenic though, and when a long time had passed in silence, he asked, "What's bothering you? Is it me? Is there something I can do to help?"

Nothing, save decide on a different destination. All his life he'd been at the mercy of where his father or his *laran* decided to send him, and the moment he thought he was free this stranger came along and trapped him again.

"If it's easier not to talk..." Aran extended his good hand in invitation.

And with that gesture came three different futures: Aran laughing, calling him useless; a rapport filled with anger and frustration; and a more pleasurable one Domenic held no hope for.

When Domenic didn't move, Aran's face fell. "I won't hurt you, if that's what you're afraid of."

"It isn't." But still, he didn't accept. He'd learned it was better not to tempt fate.

"Later, then," Aran said. "Or perhaps I will have to wile the answers out of this lovely creature." The mare had been grazing nearby, so he raised a hand, meaning to scratch beneath her jaw. She nipped at him, then swung around and landed him a stinging swat on his face with her tail.

Domenic covered his mouth with his hand, trying not to laugh at Aran's shocked expression.

"What did I do?"

"Nothing. She's not named Honey for her temperament."

"Obviously." Aran rubbed his cheek. "I was hoping that if I stuffed her with enough treats, she'd tell me *anything*."

"Stuff her with treats, and she'd soon refuse to do anything at all without them." He'd learned that when too many apples had dropped in the pasture and he'd made the mistake of letting Honey have a few too many—afterwards, she made a beeline for that spot despite his attempts to lead her elsewhere. It was good of Aran to attempt to be friendly with her, though.

But later that night, when they stoked the fire and sat near to touching, the old pang of loneliness returned.

"Will you tell me why the thought of home pains you?"

The reasons weren't for a stranger's ears, yet Domenic wished keenly he could unburden himself on someone who might understand. Aran was little like the other lordlings in the Guard; he was pleasant and was so at ease with himself and who he was that Domenic envied him.

"You know I'm not a telepath."

"Yes." The tone was observational and non-judgmental.

"I'm a disappointment to my father. The only one of my brothers and sisters without at least a little of the Ridenow Gift."

"But you have some *laran*."

"I...see things, and I can't tell which is the most likely to happen. Some of them are terrible." In a rush, he told Aran of the accident with his father's gelding along with a half-dozen other incidents that made him feel clumsy, confused and useless.

For a long time, Aran said nothing, but the easiness between them didn't change. "I'm sorry things have been so difficult for you. I know it's not easy growing up in a family that expects what you can't deliver. Did you ever think that perhaps your foresight led you to me? That if you hadn't been forced out of the Cadets and decided to live life for yourself, that you wouldn't have found me? I would have died. I'm sure of it."

"It was chance, that's all. I've never been able to see more than a few moments ahead, let alone days."

"Perhaps it was the gods' doing."

Domenic had never favored the gods, not when the only *laran* they'd granted him caused him nothing but trouble. "Perhaps," he said, and hoped he sounded convincing.

"You're not useless," Aran said. "Trust me on that."

As they lay down to sleep, Domenic ached in ways he never had before. No one, except perhaps old Di Asturien, had been so kind to him or ever stopped to understand things from his point of view. No one else had seen him as anything but a lord's son, destined to serve his Domain under his younger brother's rule until the end of his days. He was lonely for touch, and for someone who might care for him despite his worthless *laran*.

And Aran was so close, so different, and so...

He tried not to think such things, but Aran picked it up anyway. "I don't mind, you know."

"I'm not a telepath. I can't..." He'd heard stories about the rapport telepaths shared, which brought them close mentally and physically. Hurt came anew, knowing he'd never share anything so deeply.

"But I can. Will you trust me?"

He shouldn't. Aran was a stranger with secrets of his own, but his kindness had already laid Domenic open to whatever possibilities might exist. So he threaded his fingers through Aran's and risked one of the myriad futures he saw.

The rapport was like nothing he'd imagined. Except for the *leronis* who'd come to Serrais and his father's quick, brutal examination, he'd experienced none of the closeness that was supposed to be his heritage.

And this, Aran gave to him, gently filling the font of emptiness with caring and understanding. With his good hand, he brought their bodies close, closer.

Unhappy, but far from useless.

Domenic heard the thought, and accepted it as truth. But when the rapport finally ended, Domenic couldn't help but feel that while Aran knew the deepest parts of him, Aran had been particularly skillful at keeping his own thoughts secret.

What, then, was he hiding?

Pleasant as the contact had been, the dreams that followed were anything but. Domenic dreamed of a hawk, but it wasn't one of the tamed, bonded creatures his father and siblings hunted with. This raptor was huge and vicious, the wings and legs unnaturally long and thin. Neither was the bird's cry the one Domenic always thrilled to hear; this was an eerie howl, a yelping that went on and on and filled him with terror.

Domenic sat up, sweaty and dizzy, but as soon as he saw Aran retching in the gray light of dawn, he knew he wasn't the one who was ill—and, quite possibly, a fever had brought on the night-terrors that had bled into Domenic's dreams. Aran must be in more pain than he'd let on, and Domenic realized that much of the young man's charm had been to distract his guide and mask his discomfort.

After handing him a flask of water, Domenic said, "Let me check your arm."

"It's fine," Aran said, rather sharply, and kept it out of Domenic's reach.

The arm *wasn't* fine. Most likely it was infected, but without being able to see, Domenic couldn't do anything about it. In silence, Domenic gathered their things and saddled Honey. There would be no more sleep. The sooner he could get Aran somewhere sheltered where he could get the attentions of a healer, the better.

"Neskaya Tower is on the way," Dominic suggested. "They could take a look at your arm and figure out what's causing those nightmares."

Aran shuddered. "There's no time for that. I need to speak with your father as soon as possible."

His companion sounded even more stressed than before, which made Domenic ponder the reasons he might be going to see Lord Serrais. Most often, the Ridenows would get inquiries about helping with an intractable horse, hawk or hound, but there had been times Lord Serrais had been called away to aid in communicating with one of the non-human races.

And then it clicked. "Does it have anything to do with that monstrous hawk in your dreams?"

He hadn't thought Aran could go any paler, but he did, and leaned sickly against the mare. She craned her head around to look at him, and snapped at him.

"Stop it!" Domenic gave her a swat on the nose. Her sides heaved with a sigh, but at least she didn't fuss at Aran again. "Does it have anything to do with why you have two matrix stones?"

"That's none of your business."

He stroked Honey's neck and stared straight at Aran. "It is, if I'm taking you to see my father and you bring danger to him and my family. Tell me the truth. Where did you get that other matrix, and what is it?"

For a moment, he thought Aran would either refuse to say more or lie to him, but then he saw that whatever it was, it took a great deal of strength to talk about. Finally, Aran said, "There was a dead man in the Hellers. Frozen stiff. Could have been there for a month or more. All I saw was an arm sticking up out of the snow like a dead tree branch. Then I felt..." He made a gesture of helplessness as he struggled to find the word. “Something calling to me. Not quite a voice, but something palpable. I found...*it*.” He clutched at the pouch beneath his shirt. “And now it won’t leave me alone.”

Domenic had seen. “You mean that hawk? Is it some sort of god or spirit?”

“It must be. It’s in my dreams every night, tearing at me, and it won’t stop that hideous shrieking.”

“And how is my father supposed to intervene?”

“He can talk to the spirit inside. Make it understand I didn’t steal the matrix. I just...found it. I’m not going to use it to harm anyone.”

Domenic doubted simply talking to such an angry spirit would pacify it. There were too many stories of corrupting, easily misused matrices, Sharra being the most terrifying. “But that spirit didn’t give you permission to use the matrix, did it? We have to take it back where it came from.”

“Which is where?”

That was a good question, and one Domenic didn’t have an immediate answer for. “Maybe the better question is, what does it want?”

“Death. I think it killed the man who had it before me, and it tried to do me in, too.”

“But why? Did that man have anything else on him?”

Aran shook his head. “Nothing of use. A few moldy feathers. A necklace made of claws from some beast I didn’t recognize. He might have been a hunter because he had a big skinning knife, but I couldn’t bring myself to touch it.”

“But you haven’t hurt anyone or anything, have you?” Domenic asked, and again Aran shook his head. “So why is it after you?”

“How am I supposed to know? Your family is the expert on animals. You tell me.”

Domenic ignored the jibe as he tried to think through his father’s lessons and stories. This spirit wasn’t just any hawk; it was a strange, almost humanoid thing, and the terrible screeching was no mere animalistic cry. It was filled with want—and need. “I think it wants to go home. And if the one who possesses it won’t take it...”

"Then it kills them." He started to slump, and Domenic had to grab and help lower him to the ground before he fell. "Zandru's Hells, Dom. What did I get us into?"

Domenic shoved Honey's ample behind to get her to move out of the way, lest she decide to kick his friend, and squatted down. "Whatever it is, we'll find a way out of it. Now think. You've had the most contact with it. Where do you think it came from?"

"I don't—" he began, but when Domenic glared at him he changed what he was about to say. "Trees. I see trees sometimes. And a huge, thick forest."

With a sinking feeling that he knew where this was going, Domenic asked, "Your Domain is in the Kilghard Hills. What non-human race—a race with the features of raptors—might live in the forests near there?"

Aran jerked away. "It can't be the Ya-men. It *can't*. No one knows anything about them."

"Not quite. We know they go on a rampage when the Ghost Wind blows and will slaughter anyone stupid enough to get near. But as far as what gods or spirits or totems they worship..." he shrugged. "That, not even my father knows."

"You're mad if you think we're going to go look for them. The Ya-men will kill us. Besides, no one knows exactly where they are."

"So you'd rather risk dying?" Domenic was losing his patience. "If I was going to return to Serrais and face my father's displeasure for your sake, you will be honorable enough to return a matrix not rightfully yours."

"We don't have to take it back. All we have to do is to make the spirit understand."

Aran's fervor held something unnatural. He was terrified, yet unable to act on what he knew was right. Domenic eyed him. "It's not that you won't give it up—you *can't* give it up, can you? That stone has some hold over you."

Aran's lack of answer was proof enough.

"Can you try? Will you give it to me?"

Aran fumbled with his shirt and drew out the pouch. As soon as he tipped the matrix into his palm, his fingers convulsively closed around it. Gently, Domenic clasped Aran's fist in his hands, doing his best to ignore the terrible possibilities that flashed in his mind. He knew damn well that no one untrained should touch a strange matrix, let alone a wild one, but he was willing to take that risk if it meant saving them both.

And, strong as a lightning flash, the visions came stronger and clearer than before. He could see months, years ahead, and some of those visions gripped his heart with painful longing. There was one future where his father had forgiven him completely and trusted him with running the estate, confiding in him and giving him every courtesy family should expect from one another. Another showed him a little villa of his own, with sons and daughters to cherish. And a wife—

No. Not a wife. Aran as his companion and second father to his children.

It isn't real, Aran sent. *Trust me, I know. These are but dreams borne of pain and longing. The matrix gives what you want most.*

Domenic let go, shamed now that Aran knew his deepest longings. "We have to take it back before it hurts anyone else."

This time, Aran didn't argue. He dropped the matrix back inside the pouch. "All I wanted was enough *laran* to work in a Tower. I wanted to be with a group of like-minded people. I wanted the closeness."

"But they'd figure out you had a matrix not your own," Domenic said. "That's why you've been wandering."

Aran nodded. "I'm sorry I didn't tell you before. I didn't want to burden you with something that wasn't your problem." *And I would have taken that stone a hundred times over if it meant giving my father what he wanted: a son with the Ridenow Gift.*

"But it is my problem now. I found you because your laran—laran that isn't even yours—reached out to me. I rescued you and that thing around your neck. I won't risk taking that thing home. I'm honor-bound to see this through."

"The Ya-men will *kill* us."

"Only when the Ghost Wind blows."

"You don't know that. No one does."

"Then I suppose it's time we found out." He didn't tell Aran about the futures that kept appearing before him, the ones where they turned and fled and later ended up lifeless in some accident or another, or the ones where they faced the Ya-men and ended up torn to pieces, food for the creatures and their young. In only one dim future did he see success, and he clung to that vision the way he did Honey's reins as he led them toward the forests of the Kilghard Hills.

It was two days' ride before they reached the edge of the forest where the Ya-men had been seen retreating into when the Ghost Wind had subsided. Along the way, Aran had grown silent, and the merest exertion exhausted him. Although he still refused to let Domenic see the wound, his shirt sleeve had grown tight around his swelling arm. They should have taken a detour to have it seen to, but with the terrible, howling nightmares haunting both of them now, the sooner they were rid of the stone, the better.

Honey took one look at the trees, pinned her ears, and planted her feet.

Domenic sighed, though he'd figured leaving her behind would be inevitable. "I can't take her any farther. We'll have to walk."

Aran eased himself from her back, wincing when landing on the ground sent a jolt through his bad arm. "Perhaps we should have gone to Neskaya first after all."

"Too late now." He tethered Honey so she had enough length to reach both forage and water. Domenic filled a pack with food, water and other essentials and slung it over his shoulder. He nodded at Aran's chest. "Does that thing respond to you? Will the spirit come if you call?"

"I can try," he said, rather unenthusiastically.

"Then try. Hard. Maybe the Ya-men will come if they know their matrix is nearby."

"And maybe they'll rip out our throats when they find out we have it."

Domenic didn't reply, having seen that future and a dozen others play out. "Let's go."

It was rough going, stumbling through uneven footing. After only a few steps, Aran had to lean on him, which doubled his burden, and they were forced to stop several times to let him rest.

It was late afternoon when they heard the noise. It began with a faint crackle, like twigs snapping, and was soon accompanied by a chorus of raucous birds. As the sounds came closer, the birdcalls changed into a terrifyingly familiar howling and yipping. The screeching seemed to surround them on all sides and went higher and higher until it made Domenic's ears ache with the intensity. He froze, unnerved by the sound from his dreams now brought to reality. Bile rose to his throat, and his heart pounded hard enough to make him dizzy. Beside him, Aran was shaking so badly that Domenic feared his friend would collapse.

He gazed through the trees, searching desperately for their targets, but the shadows and twisted branches made it hard to discern anything. From the corner of his eye, it seemed that the trees themselves moved, but no—it wasn't the trees waving in such a jerky manner.

Domenic looked up, and up, as a dozen or so Ya-men lumbered toward them. They were nearly three meters tall, with emaciated-looking bodies that seemed as thin and spindly as the trees, but it was their heads that caught and held Domenic's attention. They were huge, with wicked, curved beaks not unlike those his father and siblings hunted with. Great, feathered plumes jutted from their skulls like headdresses, adding to the eerie, birdlike appearance.

One of them must have sensed the matrix, because it darted forward, heading straight for Aran.

Domenic just managed to step between them, heart pounding at how easily the tall, fearsome creature could tear him apart. "Don't. Please. He's hurt."

Cocked heads with eerie yellow eyes stared at him. Without his family's Gift, Domenic had no idea if the Ya-men could understand him or not.

"Look. We've come to give your matrix back. See? No harm done."

At Domenic's wave, Aran drew the leather pouch from beneath his shirt and tipped the silk-wrapped stone into his palm. His fingers closed around it, as if in spasm. One of the

Ya-men clacked his beak, and his feathers pressed flat against his head in a gesture Domenic recognized all too well.

"Give it to me." He grabbed Aran's hands and pried at his fingers, hoping that he'd be able to free it before the Ya-men hurt Aran. "Come on, Aran. Let go. It's time to give it back."

But after his first experiment, Domenic knew it wasn't simply fear that paralyzed his friend. The matrix itself kept him in its grip, unwilling to release a faithful servant.

The Ya-men waited, all poised in such a way that they loomed over the two small humans. Domenic worked frantically to free the stone. One finger. Two.

And then it was free and warm and pulsing in his palm.

It's mine now.

He wasn't prepared for the sudden rush of joy and pleasure at having such a powerful stone in his grasp. He could do anything, *be* anything.

And there was only one thing he wanted.

I have to give it back.

He meant to. That surety had stayed with him the entire journey, and he'd repeated it to himself as an incantation in order to stave off such an incident as this. But when the stone lay in his palm, he couldn't keep from staring at it, from welcoming the tingling warmth spreading throughout his body and opening his mind in the way he'd always longed for.

He closed his eyes, seeing the stone's hawk spirit, and listened to the mental cry that no longer terrified him, but filled him with promise. When he opened them, he saw the Ya-men staring at him. Waiting.

He *felt* them, too, and by instinct knew exactly what he needed to do. He'd seen his father and siblings at work enough to know that the rapport between humans and non-humans involved non-verbal interaction. Body language, images, needs, desires—these were all viable means of communication.

And for the first time in his life, Domenic knew what it meant to be a Ridenow, to *know* another creature so deeply that they could share everything with a thought. He had but to reach out to the Ya-men and—

Oh.

The sheer strangeness hit him first; the inhuman thoughts,

alien but not incomprehensible. Having worked with hawks a little himself, he understood a sight-oriented world, but *feeling* it was a rush he'd never imagined. He saw the world as they did; sharply in focus, bright, vivid colors, and heightened awareness of every sound. The feathers on their heads were for more than decoration; they monitored the wind and the very air surrounding them and transmitted a wealth of knowledge, from temperature and impending weather to the location of prey skittering beneath the leaves.

And oh yes, they were dangerous as well as fierce. In a world without walls, they had no defense the Ghost Wind, which turned them into the shrieking, violent creatures that terrified humans and had unintentionally killed more than a few. If a threat approached their nests, they would protect their young with the same intensity as a human parent. They were not bloodthirsty, though. While they were fully capable of rending and killing any palpable threat, they did not wantonly seek death. They killed to eat, and they killed to defend. The idea of revenge was beyond them.

Little by little, he absorbed bits of culture and language which he was beginning to understand but would never be able to reproduce. The Ya-men, it seemed, were equally curious about him. They conversed in soft chirps and clacks which, deep in rapport as he was, Domenic understood to be questions about the presence of the two humans and why they'd ventured so far into the forest.

I mean you no harm, he sent, using his heart and intention to convey the message. *We only want to return what is yours.*

Except, deep in his heart, he didn't want to give the matrix back. Not now. Not when he'd only just discovered what he was meant to be.

A hand, soft and warm and human, clasped his. "Don't listen to it." Aran sounded worn and exhausted. "Don't let it work its way into your soul. We came all this way; don't give in to it now."

I don't mean to. The intention, the need to turn over the matrix was still there, but the spirit inside had taken over his willpower and deprived him of the ability to do what he knew was best. It fed him more of what he wanted—more awareness.

Greater *laran*.

And he couldn't let go.

A new Ya-man emerged, this one bent and wrinkled and wearing a necklace of skulls and bones that clattered with each awkward step. The feathers crowning his head were a magnificent mix of blue and green, only slightly faded with age. This was the leader, perhaps.

But when Domenic caught a hint of the newcomer's mind, he knew differently. This Ya-man was more like a Keeper, one respected and trained in the arts of healing and matrixes, and more given to understanding the humans. When he'd made his way to Domenic, he hissed and held out a clawed hand.

Domenic meant to return the stone. With every honest intention he possessed, he willed his hand to move, to drop the matrix into the Ya-man's waiting palm.

Yet nothing happened.

The elder clacked his beak and flooded Domenic's mind with irritation. He placed his hand upon Domenic's head.

Domenic held his breath, afraid to move lest the claws dig into his skull and crush it like an egg. The elder did nothing of the sort, though. When the irritation faded, Domenic had a sense of...understanding, a communion in the knowledge about the dangers of a matrix stone inhabited by the spirit of a dangerous, reclusive race. There was also a sense of regret at having to cause the human pain. Yet, for the good of his community, the elder would do what needed to be done to secure their safety. If it meant killing Domenic to have the stone, he would.

The latter thought was so calm, so matter-of-fact that it chilled Domenic to feel it. His life was worth nothing if he put the community in danger because in the end, the Ya-men wanted what any other race wanted: a safe place to raise offspring and the means to look after one another to stay strong and healthy. The matrix aided them in this, and without human greed or lust for power to taint their desires, it worked quite well. Domenic had the sense that the spirit inside was old, older than the hills themselves, a distant ancestor of the Ya-men that had sacrificed himself in order to aid his descendants. And with that, the purpose of the matrix became quite clear: if one did not use their Gifts to aid in the good of the community, they were culled.

I have to give it back. For the good of them all, I must.

Aran squeezed his hand, and with his newly discovered empathy, Domenic felt *him*, all of him, from the awe and respect he had for Domenic's bravery in dealing with the Ya-men to the same shared longing for someone to truly understand him and the relief that he finally had. Domenic wished with all his heart that he could keep his empathy so they could share this closeness again and again—but he knew that would mean both their deaths.

So Domenic called on every ounce of willpower he had to force his hand open, and braced himself for the parting.

The clawed fingers were gentle when the elder took the matrix from him, but even so, the separation was brutal. It was like the ending of a fantastic, beautiful dream, only this was accompanied by a blinding headache as the gates of his mind snapped shut and rendered him deaf and blind to the otherworldly sensations. Now, when he gazed up at the elder's enormous head, he felt nothing but grief at being forced out of such a deep, wonderful rapport.

"I won't forget," he said, a promise to himself as much as to the Ya-men. "I will remember. And I will tell others what I have learned."

The elder made a soft cawing noise, and with relief, Domenic somehow *knew* the sound was used to comfort the small and weak. The telepathy may have been taken from him, but the knowledge of what he'd learned remained.

The elder released Domenic and secured the matrix in a pouch at his waist. Then he reached to his head, plucked a long, blue-green plume, and held it out to Domenic.

Overwhelmed by the gift, Domenic took the feather. From his brief rapport, he knew that feathers were not given lightly. They were a living part of the Ya-men, and only bequeathed to those chosen as mates or as a reward for a deed of bravery that had been for the benefit of the community. Words stuck in his throat; not that the Ya-man would have understood him, anyway.

At some unseen sign, the Ya-men turned and began to

retreat back into the woods. Domenic watched them go, feeling deaf and dumb after everything he'd just experienced. It was only when Aran wrapped his good arm around Dominic's shoulders that he remembered he wasn't alone, and he wasn't the only one grieving a loss.

Neither did he realize that his cheeks were wet until Aran used a finger to gather his tears.

It took them a long time to leave the forest. Besides Aran's injury, both of them were reluctant to leave behind such a surreal experience and to face the world of men once more.

Once they'd reached the clearing, and, to Domenic's relief, found Honey where they'd left her, the pall of silence lifted.

"Well. That's that," Aran said, sounding even more exhausted than usual. In a way, it was a relief; this was the real Aran, plain and unfettered with just the barest touch of telepathy.

"I bet you'll sleep better."

"Probably. Will you?"

"I don't know." It hurt to be merely human, knowing he'd likely never experience such a rapport again.

"I bet you're the only one with a feather from a Ya-man who's lived to tell the tale."

"Probably." He held it by the quill and ran his finger along the vane, amazed at the softness despite being so stiff. "At least my father will believe me since I have this."

"You're going home, then?"

"First, I'm taking you to Neskaya, and you're getting that arm looked after."

Aran didn't protest; he was probably tired of being in pain. "And after that?"

As always, Domenic's precognition hit when he had an important decision to make. He could leave Aran behind at the Tower and accept the inevitable loneliness. They could leave the Tower together and stake out a life of their own. He could take Aran to Serrais and tell his father that while he'd had the Ridenow Gift only briefly, he was now a friend of the Ya-men, something no other man on Darkover could claim.

Or he could forge the future he desired instead of being

trapped by what might or might not be. “After that, we can decide. Together.”

Trust

by Jenna Rhodes

Long ago, in Darkover's Ages of Chaos, breeding programs conducted by the Towers defined and bred for the psychic talents known as *laran*. As with any other human ability, these traits were not always restricted to the families in which they were most marked. Variant forms appeared throughout the population, and in illegitimate (*nedestro/nedestra*) offspring. Thus one of the most fertile areas for stories involves a character with a hidden, unclassifiable (and usually unreliable) "rogue" talent, as in this most unusual tale.

Jenna Rhodes is one of the pen names of Rhondi A. Vilott Salsitz, known for her breadth of talent in science fiction, fantasy, and mystery. (She's so prolific, she also writes as Emily Drake, Anne Knight, Elizabeth Forrest, Charles Ingrid, Rhondi Vilott Salsitz, R.A.V. Salsitz, Rhondi Vilott, and Rhondi Greening.) She's published over 50 books and numerous short stories.

He pulled Ina out of her shed, threw her on a horse, and told her to ride as though Darkover's notorious wildfires were on their heels. Clutching the reins and saddle, she wondered what the villagers thought as they pounded away into the morning mist. She needed her shed, her only home and shelter, and she knew Feros wasn't above revenge if he felt wronged, so she considered herself hired. The equal desperation of her sometime employer came through clearly, but she could ask no questions until they camped, scrubbed the horses down and gave them a meal of grain mixed with hot water, and turned them out to crop what they could. Horses meant speed. And less stink.

But they also needed food and rest, and Feros knew better

than to run them into the ground. She waited until the campfire lowered somewhat, her worn boots shoved close for heat, and ate the trail food from the pack he'd dropped into her lap.

"What is it this time?"

Ina might think her question made him frown but she knew him well enough that his face always gnarled up like that. He had ginger in his brows and a bit in his beard if there were sun enough to strike them, but clouds sulked overhead even as Feros did. Still, he had the temperament. He disliked talking, and questions inevitably bred more talking.

"I have a site."

Ina chewed on a dry crumble, her stomach protesting at not having eaten for far too long, and then nodded her head. "Got it. How far?"

"Two more days' ride."

She glanced toward the horses.

"We'll make it," he added, before turning away, and sitting down on his bedroll. He fished out a blanket with ragged ends and tossed it to her. A wind with night riding on it, cold and chill, swept over the campfire, tugging at the flames. Talk was that the red-headed folk had more than a bit of strangeness about them, even the ones far outside the lines of the powerful Houses, stretched thin by being bastards. The true reds, though, kept to themselves, mostly, and Feros no different. He had a gift for finding small treasures, and rarely in an honest way. He was greedy, too, and she was always careful when she worked with him. That gift, tentative as it was, had given them both a fatter purse when they needed it.

So what did that make Ina? Her with her tawny head of hair, her true auburn colors hidden by trousers, never to be revealed if she could help it. She had no knacks, as far as she knew, and that put her in line with most of the workers and grubbers around her, although she had a slim and supple body that made for getting in and out of near impossible openings. He'd used a trained *kyrri* if he could, but she figured she was a dram more pleasant.

Not that either of them had enough of a knack to be labeled *laran*. *Laran* meant power. Courting by one of the Houses.

Perhaps even being snatched up by the Elhalyn and given home and hearth, although there were ominous rumblings about more. It would be nice to be valued, she thought, even if only for a moment or two. Moons knew that she needed that now, as her hold on her precious shed had grown thin. The builder wanted more trade to keep it hers, and she needed to earn it. She wanted to know where they might be headed, other than into the wild lands, but Feros wouldn't tell her until he was ready, if he told her at all.

She wrapped her blanket tightly about her and scooted closer to the warmth. Feros dusted his hands off. "I've set snares," he said. "Hot meal in the morning."

That meant stamina for another long ride. Ina stifled a sigh and put her face to the frayed edge of her covering.

She smelled like horse, smoke, and blanket by the time Feros finally pulled them up at the end of a valley. What should have been green slopes lay charcoal dark, trees fallen and burnt to piles of twigs and ashes, and the odor of smoke rose thickly here. Ina brushed her hand over her eyes. A battle had been fought here and it mattered not who'd won and who'd lost. All had been devastated and abandoned now. What spoils left to be gathered up fell to the lot of Feros and his like. A thin morning sunlight tried to shine through and failed. She wanted to look away and could not. He'd brought her here to rob graves. That explained their haste, to arrive before the rest of the scavengers.

The horses blew, their flanks heaving a bit, their heads down. Feros put a heel to his, urging it back into a walk, circling the damage until he reached the ruins that must have been stonework and stronghold only a week or so earlier. How had he known? Had that quirk of his knotted and twitched until he had to ride in this direction?

Ina decided she didn't really wish to know. Finding the dead was not a talent she envied. She swung down when he did, near an epic pile of rubble, what must have been a tower, and pointed into a hole barely larger than her head.

"In there." He dropped a pouch by her feet.

Ina stretched first. She felt his eyes on her as she did, but she didn't fear him. The first and only time he'd ever tried anything with her, he'd discovered she carried hidden blades on her body, bone and sharp, and a truce had been declared between them. They had a working relationship and nothing more that stood the test of time. She got everything loosened except for one knot in the middle of her back, between her shoulder blades, that didn't seem to want to budge. Ignoring it, she knelt down and looked into the debris.

He had found a tunnel, of sorts. She put her hand out, behind her, and he slapped a thin, strong cord into it. Ina secured it about her waist. It wouldn't help much if she burrowed beyond its length, but if she did, and something happened, she doubted she would feel it. Or, at least, not for long.

She began to climb through. The rocks and edges dug at her ribs and knees as she wiggled forward. Ina stopped, backed out and dug through her jacket for her gloves, not gloves for warmth, but for tactile protection, thin but tough. Like her. Feros gave her a nod as she started back in. She crawled with light shifting in and around her, dust motes swirling on each far and between ray, and no sound but her own breathing and scrabbling progress. She stopped twice to look at the rubble and then very carefully remove a block from her path. Then she reached a point where she knew she had to see what she might be approaching. She blinked several times to clear her thoughts and her senses and took a look deep into her surroundings.

This tiny ability might be her knack, if it could be called that. She could see that which often could not be seen. The tunnel stretched before her, spiraling a bit, and then kinking off to the left and she spotted her destination. She called back to Feros.

"He's not dead."

"Believe me, he is dead. And you will be, too, if you don't hurry your scrawny little ass."

She could barely hear him, and no doubt him her, but enough to exchange those words.

Ina looked through the tunnel of debris, a cloud of dust drifting past her face and across her lashes even as she did, as things shifted somewhere far above her. She could be buried here, dead or not. But as she peered down what would be her likely only pathway, she could only see what appeared to be a living man lying trapped before her. Pale, yes, but who wouldn't be on winter's edge? Still, yes, but who wouldn't be, surrounded by shifting ruin? Silent, naturally, for who would there be to speak to, to ask for aid, to give notice that one was only lying here quietly and not dead? She shivered, as cold echoed upwards from the ground below her, and misted downward from the wreckage above. Sandwiched in, who wouldn't be cold, she told herself, and began to crawl forward again cautiously.

"You're sure?" she queried again. This was his vocation, why wouldn't he be certain, but she still held doubt.

"By the moons, girl! I touched him myself just days ago before that last arch came down. If it hadn't, there'd be no need for you, now would there? I'd've stripped him myself. The quickest in and get what we need, the quickest out. I've got a heavy cloak and winter gloves and leggings waiting here for you."

"And a fire?"

"Later, when we're away from here."

Not too far away, she hoped. Her fingers tingled and burned with cold as she burrowed closer to the fallen man, wondering what had happened here, under these arches, not even attracting scavengers except for the one who urged her onward. Stripping a corpse of whatever could be found wasn't the most unsavory thing she'd ever done, but close. Not that many people asked much of her. Too stringy. Too short. Too uncanny. That was her. Once a man had joked he could pick her up and put her in his pocket. That was when he'd had two working kneecaps. He didn't joke now. She could take care of herself, she could. But a warm doorway and good food didn't always come her way. And Feros did. A job here, a job there.

Good for the stomach, if not the soul.

She was close enough now to hear his breathing, if breathe he did. Ina paused, crouched over the broken stone and wood, to listen. Behind her, she could hear another, muted, impatient shout. Funny how the ruins shuttered it away.

Closed off the living from the dead. And the knowledge that she'd finally moved out of earshot of Feros.

Ina rested her chin on her hand. This lord had toppled here, to unknown forces, which had then brought his stronghold down upon him. Why? How? She would have to touch him, to search his finery for jewels and valuables, and she did not wish to. That was the job, naturally, and her objections unusual for her but there they were.

He did not look dead at all. He merely looked as if he were...

Waiting.

Ina's head jerked up from her hand rest. That thought, yes, that last one, had not been in her voice. She prodded at it as one might prod their tongue at a sore tooth but nothing wobbled loosely or throbbed.

Waiting. She considered that. For what? No rescue had come. Not even now, with the two of them, rescue was far from their intentions. Discovery? Hope?

"Sorry, lord," she muttered. "I'm all you've got." She wiggled forward again, a bit more boldly, as if to prove that she were able if the body tried anything. As she came even, a grinding noise sounded from above and the stones began to shift, heaving, and a shower of dirt and gravel pelted her as she ducked her face down, throwing an arm up. After long moments, the movement stilled and the debris stopped. She coughed before yelling back, "I'm all right!"

She didn't know if Feros heard her or not. If he hadn't, he'd wait a few hours before trying to dig her out or abandon her altogether. He'd probably dig in, determined to reach his treasure. That she could depend upon. She stripped her shredded gloves off for they held little protection now, and she had to search the body.

She reached out, left hand first, and caught the body by the ankle. Stone cold like a statue. Of course. Avarra, the Cold Lady, hugged him close.

She tunneled her form up next to him, pushing the little alcove he occupied wider, to hold their two forms instead of just his as she studied him. A man, not a boy, though young. Auburn haired. His eyes still open, his brow still furrowed in concentration as he held something out in his right hand, his left posed as though about to begin a movement of some kind. He'd been good-looking in a way, determined chin, a nose that looked as if had been broken and set rather than healed as most Comyn could afford. And, he looked determined.

Ina quickly removed what she could find in his pockets, trousers, tunic, and cloak. She found a nice knife tucked into one boot and considered keeping that for herself, but knew Feros would spot it in a blink, no matter where she tried to hide it. Her scant form held little curves to disguise contraband. She uncovered a gem hidden in an upper pocket, and it would pay them both handsomely, even after the uneven split. It paid to please her employer.

He wanted weapons and trade goods, but she could see no obvious weapons here.

She lifted a nicely made silk pouch and string from about his neck, sliding it up and over carefully, trying to touch the dead man as little as she could. It would have held something small yet dear, though it was now empty. She put it in her own pouch at her hip with the rest of the find. Maybe Feros would let her keep it. He might determine it of little worth and she found herself liking it more than she should. She tried never to become attached to any of her heists. It didn't pay to covet. She had little, needed little, and that proved safest for her. Nothing else to wrench away from her.

Ina rubbed the back of her hand across her nose, which had suddenly developed a stinging itch. Two scrubs and a sneeze, and she was ready to leave except for prying whatever it was the deader held in his hand.

She curled over his form to peer at his hand closely, knowing she would have to peel his fingers back and fighting her aversion to touching him, to forcing that. Through his digits, she could see another jewel, a blue as dark as a midevening sky, with stars of its own. They rode their interior sky but slowly, barely moving yet she could detect it, and thought she could stay still and stare at whatever pattern they wove forever.

The cold jolted her. So icy now that her hands burned. And her toes had gone numb in her patched, worn boots. "You must want company," she muttered to the body and reached out to do what which she'd been avoiding and began to twist a finger aside in his caging hand.

It took two pried aside to reveal the stone in all its glory. Not large, perhaps as big as an eye, but stunning, and seemingly alive. Ina looked at it warily despite the growing bitterness of her surroundings and what, she could be certain, was Feros's growling, shouting, impatience even though she could not hear it. The ruins shifted around them again, she and the lord dropping a hand or so deeper into the pit of stone. The hand holding the stone seemed to rise, thrusting its possession at her, but Ina still hesitated.

Finally, she slipped her own slender fingers into the circle of his and touched the stone.

A blinding white flash shot through her skull.

Bitter cold and then scalding heat took her. Tossed her about as if she'd fallen into a raging stream, battering her against rocks and rough water that threatened to drown her except no such stream existed. It was, instead, an outpouring rush of power, of energy, of unseen force that could not be withstood. As it swept through, it questioned her existence. Who was she? Why?

Hold. Stand fast.

She fell, twisting, into chaos that knifed her open and screamed through that void. A whirlwind took her, roiling her about until she had no sense of up or down and then began to take apart Ina's self. She shrank becoming like stone, then no, she expanded until she felt as if she were nothing more than a mist above the lands. She floated for an instance, aware her head pounded—if she still had a head—and her heart raced. Her misty form spread thin and thinner until she thought she would shred into nothingness, like a wispy of a cloud in a high wind, when she suddenly dropped back into her own body, arched in distress.

Ina panted a few breaths. When she could think slow, distinctive thoughts again, she began to back out of her access, quickly, hurriedly, in a near panic. She tugged on her line when she remembered it, and a strong answering pull helped her exit. Scrambling, heedless of the stonework moving about her, grit rising and broken timber jutting into her ribs, she got out of there as quickly as she could. At the finish, Feros reached in with his long-fingered hands, grabbed her by the shoulders, and birthed her, roughly and with a single jerk. Coughing, she bent over and slipped the star-studded stone into her boot's shaft, tugging her footwear into place and then dusting herself down all over.

She shoved her pouch into his hands as she snorted her nose and lungs clear. She could hear Feros going through their haul, muttering nice as he pawed the small knife about, weighed the cloak pin in his hand, and put the gem up to the light so he could eye it closer. One eye still squinted shut, he looked at her. "Any more gems?"

"No. Expecting any?"

"Mebbe. This silk purse was empty?"

"Aye."

"If you find anything, grasped or perhaps dropped, you'd be wise to take care. They can be dangerous, they can, these stones I'm looking for. But if you find one, that's what I've come for. Worth a lot, to you and me."

A frisson ran up her spine. Did he guess what she'd hidden? "The haul not what you expected?"

Feros shrugged. "Nice enough. Well done. Get your things and we'll be off."

She shrugged into the cloak he had thrown over her saddle, and pulled it tight to try and quell her shivering. He hadn't provided the gloves and promised leggings, but the cloak hugged her body. "Home."

"Not yet." He refilled the pouch and shoved it into his pack. "Come on."

She watched him pause at the edge of the devastation, his shoulders thrown back and his face to the wind where he took several deep breaths. *Smelling the dead.* He pointed and kicked his horse toward a destination only he could imagine.

She swung aboard her horse and felt the stone press its facets against the inside of her ankle in her boot. She thought it might warm to the touch of her skin but it didn't. The farther they rode, the colder it got until it numbed her entire foot and the bitterness began to crawl up her leg. They rode, down slope, till near nightfall and the horses blew harshly as they traveled. Ina had decided to throw up her hand and declare a halt, like it or not, when Feros pulled aside. Slipping to the ground, her leg gave way and she tumbled under the horse who stood so tired, on its own trembling legs, it didn't move a hoof.

Feros bent over and peered at her. "Problem?"

"Leg fell asleep." Sheepishly, Ina crawled out. She shucked her boot off, retrieved the stone, and tucked it into a shirt cuff at her wrist before rubbing the freezing pins and needles from her leg. The gem in her cuff began to warm almost immediately. It seemed to have a life of its own.

She got up and began to follow suit as Feros unsaddled his horse, talking to it in soothing tones with much praise and wiped it down. He heard her moving and pointed. "I'll take care of yours. You need to get down to the lake."

Dead and water. She shuddered. Very unpleasant corpses.

She opened her mouth to protest but he jerked a thumb. "Go! While we still have some light."

Ina squinted up at the Darkovan sky where light from the sullen red sun fell at a severe angle. She'd be in twilight soon, with no desire to go scavenging under those conditions, and broke into a run, her leg still pinging in protest. As she came out of the copse where they'd halted, she could see the dark waters of a lake, mostly less than one, but more than a pond, gleaming just below her. The view filled her with relief, however, as she could clearly see a small group of sturdy homes, struck though they were by the same sort of disaster that had hit her first destination. Some had been lashed by fire, and a few just fallen in pure destruction of unknown origin, but only at the outskirts. At least she wouldn't have to be pulling any floaters out of the water to finish her job. The smell of death had not yet risen from the ground as she moved cautiously forward, not knowing how many fallen would greet her or if there were any survivors. The stone at her wrist yanked at her as if someone had caught her up, forcing her in one direction. She remembered that pulse she'd had off the man waiting...for what, she'd no idea. But perhaps it had been the stone which waited and now strained to reach a goal.

Her head throbbed with the beginning wave of a headache and Ina pressed the heel of her hand to her brow. Moons, she hated these things, plagued all her life by them and they beat her down until she just wanted to curl up in a hole somewhere till they passed. A healer had told her long-ago mother that they'd pass soon enough but they never had. Now one dug its blade in cruelly behind her eyes. She pressed them shut a moment. Dizziness curled inside her skull and then leaked slowly out.

When she opened her eyes, she knew exactly where her target stood. Her hand, stone fiercely hot on her wrist, pointed to it. It hummed, promising great things. Thrilling things. Happenings that would astound and fill her with all she could ever want. It had been Waiting and she'd found it, and now carried it to their destiny. Ina walked forward, a deliberate step at a time, and could feel a vibration deep in her chest, like a cloud holding thunder and lighting and roiling about with them before bursting. Power could leap from her. She could send it striking here...or there...or even over the mountains to—where? Ina had no name for what she envisioned, but the stone did. Enemy. Target.

Her hand began to shake as she followed its line of sight. Ina made a fist, afraid to leave a finger pointing, like a knife point ready to jab. She'd become a weapon of sorts she could not understand but knew she had to stop. Nothing here lived to destroyed...or so she thought when a nearby plank moved and a small face peered out at her. Behind it, shadowed in a lean-to of timber ruins, she could see blurs of countenances.

Ina bent her elbow, pulling her arm in to her side. "Who are you?"

"All that's left. Have you come to finish us too, *vai domina*?"

Her jaw worked and her mouth formed words she hadn't considered but uttered, "What House?"

Trembling shook the barely stable lean-to as those inside reacted. "Forgive us, lady, forgive us!"

Her arm ached, each muscle tight and drawn, herself fighting her body and its instincts. And, at the back of her mind, she realized what she had in her cuff, and what Feros searched for, and what they feared.

She carried a secret of those with Gifts, terrible or useful as it might be, a gem that held those secrets even as a silken pouch might have been meant to hold it. If she were a lord or lady, she might know how to use it or not use it, but standing here, facing these poor frightened people who thought she meant to rain cold hell down upon them, Ina had no clue how *not* to do just that.

She touched her cuff. She could feel its burning. "It's armed," she said. "Targeted and meant to destroy." She managed to turn her head a bit. Maybe Feros knew how to handle it. He'd tasked her for look for them, after all, and perhaps he'd known what it wanted. She knew now, too.

It wanted to be used for that which it had been created: to bring down the heavens upon the unworthy. To call forth the lightning and the whirlwind and victory. It would not be denied in its purpose.

She didn't know how it could still live when its holder did not, but then, she knew little about such things at all. And her ignorance couldn't stop it.

The faces in hiding changed positions and now a more mature face looked out at her, distinguished by light freckles and a red-gold wave of hair that framed it. "Stay your hand, lady, and ease your mind, if you can."

"I know nothing of this!"

"Then turn away and ride and toss it as far as you can. It's not meant to live beyond its bearer. It shouldn't burn still!"

"Shut up, the lot of you!" Feros brushed up against Ina's elbow, tall and glowering, and bodies behind the woman fled the lean-to to another, deeper shelter, like small creatures running from a hunter.

"I'll have the Elhalyns here. They'll feed and house you! Just point me to the starstone holder!"

No answer came. He shook his head. "More fools they. I'll have my bounty one way or another."

"Bounty?"

"Aye. What did you think filled my purse these days? Thieving? No. The Houses are warring, sometimes petty and sometimes monstrous, but what do I care? Let them fill themselves with tales that they have mighty minds and will own Darkover. They're pollen-drunk, fooling themselves." He scratched at his chin. "The Elhalyn want to build Towers, linking small powers to make great ones. They might be delusional but they keep winter from my head. Now, don't stand there witless—find the bedamned starstone holder."

He could not sense what she had fastened in her cuff? How not? It radiated.

Ina dropped her hand to her side, though the compulsion filled her no less. She nodded her chin. "Thataway."

"You go. I'll hold here in case any more survivors emerge. Someone is bound to have a weapon."

She thought of her bone knife in her left boot. Someone always had a weapon if they could manage it.

Not all the buildings were tumbled down, but abandoned. She could see a sign or two of lightning strike, not all that accurate but close enough the ground must have shaken and the air sizzled of it. It took a clenching of her teeth not to run from it now although she could see that the village had protected areas, and the bolts somehow diminished.

She found the person she sought on the outskirts of the buildings, at the foundation of an undertaking which had only been begun but looked as if it would be massive when built. A woman sat on the rim of stone, her hands cupped in front of her, her face lean and etched in lines of fatigue, her eyes shadowed.

She looked up. "Where is Davrin?"

"I don't know any Davri—"

"Don't fill my ears with lies! You hold his matrix!"

Ina touched the starstone in her sleeve with her fingertips. "He's dead."

"Yet his stone lives."

She shrugged.

"Such things do not happen. Unless—" The woman searched her face. "It's almost buried in you, but what House?"

"I don't..." Ina stopped as the other pinned her with another fierce look. She swallowed. "I can't say if it's truth or not, but my mother once told me that my father was a lost son of Aillard." And only once had she ever mentioned it, and Ina doubted that it could in any way be true. It would never have done her any good to claim any inheritance whatsoever from that name.

The other shifted her feet in the dirt, boots sending up a small cloud. "Davrin. Was he dead when you took it from him?"

"I—I'm not sure. He didn't seem dead but once this was out of his hand, he...shrank somehow. Lady, you're asking me things I can't really answer."

"Have you done this before? Perhaps not from their hands, but from their bodies? Often wrapped in silk?"

"Twice but nothing but gravel filled it when we opened them."

Feros had been sore angry, she remembered back, although there was usually a splinter or scrap of gem left, and he'd scooped them up. She'd thought little of it, because they had always had much bigger stakes to recover. Stones that fell to dust had never interested her.

"You're a grave robber."

Ina flinched. "When I have to be."

"Come here."

That straightened her posture and she put her chin up. "No."

"Do you fear me?"

Ina shook her head. She didn't, although she did not trust the woman, either. As she saw it, the woman had little to lose while Ina had everything. Her meager life. Her shed. Her hope for a better tomorrow.

The woman, slowly and confidently, put her gem away in a small pouch that hung about her neck and into her cleavage. "There. Does that help?"

Something inside her leapt as though a vast opportunity had just opened. Ina gritted her teeth against the feeling and took a step forward.

"Another step. I want to hold your hand."

That headache that had pounded her for days and receded jumped up again and her temples throbbed. "I don't think I should."

Head tilted, Ina felt herself being keenly assessed again.

"How old are you, child?"

Ina's lip curled. "Forty turns." She relished seeing astonishment in the other.

Astonishment turned into consideration, however, and then a slow smile. "Call me Senri." She held up her hand.

She seemed relatively harmless now, and so Ina stepped into her handhold, slipping her slender fingers into the callused and worn ones of the other.

"Now hold your stone."

"It's not mine and it's..."

"I know. Dangerous. It is meant to hold the power for destruction, but knowing that, we have an advantage, you and I."

"How?"

Senri beckoned about the habitation. "We stopped it before. I daresay I can stop it again. It has to be weakened without Davrin to wield it."

Ina reached for it. And, oh, like a predator waiting to strike, it gathered and she stood in its way.

White lightning filled her mind. It grabbed her by the back of the neck and shook her, but her body fought back, turning into a mist that couldn't be shredded like flesh and bone, and it bore her away.

In a blink or perhaps it was a full turn about the red sun, she opened her eyes to another world.

Grace tempered by inner strength filled the people who passed her by, as insubstantial as she seemed now, but one stopped by her, and smiled. White-blond hair fell down about its shoulders, cascading to the hips. Gentle eyes watched her.

Not her world, no. It couldn't be. But she knew some of the peoples in it and had heard, only in dark night tales, of the *chieri* she thought she might be glimpsing now. The benevolent figure lifted a hand to Ina and tugged at her

If she had thought herself untouchable, a cloud in the sky, she thought wrong. The *chieri*, chin lifted and eyes gazing up at her, long strands of hair as fair as morning sunlight, began to reel her in. With the undeniable pull came a feeling of acceptance and good-will that would have brought tears to her eyes if she thought she still had eyes left. And yet she saw, so

Ina knew that she must and glanced down at herself to see if she were some grossly expanded creature bobbing about the sky, moon-sized to join the other four. As the being pulled her in, she felt her body collapsing into itself until she felt almost normal when her feet finally touched the ground. But looking up into the face of the gentle being who'd captured her, Ina knew that nothing would ever be normal again. And the *chieri* let her go, freed her, but she stayed with it.

What do you hold in your hand?

A soft but insistent breath inside her mind, as soothing as compelling, swept through Ina even as she struggled to stand, breathe, see, and think. She glanced down at her left hand, fingers tightly knotted in a fist over something. Feeling bled slowly back through her and she could feel something hard yet warm resting against her hold. She couldn't remember what it might be, and patted her pouch on her hip with the other hand. Items for Feros. Oh, he would be beyond furious now.

She held the starstone he coveted. He would kill her for that.

No fear, little one. You are in the Overworld, and everything lives differently here.

Yet fear crowded into her, icy and shoving, pushing her breath away until she swayed on her feet, light-headed. She crammed her fisted hand into a pocket to keep the other from forcing it open. "Who are you?"

There is no name for what I am or what I will become, and yet, you've given us one. The slender, graceful being smiled. *You might be a child of mine. Definitely a child of ours.*

Ina did not feel reassured. She felt like a nut that had been cracked wide open and then splayed apart on a table top while potential devourers looked down, trying to decide if she was worth eating or not.

Your sojourn here is brief, but you have nothing to fear. Yet.

And oh, yes that made her feel better! Ina stepped away from the being, and then, surprised she could, stepped back a second time. Whatever rein had been used upon her, it had either been let go or it no longer existed.

She should go back. With every fiber of her returned consciousness, she knew she should go back to where she had come from. While she lived. Before she froze or turned to stone as had the lord in the ruins or become something she could not recognize at all.

What lord?

"Davrin. A Comyn. Died in the fighting between his fortress and another, I suppose. Not a mark on him that I could see, though and..." Ina shifted. "He sent lightning."

The being inclined its head, its silvery blonde hair tumbling over its shoulders front and back. There was not, Ina thought, an ungraceful thing about it.

"Where am I? How do I get back?"

A breeze circled about her, a warming touch, and she wondered for a moment how stupid it was to want to go back, but there it was. Home was home.

The *chieri* reached out and tapped the back of her wrist, the one she had shoved into a pocket. Ina jumped, having thought she was out of reach, but no, the being stood next to her. She clenched her fingers tighter as the gem warmed inside her palm, tiny but insistent thing that it was, not wanting to be discovered any more than Ina wanted it to be taken from her. It buzzed with its need to tear apart its enemy.

You must take its anger, its power. Let it flow out of you, a river become harmless.

The *chieri* murmured a few more words which made them both smile sadly but she couldn't recall when she tried and, like that, it flung her out of the Overworld and back.

She stumbled and went to one knee, her hand still gripped in Senri's strong grip. "What did you do to me?"

"A better question would be, what did you do to yourself?"

Both hands filled, Ina reared back but Senri held to her tightly. She shook her head, her tawny hair loosening from its knot, and thought of the *chieri*. It was said one lived near forever, unless one of the Darkovans killed it. Did a drop or two of their blood flow in her veins explaining her childhood that never seemed to end. And if it did, so what? She would live that much longer on the edge? She pulled her hand out of reach.

"Give me your stone."

Senri looked at her calmly. "It might kill you to take it. And it would for me to lose it. Not at first, though. My mind would go slowly, and then I would die. You wish to submit me to this?"

Ina gestured about the pocket of civilization. "You have a home here. Friends. Perhaps even family. They will take care of you, as you take care of them. Me? I have a job to do."

"And that will sustain you?"

"For a time."

Senri looked her up and down. "It seems to me that you stand at a decision. Make it carefully."

Feros, returning, said from behind her shoulder, "Take what we came for. She is trying to use you, bend you to her will. Two stones! Whole! Do you know what kind of bounty that will bring me?"

"Us."

"Us?"

"A bounty for us."

"Don't be a fool. You'll get your share. Have I ever shorted you?"

"Not as long as I have my knife. But will there be a day when I have forgotten it, and you leave me behind?"

Silence met her words, but Feros scowled deeper. He threw his head back, sending his hard gaze upwards, and said, "We're running out of time."

Ina began to reach for Senri. The other leaned away but only slightly, saying, "I've never seen anyone successfully take away a stone from a living holder. They are not merely rocks...but then, you've seen the stars moving in them, I can tell you have. I've never felt *laran* like yours, but I can tell you, it's dangerous. Mortally dangerous. You've felt where they can take you. Don't do this."

Feros burst out. "I'm killing her and we're done with this. She's dying already. I scented it on the winds."

Senri canted to one side, revealing bodies behind her, bodies that had not yet begun to turn as the dead do, and scattered around their hands the familiar gray gravel of a stone that did not outlast its wielder.

Ina looked at them, the fallen bodies, most of them women, one or two young men among them, all with hair that gleamed loudly or faintly of copper. But not a hint of lightning strike could be seen among them, no charring of fire, no shattering of stone. It was as if their hearts had merely quit under the strain. As if they and their will had turned back Davrin's attack upon himself.

"You stopped him."

"We did. At great cost, but we stopped him."

"His stone lives."

Her eyebrow raised as she sat back into position, wearily, and Ina knew this woman tapped into her last resources. "Hatred," Senri noted, "can last a very long time."

Feros grabbed Ina's arm. "By the moons, stop wasting my time. I sent the beacons up yesterday. If they arrive before we are quit and done here, we'll get no bounty, and you'll have no safe winter, my girl!"

Senri smiled slightly. "A safe winter is never guaranteed for any of us, especially in these days." She looked at the starstone Ina held. "No one knew that power could be sent so far away, and with such deadly precision. I fear it won't be the last of warring." She took a deep breath to dip her fingers into her pouch.

Ina lunged and took up her hand, knowing that the woman began to summon up the last of her strength, to render one last defense. Feros threw himself forward as well, and the three of them grappled and Ina came up with both stones, one in each hand. She jumped away from them, her body shaking in her victory, yet uncertain of what she still had yet to do.

Agony came that blinded her and then, for a split second, she could feel the strength and power in each starstone, mirroring those who had bonded with them. She knew what they had intended, as unalike as night from day, and she became a bridge between them. Energy crackled. Living things they were, unknown and not understood, used by one and loved by the other and now she owned them both. She could also taste the souls of the two who had used them.

Her sight leapt outward, targeting what she both feared and sought. Her vision imaged a troop in Comyn colors and riding hard towards them, no kindness in faces of grim determination, taking the faintest of roads with the surest of knowledge.

They knew what they rode toward. They knew it as surely as they knew their own names. A storm roiled the skies on the other horizon, dark clouds rumbling ominously and closing quickly. Ina knew why.

She could give them the evidence they sought and gather a fortune for herself, or she could keep it from them for a little while longer while the rest of Darkover tried to prepare itself against the chaos these stones wanted to unleash. A sudden vision came of the *chieri* beyond the borders of her world and the last words the being had uttered, the ones she could not remember, returned to her: *Trust the timing of your life.*

I already have a home.

"Not beginning this. Not here, not today. I know it will come, for these are its times, but it won't start with me!"

The sky spoke to her in its voice of storm. Ina clapped her hands together and her world exploded. Lightning forked downward, the anger and fury rocketing down to split the earth and then gushing upward into a fountain. She could sense the others falling away from her, and then her being spilled out of the crater where she had stood. Her cloak flew off, her boots split, and she herself leapt away unseen. A river of fire and rock and scraps of her humanity ran off to the lake which swallowed it whole and washed it clean. She soared free and towards a chorus of voices that softly intoned *welcome.*

A Game of Kings

by Shariann Lewitt

One element of the romance of Darkover is its aristocratic *laran*-Gifted Comyn caste, evoking Terran nobility. So many Darkover stories involve the use or misuse of *laran* that it is refreshing to discover an admirable character with formidable abilities who does not have it—or does she? Here author Shariann Lewitt combines such a heroine with a story element not often featured—gambling and card games—but which surely must arise as the recreation as well as the downfall of bored young scions of the wealthier classes of every human world.

Shariann Lewitt has published seventeen books and over forty short stories, including "Wedding Embroidery" in *Stars of Darkover* and "Memory" in *Gifts of Darkover*. When not writing she teaches at MIT, studies flamenco dance, and is accounted reasonably accomplished at embroidery. Her expertise with birds arises in part from being the devoted servant of two parrots.

"She's cheating. And she has to be using *laran* to do it."

Ramon Aillard accused her, but the others around the gaming table nodded their assent. Some of the greatest names of the Comyn had thrown stakes in the game, and some of those with the greatest fortunes as well.

"Aren't there psychic dampers here? I thought that was one of the benefits of playing here," Ann'dra MacAran said.

"Can't anyone tell if someone is trying to use *laran* against them?" That was Elonie Aillard, Ramon's sister, who had not played in this game. She had refused to sign Ramon's IOU when he wanted to increase his stake after losing far too much to the troubled girl who sat accused in front of them. "Isn't there a *laranzu* or monitor around here somewhere? Summon one at once," Elonie demanded with just the same impatience she would summon her tardy maid to help her dress for a dinner party.

Then she turned to the pale girl who sat quivering in front of them, tied to the extravagantly carved silverwood arms of the chair. The girl in the good pink dress that showed off a slim figure had soft toffee brown hair with not the slightest hint of copper. Elonie took the three steps over and touched the neckline of the dress, felt under the silk flowers and down over the girl's breasts. Nothing. She went ran her hands over the girl's belt and opened her purse, which was bursting with coin. She opened the purse on the table and wealth rolled onto the deep red felt, some silver and a bit of gold, but most of it copper.

Tears ran down the girl's cheeks. Elonie reached into the purse and turned it inside out. Then she felt the belt carefully. "Where is it, girl? It's got to be somewhere, and it will go a lot easier on you if you just tell me instead of making me search."

"Where is what?"

Elonie slapped her across the face. "Your starstone, of course. You couldn't have managed without it. I won't touch it. We will need to hand it over to the *laranzu* who examines you. And what is your name? Then tell me where it is."

The girl swallowed hard. "My name is Nyla Connor. And I don't know what a starstone is and I certainly don't have one. If you're accusing me of stealing, I never done so."

Elonie laughed. "Oh, that's a nice touch. As if you don't know you couldn't steal a starstone. Well done. And the bit of bad grammar, as if you weren't Tower-trained and well schooled at that." She studied Nyla's hair and dress, her dead white skin, her hazel eyes. "*Nedestra*, of course. But whose? Ramon, Ann'dra, what do you think? Old Esteban Hastur? Or Lewis Ridenow?"

"It may have skipped a couple of generations," Ramon suggested. "We might not figure it out without a specialist."

"So when is that *laranzu* going to get here?" Elonie complained. "I want this taken care of now. And I want my brother's money back. All of it. This little sneak thief should be prosecuted to the full extent of the law."

Then she turned to Nyla. "And do you know what the law mandates for misuse of *laran* like this? The *laran* centers of your brain will be burned out of you and your starstone, wherever it is, will be smashed. And you'll be a cripple for the rest of your life."

The girl began to laugh.

"She's hysterical," Ann'dra said.

Elonie obliged by slapping her again, but Nyla did not stop laughing. "I have no *laran*, you stupid cow. I never did. And I never cheated, either. And all that money on that table, by any rights that's mine. These gentlemen, they wagered it free and I won it fair."

Maybe one of the men would have had to hold Elonie back from strangling the girl to death there and then had not Padric returned with a tired-looking young man in a matrix technician's blue robe and blazing red curls that looked mashed on one side.

"What is going on here?" the *laranzu* asked, blinking as he took in the young woman tied to the chair and several Comyn and well-heeled merchants complaining. Nor could he miss the mountain of copper coins on the table ringed with cards.

"She cheated," Ramon Aillard began. "We were playing Kings, and she was serving drinks and snacks. You can see from her dress, from her language, that she is not one of us. Decent enough, of course, but hardly someone who could gain admittance through the front door. Anyway, it was late and some of us had done well and weren't in a mind to go home, and wanted to stay on for a few more hands. Why not? So we set up here in the private room and the girl agreed that she would stay on later for an extra tip to take care of us. And then she asked if she could play."

"Did she have a stake?" The *laranzu*, being employed by the establishment, knew more of the game and the habits of the regulars of the King's Retreat than he might have cared to.

"No," Ann'dra admitted. "But Elonie was not playing, she was only there to back Ramon's IOUs since he had run out of cash, and she had left the room. The girl wagered herself. So..." He shrugged.

Three young men. And the girl was young and comely enough. No great beauty, to be sure, but appealing. Elonie let out a little shriek and then abruptly closed her mouth.

"You took her wager. And then?" the *laranzu* kept them on track.

"She won," Ramon said, spreading his hands. "She wiped the table. She won more than enough for a decent stake, so then we had to try to win it back. Three more times. And each time she won. Everything. No one can win like that, that consistently, without some extra help. She had to be cheating."

"And she had to be using *laran* to do it," Padric added. "There is no way she could have just cheated at the cards by herself."

"You are certain?" he asked the young Comyn. "This couldn't simply have been a case of luck, or too much to drink too late?

"Look at that pile and tell me it was just luck," Elonie said.

The *laranzu* turned to Nyla. "These are very serious charges, you understand. If this is proved true, your starstone will be taken and your *laran* will be destroyed."

Nyla sat a little straighter in the elaborately carved chair. Her toes barely reached the ground but she tried to fill the space rather than huddle. She looked the *laranzu* straight in the eye. "I keep trying to tell these people, but they will not listen. I have no starstone. I have no *laran*. And I did not cheat."

No one would play Kings with her. They knew she always won. And so Nyla sniffled, just a bit, while she served the ale and wiped down the old blackwood tables in her mother's tavern. Old Amory and his friends were in their usual corner, between the fireplace and the bar, and they'd all had at least one round too many. Nyla knew the signs—she'd been serving ale since she had turned twelve. But even in their cups they wouldn't have her. She'd tried to wheedle them since the last snow melted and if she tried again she'd only annoy them. If she annoyed them they would take their custom elsewhere.

The Green Chervine had a good reputation and excellent ale, but they were not rich. Nyla and her mother Clari lived well enough, in four spacious rooms above the tavern where Nyla apprenticed to her mother as a brewer and tavern keeper.

"You can't depend on a man, girl. Look at me. Your Da said he would never leave and then, woosh. One day he just up and was gone. I never knew where he went. He never sent word. So you got to have something of your own."

Clari had a touch for the ale. When Nyla's father had left them, all she'd had was a babe on her hip and her skill with the ale. The tavern keeper at the Green Chervine had taken her on and never regretted it. Her reputation grew as the tavern became more popular. The landlord had other properties to oversee and let her take over and run the place as she liked so long as she paid him rent at Midsummer and Midwinter.

Clari hired a girl called Stelli, a few years older than Nyla, to help with the cooking and serving, and gave her a room of her own behind the bar. Stelli got decent wages along with all her tips and a day and a half in each ten for herself. Clari was counted a good employer in the neighborhood, and kind, for people noted Stelli had ways. She took her time and spent too much on her dress, and flirted with the handsome customers when others needed service. But she cooked well enough when she'd a mind to, and so Clari kept her on.

It was Stelli who taught Nyla to play Kings, one early evening during a heavy storm when custom was light and time heavy on their hands. Stelli had a deck of cards and Nyla picked up the game quickly. Raul the groom and man-of-work joked while he lost every hand and said that he could win if he wanted to, which made the young women giggle outrageously.

Then Stelli began to teach her the complex betting system. Raul clearly didn't follow, but something snapped in Nyla's mind. Like unfolding shapes and putting numbers together and taking them apart when she was barely walking, she could see clearly into the whole pattern of how the game worked.

They played the next hand. And the hand after that. And Nyla won. Not just by a little, but cleaned up the pebbles they used as betting counters.

"You're cheating," Stelli accused her.

"Not," Nyla countered.

"You think because you're the boss's daughter you can do

whatever you want. You think you're better'n us because your Ma runs the tavern. Well, you're a liar and a cheat and I'm going to tell everyone that you're a cheat and no one will ever play with you, ever." Stelli stomped off.

Nyla, hurt and confused, tried to explain, but Stelli disappeared into the kitchen and dinner was stringy tripe stew, which Nyla hated.

Nyla had a gift for numbers—and for playing Kings. But she had little idea of how she could earn a living at either of those. By the time she turned fourteen she had begun to do all the accounts for the tavern and proved quite good at it. She enjoyed it far more than she enjoyed brewing. Certainly more than lifting the great kettles of hot water to immerse the bluegrain malt. Then came soaking and mashing and clarifying and sparging, all of it heavy labor. Nyla was willing to work hard, but brewing was constant, backbreaking effort. And she had a good head for bookkeeping.

Doing accounts for their neighbors, for Ker the butcher and Donal the baker who provided the tavern with bread sounded far more interesting and exciting than brewing ale. But she also knew that her mother would never agree. Her fate had been decided; she was to be an alewife and tavern keeper like her mother. If they did well together, they would buy the tavern outright. That was Clari's dream.

She walked home from the market as she had done every day since her birthday, wondering how she could manage to change her fate and her mother's mind. That day there seemed to be a crowd at the tavern when she arrived, far more than would be normal at this hour. While still in Thendara, the neighborhood was nowhere near the centers of government or trade, nor near the Trade City and Port where the *Terranan* lived and did their work. Indeed, Nyla had never seen one of those mythical creatures. She had rarely seen one of the great nobles, either, and then just a glimpse of some Guards cadet with brilliant copper hair on a tall horse or a closed litter with a house crest, always on the single great street that cut down the middle of the district into the center of Thendara. Everything she needed and everyone she knew was right here.

Her mother would need help serving their ale to such a

crowd, and maybe some food, though why all these customers had come so early confused her. Normally only a few people, mostly men, would be in the tavern this time of day. Two or three, either out of work or taking a rest between deliveries, or a late luncheon or early supper.

The crowd filled the street in front of the tavern but the door was locked and barred. In all her life Nyla could never remember the tavern closed and fear ran through her. Her mother? What happened?

She saw Donal at the edge of the crowd and tugged at his sleeve. "Donal, where's my Ma?"

"Your Ma's gone for the Guards. Stelli's disappeared and taken money. All we know is that Clari barred the door and flew out screaming that she'd skin that wench alive if she caught her. Your Ma made quite a scene, she did. Biggest thing that ever happened around here since Margalie ran Haydn out of the house with the pitchfork, and him stark naked in the middle of a snowstorm. Remember?"

There had been no forgetting that. Nyla did her best to smile. "Thank you, Donal. I mean it. You've been a great friend. But I can manage for now."

The baker nodded slowly and Nyla opened the tavern doors. Then she stood up on a stool and banged on a bucket with an oversized wooden spoon. "We're open for business, everyone. I've got good ale in the back ready to serve, and we'll have a supper ready soon. So if you're here to gawk, go someplace else. If you're here to drink, sit down and let me know, and I'll bring you your drink."

"Should be easy enough to test to see if I have any *laran*," Nyla suggested. "They did it before, when I turned fourteen. And the *leronis* from the Tower, the one in the white robe, said no, not even a trace."

"She could be lying about that," Elonie said.

"Mmm," the *laranzu* said. "Easy enough to check."

"But what if she's got one of those strange hidden gifts," Ramon said.

"You mean like ours?" Elonie pointed out.

Ramon raised one eyebrow, the very picture of the

decadent youth about town. "Precisely. Maybe even a relative. That would be interesting, wouldn't it?"

Elonie bristled, but the *laranzu* smiled. Even Nyla shook her head at the ridiculous premise. Her, related to these arrogant swells, that would be a tale. She hoped, to the bottom of her toes, that she had nothing whatever to do with them. Nobles, indeed. Everyone she knew in the tavern, excepting Stelli, of course, had more real nobility than she'd seen this one night at the gambling den of the rich and mighty. In fact, the rich and mighty had impressed her very poorly indeed.

"I would prefer to have a monitor do this," the *laranzu* said. "I can do it, but a monitor would be far better. And if someone is adept at hiding their *laran* so well, then it would take a very highly skilled monitor to catch it."

"I don't care whether you have to wake the Lady Keeper of Hali Tower herself. I want her punished and I want my money back. Now." Ramon never raised his voice, but the hard look that accompanied his soft tone made Nyla want to shrink back into the great chair that held her.

The matrix technician sighed. "What about truthspell? She would be compelled to answer honestly, and that would end matters."

"Wasn't there some family that could lie under truthspell?" Elonie asked.

"That was a million years ago, and they were all destroyed. I think you're being over cautious," Padric said.

Elonie bristled. "Well, maybe you lost rather less than Ramon did. He had a lot more coin than I had suspected, or I never would have permitted..."

"Elonie!" Ramon drew out the syllables and even Nyla winced. Clearly the lordling disliked his sister holding his purse strings.

"Please, let's get on with this," the technician said. "If everyone will take a seat. And untie Nyla, she isn't going anywhere."

Ann'dra shrugged but untied the cords that bound her. Nyla flexed her fingers and toes and rose, finally, stretching out her legs. The technician indicated a small stool for her right in front of him, in the middle of the semicircle of the others. Then he took a small bundle from around his neck and unwrapped it carefully.

The blue light that came from that stone lit the gaming chamber with a cold, unreal light. He said words that Nyla did not bother to listen to, for she felt them inside her head and with her entire body. Her whole mind, even the nerves that ran through her arms, her legs, her spine, felt the deep pull of that incantation. She could not keep quiet, and she could not say anything but the truth.

All of the truth.

So she told them about the tavern and Stelli and the way she had always played Kings. And that she had been properly tested like everyone else and had no shred of *laran*. None at all.

"Ask her how she cheated," Ramon demanded. Nyla heard the question and yet did not hear it. She only responded when the *laranzu* spoke.

"How do you win so easily?"

"It *isn't* easy," she replied. "But I know that, with a fresh deck, there are thirty-four thousand two hundred twenty possible hands in Kings. Depending on how many players, and how many cards each player discards in the first round, I can eliminate up to twelve thousand one hundred and twenty of those. Tonight with four players, and two discarding two cards in the first round, I knew there were only five thousand six hundred and seven possibilities left."

"That isn't possible!" Ramon interrupted.

"I agree, it sounds absurd. How is it even possible to keep this all in your head? Or are you making up these numbers?" the *laranzu* asked.

Nyla looked at him, confused. "I am *not* making them up. I just know how many, that's all. People are good at different things. Some people can sing beautifully, others cannot carry a tune. Some people can make the most delicious chervine pie you've ever tasted and others, well, you'd rather eat day-old nutbread with moldy cheese than whatever comes out of their pots. I can see numbers work. I was born that way. And cards are just numbers with fancy pictures on them. I just do it, that's all."

"Besides, five thousand whatever is still a lot," Ann'dra said. "You can't bet on those kinds of odds."

"No, of course not," Nyla agreed. "But after the second round of discards that number goes down again, depending on the number of discards. I remember there were a lot of discards in the second round there, so we were down to under five thousand possible hands remaining. Since my stake had been for three full games, and the custom is to use a single deck for three games, by the second game the probabilities were down to the very low hundreds and I could be confident of how to discard and play my own hand against what I knew were the only possibilities left among the cards remaining in the deck."

"But you can't tell us how you can calculate those numbers?" Elonie asked.

"Not exactly."

"Then she is cheating. You, send for the Guard now and have her locked up for thieving and deceiving her betters," Elonie directed the *laranzu* as if he were a servant.

The *laranzu,* who had been about to send for the Guard, hesitated. Then held up his hand and shook his head. "I think we need to learn a little more to make that decision. And you, Elonie Aillard, are not the judge here."

"Neither are you," Elonie said.

"Elonie," Ann'dra tried to interrupt, but Elonie didn't listen.

"You are merely an employee here, and you serve us," she continued.

"Elonie," Ann'dra tugged at her sleeve to get her attention, but Elonie merely brushed his hand away.

"What right do you have to disobey me? Do you know who I am? You've got *laran*, but that doesn't mean you outrank us. You just work here..."

"Elonie, that's Mikhail Ridenow," Ann'dra said, his face burning red.

But Elonie would not give up easily. "Really? Are you certain, Ann'dra? How do you know that? What would Mikhail Ridenow be doing working here at night when his older brother is the heir of Serrais? You must be mistaken."

"He was training at Hali with me when I had my season," Ann'dra said. Then he turned to the *laranzu.* "I apologize for my friend, Mikhail. She is very upset over Ramon's loss, and her father will hold her responsible."

Mikhail Ridenow looked at the girl curled in upon herself in the chair, and then at Elonie Aillard, still wearing a haughty expression. He turned back to Nyla. "You still clearly have done something—not usual. Probably wrong in a way that we don't quite understand, and you are hiding something. And we will find it out and understand it. So. I will be reasonable. These young people are decent and fair. They only want what is theirs. You can leave the money and walk away and no one will come after you. You get away with what you've done but you never come to this part of the city again, you never gamble again, and you leave every single coin you wrongly won on this table. And you are free to go. Do you understand?"

Elonie smiled, a thin, cruel expression that promised only pain.

Nyla shuddered and shut her eyes to keep the tears from falling. She would not cry in front of them, she would not, and yet she could not keep the wetness from her face. She had not cheated, she knew it, but they were Comyn and there were four of them, five counting the *laranzu.*

And if she walked away from that pile, she and her mother would never recover. They could not pay, not the rent, not the bills for supplies, not even Raul's wages.

"And if I don't?" she asked, failing to keep the quaver out of her voice.

"You will be punished when we learn how you have managed this," the *laranzu* said. "And we will, even if we have to use force or forced rapport. So I would advise you to take the offer. It's the best you'll get."

Nyla took a ragged breath. Her mind fought her body as her stomach threatened to retch and her muscles shuddered. So very easy to just give up. To walk away. To pretend this night had never happened.

But they had no reserves. She'd spent the last to get here, stolen them if she were honest. Her stomach heaved. Her chest shrunk against her ribs. Her knees pulled up against her belly.

She shook her head.

"No. I won fairly. Those winnings are mine."

Stelli had stolen all the savings Clari had kept in the jug in under her bed.

"And Stelli! What did we ever do that she should repay us like this?" Clari went on, again. "She had plenty to eat and her wages every ten day and her own room here that I never entered. And she was only a decent cook when she wanted."

Now Stelli and the money were gone. And the debts were due. Not just the suppliers, which they might be able to manage with the little stash of coins she had tucked into her mathematics notebook, Nyla thought, if they could put off the rent. The rent on the tavern itself was the one expense that they could not afford and it was due in a tenday. No matter how good the custom, they could not make up the amount in that time.

"Don't look like a rabbit-horn looking at the pot," her mother scolded, and then smiled. "I'll figure out something. I've been through worse. When your father left I didn't have anything but you on my hip and two jugs of ale, and here we are now. We'll manage."

That evening the tavern was packed with gossips as well as regulars and everyone wanted to know what had happened. Had Stelli really stolen all their money? Were they going to remain open? Did they need a new cook?

Nyla tried to seem calm as she answered, but inside she was churning. She couldn't tell anyone about the amount of money missing and the rent that was due. Most of the neighbors believed that they owned the tavern. Ownership had always been Clari's dream.

If only she could earn something more. That evening as she served the ale, the regulars all came in. In their usual corner she saw Old Amory with his friends, their cups full, playing Kings. During a quiet minute, when everyone had been served and paid, she wandered over toward the game.

Amory gave her a large smile and shook his head. "Oh, no, Nyla. We're on to your tricks. You can come and bring another round soon as we finish this hand, but we're not dealing you in. Bad enough to lose everything. But to a little girl? Downright humiliating, you know. How'd I ever tell my wife?"

She smiled back and shook her head. "Don't want in at your game, gentlemen. Your stakes are too low. But if you know about some other game I could join where maybe they don't know me and where they're playing for more..." She left it open and tossed her thick brown braid over her shoulder.

"Oh, ho, the little lady wants to go uptown," Burl said.

"Burl, don't tell her. It'll only make her sick and she'd never get in, anyway," Amory said. "Let's have another round of Kings and call it a night."

But Nyla hadn't gone far and she arrived with another pitcher full of beer as the men played. She waited on her customers, every bench and stool full, and twice the work without Stelli to help. She had to enlist Raul to carry in platters and mugs, though he often confused what order went to which table, but her mother was too busy between the kitchen and the bar to spend any time on the floor.

And so Nyla slipped over into Amory's corner and set down another pitcher as she removed the empty one. Once more, and then once again. The men were not so drunk that they couldn't move, but they were talking freely and not taking any care who heard them.

She judged when she thought they may talk to her, and she had plenty of experience judging drunks. "So Burl, you say you know a place where the rich play cards?"

"Oh, like the likes of us could ever set foot in there," Burl said. "All full of redheads. I don't know how much you need for a stake just to walk in the door. But..." and here he winked at her, "you'd clean up in there. No one would believe you had any reason to be there. I don't know how you win. They might say you cheat and in that crowd it would be pretty dangerous. Guards and swords all over the place."

"How do you know all that, Burl?" Amory asked.

But Burl shook his head. "Had a job inside the place once. They need woodwork like everyone else and I made a fortune on the new bar they installed. Wish you could see it, blackwood inlay with silverwood, real delicate patterns all around the edges. Best thing I ever done, I'm telling you.

Twenty-eight layers of varnish to get it glow." Burl's face shone and his hands caressed the plain table in front of him as if it were the finest inlay work.

"So where is the King's Retreat?" Nyla asked.

"Oh, far away. Down near Comyn Castle. You just go down the big road until you get to the Temple of Avarra, and then turn up the little street on the side of the portico and keep going around the back of the fancy linens shop. Then you come to a bigger road, turn right on that and go a short way. It will be across the street and looks like a private house. Private palace, more like. But you'll know it because there's carvings of all four Kings over the door." Then Burl looked at Nyla. "You may play better than them, but they'll never let you in."

Dom Rafael Ardais came after breakfast with four Guards and two monitors from the Tower at Hali. That was to say, after breakfast for those who could afford it. Since Nyla's winnings had been confiscated, only the matrix technician had made provision for a cup of *jaco* and an extra nut pastry. She drank the *jaco* but had little appetite for the pastry, which wasn't particularly fresh.

Dom Rafael, for all that he had been assigned to look into the case, did not bluster or threaten Nyla. Instead, he listened to Elonie, Ramon, Ann'dra, and Padric tell their story, which hadn't changed since they had pounced on Nyla the night before. Elonie still told most of it and the young men either nodded or voiced their support, and Elonie still insisted that Nyla had cheated with *laran*. Or if she had no *laran*, she had cheated in some other way unknown to them.

Dom Rafael listened, and then called on the monitors. They were gentler than the matrix technician, certainly. Nyla felt only the slightest disorientation as one, then the other, entered her mind and did—whatever it was they did. She had been tested when she had turned fourteen, as all children were, and had been told she was head-blind. Since life, or even a season of training in a Tower sounded miserable to her, she was quite relieved to learn that she would not have to endure it. So far as she and all her friends knew, Towers were only for Comyn, not for them. The only way they would get in would be as servants, and if they had the slightest shred of telepathic talent they had no doubt they would still be treated as servants by the high and mighty. Nyla had other interests and other plans.

Now two more *leroni* agreed that she truly, seriously, had not the slightest trace of telepathic ability.

"So how did she do it?" Elonie demanded. "She had to have cheated. No one has luck like that! No one can win all the time. She gave us some story about remembering all the cards that had been played and then knowing which must be still in the deck and which in play. That is impossible. Everyone knows that."

But *Dom* Ramon listened carefully and seemed to turn the notion over in his mind. "And she said that under truthspell? That she could do such a thing?"

They all agreed that Nyla had done so, and both monitors agreed that Nyla could not beat a truth spell.

"I have an idea," *Dom* Rafael said. "I would like to consult with someone, though, and I would not like to stay here, nor would I like this girl to be kept prisoner in this place. Would you all agree that I could take the girl, and the contested winnings, to my quarters in Comyn Castle? She and the money will be quite safe there. The Guards will be with us. You may, of course, accompany us, or retire to your own quarters in the Castle. I would need to contact the person I think may help and see when she might be available. Then I will let you all know. Will you find that acceptable?"

The four young Comyn looked at each other. Elonie Aillard appeared to want to speak out, but the others clearly seemed unable to counter *Dom* Rafael. How could they? He was not only the Head of his Domain, but one of the most influential members of the Comyn Council.

Nyla knew none of these things, and wondered if they had spoken telepathically to reach agreement. But she could not miss Elonie's resistance and grudging acquiescence. Nor did she know whether to be relieved or more afraid.

Nyla went to get another round for the regulars. She didn't know quite how to get in, or how to get money for the stake, but at least she had a place to go. That was a start.

She began by asking around. No one in the neighborhood had ever been anyplace so fancy as the King's Retreat except Antonella, who had worked as a seamstress for the fine ladies before her eyesight had gone bad with age. Antonella had, to Nyla's knowledge, never come into the tavern, but she managed an introduction through two regulars. So on a slow afternoon she stopped by Antonella's with a basket of leftover rabbit-horn pie, a loaf of bread, and two berry tarts.

The older woman greeted her cheerfully and invited her into her small but immaculate home. "Sit down, sit down," Antonella said, indicating the more stable looking of the two stools. "Let me get you some honey tea. I know your mother is a brewer, and a fine one, but I'm sure you would like some honey tea."

Nyla felt her face flame. Honey, and even tea, must be a great extravagance for this woman. Her children and grandchildren kept her fed, and she owned the tiny cottage, which Nyla could see had only a single room.

"That would be very nice, *mestra*, but I've just come from home and I'm very full. I've even brought you some samples of our food."

"No, no dearie, I don't need to take charity. I've plenty. My Derek and Dorcas, they're twins, you know, they do very well by me. I want for nothing, and Derek's eldest, Ewan, is now grown and is a journeyman carpenter, and he never forgets his old gran."

"And now, what brings you here?" Antonella asked. "For sure as I do love rabbit-horn pie, I also know that you have some for some purpose beyond bringing it to me."

Nyla hung her head. "I heard that once you were seamstress to noble ladies."

Antonella laughed. "And why should you be so sorry to ask me about that? I enjoy remembering that time, working with those beautiful fabrics and such exquisite designs. Oh, the dresses we made! So what do you want to know?"

Nyla swallowed hard. "There is a gaming house called the King's Retreat..."

"Oh aye, I've certainly heard of that that place," Antonella cut her off before she could even finish her question. "Not a place for nice young ladies, or gentlemen, either. Heard whole fortunes won and lost in a single hand. But why are you interested in the King's Retreat? Not that they would let you in the door. And they know their own, all the rich who come and go."

"Do you think I could get work there?" Nyla asked.

"Hmmm. Maybe. They go for pretty girls, but you'd have to show yourself more." She studied Nyla critically and ordered the girl to stand.

Antonella circled her, passed her hands over Nyla's chest and narrow waist. "Hmmm."

"I think I may be able to make this work. Dorcas's second daughter, Kindra, is my apprentice. And I think..."

"I need to get there soon. As soon as possible," Nyla interrupted.

Antonella sighed. "Of course you do. Ladies always want their dresses yesterday. But it will cost, and copper. I doubt you can afford it."

Nyla swallowed. There were the coins she had secreted in her notebooks, the ones Stelli had never found. Enough to pay rent on a room for a few tendays until she and her mother could get work. And if she squandered them on a dress fine enough to admit her to the King's Retreat, even as a serving girl, there would be no going back. If she didn't win they would be on the street.

And if she didn't? They still couldn't pay the rent.

She nodded to Antonella. "I'll have the money. This evening."

She managed to slip out after the dinner rush. Antonella's granddaughter was older than she. They stripped Nyla and discussed her as if she weren't there, and then they measured. Finally Nyla put her clothes back on and Antonella held up lengths of fabric under her neck. Not the blue. Not the green at all. They rather liked the pink and the cream with the pink and lilac flowers painted on the edge.

Antonella dismissed Nyla and told her to return in two days' time. "And you shall return the dress after you wear it. We will be able to recut it and reuse the fabric."

"But I paid," Nyla protested.

"Not enough to cover the full cost of the fabric," Antonella explained. "And there is the matter of the extra labor to make the rush."

When Nyla returned she had to admit the dress was beautiful. And flattered her like no garment ever had.

So she had put on the dress and found a ride at least part of the way to the Temple of Avarra. She had found the King's Retreat easily enough, and went around to the back to ask if they could use a serving girl. Antonella had been right—she looked very pretty in the dress with her hair held in a butterfly clasp at the base of her neck, and her eyes widened just a touch with Antonella's paints.

The man who spoke to her asked a few questions, but mostly he stared at her, at her face and her chest, which had been left carefully and modestly exposed. And at her small waist, gently suggested, and how the soft fabric draped to show off her legs. Clearly she had all the important qualifications for the job.

She served drinks and snacks, bringing around a tray as the players played. And she studied the cards and the players, too. She expected to have to spend a few days before she found an opening, but then when three of the more reckless and drunk young men decided to stay late in the private room, she saw her chance.

Though *Dom* Rafael and the Guards had her in custody, she rode unbound on the horse in front of one of the Guardsmen. They would have given her a horse of her own, but when confronted by the towering animal she had to admit that she couldn't ride. The Comyn youth who helped her up and steadied her in front of him had been quite pleasant.

Dom Rafael rode up beside her. "Don't worry so, girl. I believe you. I'm a good enough telepath myself that I know the monitors are right. And as for cheating, well, that bunch deserves a lesson if you did. And if you didn't, good for you. But you've nothing to worry about. Those boys need some fear shook into them, and nothing like losing a respectable fortune to do that. They're going to have plenty to explain to their fathers now, and I think they're going to have some hard lessons to learn that being Cadets didn't teach them. But I am curious about you. You're not *nedestra* Comyn, are you?"

"No sir. Or if I am my mother never hinted at it. She's a tavern keeper and my father took off long ago. He was a glassblower, a journeyman my mother always said, who went off to take a journey."

Dom Rafael nodded. "Well, you should enjoy your stay at Comyn Castle with no fear over your head, for I think you have not known the like of it."

And certainly the Head of Ardais Domain spoke the truth. They rode into the portico and the Guard lifted Nyla gently to the ground. She followed *Dom* Rafael through long corridors lit with gently glowing lamps and windows as tall as she. They turned and turned again and walked across a courtyard with a fountain and a balcony planted with fragrant flowers. She felt as if she had walked blocks through her neighborhood before they came to *Dom* Rafael's apartments, where they were met by a middle-aged woman with a tray of *jaco* and damp towels. She offered these first to the older lord with a curtsey.

Nyla blushed. She had not realized that she should curtsey to the *vai dom*. She didn't quite know how. But then the woman came over to her, and Nyla could see that she was about Clari's age, and her eyes were lined from years of smiles. "Now you must refresh yourself from your very long and trying night. And then you shall have a bath and a good solid meal and sleep, for it will be some time before the Terran can come, if she is available at all. So we'll have you put to rights."

She smiled and steered Nyla into what seemed to be a dream. A full bath, fragrant petals floating on the surface, stood in the middle of a room tiled in polished blue stone. Various soaps and bottles of ointments sat ready for use on a table within easy reach. A girl just about Nyla's age stood next to them. "Now get in and I'll take care of you," the girl said.

Nyla had never imagined such bliss. The girl asked questions about her hair and skin before choosing the correct shampoos and soaps, which were followed by oil and a massage after she stepped out of the tub. And that was followed by ointment and a thick, absorbent robe, and then the girl led her into a tiny chamber to breathe soothing incense.

The older woman fetched her to a private meal, a table set with foods she had never seen. Indeed, the only items she recognized were the nutbread and the bowl of berries. Exotic spices and delicate sauces created flavors she had never dreamed. Only the ale disappointed her, for it lacked the crisp clarity of her mother's brew.

If she came through this with the fortune she had won, if she saved the tavern and some to spare, she swore that she would send *Dom* Rafael a full barrel of her mother's best.

Full, the older woman took her through a thick door to a bedchamber Nyla thought surely must have been fitted out for a daughter of the house. A carpet thicker than her mattress back home tickled her feet and a giant bed with embroidered yellow hangings had been turned back to invite her. She put on the white nightdress that had been laid out, and while it was plain, the fabric was softer than flower petals in the bath. The sheets, too, had been made of the same fabric, and Nyla wished that she could stay awake simply to luxuriate in the sensations. But she fell asleep before she could finish the wish.

When she finally awoke, she had some time to explore the suite, to enjoy the view out the window over an inner courtyard planted with fruit trees. Her pink dress, cleaned and folded, lay on a chair, and a blue dress had been laid out on the small divan. She took the hint and tried it; it fit and looked good, though it did not emphasize her figure quite so much as the one Antonella had made.

"Oh, good, you're up," the young woman who had given her the bath said as she entered the room. And then she frowned. "You put on the gown yourself? Before I dressed your hair?" She shook her head. "Well, sit down and we'll take care of your hair now, I suppose."

The only time anyone other than her mother or herself had touched her hair was when Antonella had put it into the butterfly clasp. The girl brushed and combed, rubbed in ointment, braided, and did all manner of things, some of them uncomfortable.

"Now let me redo these clasps, and you need a petticoat and here," she gave a tug. Finally, after more adjustment, she took Nyla to the mirror. "Now you look a proper *damisela.* Cook sent up some breakfast for you."

"But I went to sleep in the morning," Nyla said. "It should be evening now, or maybe night."

"You were so tired you slept all the way through, all the day and the night too. It's morning now, early, but *Dom* Rafael likes to start early. The Terran arrived last night and there was a great feast and she asked about what you did then. But he said to let you sleep and that we'd finish up all this business in the morning. And besides," she giggled, "those young Comyn who lost their fortunes, not only are they here, but *Dom* Rafael had time to contact their fathers, too. So it should be quite a show. I expect to come with you and watch."

"Certainly," Nyla answered, without knowing who the girl was or why she should be included.

"Good. A *damisela* should not go anywhere without her lady's maid."

So Nyla ate a sumptuous breakfast and was led to *Dom* Rafael's audience room. He sat in a chair carved even more elegantly than those at the King's Retreat, and at the table in front of him sat three men of his own generation, sober and angry. The Comyn she had played cards with, along with Elonie, sat behind them, and the pile of copper she had won made a respectable showing in the middle.

Across from the Comyn gentlemen sat a woman in a skin-tight gray suit. Her skin was brown and her hair, glistening black and braided, and of everyone at the table only she appeared relaxed and almost amused. This must be the Terran. Nyla had never seen anyone like her before.

"Come, girl, sit here next to me," *Dom* Rafael said, indicating the seat between him and the Terran. Somehow, even facing the scowls from across the table, Nyla felt safe between *Dom* Rafael and the Terran.

"Now, Nyla here stands accused of cheating in a game of Kings," *Dom* Rafael started.

"Why do you have a Terran here?" Ann'dra's father demanded. "You know we can't discuss these charges in front of a Terran."

Dom Rafael smiled. "Oh, but this Terran is an expert in

exactly what Nyla did. Everyone, please meet Dr. Ashanti Scott, who is an expert in the mathematics of probability."

The Terran smiled and nodded at everyone. Everyone sneered and huffed at the Terran, who immediately took the floor.

"This particular form of winning is known to us. Nyla, please explain exactly how you won game after game and managed to amass such a great fortune in one night?"

Nyla bit her lip. "I tried to explain before. I know how many are in the deck and which cards are discarded. And so I know how many hands are possible depending on the number of discards and how many cards are in the deck. Since it is customary to use one deck for three games, and each game is three hands, by the second game there are usually fewer than a thousand possible hands left and I have a good idea of how to manage my own hand to advantage. By the second round of discards in the second game the number of possible hands has dropped so dramatically that I usually have one in three to a one in six chance of winning. By the end of the third game, at least if we have at least four players for all three games, I have better than a one in four chance at worst."

"How long have you been able to do this thing?" the Terran asked.

"All my life," Nyla admitted.

"Do you go in with set parameters?" Dr. Scott asked.

Nyla shook her head. "I just do it for each round, since the numbers change depending on the number of players and how many they discard each round."

"Let me ask you a question," Dr. Scott said. "Let's say there are two horses galloping at each other, and they are each running at fifty miles an hour. Do you know miles an hour?"

Nyla blinked and nodded.

"And the horses are a hundred miles apart on the road. And let us say there is a fly on the nose of one horse. And let us say that the fly is flying at seventy-five miles an hour back and forth between the two horses. How much distance will the fly cover before it is squashed between the horses?"

"That is a stupid question," *Dom* Felix Aillard interrupted. "The horses would turn aside and never meet. And that's too far and too fast for horses to run in the first place."

Dom Rafael managed not to wince. "Answer the question, child, if you can, for I do not quite understand it."

"Seventy-five miles," Nyla answered immediately.

"How did you do that?" Dr. Scott asked gently.

"I just added up the number of times the fly flew, along with the distance the horses covered while they were running."

"That's—just not possible," *Dom* Lewis MacAran said, his eyes bulging.

Dr. Scott smiled. "She is correct. We know this ability very well. Nyla is extremely talented—in mathematics. This is the origin of my own field of study. She had not cheated, though gambling establishments do keep records of people with her abilities and tend to keep them out. She has used extremely advanced mathematics, probability theory, to figure out where the cards should be and how they will fall. But it is not cheating. It is a talent for mathematics. I would recommend that you send her for advanced study."

The three older Comyn across the table looked as if they wanted to tear the Terran limb from limb, along with Nyla, but Dom Rafael shoved the mountain of money in Nyla's direction. "So you are saying, Dr. Scott, that this money was honestly won?"

"Absolutely." The Terran smiled broadly and seemed to want to bounce in her seat. "And if you have no place here to send her for advanced study, may I suggest the Terran Academy, where I did my own degrees? I think she would fit in quite well there."

At that, Nyla stood. "What about my mother? I need to get home and give this to her immediately. We have the rent to pay and she's probably frantic about me. And I can't go off to some Terran place forever."

But Dr. Scott did not stop smiling. "It's not forever, only for a few years, and you can come home for holidays. We'll talk later, and with *Dom* Rafael as well."

And then *Dom* Rafael waved his hand and the door opened, and Clari walked in. She ran to Nyla and hugged her tight. And then she looked at the mountain of copper. "This is enough to buy the tavern," she said as if in a dream. "Is it truly yours?"

"Yes, mama," Nyla said. "Now we can go home."

Wind-Born

by Pat MacEwen

Characters journey to Darkover for many different reasons and engage in a wide range of occupations once there. In *Stars of Darkover*, the first of these anthologies I edited, Steven Harper's "Kira Ann" featured a narcotics cop on the trail of a drug originating on Darkover. This current volume includes a forensic scientist and a sociologist (both women, interestingly enough). Marion never portrayed a forensic scientist, in part because detective policing was not part of her knowledge base. But it stands to reason that as the interactions between Darkover and Terra continue, there would be interest in and a need for specialists in crime investigation. On Darkover as on Terra today, the results do not always align with expectations and good scientists follow the evidence wherever it leads.

Pat MacEwen is a physical anthropologist. She works on bones from archaeological sites and does independent research on genocide. She worked on war crimes investigations for the International Criminal Tribunal, after doing CSI work for a decade, and was once a marine biologist at the Institute of Marine & Coastal Studies at USC. *Rough Magic,* first in a forensic/urban fantasy trilogy, *The Fallen*, is out from Sky Warrior Publishing. *Dragon's Kiss*, a YA fantasy about a crippled boy who can talk to dragons, is also out from Sky Warrior. She writes mystery, horror, science fiction, and fantasy. Her work has appeared in a *Year's Best SF* anthology. It has also been a finalist for the Sturgeon Award, and made the Tiptree Honors List. Her hobbies include exploring cathedrals, alien-building via nonhuman biology, and trawling through history books for the juicy bits.

Gillian wanted to lay down and die, right there in the snow beside the corpse. Why not? His career was over, and so was hers. The big difference? All of *his* problems were now resolved.

If she could just seal up her survival suit and take a nap, it might help. A little. No chance of that, though. Not with the Terran Envoy, Byron Lamar God-Damn Vanger himself, on scene. If she did take herself out, the son of a bitch would probably just shoot her ass full of stasis drugs and have her patched up again soon as they got back to base. Then he'd dock her pay for the time it took to heal.

They can't do that to you, though, can they? she asked her silent subject.

No answer, of course.

The body had been reduced to bones, and most of those were broken.

Gillian picked up one of them and fingered its long curved blade-like edge—all that remained of somebody's shin. It was shattered halfway down its length, and when she looked into the central cavity, it was empty. There were, however, several impact points around the jagged end where something pointy had been used to smash the tibia. Perhaps a hand axe. At the other end, there were deep, v-shaped incisions slicing across what had once been half of a knee joint. The same was true of all the long bones.

She dropped the shinbone into a bag and stripped off one glove to scratch a sudden, nagging itch at the back of her neck. And then froze when she realized what that meant.

"Well?" said Vanger.

Gillian glanced up at the man with more than a little irritation. "He's definitely dead."

Wrong move. She knew it the moment the words left her mouth, but could not call them back.

The Envoy advanced on her, looming, bear-like. "You trying to be funny, Haut Specialist?"

Damnation. His use of her former rank was no accident. It was a weapon thrust into her very core. She rose to face him, refusing to retreat by so much as a single millimeter. "No, sir. I am trying to examine the body. You've given me all of six minutes to do that, and I have no sense of context at all yet."

"Context!" Vanger shot a glance at their companions, an Amazonian figure in boiled leather armor, and a balding man in a fur shirt and elaborately embroidered brown cloak. The latter, Lord Darriell, looked more like a librarian than a nobleman, but he'd been sent by the Comyn Council, so he was a big wheel of some kind. Both watched them closely and that, she could tell, did not make Vanger happy.

"Look," she snapped, "I landed on this medieval mudball a whole three hours before you assigned me to this case. If you want me to get it *right*—"

Gillian broke off. Her ill-considered use of the term 'mudball' had brought their military escort's head around about as fast as if she had slapped her. The red-headed local inhaled sharply, her nostrils flaring, but then the librarian laid a hand on her forearm. She glanced aside at him, regained control of herself and said nothing.

Vanger, on the other hand, locked his gaze to hers and attempted to turn up the heat. Which would have been rather nice if it had actually worked, since the mountains were warmed not at all by the dim red giant glowering overhead, nor yet by the coming of what she'd been told was considered spring hereabouts. It would have been called midwinter back home. Cottman IV was a frigid planet. Cold as hell.

And now you're stuck here, Gillian reminded herself. Make the best of it, you fool. Don't start burning bridges Day One.

So she took a moment, and a long deep breath, and attempted a professional stance in spite of the itch and brain-numbing travel fatigue. Four days wasn't enough to recover from orbital transfer, a new time frame, the alien zeitgeist, and a tidal wave of depression. Especially not when it had to be done on horseback, something she wasn't used to at all.

"I need at least five more minutes for a DNA match to confirm the ID," she told Byron Vanger. "But this *is* a man, by his pelvic bones. What is left of his gear and his clothing is Terran, so he probably is your missing attaché. And I don't have a cause of death yet, but there is clear evidence he has been butchered. Consumed. In my opinion—cannibalized."

That did not go over well with anyone.

"*Canni*—" Vanger cut himself short with an obvious effort. "You mean..."

"His body was disarticulated with a very sharp blade of some kind. Probably volcanic glass, judging by the incisions and the bits of broken obsidian. The flesh was removed. Then his long bones were smashed, so the marrow could be removed. So far I haven't seen any signs of charring or pot polish on what's left, so my assumption is, they did not cook what they took. They ate him raw."

That was entirely too blunt for the Envoy's delicate diplomatic digestion. "You can't know that."

"I can," Gillian answered. "I do. This *is* my specialty."

"Not anymore," Vanger all but snarled at her. "Your *reputation* precedes you, Specialist. Why on Earth they didn't throw you in prison—"

At which point, he remembered their audience.

"Then take me back to base," Gillian growled in return. "Officially, sir? I'm just a Spec One on another underfunded off-world archaeology team now. Whatever I find here, you can't use it in court. You can't even put my name on the report."

Vanger knew that. He had to. He'd read her restricted file, or he wouldn't have known anything about her forensic rating. Her once-upon-a-time rating. Now any case that relied on her testimony was doomed to dismissal. And she herself would be facing new charges if certain officials back home found out she was working a crime scene of any kind.

Bitterness threatened to choke her but Gillian fought hard and swallowed it. She clung to one cold hard fact. He'd brought her into the Hellers because of her skills, hadn't he? He knew exactly why she had been sent here, in disgrace. Or thought he did, and yet he'd ignored her mission orders for the sake of his own pressing need. Which was what, exactly? The thought brought new life to that itch at the nape of her neck.

A simple death investigation could have been handled by the military. By bringing her into this, Vanger was taking the needless risk of offending his own superiors. So he must think this was serious. Why? Because of his own relationship with the victim? Or was it the victim's rank? His involvement in something local? Why *was* Vanger inserting himself into this?

Nine times out of ten, Old Man Jenner used to tell all his graduate students, a murder is the result of the victim's own bad choices. And in the case of the tenth victim, who is truly innocent, you don't ever admit it but you work harder to solve the case. You do whatever it takes for *that* vic.

Gillian sighed. I wish I'd never met you, old man. Never listened to all your damned stories.

No point now to regretting her choice of mentor then, however. Instead, Gillian bagged up the rest of the bones and a few stray shreds of frozen tissue. Likewise the debitage. The chips of obsidian someone had knocked off to sharpen a blade would be traceable to a point-source, probably in these same mountains, and stylistic aspects might point to the knapper who'd made the blade.

Reluctantly, she let Vanger take charge of the missing man's saddle bags, his broken com unit, and the tattered shreds of his boots and clothes since Terran tech wasn't supposed to be shared with the locals. *Fine, let* him *haul it home,* she thought, trying to stretch out a muscle spasm in her shoulders. Then she set a sampling bot-swarm loose to collect all the various bits of blood spatter, most of which would belong to the victim. If he'd fought back, however, or the killers had been careless, some of them might derive from suspects. Then she rose and slowly turned around, allowing her suit to record a panoramic view of the scene from its center, a match for the ones already taken from several other vantage points by those who'd found the body five days ago.

Four trails led away from that point: one downhill and one level but curving out of sight within ten feet among the trees. Another led to the mouth of a sizeable cave, and one headed up a steep northern slope too rocky to offer much in the way of footprints. The intersection of those four pathways was open space despite the dense tree cover at this elevation. Most likely, this area would turn into a boggy meadow as the leftover snow melted. She could see thickets of green stuff already sprouting tiny blue bell-shaped flowers at the sunnier end of the lea. The local equivalent of crocus, back home?

It was not a site she would have chosen for an ambush. And

the meadow was certainly not the full extent of the crime scene. Gillian headed uphill, ignoring the leaden weight of her own feet, leaving the others behind. She'd automatically chosen the most difficult direction first, and promptly found herself breathless.

"You should beware the altitude. You have not had time to acclimate," said the red-head, who'd somehow managed to follow her without Gillian or her suit even noticing.

Whirling around, Gillian found her right hand had made its own decision and landed on the empty holster where her side-arm should have been. The other woman reacted by taking a long step back as she drew a sword from the sheath on her back. An honest-to-God sword!

It startled Gillian even more than the woman's voice had, jogging her memory into gear despite her weariness. There was a semi-feudal culture here, and some kind of compact in place that forbade all weapons other than the hand-to-hand type. Why? She couldn't remember. Hadn't cared. Hadn't bothered with most of the briefing material.

"Please don't sneak up on me." Gillian managed to say it evenly, and to mostly suppress a surge of rage as prickles spread from the back of her neck down the length of her spine and fright transmuted itself into anger.

"My apologies," said the red-head, sheathing the sword. "I am here to protect you."

Are you? Gillian wondered. The itchiness said otherwise. An instinctive reaction, and she'd learned to trust it, sometimes even more than the evidence.

"What are you looking for?" asked her escort. "Perhaps I can help."

Gillian hesitated. Much as she might need some local expertise, there was something wrong about all this. About all three of her companions. She'd kept to herself on the long ride into the mountains, at least in part so that she could brood about her new so-called "career." But the truth was, they made her feel flea-bitten. Testy. Unwelcome in spite of the Envoy's insistence on bringing her into this whole bloody mess.

"I'm looking for suspects," she said finally. "Which way they came. Which way they left. Anything they left behind, either way."

"We've already tried tracking this route, but Ya-men are cunning. They can take to the trees and use high ways and byways we cannot."

Ya-men?

Something stirred in her memory. Stone Age people? A query aimed at her implant's limited database brought her very little specific information. Humanoid indigenes. Very tall—up to 2.7 meters. No language cache on file—why? Did they not have language? Or was it something untranslatable?

"Whatever it is you're looking for, we should not linger long," said the other woman. "We are not safe here. The Ya-men might well return, and there's been no rain for two days now."

No rain? Why should that matter?

Rather than ask her, Gillian released her bot-swarm again, and this time she was rewarded with several deposits of semi-fresh scat alongside the next flat stretch of the trail. Upon checking the chem-analysis, Gillian told the red-head, "Your trackers missed a few things. I'm getting a match for Ya-man DNA, according the database."

The other woman's face clouded over. "The Ya-men travel through here on a regular basis. Of course they've left a few piles behind. They don't normally bother with burying their feces."

"Feces containing human myoglobin."

"What?"

"It's a protein specific to muscular tissue. To meat." Gillian showed her the read-out, knowing it was unlikely the locals understood anything about protein structure. They really weren't much more advanced than the Ya-men they apparently considered total savages. How had even a colony lost for millennia failed to advance once again in terms of basic biology? Tech or no tech?

The chem-kit pinged again.

"Most of them are about four and a half days old, according to the protein degradation profiles. Which fits right into the time frame," Gillian remarked. When that drew a blank look from the other woman, she explained. "It takes twelve to fifteen hours for meat to pass all the way through the gut. And the victim has been dead for five days and change."

A third ping, louder this time, echoed off the rocks.

"And...it's a match to the attaché's somatic profile." Then, when this news also had no discernable impact, she tried using simpler terms. "The shit contains the remains of the dead man's muscles. It proves what they ate and digested was...him."

Still nothing.

"You don't seem to be surprised."

"Why should I be? These things happen when the Ghost Wind blows."

The *what*?

Oh! Somehow she'd missed it. A hazard flag was attached to the Ya-men file. Some sidebar about flower pollen and its outsized effects on the various humanoids here.

Something flickered in the Amazon's eyes. A dark orange-red shimmer that was nothing to do with the escort's hair. And again, that odd itch arose at the back of her neck. Gillian scratched at it, knowing that wouldn't help since it wasn't a skin problem. It was her body reacting to something subliminal. Something she'd seen or sensed at an unconscious level. But what? Damn it. She made herself stop, brought her hand back down and tucked it into her duty belt.

To distract herself as much as anything else, she said, "I'm sorry but I'm afraid I've forgotten your name."

Hadn't bothered to take it in, really, despite four long days on the trail with her. And suddenly Gillian was grateful Vanger hadn't followed them up the steep slope. He would have put an entry in her file over such an egregious offense to his beloved diplomatic standards. But the envoy and the librarian had stayed put in the semi-frozen meadow.

"It's Creidne n'ha Camryn," her companion replied, annoyance apparent in her tone. She was ready to say more but broke off at the sound of a rockfall somewhere above them. "We're not alone," she said quietly.

"Maybe not," Gillian said. "Some of those piles I just sampled were only a day old."

"Why didn't you *say* so?"

Gillian had no good answer beyond being dead tired. Then a cold whiffet of air brought a breezy resinous scent up the trail and the woman's expression switched instantaneously from irate to alarmed. She made a grab for Gillian's arm. "We must go. *Now.*"

Gillian stepped back, evading her grasp, unable to trust anything she said. Not while the skin on her back crawled over itself. As the wind stiffened, that strange odor it carried, a little like rosemary, hit harder, making her sneeze several times as it caught in her throat and tickled her nose.

Somewhere above them, more rocks rolled down the trail. Something snuffled the air, then whuffed out a low growl and leaped at her. Acting on instinct, she pivoted on one hip, using a jujitsu move to send all of that mass flying past her.

The thing hit hard, but rolled with it, coming back up on all fours with sinuous and lethal grace. A cat of some kind? With a *bird's beak*? No, that was a helmet of some sort. A Ya-man, she realized. Oh, *hell*.

It leaped at her once again, but squalled as a sword bit deep along its hindquarters. It whirled in mid-air, swiping furiously at the Amazon with claws befitting a tiger. Were they its own? Or borrowed, too, like the bird beak? Creidne danced backward, avoiding the claws, and then took another swing, but the creature dove underneath it, then launched itself and knocked her flat.

"No, you don't," Gillian cried. Pulling a tissue-sampling trochar free of her duty belt, she jumped onto the Ya-man's back and plunged it into his grimy neck, what little of it she could see through the feathers that also adorned that weird, bird-like headdress. The Ya-man yowled, rearing back to swipe at her. Then a sword's point erupted through his ribs, alongside his spine. It nearly skewered Gillian too, so she let go of him and her trochar and fell away on the downhill side of his convulsing body. Momentum carried her back down the trail like a cannonball on the loose. If not for the impact-resistant qualities of the cloth her suit was made of, Gillian would have been stunned, or worse, by the multitude of collisions with various rocks and trees and shrubs that followed.

Gillian cried out, as much in surprise as fright. What emerged wasn't words, though. More like grunts and whoofs as the air was knocked out of her lungs in spite of the suit. When she finally came to a stop again, Gillian found her lower half wrapped around a black boulder covered with lichen. The basalt did not penetrate any part of the suit, but the overall *wham* left her motionless for a few critical seconds.

Long enough for the wind to find its way into her nostrils again, and then into her body as she recovered enough to pant, and then to groan. Her lower back was already so sore and stiff from four days in the saddle, this new insult was all but crippling. Her legs refused to respond for a moment, and she could do nothing but listen while something further up-slope howled. As more voices joined it, the various 'songs' melded into a blood-chilling serenade that would have done a wolf pack proud.

More Ya-men? She tried her comm unit, hoping to warn Vanger. No go. She'd broken it.

Okay, what else could she use as a weapon? She had a small hand laser, meant to cut through wood or thin metal. She palmed it, triggered the energy pack, and aimed the beam back up the trail, at whatever was scrabbling down it at such a frightening velocity. When the red-head burst into the open, half sliding, half running down the rocky slope, Gillian swore. She pulled the faint red beam upward and sideways and so, accidentally, brought it across the dark eyeholes of another enormous feather-crested helmet. The Ya-man wearing it screamed and tripped, and then his head fell away altogether as Creidne turned and lopped it off with her already bloody sword.

On reaching Gillian's side, Creidne grabbed hold of her suit's torn collar. She began dragging Gillian downhill.

Sparks erupted. Like distant fireworks, but not that far off. It formed a weird nimbus around the Renunciate's red hair. The whole world was pinker than usual, too. Much more than the red giant that was its star could account for. More like what Gillian had sometimes experienced during her youthful experiments with cannabinoid variants. A strange cloud of static engulfed her as well, and somehow it began squeezing her head as small waves of heat rolled across her face, just as if she were too near a fire.

"What's happening?" Gillian asked herself. Aloud, to her own surprise.

"It's the Ghost Wind, you idiot!" Creidne spat. "The Ya-men are going berserk again. They'll eat us, too, if we let them!"

Truth. Irrefutable. Gillian's skin said so, the prickles all vanishing. "I don't...I don't understand."

"Of course you don't." That was a snarl as much as a sentence. "Look. I can't carry you, so get up. We need to get back to the horses. We've got to get out of here."

When Gillian still didn't move, Creidne struck her, an open-handed bloody slap. "Do it. Or die."

And that too was true. No room for doubt. Certainty she'd never felt before whacked its way through her confusion like a mental machete, and Gillian climbed onto her feet. Groaning against her body's protests, she turned back toward the trail and found Creidne's hand gripping her own.

"Oh, shit," she muttered, but found that she needed the woman's strength—of mind as well as body. Stumbling over the rocks and tree roots and each other, the two of them set off downhill with all the speed either one could muster

It wasn't enough.

By the time they made it back down to the meadow, the horses were gone and so was the damn librarian. Only Vanger remained, and he lay flat on his back with a bloody gash across his forehead. Hoof-shaped, by the clean curve of its edge. When she called his name, Vanger's head turned her way, but the envoy showed no other sign of awareness. There was, however, a dusting of pale golden powder on his face and his suit, so that might be the pollen at work. It was certainly working on her, Gillian thought, her confusion returning.

At her side, Creidne spat, "Sharra's tits!" as she let go of Gillian's hand and sank to her knees. Her other hand was dripping blood. Her own. Copiously. The Ya-man, one or the other, *had* done some damage, then.

Stop the bleeding.

Was that thought her own? Gillian shook her head. She had

no idea. Something about it was unfamiliar, and yet it felt welcome as well. Enticing, even. And the simple command was certainly apt. When she looked down at Creidne's arm, the leather armor was sliced across by three long parallel slashes a bare hand's breadth below the shoulder. The sleeve underneath was totally blood-soaked.

Gillian used her laser to cut away the rest of the leather, and then the sleeve. She fished the longer styptic bandage out of her duty belt, wrapping it once around Creidne's arm and letting it seal itself in place. Not much she could do to replace the blood volume already lost, though. She had a more complete first aid kit in her pack, but that was still strung from her horse's saddle, wherever the silly beast had gone.

Once again, she heard that weirdly melodious howling from somewhere above them. More Ya-men. Closer by far. So maybe the horses were smarter than her.

This time it was Gillian telling Creidne, "Get up, damn it! Do it, or die!"

The look Gillian got in reply struck her dumb. Rage and fear lived there, but so did a darker thing she could name nothing but guilt. Or maybe it was a dark resignation. Was the Amazon going to just give up and die now? What the hell?

Damn it. The world was engulfed by that sweetish want-to-be-rosemary scent, and her mind was whirling in seven directions at once. Where was Lord Darriell, the double-damned librarian? Maybe he'd gone to get help from the rest of their party, the eight armed horsemen they'd left behind at the last village. At Byron Vanger's insistence.

At the time she'd approved. They didn't need a whole troop of untrained humans and horses, too, tromping on the remains or the evidence. Now, though, she wondered about it. What was Vanger trying to hide? And from whom?

Never mind. Get Creidne moving. If not on her own behalf, somebody else's.

"You've got to help me," she told Creidne, who peered at her with an owlish frown, but finally surged to her feet again. Then, each of them taking a grip on his collar, they hauled Vanger's bear-like bulk across the meadow, toward the cave she'd seen earlier. Hard work at the best of times, and this was surely not that. Without the occasional ice slicks easing the passage of Vanger's broad behind, it might have been impossible.

It was also pointless. The cave might serve as a reliable shelter from the weather but it was indefensible. Too large, for one thing. The ceiling was a good three meters high and the opening at least five meters wide. The well-used trail they were on led straight to it, and there was no exit but this one.

We're trapped, she thought. *We can't stay here.* But Vanger could not be moved further without help and horses. Abandoning him might be their only option.

A tempting thought but one that vanished at the sound of hoof beats. Whirling about, she and Creidne both cried out when the librarian reappeared at the edge of the meadow, pelting along the southeastern side. His appearance now warlike, impressive, in fact, the Comyn lord was astride Vanger's two-tone horse, and leading two others, but of the fourth mount, her own, there was no sign. There were at least twenty Ya-men, however, in hot pursuit and maybe forty meters behind him, all loping along on foot.

They were giants! A third again as tall as the Comyn lord. Nearer twice her own height. And they all wore those same feathered helmets, or were they headdresses, adding to that overwhelming dimension. Good God. She hadn't realized how big they were in the midst of things.

What's worse, this group all carried spears, and several cast them at the man in flight. They missed him but succeeding in hitting the hindmost of the three horses. It screamed and stumbled, but kept going. Then then two more lances struck home and the animal foundered.

They swarmed it, leaving the Comyn lord free to finish his race up the trail, headlong, hurting in some way that kept him bowed over the neck of the horse he rode, clutching his ribs with one bloody hand. On reaching Creidne, he flung his reins her way and slid off to land in a heap at the mouth of the cave. Creidne needed no orders. She led the man's well-lathered mount inside, letting the other horse follow on its own, then turned back. With her sword in hand and her injured arm tucked inside her sword belt, she placed herself between

Darriell and the boiling troop of Ya-men below.

Gillian stepped forward, taking the man's arm and helping him rise.

"Hurry!" he told her. "Inside!"

To Creidne he said something more but in *casta*, which she could not follow. Her comm's translator seemed to be broken too. Perhaps in her tumble down the upper part of the northern trail. *No matter*, she told herself. *We're all dead anyway. There's no way we're going to hold* that *off with nothing but swords and a laser sampler*.

"Have a little faith," said the Comyn lord, so on point as to make her jump away from him. He ignored that, bracing himself against the rock face at the cave's entrance, one foot planted in the small stream of melt-water making its way from a spring within down the slope to his right. He fell silent, although it was hard to tell with all the noise made by the dying horse and the Ya-men...oh, hell. They were taking *bites* out of the struggling beast, like a pack of lions. Like animals.

While her attention was centered on that, something shimmered. Cool blue and white. Icy. Wet!

Something shifted inside her head and she saw that a waterfall now took the place of the stream. It appeared to originate much higher up and cascade down the face of the slope to crash into the small pool already formed there. The melt-water widened its path and obscured the soft earth where they'd all left their footprints. A small cloud of mist hid still more. And the cave? Was invisible. Hidden behind it all.

"Now, then. Be *quiet*," Lord Darriell ordered.

What? Did he think she was going to start singing? Or screaming? "But..."

"Shush!"

As if she were a child. Gillian's head rose, but then she froze, hearing footsteps in grit or gravel, and nobody inside the cave was moving. She heard voices too. Grunts, really. No recognizable words. And then, through the shimmer of the waterfall, she saw three very tall silhouettes. They were bent over, probably scanning the ground outside. Sniffing it, actually, in between their wild gyrations. *Searching for us*, she thought, fingering her little laser. Would it work through the waterfall? Was the water even there?

"No, it's not," the Comyn lord whispered, laying his hand on hers. "Don't. You will only betray us to the rest of them, even if you succeed."

How did he know what she had in mind?

"I used *laran*," he answered. "Just as I did in creating the waterfall. I reached into your mind and I shaped your perception, and theirs. So they'd see what I wanted them to, and not you or me or the others."

Was he talking about telepathy?

"Not really. *Laran* has many forms. I do have a touch of the Alton Gift, but it's limited. Using it like this is exhausting, and I need...I need to lie down."

Collapse was more like it. He sagged, and Gillian did what she could, easing his slide down the rock wall. He ended up at Creidne's feet, but when Gillian examined his injury, it was not the sucking chest wound she'd feared. Merely a gash where something, a spear's tip perhaps, had sliced into the muscles along the ribs, but not into the bones themselves. Applying the other styptic bandage in her mini-kit was all she could do for him since the horse gone missing was hers and her fully-stocked first aid kit had gone with it.

Creidne ignored them, maintaining her careful watch even after the Ya-men outside gave up their search. Only when they had rejoined the noisy group feeding in the meadow did she allow herself to give in to her own pain and weariness.

"We all need rest," said the Comyn lord, by now laid out flat on the smooth sandy floor of the cave. Creidne nodded and stretched out beside him. That left a rather narrow space between the Renunciate and Byron Vanger. Gillian shivered, and wanted a share of that warmth. Or was that the librarian's work?

Did it matter? She was hurting, too. And so cold. So very tired. She lay down in the remaining space, taking great care to avoid jostling Creidne's injured arm. It was still cold, but sandwiched between the Renunciate and the envoy, she felt warmer. Safer. She drifted into a dreamy state, somewhat nightmarish because of the feasting and madness going on just a couple hundred meters away, but she found she could tune that out, more or less, if she focused on other things. Everything being pink, for example. And Creidne's nearness. Her strength, and her courage. At first, it had been so strange to her that Renunciates even existed, like nuns in arms, but there had been men's groups like that at one time, hadn't there—Knights Templar? Things like that? What were they really all about?

She felt like wrapping her arms around Creidne and hugging her. Maybe kissing her too. Maybe more than that. Maybe...no. No, not with that injured arm. Couldn't risk it. Could not hurt her further, not even for the sake of their shared heat. There were other choices though, weren't there? Like Vanger, who lay on her other side. He was a big man, burly, and warm and fuzzy, underneath all those clothes. Was he also proportionate? Interesting question. And one she could answer so easily.

Gillian let her hand drift his way, let it rest on his leg for a moment, then glide upward. What would it hurt to find out? Anything? Anybody? They were, after all, just two Terrans trapped in a cave. Who'd object if she explored a little bit? What would he feel like?

Gillian found her hand had made contact, had already opened the suit, had begun to massage what it found within. Worse yet, his body began to respond. This when he was unconscious! And somehow that is what abruptly woke her up from that strange erotic dreaminess.

"What the flaming *hell*?" she asked herself. "What *are* you doing?"

An attraction to Creidne—that made some sort of sense even though she had always before been drawn to men. It would be insane to trust the woman on any level, but there was no denying the fierceness in her, nor yet the intelligence. And she might be plain by Terran standards but there was a certain magnificence to the strong bones in that face, to the auburn hair now escaping its bounds.

Why she'd want any part of the envoy, however—NO. Not if he were the only man left on the planet. In the whole flaming galaxy.

A red-hot tidal wave struck her. Pure shame. It yanked her

hand out of his suit. It set her to pawing her duty belt, searching for steri-cream.

"Easy," said someone. The Comyn lord? Oh, hell. Had *he* seen? "It's all right," he whispered. "The Ghost Wind is blowing. There is no blame. No right or wrong to what's done here and now."

No. *That* she would not believe.

Had she said that aloud?

It would seem so. The man reached over Creidne's still form and stroked her cheek. "It's the *kireseth*," he told her. "It is also an aphrodisiac. It has led to a great many strange...encounters. Even some hybrids. Of humans and...others."

Did he mean the Ya-men? But that was impossible. Anything that big would do too much damage!

He chuckled. "Where do you think *laran* comes from? Not Ya-men, no. But the old ones? Oh, yes. The *chieri* are part of us. Some of us. You, though. You are a surprise. I would not have thought a Terran would have your Gift."

"What are you talking about?" Gillian, finally finding the steri-cream, used it to clean her soiled hand with a vengeance. Would that she could use the stuff to scrub her mind too, of the memory.

"That can be done," said Lord Darriell. "But at the risk of your *laran*."

Her hands froze. "*My laran*?"

"Are we not speaking by way of the Gift we share?"

That's when she realized she was biting her lip in an effort to keep control. She hadn't said a word, physically. Neither had he. The sounds of breathing filled the cave, human and horse. But the rest of it came from outside, from the Ya-men. Who could not seem to locate the cave, or its hunkered-down contents, despite the trail leading straight to them. All because of what this man had done with what he called *laran*.

"The Ghost Wind," he whispered, "has many effects. It can enhance a latent Gift, like your perception of lies, of guilt."

Was he talking about ESP? But she had none.

"Do you not?" This time he stroked her neck, setting off cascades of itchiness. Everywhere. "You have been using it most of your life. Unaware, I can see, of what it really is."

No. I'm dreaming all this, Gillian told herself. It's the damned pollen. It's giving me hives.

Another caress, and the itch faded out of existence.

"How did you do that?"

"How do you know who is lying? Who is truly guilty?"

She snorted. "If I *could* do that, I wouldn't be here, would I?"

No. I'd be well on my way to a major promotion. For catching a kid killer. Famous? Oh, yes, indeed. But not for faking the evidence. For framing an innocent man because I am an ethnic extremist, a renegade who hated him, his race, and his politics.

"But you *do* hate him."

She didn't bother to answer. Let him use his blasted "gift" to see what boiled up out of her soul at the thought of that monster.

"So how did you get it so wrong?" he inquired, his tone mild as milk tea. Again he caressed her neck. Her face. Even her carefully sterilized hand.

"I...wasn't wrong," she said, suddenly breathless. Quivering with renewed desire.

But that faded too, like the itch. "I apologize," he said. "I...lost control for a moment. I would not be...such a man."

Truth. It startled her, both knowing that and getting it from a man who was still high on her suspect list. Or was he using *laran* to beguile her?

"What did happen, then?"

She did not want to talk about that, about precisely how they'd set her up, making it look like she had planted evidence. How they then used her passionate defense of the truth to convict her in the public eye-of malfeasance, misprision of justice, and madness.

He knew anyway. Damn *laran*!

But he didn't ask questions about that—her folly in pursuing the whole thing, or her downfall. He said only, "*That* is what brought you to Darkover?"

She nodded, using her face to stroke his hand. "They gave me a choice—accept off-world exile and a transfer to archaeological studies, or go to prison."

The concept of prison seemed new to him. She felt the question he didn't ask, and replied, "I just...I couldn't do that. I don't think I would have survived it. I knew too much. The man I accused was too important."

Then the irony struck her. "I thought I'd be *safer* here."

They shared silent laughter while, outside, the Ya-men continued to scream and howl and do further violence to the poor horse they'd taken down. She was glad of the animal's silence at that point, poor beast. She hoped it could no longer feel what they did to it. Gillian was happier still, hours later, when all went suddenly quiet outside.

The reason? Rain.

At Lord Darriell's insistence, all of them washed off as much as they could of the pollen, using the shockingly cold melt-water in the stream that was no longer a waterfall. That helped to clear away much of the pink fog engulfing her senses, although it did nothing to ease her fatigue or the aches and pains of her bruises. And Vanger was still unresponsive.

Her neck started itching again as she stared at his blank face. She turned to the Comyn lord, now consulting with Creidne in muttered *casta*. "What have you done to him?"

The man—*was* he an Alton?— turned. "The envoy has a head injury. He was kicked by his horse."

"Then he should be unconscious, or sick. Or maybe confused. But not just...missing in action."

"What did I tell you?" he said to Creidne and nodded toward Gillian.

That's when he noticed the laser sampler in her hand, aimed at his chest. When the Amazon reached for her sword, Gillian shook her head. "You say I've got a gift. You want to know what it's telling me? What it's been telling me, all along?"

Neither one took the bait.

"You're all lying. You two, the envoy, even the dead man. You're all guilty of something...something heinous." Just what she could do about that, though, she didn't quite know. She could hardly arrest them on what she had so far. And she wasn't in much better physical shape than all three of her living suspects.

"I think none of this was an accident," Gillian said. "You're all here for a reason."

Lord Darriell raised a hand, palm out in a conciliatory gesture, preparing to take a step forward.

"Don't bother," she told him and nodded toward Vanger. "Whatever you did to him, undo it. Wake him up."

"That would be...unwise."

"I really don't give a shit."

"All right. But first, let me show you what his man, Macon, was doing here. What *he* came for, now that Macon is dead." Darriell pointed at the two-tone horse at the back of the cave, the striking black and blond piebald animal that had been Vanger's mount originally, and then the Comyn lord's. It still bore the well-worn saddle and bedroll and other gear Vanger had brought with him. Likewise, the saddlebags he'd laid claim to, out there at the crime scene.

Gillian nodded her assent, then backed off a few steps to let him pass and still keep the laser trained on both the locals. It wasn't likely the laser would do all that much even at close range, not with its energy pack half-drained, but they didn't know that, did they? The horse didn't care. It seemed to welcome the man's attention, nickering to him and lipping the cloak falling over his shoulder. He untied the leather thongs securing the bags to its saddle and pulled them free, then carefully laid them at Gillian's feet.

"Back off," she told him before kneeling down to undo the loops holding the saddle bags' flaps shut, despite being overstuffed. Inside were specimen bags of the type she herself used. And every single one contained the odd little bell-shaped blossoms that she'd seen growing in the meadow. They'd all opened fully, and had stamens standing up, most of them dusted with the very same shimmering golden pollen she'd just washed off her own face. What had Creidne called them? Starflowers.

"*Kireseth*," said Lord Darriell. "It's the source of the Ghost Wind. We use it to test our children for *laran*. And to train them in its use. But it's dangerous. You've seen that."

Oh, yes. If only for what it set off in the Ya-men.

"It is illegal to harvest the flowers. Forbidden to all but the Tower-trained."

She flicked a razor-sharp glance at him, and was surprised by the blush flooding his pale cheeks with color.

He cleared his throat and carried on. "We, ah... In the Towers, we use a multiple distillation process to render it safe. Relatively safe. We...take the aphrodisiac out of it. Some other things as well, so that the mind remains...unclouded. The liquor we make is called *kirian*."

He paused, clearly uncomfortable. She snapped at him, "*So?*"

The man flinched, but met her eye squarely. "We believe your people have been trying to develop their own form of *kirian*. So they too can acquire and use *laran*. We cannot allow that."

Creidne blurted, "The *bastards*! They've done *so* much more than steal starflowers."

Meaning...what?

Gillian got no chance to ask. All of a sudden, the cave dimmed and something squeezed into her mind like a liver fluke worming its way through an inward passage that she'd never known was there. Damn it all! Had to be Darriell's work. He was using his "Alton" Gift again, this time against her will. She fired blindly and swept the little laser beam sideways to try and take out both the locals. But she couldn't see whether she'd even hit them or not. Couldn't see the damned *cave*.

Instead, she found herself in a cell. Behind steel bars. In a body that wasn't her own. Wasn't even a woman's. And it was in such a state—full arousal. The mere presence of that priapic excess held her motionless, stunned by the need surging through every vein, every fiber. Before her—him? —there was a girl. Darkovan, by her appearance and clothing, which she wasn't wearing.

Like him, she was naked. And fully aroused, by the size of the pupils in her eyes. But so young. The girl couldn't be more than eleven or twelve. Frightened, too, underneath all the rest. And he couldn't quite figure out what all this was. That pink fog had returned and his mind couldn't cut through it. Couldn't decide anything.

"Well? What are you waiting for? Have at it, boy!"

When he turned his head, the dead man stood there. Macon. The attaché who'd been eaten alive. But here he was, whole. Or was he? The man had his pants open, had his hands on his own organ, but his was flaccid. The man kept stroking it, muttering things he did not want to hear, but it didn't respond.

"Come on! Get to it!" Macon cried. Reaching out with his free hand, the man pushed him toward the girl. Pushed him from the inside, too. With *laran.*

How could *that* be?

He saw the vials, then. Three of them. One for each. Empty. And the liquid they'd swallowed—was that what was causing the fog? The overpowering need?

He shook his head, but the worm inside slid between him and the thing that protested, that gibbered in terror, while he advanced on the girl. Fell on her. Parted her thighs and gave free reign to that driving force within while she cried out in sudden pain. Blood spurted. Oh my god. She was a virgin, and that thing inside him was reveling in it. *Sharing* in it.

Gillian convulsed in an effort to tear herself free of that vision, that horror. She fell to the floor of the cave and buried her face in the cold sand. Only the lack of air brought her back up again. Even then, she couldn't breathe. Couldn't find herself for a long moment. She'd been someone else, and now nothing felt right. Felt like *her.*

"It's all right," said Lord Darriell. He was cradling her, had somehow pulled her into his lap and now sat with his arms wrapped around her. "I'm sorry. But there was no other way you would believe me."

"But...who was...who was I?"

"My half-brother," said Creidne. "Macon was using him in his experiments. He has...had *laran,* though I don't. That bastard was *riding* him..." She broke off, choking on her next words, but finally managed them anyway. "He...Iason killed himself. He couldn't bear what he'd done, after. Done to so many girls like that."

Gillian wept, and allowed the Comyn lord to rock her gently, murmuring into her ear as he did so. She didn't know what he was saying. He whispered in *casta*, perhaps to himself as much as her.

Had he shared in all that, too?

"Yes. And not for the first time. I tried...to help Iason," he told her. "Tried...and failed. I failed him and his family. I will *not* fail my people."

The steel in his voice was as sharp as the sword Creidne wielded, the blade marred where something had cut through the finish and one of the runes embedded along its length.

Laser cut, Gillian thought. Somehow the Renunciate must have used the bright blade to deflect the beam. But had not used it on the beam's owner. Yet, she was quite certain now, Creidne was a murderer.

"Yes," said the man holding her. "Creidne offered her services to him in Iason's place. And she brought Macon up here, and promised him plenty of *kireseth*. Only she timed it so he would encounter the Ya-men during the Ghost Wind. She made certain he would be consumed by them, leaving no evidence of his crimes. Or of hers."

It would have worked, Gillian told herself. It would have looked like an accident, if not for me and my itch. My...*laran*?

But... "What are *you* doing here?" she had to ask.

He let go of her, let her climb out of his lap and find her feet and stare down at him. He spread his hands in supplication. "I have to know what part Vanger played. And if there's anyone else involved. We cannot let them go forward with this."

"Are you going to kill him, too?"

No answer. Just that look. Wounded and angry and utterly set upon this task he'd assigned himself.

It's my duty, too, she thought. Screw archaeology. This is my real job.

"Okay, then. Let's find out. Wake him up."

The man shot a hard look at Creidne, who flung one of her own at Gillian, but nodded. Thereafter, it was the work of minutes. As if waking up from a dream, Vanger blinked at them, rubbed his face with both hands, and encountered the gash on his forehead, muttering, "Ow."

Then he sat up, frowning as he eyeballed the cave. "Where

am I?"

"We came under attack by the Ya-men," the Comyn lord told him. "One of the horses panicked and kicked you. Do you remember?"

"We took refuge here," Creidne added, "because of the Ghost Wind."

The envoy got up, awkward and stiff, perhaps dizzy as well. Then his gaze fell upon Macon's saddlebags. "What are you doing with that?" he demanded, striding toward them.

"It's evidence of a crime." Gillian fought hard to say it in a matter-of-fact tone. To keep it impersonal. She put herself in his path and he stopped short of barreling into her.

"What are you talking about?"

"A treaty violation," Gillian told him, feeling the itch set in. "Willful abrogation of common law strictures, as maintained by the indigenous culture. Specifically, harvesting *kireseth*."

"Are you accusing *me* of a *crime*?"

"Am I?" She gave him her best and most guileless expression of puzzlement. "Well, Macon *was* working for you, was he not?"

Vanger's broad face darkened. "That project is none of your business." Then, glancing aside at the other two, he leaned over and hissed at her. "It's classified. At the highest level."

"So you *did* know about it," Lord Darriell said.

"He not only knew about it. He came out here to cover it up," Gillian told him, resisting a powerful urge to scratch both her neck and her scalp.

Vanger rounded upon her. "Have you gone insane? Are you taking sides with *them*? You're a citizen of the Empire! They're...*barbarians*. They're *nothing*."

"Oh, dear." Gillian shook her head and sighed. "You knew what Macon was doing too, on the side. Didn't you? All those vicarious rapes. All those girls."

For an instant, the envoy goggled. "You can't...how could you..." Then, fury blasted its way through his shock and he bellowed, "*How dare you*! I will not tolerate this nonsense. You and your...your *fixations*! Your hatred for any man in a position of authority!"

So that was how he intended to play it. The back of her

neck flared red-hot. Her hands and forearms as well, erupting in a rash that resembled goose bumps except for that livid heat. It reached inside her, too, finding a home in her throat, which began to swell up as she backed away from the envoy.

He followed her, growling, "It's treason this time around."

Her throat closed up entirely. *Anaphylactic shock? Are you* kidding *me?*

Then, as Vanger reached into his own survival suit, into some hidden pocket she hadn't encountered during her pollen-induced explorations of his physique, she flailed at the air she could not pull in, and he produced a needle gun. He fired first at Creidne, who'd drawn her sword, one-handed, and rushed him.

The Amazon went down. The envoy turned her way again. Tunnel vision set in. Now the gun was all Gillian could see, everything going black at the edges amidst a roaring in her ears. *He will kill us all to keep this secret.* The laser sampler—where was it? She brought it up, taking aim.

Too late. The needle gun chattered, and Gillian fell into the darkness.

Some time later, she surfaced again, and found herself in the Comyn lord's embrace.

This is getting to be a bad habit.

It felt too nice to be worth a struggle, so she simply lay there. Until it occurred to her to wonder. *Why am I still alive?*

And then, *Creidne!*

"She's all right," Lord Darriell told her, stroking her cheek with his fingers, but keeping his grip with the other hand, making her stay put. "That armor of hers. It's only leather, but it's proof against a lot more than you'd think."

"But..."

"She'll be back in a moment. She's tending the horses."

"Vanger?!"

He turned her head, gently gripping her jaw, so that she could see him where he lay among the rocks. Oh. The envoy's dark eyes were wide open, the one charred, the other one sightless, the pupil blown so that the whole eye looked black. His big body lay perfectly still. And there wasn't another mark on him, other than that nasty gash in his forehead.

"What...what happened?"

Darriell shrugged. "Well, you took his eye out. Then, while he was still trying to shoot you, a blood vessel burst, I should think. In his brain. All that excitement, him in such a rage... Well, I expect your people will find it's that untreated head wound that did him in."

With help, she thought, from the Alton Gift.

"Plus, if we leave him outside for a bit," he remarked, "where the ravens can get to him, that eye will go away."

Leaving no evidence whatsoever of what really happened here. Only what she had already collected. If she let *that* theory stand...well, then Macon had died of a misadventure. Natural causes, and nobody's fault. Blame the Ghost Wind.

And Vanger?

Another accidental death. No one to blame, and most likely no record of his little project.

So? Is that the story I'll tell?

"I don't know. Is it?" Lord Darriell asked her.

Finally, he let her sit up and massage her still slightly swollen throat. On her lips was the taste of something like chicory. Same thing she smelled on his breath. Oh. So that's why she wasn't dead. One more reason, anyway.

Was that what all this came down to now? Her past? Her future? Her choices?

Okay, then. Make one.

Both guilty parties, she told herself, have been removed from this equation. And no good will come of revealing the truth. But here, at least, the truth still matters.

I can live with that.

Snowquake

by Robin Wayne Bailey

I love the idea that Darkover is filled with forgotten pockets of history, hidden secrets, and the like. Given the inaccessibility of the mountainous terrain of the Hellers range and The Wall Around the World, it's not surprising that people occasionally stumble upon these mysteries...or are drawn to them.

Robin Wayne Bailey is the author of numerous novels, including the *Dragonkin* trilogy and the *Frost* series, as well as *Shadowdance* and the Fritz Leiber-inspired *Swords Against the Shadowland.* His short stories have appeared in many magazines and anthologies with frequent appearances in Marion Zimmer Bradley's *Sword and Sorceress* series and Deborah J. Ross's *Lace and Blade* volumes. Many of his stories have been collected in two volumes, *Turn Left to Tomorrow* and *The Fantastikon: Tales of Wonder*, published by Yard Dog Books. He's a former two-term president of the Science Fiction and Fantasy Writers of America and a co-founder of the Science Fiction Hall of Fame. His latest book is *Little Green Men—Attack!,* an anthology co-edited with Bryan Thomas Schmidt.

Jenna Barron strained against her safety straps to stare out the passenger window of the Aldaran aircraft in which she rode. "It's going to be bad. Really bad." She shivered in her coat, not from cold—the craft provided adequate heat—but from the violence of her visions.

"We're wasting our time out here." Fighting turbulence, Alan Stone worked the craft's controls with consummate skill as savage winds battered them. He ignored the blowing white wall of snow outside, and fixed his attention on altitude and attitude, on terrain warnings, weather radar, and de-icing monitors.

Jenna couldn't see the aircraft's wing tips. She couldn't see anything except the ominous, vague shapes of the Hellers. Fear gripped her, but it wasn't from the rolling and pitching of the plane, rather from an onslaught of precognitive flashes—images she didn't understand, of people in fear and anguish, and looming foremost in her mind, the collapse of the Wall Around the World.

A sudden downdraft snatched the craft and, for a moment, they hung upside down in their safety straps. The terrain warning alarms screamed. Alan Stone shouted frantic curses as he fought with the throttle and rudder to regain control. An icy mountain loomed directly ahead, barely visible in the churning snow and mist. Jenna instinctively threw up one hand to protect herself, sure that they would crash.

But weather patterns in the Hellers were unpredictable. They barely escaped the savage downdraft only to be caught in an updraft that bounced them five thousand feet higher.

"I'm going to be sick," Jenna muttered.

"I warned you," Alan said. "It's a fucking roller coaster up here. The weather is crazy."

Jenna squeezed her eyes shut and swallowed. "Darkover has never seen this kind of snow and cold," she said. "Even in the Lowlands it's bad. Rivers are frozen. Some reports say that half of Thendara is blacked out and without power."

Alan Stone sneered. "Yeah, the Comyn Towers have battened down, too, the bastards. They could be of some help out here."

Jenna shared her pilot's contempt. "Since when were the Comyn ever of any help? They have their own agendas."

The attitude indicator flashed red as a severe cross-wind blasted the small aircraft and tilted it nearly thirty degrees. Alan shouted another blistering string of curses as he struggled to right the plane. On the port side, the sky turned blue-white for just an instant. A series of weaker flashes followed that.

"Snow-lightning," Alan grumbled. "You're the precog, Jenna, but I'm making a prediction of my own right now. If we don't get out of this storm, we're dead."

"Keep searching, Alan," Jenna answered. "This plane is Terran technology. It's supposed to be un-crashable." She wasn't sure she believed that, but just in case, she moved one hand closer to the emergency transponder on the console.

"You don't even know what you're looking for, Jenna," Alan Stone said. "And this storm is playing hob with our communications. It's impossible to get a signal out. Right now, we're shut off from everything."

"Something has happened out here, or is going to happen," Jenna muttered to herself. "I have to understand it." She touched her forehead with a pained expression.

For the first time, Alan took his eyes off the controls and stared sideways at her. He was a hard man, not given to sentiment, yet the blank expression on Jenna's face startled him. "What the fuck are you talking about? Jenna?"

She blinked and shook her head as if awakening suddenly. "None of it makes sense," she answered. "These flashes—so disturbing."

"Flashes of what? What are you seeing?"

She shook her head again and stared out the window. "That's just it, Alan. I don't know. You said the weather was playing hob with our communications. Well, it's like something is playing hob with my precognition. Something's reaching out to me—something powerful.

Alan gave his attention back to the controls. He and Jenna had known each other too long, since childhood, one of Terra and one of Darkover. It was a rare pairing, but they got along well and could read each other's moods and emotions. Whatever Jenna was experiencing, whatever drove her to commandeer a plane and a pilot in such weather, he trusted her. She was a woman who could handle herself.

Jenna gave him a sidelong look, then turned away. She hadn't told him about the constant headaches, two days' worth since the strange flashes began. Once more, she stared out the window into the frigid maelstrom. The increasing turbulence rattled her in every joint and bone, and she clenched her hands together in her lap until her knuckles turned pale. She couldn't see the Hellers at all now. The storm concealed the towering mountains in shifting white shrouds. Yet, she could feel them out there, no longer content to just be mysterious. Now, with their treacherous peaks and sharp-edged cliffs, they were something else, something atavistic and alive, and they regarded the small aircraft with malevolence.

"Kostigar," Jenna murmured.

Alan glanced over at her again. Her eyes were closed, her face without color. "What did you say?" he asked. "What's Kostigar?"

Jenna snapped. "I don't know, all right?"

"But what language is that?" he persisted.

Jenna closed her eyes again almost as if she was falling asleep. "I don't know," she repeated. "But it's right below us."

He leaned toward the window on the pilot's side and stared downward. "In this damnable storm, I don't see anything."

Jenna looked toward the ground, too, and shivered. "Something's horribly wrong, Alan. I can feel it! Mark the coordinates and contact home so they know where we are."

"We lost the satellite feed and communications, even the auto-nav an hour ago." Alan spoke with a set jaw, his tension palpable. "I'm flying by instruments and the seat of my pants."

Jenna bit her lip and stared groundward again. "I guess I'm not surprised," Jenna said. "Most of the planetary satellite grid is down because of the storm."

"You insisted we come out here!" It was Alan's turn to snap. "I told you it was a mistake." Then he shrugged. "I'll circle around if you want."

We're lost, Jenna thought. New visions cascaded through her brain, icy images of angry faces; the mountains glaring; storms and winds all full of dark intelligence. She didn't dare tell Alan. He would think her crazy. *This storm will devour us.*

The plane banked into a left turn as Alan attempted to circle back, but the wind surged with a howl and shriek heard even inside of the cockpit. The craft flipped over again. This time, Alan wasted no breath on cursing. He hissed once as he fought the yoke, his eyes wide, his lips pressed into a thin, bloodless line. He radiated uncharacteristic fear, and that made Jenna afraid. She reached across and clutched his arm, but he shrugged her off. *Too focused for sentiment.*

Jenna remembered the emergency transponder and reached a hand toward it. Then she gasped, and the gasp became a scream as a face took shape in the battering snow and ice and pressed itself right up against her window. It snarled as it regarded her with hungry eyes.

And it was not alone. She saw them now, evil things in the icy tempest that meant Jenna and Alan no good. They surrounded the craft!

Alan caught her wrist in a bruising grip, her finger just inches from the transponder. “Leave that alone!” he shouted. “Two rules for passengers! Say nothing—touch nothing!”

Jenna’s stomach lurched as Alan leaned hard on the controls and rammed the throttle forward. The plane shuddered as it bucked the winds and righted itself again. She shot a look out the window. The faces were gone. *That wasn’t some precog vision!* she told herself. *It was real! They were real!* She put a thin, gloved hand against the cold plexiglass, and the heat outline of her palm and fingers made an imprint that quickly disappeared. *But were they real? I’m not sure!*

Her headache worsened. Why hadn’t she noticed before how claustrophobic the cockpit felt? How little room there was to move, to stretch! The air tasted stale; she felt strangled by her clothing. She clutched Alan’s arm again. This time he didn’t shrug her off, but covered her hand with his own.

Why did she hold back? Why didn’t she tell him? *This storm wants us!*

A shrill alarm sounded, and multi-colored lights flashed on the console. “Ice!” Alan shouted. “The boots didn’t inflate fast enough! It’s overwhelming the de-icing tech!”

Great wet globs of sleet and ice slammed the fuselage. It pelted the windows, stuck, and obscured any possible view. A dangerous, clattering rattle filled the ship as balls of ice rapidly impacted the hull and wings.

Alan tapped the altitude gauge before leaning back in his seat. He tried the flaps. They were frozen. So was the trim. “The wings are iced up. We’re going down, Jenna.” His voice was frighteningly calm as he reached across the space between them and took her hand in his, but it was his sudden show of sentiment that scared her the most.

Her head slammed against the window. Her knees banged into the console. Alan’s body bounced against hers with jarring force as the small plane skipped, bounced, and slid over an icy field, scattering pieces and parts in its wake. *This is my fault! I insisted we fly! My visions! Kostigar. What is Kostigar? I've killed Alan!*

Jenna Barron passed out, thinking she was dead, too. Her head hurt so much, the pain almost too much to bear, but she thought about the emergency transponder she had not triggered, about Alan whose hand she still held.

She woke cold and chilled to the bone, and scared, aware that she was no longer in the plane. Through half-open eyes, she saw the faces in the storm. They were back, looming with menace and anger, not satisfied to have knocked her from the sky. *Darkover is a strange world, but this is beyond strange—beyond Darkover!*

She slipped into unconsciousness again, dreamed a jumble of dreams, and once more woke. She ached in every part of her body, feeling as broken as the shattered plane. Alan sat with her now, doing his best to keep her warm. *Not dead!* He held her head on his lap in the dubious shelter of a smashed wing.

"Be still, Jenna," he said. "You have a concussion."

She took surprising comfort in the closeness of his body, the gentleness of his touch. She had never thought of Alan as gentle. Yet she struggled to sit up. The chill of the snow upon which she lay was too much. It stabbed her as with tiny needles, pricked and tormented her. She listened to it falling from the sky, blowing, striking the metal wing with ringing, angry force. It wanted to get to her and to Alan.

The ground shook suddenly. It began as a slow vibration. She felt it in her sore body, a vague awareness that she doubted at first was real. But it grew, and the snow around them began to ripple and shift like white water on a white sea.

"It's a quake," she told Alan whose arms tightened around her. "I saw a quake in my visions. A lot of quakes." A deep humming sound rose up from the ground, and that became a growl, and then a rumble. Alan tried to stand and fell back against the broken wing. He banged his head against a twisted flap. The wing, itself, shifted and shook. Alan grabbed Jenna's hands, pulled her to her feet and away from the wing lest it fall on them. Jenna clung to Alan, and they both fought for balance as the ground tossed beneath them.

"Did your visions show you this?" Alan asked.

"The quake?" Jenna answered. "I told you I foresaw quakes."

"Not quakes," Alan said. "This."

He drew her closer, tilted her head upward and kissed her.

Jenna recoiled, drew back and slapped him. "It took the biggest storm in history, a plane crash, a near-death experience, and an earthquake to make you do that!"

"I didn't want you to think I was easy," Alan said. He kissed her again. But then he pulled away. "That was nice, but we have practical problems to consider." He reached into his coat pocket and extracted a pair of tinted aviator goggles. "Put these on."

Jenna rolled her eyes. "There's the Alan Stone I know." Her lips still tingled from the intensity of his kiss, but he was all focus and business once again. She accepted the goggles and pulled them over her eyes. "What about you?"

"I only had one pair in the cockpit. You wear them. I did manage to salvage a few things, though."

He looked toward the shattered wing, which was now leaning at a different and more precarious angle. With no more word to Jenna, he waded through knee-deep snow toward the wider section that had shorn off from the fuselage. A small backpack lay half-buried. Alan picked it up and shouldered it, then moved quickly back to Jenna's side. "It isn't much," he said.

Jenna wasn't listening. As snow and ice continued to pummel her, she stared past the wing at the long trail of metal debris. The cockpit or what remained of it looked like the corpse of a frozen bug whose wings and tail had been plucked off by some giant child. Pieces of the fuselage, fragments of propellers, a shattered radar pod, a landing gear, and more littered the snowscape, all of it covered and caked with ice so thick that no marking could be seen.

"How did we survive that?" Jenna whispered.

"My masterful piloting skills," Alan answered, "and this unexpectedly smooth snow field where one shouldn't be."

Jenna pulled up the hood of her coat. Even with the protective eye wear, she could barely see as the lenses quickly fogged, and if she looked into the storm, the wet sleet coated them just as it had coated the windows of the plane. Still, she looked around. "Where do you think we are?"

"Kostigar?" Alan Stone answered simply.

Jenna thought it a poor joke. "There's nothing here!" she answered. "I don't even know if it's a place. I don't know what it is. I just keep hearing it in my visions." She thought of the faces she had seen out the window. Maybe Kostigar was one of them. Maybe they were Kostigar?

Alan adjusted the small backpack as he put his arms through the straps. Then he scooped up a handful of snow, compressed it into a hard snowball, and threw it toward the horizon. "You said it was right below us," he insisted. "Maybe it's buried."

She frowned and studied him, wondering if he had hit his head too hard in the crash.

He explained. "That quake you just felt came out of the Hellers. There must have been an avalanche—probably several—and the snow followed a natural path down the mountainsides to make this snowfield. Lucky for us. But what if something wasn't so lucky? I trust your visions, Jenna. You're an Aldaran precognitive."

Jenna shuddered. Alan's explanation made twisted sense. In her visions: *people in anguish, lives crushed, shock and destruction.* But nothing clear, just flashes and a relentless urgency. Her head pounded, but from the concussion or from some other cause, she couldn't say. Her gift, her precognition, everything seemed scrambled. Was she seeing the future in her visions, or had she had seen the past?

"So, what do we do now?" She gazed hopelessly toward the cockpit. "I don't suppose the transponder is still working? I didn't throw the switch."

Alan barked a short laugh. "You don't have to throw a switch," he answered. "Every plane has an automatic transponder. We just can't count on any signal getting out with all these mountains and this mega-storm." He took a deep breath as he turned in a slow circle and looked around. "The first thing we need to do is get out of this valley as fast as we can. Normally, I'd want to stay close to the plane, but we don't know if these quakes have stopped. If there's another avalanche, it will follow the same path, and we don't want to be here."

"But we can barely see anything!" Jenna protested. She wiped a hand over her goggles. "I can't even see the Hellers, the largest mountain chain in the world!"

Alan grabbed her by the shoulders. "You're a precog," he said. "A ranking member of the Aldaran family, and one of the most powerful precognitives in a generation."

Jenna didn't understand. Maybe it was the cold that numbed her right through her coat. Or the maddening snow and sleet that continued to assail her like frozen bullets. She tried to look around, but no single feature, not even the mountains, stood out in this white hell. She pressed a hand to her head and tried to wish the pain away.

Alan shook her. "You're going to get us out of here. Your visions are going to guide us through this storm and show us the way. Maybe to some bandit village or a *chieri* stronghold. But anyplace safer than this."

Jenna pushed the problematical goggles up and gazed at Alan's face. *He has faith in me.* The sudden realization hit her with a strange force. She wasn't at all sure that she had such faith in herself.

A long and horrible wail tore through the howling storm.

"Great," Alan said, scowling. "Banshees. As if we didn't have enough trouble." He reached into another jacket pocket and extracted an old Terran revolver, then checked the cylinder to count the shells. That done, he put the gun away again. "Choose a direction, Jenna Barron, and don't deliberate too long about it."

Jenna took a step back and looked shocked. "A pistol?" she cried. "You know such Terran weapons are forbidden! It's one of our strongest taboos! Where did you get that?"

The banshee, unseen in the storm, howled again. Then another, perhaps its mate, howled a higher note. Banshees were blind creatures. They didn't need eyes to hunt prey. Their sense of smell and ability to read heat signatures were more than enough.

Alan dismissed her outrage. "I'm a Terran," he answered bluntly. "It's not my taboo. And we have bigger problems right now than your delicate sensibilities."

Jenna regarded him angrily, but she pulled her goggles back over her eyes. He was right about immediate problems, but possessing a gun could get him banned from the Aldaran territories, and she found just the sight of such a weapon—offensive.

The banshees screamed again. The sound had a powerful way of making her focus. She didn't yet know where they were going, but she chose a direction and trusted herself. She hoped it was away from the predatory birds. "This way," she said.

The snow was deep, well above their knees in some places. More than once, Alan had to pull her out of a drift when she slipped in above her waist. The wind battered them. It seemed determined to hinder their every step. She pushed back the edge of her hood and glanced at the sky, and a previous thought returned. More than a thought, really. A realization. *It wants us. This storm wants us.* She didn't know how or why, but she felt its hunger.

The sleet continued to fall. Here and there, all across the snowscape, it began to pile up on itself in strange ways, creating little shapes, grotesque sculptures, with heads and twisted arms. The snow and sleet continued to enlarge them, and they multiplied.

"I've never seen a phenomenon like that," Alan whispered. Jenna shivered at the unsettling note she heard in her companion's voice.

This is a horror story. She felt the Hellers, the ponderous weight of the mountains all around her, as if they were alive and breathing on her neck. She sensed, also, with undeniable certainty that the Hellers were angry, that the mountains resented them, regarded them as unwanted invaders.

Invaders. That's why it smashed Kostigar.

Kostigar again! What was Kostigar?

Once more, the ground began to shake. There was no slow buildup this time, no hint or hum, just a deep rumble that knocked Jenna and Alan off their feet. Jenna fell forward, planting her face in a deep drift, for a moment buried as the drift collapsed over her. She panicked, unable to move as the weight of the snow pressed her down like a foot upon her back.

Alan found her somehow. She felt his frantic scraping and digging, and the lessening of the weight on her body. Then, a strong hand squeezed her right shoulder and another grasped her left wrist, and she was yanked from the deadly trap and set on her feet again with Alan's arms tightly around her.

In the unseeable mountains, the deep rumbling continued. To Jenna, it sounded angry and disappointed, cheated of its prey.

Jenna leaned on Alan for a moment, bone-tired and aching in every joint. Then, embarrassed, she backed up, grabbed a handful of snow, and pressed it into her mouth for much-needed moisture. "We can't stop," she said.

The banshees howled, as if to drive home her point. The deadly, wingless birds were still on their trail.

She trudged onward, leading the way. Through her goggles, she studied the snowscape as best she could, mindful now more than ever where she put her next step, lest she tumble into another snow pit. But the world was indistinct to her, shades of white upon white and more white. It was as if, she thought, they had crossed into some other realm, some hostile dimension that was no longer Darkover.

Those shapes, those things of ice and sleet, those—creatures!

Jenna swore that they moved sometimes. They seemed closer now, as if they schemed to surround the pair of invaders. What horrible trick of meteorology had made them? To what purpose?

Her heart pounded, not from exertion but from a growing terror. They were lost, and it had to be getting late, toward nightfall. What time had they crashed the plane? Her legs ached dreadfully from wading in deep snow and from battling the winds. And the banshees. The banshees!

Her head throbbed. She pressed a hand to her temple as her senses suddenly reeled, and she knew she was falling again. This time, Alan caught her and eased her down.

"You have a concussion," he reminded her. "You need to

rest. You've done well, though, leading us."

He lied. Jenna could see it in his eyes. She could always read him. But for now, she said nothing. She ached too much and couldn't focus.

Alan unslung the small backpack he wore. He had tried to tell her what was in it, but she hadn't listened. Now he withdrew a box. It was no bigger than a shoebox, but bright red in color and made of nylon or rubber, she thought, but maybe some other material. She pushed up the goggles again to see it better, but Alan touched something, some small button or trigger on it, and the box hummed as he set it down.

A moment later, it began to expand. In better circumstances, it might have made Jenna laugh to see this scarlet bladder swell and grow so quickly, to watch it sprawl upon the white snow. She grasped immediately that it was becoming a shelter, and she sat up, intrigued.

"Inside," Alan said, holding back a flap.

Jenna crawled inside, and Alan followed. The tent was too small to let them stand. They could only sit closely together or stretch out on the floor. But it had one amenity. A tiny control just inside the flap blinked. Alan touched it. The blinking became a small, steady glow.

"Now, we'll have heat. The battery will last only for a few hours, but you'll get warm. We shouldn't stay here that long, though, so rest now while you can. I'll keep watch."

"Watch for what?" Jenna muttered as she lay back.

The banshees answered that question with a long screech, and Alan drew his gun.

She hated the sight of that weapon.

Jenna fell asleep, but it was a fitful rest full of dreams and nightmares and images she didn't understand. She woke twice, each time feeling as if she was not alone, but Alan was not beside her. Once, she crawled to the tent entrance and pushed back the flap, only to recoil, gasping. The sleet creatures were much closer now, almost upon them. They radiated animosity and malevolence. Like the mountains. Like the storm.

She fell asleep again, fearful for Alan. Where had he gone? Maybe the storm had taken him. *The storm wants us.* Without waking, tossing and turning from one side of the tent to the other, she called his name.

Then out of the chaos of her dreams, came one clear vision—a black-sleeved arm sticking up, bent at the elbow, from the smooth snow, one pale frozen finger pointing a direction.

The angry howling of the banshees and a loud gunshot shattered her uneasy sleep. Jenna scrambled out of the tent, stood up, and called Alan's name. The wind seemed to have lessened, and although it was night, she could see the vague outlines of the Hellers looming over her even closer than she had anticipated.

She turned, searching for Alan, and noted that the once-red shelter was now coated white with ice and snow. A second gunshot jerked her around again, and this time the sound echoed off the mountains. She couldn't tell where the shot came from. "Alan! Alan!"

A shape came running out of the mountain shadows. Running was not the word. It lurched and stumbled through the deep snow with frantically waving arms, seeming more like a comical marionette than Alan Stone. And yet it was he.

"Jenna! I got one!"

"You left me alone!"

He hugged her tightly, the pistol still in his hand, the smell of gun smoke still strong. "The birds were getting too close. I lured them away from the tent, and I got near enough to take a shot."

"In the dark? You must have been awfully close!"

Alan laughed. "Well, they didn't take a bite of me. Not for lack of trying." He turned serious. "How are you feeling? Well enough to travel?"

Jenna frowned. "Why leave here? We have the tent and heat."

Alan shook his head. "I told you, the battery has a short life in weather this extreme. It's probably dying already. And we're still too close to the mountains. Another quake could mean another avalanche. We need to go."

A lone banshee cried in the darkness.

"Damn!" Alan muttered. "I thought killing one would discourage the other."

As soon as they left the tent, the storm picked up intensity again. Jenna pulled down her goggles and, stumbling, led the way. She carefully avoided the eerie ice creatures and picked her way around them. She thought of them now as ugly spirits, alive somehow, moving only when she wasn't quite looking at them, always trying to maneuver closer. She feared if one should ever touch her that it would keep her and never let her find home again.

"There's something over there," Alan said suddenly. He pointed. Although it was dark, some darker form revealed itself against the whiteness of the snow. Alan took the lead and moved toward it, one hand on the gun that was back in his coat pocket.

Jenna knew what it was before they quite reached it. She had seen it exactly in her vision: The black-sleeved arm thrusting up from the snow, one finger pointing.

"Poor guy," Alan said. "Some bandit, probably. I wonder what he's pointing at? The mountains? The avalanche? Maybe he saw it coming."

Jenna remained silent. *Something coming, but not the avalanche—something else.* In her vision, she thought the dead man was indicating a direction, perhaps the way for them to go. Now, she wasn't sure at all. "We've been going in circles," she said. "Whatever Kostigar is, I think it's still below us under the snow. I don't know how, but I can feel it."

She turned her gaze skyward and a scream choked in her throat. In the storm above, she saw the monstrous face again. And other faces, too, all angry and threatening.

This time, Alan saw them. "What are they, Jenna? What magic is this?"

Somewhere behind them, still on their trail, the banshee screamed.

"Follow the dead man," Jenna urged. On an impulse, she leaned down and touched the tip of one finger to the finger of the frozen corpse. *He's pointing the way! But to what*? In the instant of contact, a flood of images poured through her brain. Some she had seen before in earlier visions, but many were new and frightening and promised to overpower her.

Alan snatched her hand away, breaking the contact. "Jenna! What happened? What did you see?"

Jenna didn't answer at once. She looked up again into the sky. The air flickered with more snow-lightning, but the strange, angry faces were gone. Still, she felt their presence near and watching. "Something has happened here, Alan," she answered, trembling. "I wish my visions were clear!"

She took the lead again, setting a course in the direction indicated by the dead man. Her head continued to ache, and her legs felt like lead from hours of deep-snow hiking, and with every breath the cold air raked her raw lungs. Worst of all was the oppressive fear, the sense of an otherworld malignancy purposely directed at them.

The direction she had chosen, the way indicated by the dead man, took them ever deeper into the Hellers. A slow cascade of visions, just fragmentary glimpses of things she didn't understand, began to fill her brain. She fought to make sense of it and to keep her course at the same time.

Then Jenna gave a gasp of despair. At her feet, now half buried in the snow, lay one of the wings of their aircraft. And not far ahead was a shape that she knew was the fuselage. She had been right—they were traveling in circles.

Not far behind now, the banshee laughed at them.

Jenna pushed back her hood and cast off her goggles. The Hellers stood sternly before her as if in judgment. "I don't understand!" she shouted into the wind, and her voice echoed strangely off the cliffs and peaks. As if dreaming, she remembered stories and tales about the Hellers and an ancient Darkovan god who ruled them. She didn't believe in gods, nobody did anymore, but out of desperation, she flung out her arms and shouted a very old name.

"Zandru!"

Snow-lightning danced across the sky. The wind roared and struck Jenna with such force that it blew her backward into Alan's arms, and they fell together amid parts of their shattered plane. Jenna started to scream, but suddenly a singular vision jumped out from among all the others in her head, and for a moment she lay still as death.

"Help me up, Alan," she said, calm again. "I know where we're going."

Alan stayed close to her, sometimes taking her elbow when she faltered. As they moved away from the wreckage for a second time, the wind began to subtly weaken. The snowy ground rippled and shifted before their feet, and the ground vibrated with a soft, building hum.

"Another quake!" Alan shouted.

"It's going to be bad! Really bad!" Jenna answered. Then, she stared ahead and pointed with one finger exactly as the dead man had pointed. The storm blew heavy veils of snow into the air, and the wind parted those veils to reveal—something. "That's where we're going!" Jenna cried.

The ground began to shake as, hand in hand, they lurched toward a low structure, the top of a conning tower, maybe, or a gigantic rocket fin. "It's a ship," Alan said as he fought for balance. "Why didn't we see this before?"

"Because it was hidden from us," Jenna answered uneasily. "Or maybe it wasn't there."

Most of the vessel was buried beneath ice and snow, probably by the same avalanche that had formed the snow field. What remained rose up to twice their height. It appeared intact, but closer examination revealed one side caved in. While Alan circled the strange structure, Jenna hugged herself and looked around at all the sleet and ice monsters pressing ever closer. *How do they withstand the ground's shaking and trembling? Why don't they topple and shatter?*

"I don't recognize this hull configuration," Alan shouted from the other side of the structure. "But there's an access hatch over here!" He came hurrying around to face Jenna. "A goddamned door!"

With the ground still shaking, Jenna trudged around in Alan's footsteps. "We have to go inside."

"That could be suicide," Alan warned. "Another avalanche will bury this valley again. We'd be trapped."

"We have to go in!" Jenna insisted. She put a gloved hand to the hatch and tried to pull it open, but deep drifts held it shut. Alan took her place and tried to muscle it open with no luck. Jenna fell to her knees and began digging in the deep snow, scooping handfuls and throwing them aside. Alan also began digging, until they had enough of the hatch exposed. Alan then rose up, seized the cold metal edge, braced one foot against the structure, and yanked with all his might. Reluctantly, the hatch slid back, leaving an opening just wide enough for Jenna, but not for Alan.

"I'll go first," Jenna said.

But before she could squeeze inside, a terrifying screech sounded behind them, and the lone banshee that still followed them charged. The shaking ground didn't slow it, nor did the rows of ice monsters blocking its path. Jenna had no time to react. The giant bird knocked Alan aside and fixed its hunger on her, slamming her against the vessel's hull. It raised a claw and slashed at her, ripping open her coat. Its beak snapped at her face.

Sprawled on the snow, Alan drew the gun from his coat pocket and hastily fired. He fired again and kept firing. The banshee screamed, turned and lunged at Alan, knocking him down. The gun went flying. The banshee pinned him with one claw and raised its other claw to slash him open.

The gun boomed in Jenna's hands. The powerful recoil knocked her back against the ship's hull, and she stood there trembling, pale, her muscles locked, unable to lower the forbidden Terran weapon.

Red blood splattered over the white snow, over the walls, over Alan, but the banshee toppled sideways, dead. Alan, however, didn't spring up. He stared with empty eyes at the beast, then uncertainly at Jenna and the still-smoking gun. Jenna pulled herself together and lumbered to his side.

"Alan! Alan! It's all right! The banshee is dead. I'm fine!"

Alan's gaze slowly focused on her, and he reached up to touch her face. "I thought it killed you," he said.

She grinned and showed him the tatters of her coat. "I was lucky."

"You fired the gun," Alan noted. "I thought the weapon offended you, but you picked it up and fired."

"I had to, to save you." She gave the weapon back to Alan. Her hands felt almost numb from the force of the blast. A part of her still felt dishonest for having used it, and the smell of the gun smoke still clung to her gloves. "But we won't speak of this to anyone, Alan. We don't dare incur the penalties."

She helped him up, and then turned her attention back to the access panel. "I can just squeeze through," she said.

Alan wouldn't hear of it. He grabbed the panel once more, braced his foot against the hull, and strained until it gave another few inches. Jenna passed inside easily, but Alan had to remove his coat and barely managed to squeeze through. Then he gasped and stuck his head back outside for a deep breath.

"There isn't much air in here," he said when he turned back to Jenna. "Are you all right?"

"I noticed it," she answered. "It's not lack of air. It's something *in* the air. Alan, some things are starting to become clear to me. This ship is alien."

"Maybe we shouldn't be here," Alan suggested.

"I *have* to be here," she answered. "This thing has been calling to me. It's calling to me now." She gave him a sidelong look. "And when did you become such a nervous nelly?"

He frowned. "Plane crashes have a way of making the bravest men see the light."

"Speaking of light," Jenna said, "I could use some." She took three cautious steps away from the access hatch and, as if in answer, the interior walls began to glow with a soft blue radiance. "What do you know? Panel lighting."

"It still works," Alan answered. "But the heat is out. It's freezing in here."

Jenna wasn't listening. A new flood of images washed through her head, so powerful that she lost awareness of Alan and even the storm outside. She walked out of the room and into a corridor. The panel lights came on as she approached and faded out as she passed. Alan kept up with her, shivering, whispering her name only once, aware of her precognitive state, as she navigated the corridors and descended levels as if she knew them.

Finally, Jenna stopped. Alan looked over her shoulder into the next corridor and gasped again. The panel lights came on, and he cursed. Bodies lay everywhere—small, twisted, and broken. Alan moved carefully past Jenna into the hallway. He observed the anguished faces, the expressions of shock and despair, but he avoided touching any of them.

Jenna shuddered. "They look like the ice creatures." She pointed to rows of white doors or hatches on either side of the hallway. "Open them."

There were small rooms, what might have been conference rooms. Another, larger room was obviously an astro-lab of some sort. Another, still larger chamber seemed to be a command center. Little dead bodies lay scattered around, some still strapped in chairs at their stations.

"It's horrible," Jenna said. She kneeled down before a body strapped in its seat before what she felt sure was a navigational arrangement. "I understand it now, all the visions that didn't make sense. They're clear. I know what Kostigar meant."

Alan shook his head slowly as he bent over an alien computer and punched some buttons. "Well, don't keep it to yourself."

"It means several things. It's what these people called their home," Jenna answered. "And this ship. And themselves." She leaned over a navigational star chart on a broken screen and noted what appeared to be a small notebook on the console. She picked it up. Just touching the notebook brought a cascade of images. *Not images—memories*! "No wonder nothing made sense. All the flashes, all the impressions I'm picking up and couldn't understand—they're alien. They were psychics, Alan!"

Alan looked suddenly angry. "They crashed in the storm just as the first humans crashed on Darkover. The avalanche took them by surprise." He looked sad and thoughtful. "We don't even know why they were coming here."

I called him unsentimental. Jenna tucked the notebook under her jacket and touched Alan's arm. She wanted to kiss him again as they had kissed before, to reassure him, but something held her back. Later, she would explore that.

The deck began to shake. A few of the panel lights flashed and exploded. Pieces of machinery collapsed. *It's going to be bad, really bad!* She grabbed Alan's hand and together they ran as fast as they could through falling debris and buckling hulls until they made it back to the hatch through which they had come.

Outside, the storm raged and the ground shook. The grotesque ice creatures were toppling and shattering. Jenna found it difficult to stand. She stumbled back against the vessel, tripped over the banshee carcass, regained her footing, and nearly fell again. But Alan caught her and held her, and they both looked toward the Hellers as the ground churned beneath them.

Jenna reached out and touched the hull. It still called to her. The ship and all the area around called to her. Even in death, some aspect of the creatures still lived as waves of psychic energy. Those would fade in time, but now they were still strong.

"Listen," Jenna said as she clung to Alan. "They've found us."

"Another vision?" Alan asked uncertainly.

"No, it's real. The transponder worked."

An Aldaran search copter plunged with reckless speed through the storm, but on a trajectory that would pass the alien vessel. "They're headed for the wreckage," Alan said. "Our wreckage."

"No," Jenna said. "They saw us. They're circling back."

Battered by wind, the copter rocked a foot above the snow, not daring to touch down. In the Hellers, thick clouds of snow, sure signs of an avalanche, roiled into the air, and great walls of snow slid into the valley. The pilot struggled to keep the craft stable. Desperately, Alan grabbed Jenna and flung her through the copter's open door. She cried out as her jacket tore open and the thin notebook she had taken from the navigational station went flying. She cried out again as she watched it sucked into the air and blown across the snowscape like an escaping bird.

Without a moment to spare, Alan leaped inside and the copter shot upward. Uncounted tons of snow crashed over the alien ship, burying it, sealing it forever with all its secrets, all its dead, inside. The sudden immense air pressure bounced and tossed the copter and all its passengers, and Jenna screamed once, fearing they would crash again.

But they didn't crash. They rose ever higher into the

furious storm, leaving the Children of Kostigar farther and farther behind.

"What just happened here, Jenna?" Alan asked. "What happened to us down there?"

Jenna pressed her face against a window. The face—that hideous face—glared back at her from the storm's heart as if angry that she had escaped. Snow-lightning flashed in its eyes, and its lips blew gales of ice and snow.

"I don't know," she answered. "I think we crossed a border into some dark fairyland, a different place with different rules—alien rules." She stared back into the eyes of the storm itself until her breath fogged the window. "We were invaders. But also guests." She took a deep breath and leaned back in her seat. Her headache was a little better.

She thought of the lost notebook.

Something wanted us to know a secret.

Alan put his arm around Jenna. "Maybe they were the invaders," he said quietly.

Jenna closed her eyes and leaned her head on his shoulder. "Darkover is strange. Even alive, I sometimes think. I wonder sometimes if it wants any of us here."

A silence fell between them as both Jenna and Alan contemplated that. Then, Alan kissed the top of Jenna's head. "I saved something," he said softly. "I took it from one of their computers." He reached into a pocket and withdrew a battered data chip.

Jenna snatched it from him and turned it over in her hands. "I wonder what's on it? I wonder if we can read it?

Alan drew her even closer. "You wonder a lot of things, Jenna Barron."

She leaned toward the window again and looked out. The faces were gone, but she felt them out there as she had before. On the ground far below, in the deep mountain ranges, she could see the quakes shaking the cliffs, breaking the mountain sides. She reached for Alan's hand.

Through the intense clouds of snow and sleet, it looked as if the Wall Around the World was collapsing.

Tricky Things

by Robin Rowland and Deborah J. Ross

Darkovan culture relies heavily on the concept of honor. Oaths are regarded extremely seriously, with full recognition of the power of a solemn promise to alter the minds and hearts of both parties. But what happens when an oath is extracted under duress? In contemporary Western jurisprudence, such oaths are not considered binding, but Darkover is not Earth, and the added element of *laran* changes everything.

Robin Rowland lives in Kitimat, British Columbia, a town in a northern mountain valley, which he says has a microclimate that closely resembles Darkover. Before retiring to his old home town, he spent 30 years as a news producer and photographer for Canada's television networks. In 1995, he co-wrote *Researching on the Internet*, the first computer manual on how to search the internet. He is mostly a non-fiction author, specializing in historical investigation, including two books on Canada's Prohibition gangsters. During the Second World his father, who became a prisoner of war after the Japanese occupied Singapore, was forced along with the other prisoners to take an oath not to escape from the prison camp. That became known as the Seralang Barracks incident and a full account is found in Robin's book *A River Kwai Story: The Sonkrai Tribunal*, and the original idea behind this story.

Deborah J. Ross writes and edits things.

During the tumultuous Ages of Chaos, ordinary folk went about their lives in isolated communities, secure in their belief that they had no part in the wars of the great Domains. Thus, Garvan Carganan, at eighteen years the eldest son of the Warden of Nira Plateau, made ready to transport a load of *laran*-preserved fish to Lord Riedel Storn. His cargo was no ordinary fish, but the exquisitely delicious Bronze K'bradon, spawned high above his family's holdings. The annual catch was the high point of the year. As the time drew near, emerald spearbills perched along the streams, ready to swoop down and pick off the migrating fish. The earlier the spearbills arrived, the more bountiful the catch, or so the people of Nira believed. Then hawks gathered, wolves patrolled the river banks, and scorpion ants emerged from their dens to scavenge whatever was left behind.

After Garvan loaded the canoe, his father handed him a copper plaque, the Storn oath of safe conduct that would ensure his safe return. The people of the Nira Plateau owed no fealty to any Domain, yet for generations, the Carganan family had sent their best fish to the lords of Storn, who ruled the mountains and valley lands to the south and east, ever their friends and allies.

As Garvan set out, the *water sense* that he had inherited from his ancestors, a prickling sense that warned of dangerous rapids and guided them to the best fishing spots, itched the back his mind. With the sun high in the clear sky, the weather posed no threat, being one of the few hot days in the brief mountain summer. Birds sang in the trees to either side of the river and the currents flowed gently, smoothly. The warning itch soon faded away in the tranquility of the day.

Two hours after sunset, Garvan reached the tavern at Felton Woodhead, and the next day he took the riverboat upstream. It was a good trip, and fast, for he reached Storn well within the span of the preservation spell. He had hoped for a word with Morgan, nephew to Lord Riedel, with whom he'd passed a few summers when they were younger, but there was no sign of his friend. From Storn, he proceeded on foot toward Nira Plateau, for he had been given leave to attend a local festival, where he hoped to spend his own money on a gift for his father.

Garvan was not a half hour on the road when he came upon a checkpoint, a barrier blocking the road that was manned by soldiers wearing Storn colors. To one side stood a weathered building, perhaps an old inn no longer in use but not yet fallen down. He touched his jacket, feeling the outline of the safe conduct. Whatever was going on had nothing to do with him, he told himself, yet his heart sped up as he approached the barrier. Two soldiers came forward, moving to either side.

"A fair day to you," Garvan said politely. "Please allow me to pass."

Without a word, the soldiers sprang at him. One grabbed him by the collar so roughly that Garvan lost his balance. Garvan would have gone sprawling had the second not seized his arms and twisted them behind him. Garvan recognized the hold from wrestling, a hold he could not easily break without risking a dislocated shoulder or worse.

"What are you doing?" Garvan gasped. "I've done nothing wrong!"

"Shut up!" The two soldiers began dragging him toward the building.

"But I have a—"

"I said *shut your trap.*" The first soldier cuffed the side of Garvan's head. Garvan's ears rang with the blow.

"Lad, you've just met Lord Riedel's press gang," said the other soldier, not unkindly. "Welcome to the Storn army."

Before Garvan could recover his senses, his pack was searched for weapons, shoved back at him, and he was propelled inside the building. Still reeling from the blow to his head, he tumbled to the floor. The place smelled of dust, mildew, and old beer, not to mention the waste buckets in the far corner. He pulled himself up and saw faces, a half dozen boys and young men.

"Zandru's purple balls, not another one," someone groaned.

"There's been a mistake," Garvan said. "I'm from Nira Plateau, not Storn."

"You think that makes a difference?" another man sneered.

"It appears that they care not where you are from," came another from across the room. A tall, fair-haired youth approached. "My name is Octavien, and I am pledged to wear the robes of a novice at Saint Valentine-of-the-Snows."

A young voice chimed in. "Me da told me yesterday that guards were blocking the road, although no one knew why, and to stay clear of it. I wisht I'd a-listened to him now."

Garvan paced the large common room. There was no way out, for the back rooms had were boarded up and the shutters had been nailed shut. The single exit was the door guarded by the soldiers. When he finished his circuit, the others made room for him on the long bench that was the single intact furnishing. He glanced at the wreckage of tables and other benches, wondering if he could fashion a weapon from the long splinters. Once he had time to calm down, however, he decided that it was foolhardy to go up against trained fighters with only a piece of wood. Besides knowing how to wrestle, he was fairly good with a sword, thanks to his summers with Morgan Storn. The best course of action was to wait for someone in authority to remedy the mistake.

As the night wore on, more men, most of them young, were shoved into the hut. Many of the newcomers were drunk. A few howled out off-key drinking songs until the others told them to shut up so they could sleep. Garvan settled on the dirty wood floor beside the boy who'd been promised to the monastery, and tried to ignore the snoring.

When the first red rays of dawn crept through the crevices, the door swung open. Along with the others, Garvan stumbled into the chilly morning. Most of them stood there, shivering and blinking in the dawn light. One of the soldiers handed out chunks of stale nutbread and allowed the conscripts to dip water from a barrel of none-too-clean rainwater.

Summoning his most confident air, Garvan approached a tall, beefy man wearing a sergeant's insignia. "Excuse me, sir. There has been a mistake." He pulled the copper from his belt pouch. "I have Lord Storn's oath..." His voice fell when the officer's gaze slid over the engraved words and he realized the man could not read.

"Ye canna bribe me with metal, boy. I'll take it that ye knew no better, but that's a hanging offense, that is. Now get back into line."

Garvan took his place beside a rough-looking lad, perhaps a year or two older, one of those who had been drunk. Now the youth was sober and pale-faced.

"I'm Cayo," the lad whispered by way of introduction. He glanced at Garvan's pouch, where he'd replaced the safe conduct. “What’s that you got there? A charm?”

“My name’s Garvan. It’s a safe conduct from Lord Storn.”

“Keep the copper to trade, Garvan. You be needing it.”

The group of conscripts marched up the road under the watchful eyes of the Storn soldiers, some of them mounted. Garvan, seeing the poor condition of his comrades’ footwear, was grateful for his stout boots, and also for the days of travel that had accustomed him to long walking. Even so, he was glad when the sergeant called a rest stop and ordered another round of bread, which was clearly the midday meal. The soldiers received dried meat and fresh apples in addition to the bread.

One of the older conscripts took advantage of the stop to dash for the nearest line of trees. A mounted soldier rode after him and returned a short time, dragging the runaway behind his horse. The soldier halted his mount where the rest of the conscripts could clearly see the man’s condition, the darkening bruises and the raw abrasions on the side of his face and showing through the shreds of his shirt. “Get back in line—at the front,” the soldier said. Although it obviously pained him to do so, the man complied. Garvan, watching in shock, recognized the symptoms of a broken collarbone, although there was no offer of treatment.

They slept that night in the open, huddled together, while the soldiers enjoyed tents around a fire. Fortunately, the weather was mild for late spring and there was no snow.

The road began to rise as the countryside turned mountainous. On the third day, Garvan, who was marching near the end of the column, passed the body of the man who’d tried to escape. There were no more attempts.

Toward the end of the fourth day, they arrived at an encampment where the road branched. A wooden fort controlled the crossroads and the village some distance beyond. Here they joined other conscripts, many of them farm and forest boys. The entire troop was herded into a central area, in front of a massive, spreading silverleaf tree. Off to one side stood ranks of tents, far too many for the number of officers present. Garvan spied another area where meat roasted over long firepits. His stomach rumbled at the smell.

"Get in line!" barked the sergeant from Garvan's group. Everyone shuffled into ragged order. Garvan ended up between Octavien, the pledged monk, and Cayo. Ordinarily, Garvan would not have sought Cayo out as a friend, but they'd marched together for enough days now that having two men he knew by his side gave him a rough sort of comfort.

Five officers strode to the front of the assembly. The oldest, with grey hair and beard, barked, "What a bunch of rotten root rats! You are now soldiers of the Army of Storn, and you will be trained to fight for Lord Riedel Storn, and—if need be—to die for him. You will now all take the oath of allegiance to Storn."

Muted protests rippled through the assembly. Garvan's belly clenched. Beside him, Octavien murmured his *cristoforo* prayers through muffled sobs. "Holy Bearer of Burdens, save me from this dishonourable fate..."

"Save your breath for the oath," muttered one of the others.

Garvan wavered on his feet, irresolute. What should he do—what *could* he do? If he took such an oath, he'd never see home again, not even if the mistake was later cleared up. An oath meant forever, or until Storn's enemies killed him.

"Look up," Cayo whispered.

Then Garvan saw the archers in the branches of the enormous tree in front of them. He spied two...three. More appeared behind them along the top of the fort wall.

"Raise your right hand," commanded the grey-haired officer.

To either side of the conscripts, soldiers drew their swords. One of the archers caught Garvan's eye and with a menacing smile drew his bow. Garvan's mouth went dry. Octavien fell silent. A hush descended upon the assembled conscripts.

"Repeat after me: I—give your name—do swear by Aldones, Avarra, Evanda, and Zandru—or whatever other gods you believe in—to well and truly serve Riedel, Lord of Storn, his heirs and successors. I will resist and smite the enemies and defend the House of Storn. I will fulfill my duty until my death or discharge. I swear it on my life and honour."

Garvan raised his right hand, along with the others. With his left, he felt the safe conduct in his belt pouch and reflected on the worth of such a promise. Under the laws of honour and age-old custom, he was now bound to the army of Storn. He had never felt so alone.

The oath completed, the conscripts filed over to the firepits, where they were given wooden eating trenchers and served slabs of meat, along with the usual nutbread. Garvan found Cayo, Octavien, and a couple of the others he knew. They settled, cross-legged, on the ground. Cayo had a small knife that hadn't been taken from him, as did Garvan, and they shared the knives around.

Octavien stared at his untouched meal, tears running down his cheeks. "What am I to do? I was pledged to Nevarsin. I dreamed of becoming an herbalist, not a killer."

"*Pledged.* You weren't a real monk yet, were you?" Cayo asked.

"No," Octavien admitted. "But that had been my dearest wish—"

"What does it matter?" Cayo interrupted. "You took the oath with the rest of us. We're all Storn soldiers now."

"I had no choice!" Octavien whimpered. "I should have done something—stood up to them! I am such a coward. Now it's too late."

Garvan, remembering the corpse beside the road, said nothing. What choice had any of them had?

"Well, your *cristoforo* god chose a different path for you," Cayo said. "You took the oath, so you're a soldier now. That's got to be less boring than washing dishes and mopping floors." He paused, his mouth spreading in a devilish grin. "Even if it was in an ale house."

March, march. Left. Right. Soldier's Oath. Left. Right. Double-time. Soldier's Oath. March, march. How to handle a sword and dagger, a sword and shield. Digging latrines. Scrubbing root vegetables. March, march. Left. Right. At the end of each day, the recruits were so exhausted, most of them fell asleep over their dinners. At least the food was plentiful, if plain.

As the days passed, the squadrons settled into working together. Garvan's sword skills had gotten rusty since those summers when Morgan taught him, but soon his muscles remembered the moves. He found himself ranked at the top of his group. The drillmaster took to using him to try out the others, knowing that Garvan had enough control to minimize accidental injuries. When left to choose his own sparring partner, Garvan often ended up with Cayo who, it turned out, knew something about fighting with knives.

From time to time, riders would gallop up the road, carrying messages for the officers and gossip for everyone else. From one of these, Garvan learned the reason for the conscriptions. For generations, an uneasy peace had held in this part of the Hellers, but now war threatened between Storn and the ambitious lord, Frazer Lanart. It was rumoured that he, being related to the Altons, possessed their Gift of forced mental rapport. Whether or not this was true, he seemed bent on conquering all the neighbouring kingdoms. For the first time, Garvan found a reason to fight—not for Lord Riedel Storn, but for his nephew and heir, Morgan.

As if in a dream, Garvan remembered those summers with Morgan, gazing into the endless mountain skies, wishing the summer and their friendship could go on forever. They'd spent hours exploring the ruins of an old keep, pretending they were liege and paxman. They'd been too young to exchange formal vows, but in their own way, they had pledged to one another with all the loyalty their boyish hearts possessed.

The captain announced a competition between the conscripted squadrons, with the reward a half-day in the village and ten *reis* each to spend there. The men trained even harder, and the sergeants took careful notice of their skill level. In the middle of an afternoon's training session, the sergeant of Garvan's team called him over. He pointed to Octavien and Tal, the skinny boy who wished he'd paid attention to his father's warning. Neither one of them was doing well. In fact, the two were the worst in the entire camp. Garvan, watching, thought it a wonder that they hadn't killed themselves yet. They were still using wooden practice swords instead of the short, heavy blades they'd all been issued.

The sergeant grunted his opinion. "Got a ways to go, those

two."

"Yes, sir," said Garvan.

"An army runs on teamwork."

"Yes, sir."

"So you and the alehouse rat will bring your buddies up to scratch or you'll all pay for it."

That night, as they sat around with their trenchers of grain-porridge, Cayo tapped Garvan on the shoulder. "Just how did the 'fish boy' from Nira learn to sword fight like a Comyn lord?"

All Garvan wanted was to sleep. Every joint and muscle ached. But talking about happier times would take his mind off the present. "When I was a boy, I spent a couple of summers at the Storn mountain hunting lodge. One day I got lucky and I knocked the sword from Morgan's hand. He lost his temper and came after me. I dropped my sword, grabbed him, and wrestled him into the mud of the exercise yard."

"You're joking!" said Tal, who'd been listening.

Garvan shook his head. He remembered the scene later that day when Morgan had lain in wait for him and demanded to know the trick. "After that, every time we could get away, Morgan and I went up to our favourite meadow in the hills above the lodge. I taught him to wrestle, and he taught me the sword."

Cayo clapped Garvan on the shoulder. "Let's do the same with Octavien and Tal."

Training began as usual at red dawn and lasted till supper, leaving the trainees bruised, battered, and exhausted. Each night, however, Cayo and Garvan took Octavien and Tal back to the field for another hour of training. At Cayo's insistence, Garvan taught them wrestling as well as swordplay, and Cayo shared his nastiest knife fighting tricks. As Cayo said, "You never know when it might come in handy." Although Tal and Octavien improved, their squad never won the night in the village. At least, Tal could now hold his own with a blade. Octavien turned out to be a fair wrestler, although hopeless with a sword. He likely could not bring himself to kill another man. Garvan fretted what might become of his friend in a battle; on impulse, he asked the sergeant if Octavien might be assigned to the healer's tent. The sergeant looked surprised, then thoughtful, then said he'd see what he could do.

A tenday later, another courier arrived, this one on a horse so lathered and blown, it had to be put down. Word spread like wildfire through the camp that war had come. The Lanart forces had overwhelmed Storn at the border. Morgan now commanded the fortress of El Lobo Negrón, hoping to halt the advance. The camp made ready to depart the following dawn.

They marched long and hard, not stopping until the gathering shadows made the mountain trails too dangerous. Finally, with only a day's travel to go, they spied the distant walls and towers shining like obsidian in the westering sun. The fortress, it was said, had been built by *laran*, its black stones shaped so accurately that not even a blade of grass could find root between them.

Sergeants took up the cry: "Double time! Double time!"

The road was steep. Garvan and his friends gasped for each breath, but they stuck together. The bloody sun was setting as they neared the watch towers. Bodies in the colors of Storn and Lanart littered the road to either side. The Storn forces hurried inside and the gates clanged shut behind them. The column stumbled to a halt in the middle of the stone-paved central courtyard. Here they joined another body of men, their ragged uniforms streaked with blood. Although Garvan's company was weary from the last uphill struggle, these men were in worse shape, for they had clearly just survived a bitter fight. Pallets had been set up along one side of the courtyard, and many of them bore bodies that were completely shrouded. A few older men, healers most likely, moved among the others, whose agonized moans sent shivers through the new arrivals.

"Form into ranks!" a sergeant yelled. Weary as they were, discipline took over and they obeyed.

A handful of officers left the keep and came to stand before them. It was a moment before Garvan recognized Morgan as chief among them, older and taller, but with the same red hair and storm-grey eyes.

"Men of Storn, you are most welcome among us." Morgan's voice, a fine baritone, carried well. "I will not hide from you how perilous our situation here is. Frazer Lanart's advance guard made an attempt on the fortress earlier today. We repulsed them, but with heavy losses. His full army will be at the gates by morning. We have few rations, and the summer drought means the mountain streams are low, although the castle well is, praise Aldones, full and clear. Know this: Lanart's army cannot pass as long as we hold El Lobo Negrón. We must hold fast! The fate of Storn rests upon us."

A ragged cheer answered him. With such a leader, Garvan thought, they had a chance and more than a chance.

"Stand by for inspection!" came the call.

As Morgan and his senior officers proceeded along the ranks, Garvan could not keep eyes front. He looked down the line, searching for his old friend. Morgan glanced up the row and their eyes met. A moment later, Morgan stopped in front of him.

"Garvan? Garvan of Nira?"

"Yes, Morgan. I mean, *vai dom*."

"By all the gods, it's good to see you!" Morgan clapped him on the shoulder. Garvan felt a fleeting moment of rapport between them, intensified by the physical contact. "Report to me when parade is dismissed."

An hour later, a corporal ushered Garvan into an office and sleeping cell that had once been the garrison commander's quarters. Morgan, who had been poring over maps spread over a battered old table, came over and took Garvan's hands in his.

"Garvan. Come, sit—" Morgan led the way past the table to the unlit fireplace, where two chairs of leather straps over wood had been drawn up. "I'd offer you something to drink, but it would be the same well water the men receive."

"That's all right, sir."

"Morgan, as we once were. At least in private."

Warmth suffused Garvan's face. "Morgan, then."

Morgan settled into his own chair. "How did you end up here?"

"Lord Riedel's press gang," Garvan replied. "I brought the Bronze K'bradon to Storn as is our custom. After I left, the press gang seized me." Garvan pulled out the copper plaque. "The safe conduct meant nothing."

"Just like my uncle," Morgan muttered. "He was never one to respect an oath to anyone but himself."

"One way or the other, I took the oath of allegiance to Storn."

"If I know men, your friends in your platoon are worth a thousand oaths to my uncle."

Memories surged up in Garvan, almost overcoming him. Here was the friend he remembered, the young lord to whom he had pledged his loyalty. But did Morgan remember, too?

"What is it, *bredu*?" Morgan asked in a low voice.

"Morgan, do you recall that day in the mountains? When we went up to that old, fallen-down keep above the meadow? It was just the two of us: I the boy from Nira, and you a Comyn, a Storn."

Morgan was smiling. "Yes, I recall it well..."

"That day, I swore an oath, an oath of allegiance to—" Garvan laughed, "—to Morgan, Lord of Storn. Later you told me never to mention it, in case your uncle should hear." He paused for a second. "That oath I took first and I took it willingly, even though I was not of age when such things are proper. *That* oath I will fulfill."

Before Morgan could reply, a sudden outcry rang from below. "Fire!" followed by more shouts and cries: "Fire! Fire!"

Morgan raced downstairs, Garvan at his heels. An eerie glow lit the courtyard, first orange, then red, then white, then yellow then orange again. The keep itself was untouched, but the hillsides beyond were surrounded by towering flames. Gigantic plumes of fire surged almost to the peaks above. Garvan's knees threatened to give way under him. He'd heard of such manifestations but had thought them things of legend, or atrocities so against nature that no sane man, be he commoner or *laran*-Gifted sorcerer, would perpetrate them.

"Aldones save us!" someone shouted, echoing Garvan's unvoiced prayer.

The men in the courtyard stopped work, and dozens more rushed out of the barracks, then froze at sight of the uncanny fires. The lookouts along the wall retreated from their stations, arms thrown up to shield their faces from the heat.

A boy ran across the courtyard. "Lords," he gasped. "The

sergeant in the tower told me to say the fire burnt up all the trees—all the bushes—all the grass—in only a few moments. It continues to burn but, sirs, there is no more fuel. Is it magic?"

"Not magic, lad," Morgan said. "*Laran.*"

"But there's no cinders, sirs," the boy continued as if he had not heard. "The smoke rises but no sparks as from a forest fire."

Morgan dismissed the boy with a kind word and then turned to Garvan. "With our only military *laranzu* dead, there's little we can do to defend ourselves. I sent to my uncle, begging him to dispatch another, but he refused. He said those precious resources were needed elsewhere." He paused, clearly restraining himself from openly criticizing his kinsman.

Garvan studied the flames. "Why keep to the mountainsides? Why not use *laran* against the walls themselves? If they launched a direct attack, we would all be burned meat by now." And yet, he could not help thinking, he could imagine no more noble end than to die at the side of the man he'd sworn himself to.

"Lanart wants the fortress intact," Morgan explained. Then: "Sergeant, get your lookouts back on the wall. We need to know what's going on."

The lookouts reclimbed the inner stone steps, hesitating at the heat. All but one turned back, and even at this distance, Garvan saw the blistering burns on their faces and hands. A few moments later, the single stalwart stumbled back down. He collapsed and fell the last few steps, and two of the other soldiers carried him to Morgan. Garvan could barely look at the poor man, so severe were the burns. In places, the skin looked charred. He wondered if the man could live, and prayed that Octavien's Bearer of Burdens might ease his pain.

"The fire comes no closer than the ditch," the wounded lookout said between barely-suppressed moans, "but there are no gaps, not even in front our gates. We are encircled, *vai dom*. Besieged." And with those words, he lost consciousness.

The men who had assisted the lookout paled, but recalled themselves when Morgan commanded the lookout to be taken with all tenderness of care to the infirmary. "I wish I had a Tower-trained healer to attend him," Morgan confided in

Garvan, "or a dozen, to reward such valor."

Very soon afterward, the flames surrounding the fortress leaped higher and higher, bathing the highest clouds in a ruddy glow. The sound was the most frightening part, however. The roar of a forest fire, like continuous thunder, accompanied the crackling, hour after nerve-wracking hour. There was nothing any of the defenders could do, except endure it.

That night, when the cooks went to the well to get water for breakfast, they found it had gone dry. Word spread quickly through the fortress. Thirsty men stood around the courtyard, grumbling.

One of the sergeants strode across the courtyard, causing the men to leap to attention. "Silence in ranks! Stop acting like a troop of babies in need of your nursemaids. We still have cisterns, so we still have water." He paused. "We'll go to half rations. The cooks are already at work for breakfast."

The chow line that morning was quiet. Breakfast was dry nut porridge, rabbit-horn jerky, and bitter *jaco*. The sun shone scarlet like fresh blood through the flames.

"This ain't good," Tal said to Garvan and Chayo as they stood in line. Octavien had been assigned to the healers and took his meals with them as their duties permitted. "Me mam used to slow bake turkey-cock pie. That's what we're going to be, slow-baked pie."

"Something's going to change soon," Garvan said.

"You got *laran*?" Cayo asked.

Garvan had always thought of *laran* as an exotic talent, belonging only to great lords and *leroni*. That summer with Morgan, he could have sworn he *felt* a mental bond, and since arriving at the fortress, that inkling had grown into certainty. And then too he'd always had what his family called "water sense," which often warned of danger.

"I've got a feeling," he replied.

The sun had passed the topmost towers when the flames directly in front of the gates parted and an emissary bearing the Lanart colors and a flag of parlay emerged. After being admitted, he was escorted to the keep. Negotiations between him and Morgan went on for several hours. Officers tried to keep order in the courtyard but stopped short of confining the entire army to the barracks. Storn soldiers stood around in their squadrons, all those who did not have active duties. After a time, the emissary emerged. Garvan, standing with his friends, was too far to read the man's expression. The keep doors remained closed through the succeeding hours in which the emissary made several more round trips.

Finally Morgan appeared on the steps of the keep, his face reddened by the flames. His copper-hued hair looked as if it, too, were on fire. Through their mental connection, Garvan sensed his friend's desperation. Within a few minutes, every man in the fortress had assembled. They fell silent facing their commander, not at formal attention but with a focus born of equal parts hope and despair.

"A choice lies before us, my friends," Morgan's voice carried through the courtyard. "A choice we must make, not out of fear but the hard reality of our situation. Our water is almost gone, as you know. Other supplies, including healing herbs, are exhausted, and our wounded will surely perish without them. Frazer Lanart has given us an ultimatum. He has a dozen *laranzu'in* in his service, and he swears he will burn us alive in the castle unless we surrender. I believe he will do it. Our only option is to accept his terms."

He paused, his shoulders rising and falling as he gathered himself. Not a whisper of breath could be heard in the courtyard. "In exchange for his clemency, everyone here must swear allegiance to the Lanarts, foregoing all previous oaths to Storn."

"An oath is an oath!" came a voice from somewhere behind Garvan.

"We'll not forsake ye, m'lord!"

"Death before dishonour!"

"Silence!" Morgan cried. "Every man here is free to choose not to take the oath. But Lord Lanart has made it clear that anyone who refuses will face hanging."

"Saint Valentine protect us," Octavien whispered.

"Zandru, more like," Cayo spat.

"Frazer Lanart has assured me that he will not order us to fight against Storn. He is not fool enough to do that," Morgan went on, his voice resolute. "I cannot command you, but I beg you to accept his terms. There is no shame in preserving your lives. Every man here has fought well and bravely. You have done everything possible to defend the House of Storn, and therefore you may surrender with your honour unstained. I urge you to keep your lives, which are equally precious to me." Morgan concluded by saying that Lanart had given them until the following dawn to make their decision. Then he dismissed the assembly.

As the men turned away, either back to the barracks or to mill around, talking in the courtyard, Garvan made his way to the steps of the keep. Morgan had not moved. Garvan, coming to stand beside him, thought that a word, a touch, a breath, might shatter him. But the next moment, Morgan touched Garvan lightly on the shoulder.

"I am grateful for your company, *bredu*. Come inside, for I have private words that I must say to you."

Once inside the commander's quarters, they both sank into chairs around a cold, dark hearth. For a time, Morgan said nothing, staring into the emptiness. The skin around his eyes looked bruised. Garvan needed no words to understand his friend's anguish. The psychic rapport between them shimmered invisibly.

"I do not fear for the men," Morgan said. "I did not flatter them when I said they had served honourably. Frazer Lanart is many things, but he knows the value of a good soldier. As for my own fate—" he made a dismissive gesture, "—that was sealed on the day of my birth. I have always known I would end up a pawn in the wars of greater men."

"No!" burst from Garvan. "Don't say that! You begged the men to not throw their lives away for the sake of an oath. Surely you—*you!*—are worth as much."

Morgan shook his head, a fleeting, weary smile on his lips. "But you, my old friend, I would not expose you to the burden of fighting for yet another realm not your own. There is little enough I can do to shield you, but what I can do, I shall."

"Me? Morgan, you must think of yourself, not me."

"The best way I can protect you—and you must do this of your own free will, Garvan—is to take you as my paxman. That way you cannot be held accountable for any actions given under my orders. Nor can you be treated as a common soldier, but according to the rules of honour."

Paxman? Their *laran* rapport deepened. It whispered in Garvan's mind, words he could not comprehend. Yet.

Stalling for time, Garvan drew the battered safe conduct copper from its pouch. "Morgan, I am your friend, and I will follow your commands. I love my brothers in my squadron—Cayo, Octavien, Tal, the others. At the same time, I am still angry that my safe conduct was ignored, that I was compelled into the Storn army, forced to take the oath to Lord Riedel. Now I am going to be forced take a second to Lanart. An oath is an oath, sanctioned by the gods. I want to be your paxman...but I am not sure that I am free to take *any* oath. To which of them must I be true? Does the one not cancel out the other? And if I break faith with an older loyalty, what does that make me?"

As if reflecting the passion behind Garvan's words, the flames rose even brighter for a moment, reflected against the fortress walls through the open windows.

"Oaths are tricky things, indeed," Morgan said in a choked voice.

"For generations we of Nira have called ourselves free people, servants of no Domain. But we also believe that an oath is binding and that oath must be given—and taken—honestly." Bitterness filled Garvan as he said, "The great lords play with oaths without conscience. Just like they play with the lives of their own people."

Morgan took Garvan's hand. In Garvan's mind, the instantaneous psychic rapport was like a mountain hidden behind clouds, when the clouds thinned away. He knew in that moment how much Morgan was hurt and angered by his words, but through the anger Morgan accepted the rightness of the accusation. Garvan also sensed Morgan's fear, fear of what might happen to his dearest friend, and for the army he commanded, and for what was to come next at the hands of Lord Lanart.

Then a terrible certainty descended on Garvan's shoulders: in order to defend Morgan from that fate, perhaps his only chance to keep Morgan alive, he must accept this new oath. He took the fisherman's knife from his belt and handed it to Morgan.

"I will be your paxman," Garvan said. "I take this obligation as an adult, fully capable of such a commitment, not the boy I once was. If my soul might choose, I would hold fast to that first oath we made to one another so many years ago."

Morgan took his dagger from its sheath and held it out.

Around the walls the flames roared.

The moment Morgan informed Lord Lanart's emissary of the surrender, the flames ceased. Instantly the day became chillingly cold. Morgan stood on the steps of the keep, Garvan as his paxman beside him.

"Stack your weapons by the gate, with the exception of personal knives or daggers." Morgan ordered. "Put essentials into a travel pack; gather what supplies you can carry. This is not going to be an easy march."

The gates swung open and the Lanart general, flanked by a circle of Tower-trained *laranzu'in*, rode in. The oath was administered to everyone, but not to Morgan and Garvan. Morgan was to make his surrender directly to Lord Lanart. This was to be an oath of personal fealty. Morgan would be no more than a bound servant. Garvan sensed the effort Morgan put forth to retain his dignity.

The remnants of the Storn army trudged out of the fortress and turned down the pass toward the Lanart lands. They left seven corpses hanging from the battlements, men too stubborn or too weary of living to swear themselves to their enemy.

The Storn troops made journey barely walking, more like stumbling, with just enough food to sustain them each day. Some who tried to escape were tracked by Lanart scouts; their heads brought back to the makeshift camps. Others failed to wake in the morning. After several tendays, they came within sight of Castle Lanart. Here they made camp and were supplied with food. Healers attended those in need of care. Some still grumbled about the oath, but more quietly than before.

At last the expected summons came. Hands bound and accompanied by Frazer Lanart's personal guards, Morgan presented himself to his new liege. Garvan accompanied him, aware of how they both looked—haggard, their clothing trail-stained and torn. Every weapon, including the fishing knife and the dagger they had exchanged, was taken from them.

As they entered the presence chamber, Frazer Lanart looked down on them from his throne, its upholstered back emblazoned with the colors of his House. He was a tall, muscular man, with dark red hair, cut short, and a slightly darker beard shot through with threads of silver. Two other men flanked the throne. The one to Lord Lanart's right must be his paxman, while the second was clearly a senior *laranzu*. The paxman came forward, directing Morgan to kneel. Garvan followed, the appropriate two steps behind, but remained standing.

"So, Morgan Storn," Frazier Lanart said, "you have given up your hopeless resistance. That shows good sense, for which I give you credit. I will in turn honour my agreement to spare the lives of all those whose loyalty is now assured. I will have need of an expanded army in the times to come."

"For that I am grateful...*vai dom*," Morgan said.

Frazer Lanart made a dismissive gesture. "It was sufficient for lesser men to take an oath all together. If one or two prove faithless, that is no matter. There is no shortage of gallows nooses. You, on the other hand—you will take the oath to me here, where I can hear the words with my own ears and see the truth in your eyes. This may be an oath under duress, but you will take it willingly."

Morgan said nothing. Garvan felt their *laran* rapport like a web of spidersilk gently dropping across their shoulders. Binding them together with invisible threads. Through it, he sensed the power of the *laranzu* as he took out his starstone. Pale blue light flared, filling the room and glimmering on the faces of everyone present.

Truthspell.

Garvan's belly clenched. He had heard of such things, although never thought to see it in life. Morgan could not lie, not in the slightest particular, or the deception would be instantly unmasked. From where he stood, he could not see Morgan's expression, only Frazer Lanart's look of expectant avarice, of hunger for power over his defeated enemy. Garvan reached out in his mind to Morgan, and felt Morgan's invisible hands slip into his and hold fast.

The paxman recited the words Morgan was to say, phrases that went beyond the usual pledge of loyalty. Frazer Lanart meant to bind Morgan as tightly and irrevocably as any Dry Towns slave. The recitation completed, silence fell on the chamber. Morgan remained as he was, on his knees, unmoving. Barely breathing.

"Well, man?" Frazer Lanart broke the tension. "Those are the words you are to say. What are you waiting for? Andres, tell him again—"

"No." Morgan's quiet voice resonated in the chamber.

"No? What do you mean, *no*?"

"No, I will not take such an oath." Morgan tilted his head in the direction of the *laranzu*. "Nor will I insult this man by swearing falsely."

"You—you will swear to me!"

Garvan could not see Morgan's expression, but Frazer Lanart was facing him directly, cheeks suffusing with ugly red. Lanart's eyes bulged and his lips drew back from his teeth.

"You will..."

Through their psychic bond, Garvan felt a wave of crushing pressure emanating from Frazer Lanart toward Morgan. It slammed against Morgan's natural shields, which shuddered and then held. But the energy streaming from the Lanart lord was no ordinary *laran*. Garvan had never sensed anything like it before. It seared and burned, akin to clingfire. Morgan trembled under the assault.

The *laranzu* recoiled, color draining from his face. The blue light of truthspell wavered and then winked out.

From Morgan's mind came a voiceless scream, as if he were being flayed alive. The integrity of his mind was failing fast. And then— Garvan knew what would happen. The Lanarts were related to the vastly powerful Alton Domain, and the Altons had been bred for the Gift of forced rapport. Frazer Lanart would take over Morgan's mind and dictate his actions, his very thoughts. Morgan would cease to be the man Garvan knew and loved, if he survived at all.

Hold on, Morgan—I'm here! Garvan threw the weight and force of his own mind into the bond between them. In a flash he caught the image of their joined hands—Morgan's grip going limp as lightning branches sizzled along his psychic channels—Morgan's mind howling in agony—his own invisible fingers tightening. Reeling his friend close and closer. Throwing his arms around Morgan. His own resolve hardening—a flare of hope from Morgan, then a burst of renewed strength—the two of them reinforcing each other—

The pressure from Frazer Lanart's Gift eased—a sense of puzzlement like a whiff of poison smoke—then came another blast and another, each splattering ineffectively against the shield of their combined *laran*. There was no dividing line between their minds, utterly open to one another, made stronger by the oaths freely given. No division, no difference—as smooth and unblemished as polished steel—or the finest mirror.

And like a mirror, their joined minds turned reflective. Neither had any thought of counterattack, only of preserving the person most dear to him. The attempted forced rapport found no crevice, no opening—only the perfectly twinned image of itself.

Back sped the power that fuelled the assault, back at Frazer Lanart's unguarded mind. For a moment, the hurricane of destructive energy engulfed them all. Had he been able to do so, Garvan would have turned away from the devastation that followed, but he dared not falter in his part of the shield. Dimly, as if through a shrouded veil, he sensed the waves of corrosive mental energy surging into Frazer Lanart's mind. As if drawn by a magnet, the power poured into the *laran* centers of Lanart's brain, the origin of his psychic attack. Then Garvan's internal vision went opaque until he seemed to be floating in an ocean of azure-tinted light.

Slowly, slowly the light resolved. He felt Morgan's mind,

linked to his through their rapport, the rapport that had arisen and been nourished by their love for one another. Moments seeped by. The *laran* bond fell away, leaving him separate and breathless.

He could feel his body again. Vision returned. He was still standing, impossible as that seemed. Morgan knelt on the carpeted floor, although he had fallen forward and braced himself on his hands. And Frazer Lanart—Frazer Lanart slumped in his throne. For a moment, Garvan feared he might be dead, with those staring, whitened eyes and slack mouth, the drool dripping onto his chest. But that chest rose and fell, stuttered, and rose and fell again.

The paxman rushed to his master's side, crying out his name. The *laranzu* examined Frazer Lanart with starstone and mind, and shook his head. Garvan was no healer, but he did not think the Lanart lord would survive very long. In the commotion that followed, the stricken man was carried away, his wife and heirs sent for, and his generals summoned. By this time, Morgan had regained his composure enough to argue the case that he and Garvan had nothing to do with Frazer Lanart's condition. Indeed, the *laranzu* himself declared that, since they were the victims of a *laran* attack and had not made any overt counter-attack, they were innocent.

"This is the end of the campaign," the most senior of the generals declared. "Our duty now is to the next Lord Lanart and the stability of the realm."

Morgan faced him. "The matter is not so simple. I could well bring charges of unlawful use of *laran* against Lord Frazer Lanart—who still lives—or against his heirs. A court of Comyn peers will rule in my favour and then, I swear to you, I will exact revenge."

The general, clearly taken aback, said, "I cannot act for Lanart. Only Lord Frazer or his heirs can do that."

"You can issue *military* orders for their benefit. And you will."

"What terms will satisfy you, *vai dom*?"

"I do not ask you to put Lanart at risk, only that you keep to what is yours. You will therefore release my men and withdraw your forces immediately from El Lobo Negrón. And you will give me your personal pledge that when the matter of the inheritance of your House is settled, you will advise that no further invasion of Storn be attempted. I will not hold you responsible for the results of that counsel, only that you give it."

The general bowed his head. Garvan thought the man might have knelt, had he been less proud. "That is more than any man could ask. I will issue the orders, and I will plead your case to the best of my abilities. May the gods strike me dead if I prove false."

Morgan remained at the castle only long enough to ensure that all the Storn soldiers were released from their enforced oath. Garvan stood at his side as Morgan announced that the men were free to return to their homes or to continue in his service, as they wished.

"My uncle conscripted your service," Morgan said, "but you have proven yourselves loyal. I will not hold a single man to a promise given under duress. I welcome those who chose to remain, and for those of you who go your own way, I say to you, *Adelandeyo*. Go with the gods." As the meaning sank in, more and more of the men cheered.

The sergeants set about organizing those who chose to return to El Lobo Negrón with Morgan, the better part of the forces. While they were preparing to march, Morgan took Garvan aside.

"And you, my friend, you have but to ask and I will release you, too. You are free to choose—return to the wilds of Nira and your family, and catching those delicious fish—or remain with me."

For a long moment, Garvan did not know how to answer. He remembered his words from the night he had formally become Morgan's paxman: *"If my soul might choose, I would hold fast to that first oath we made to one another so many years ago.*

If my soul might choose...

Confusion vanished like morning mist. "I must go home, so that my father knows I am still alive, and to relate all that has happened. But then I will return to your service. Morgan, I offered you that oath with my whole heart—" He broke off, unable to say more.

"As I did to you," Morgan replied, grasping Garvan's hands. "And I will honour it, and you, to the last of my days. For oaths may be tricky things, but the word of such a friend and brother is worth more than all the kingdoms of the world."

Crème de la Crème

by Deborah Millitello

A few years ago, I participated on a panel considering story endings, and scribbled the note: "What do we want to stay in the reader's mind—cliff hanger or chocolate on the pillow?" This delightful tale is very much the latter, in more ways than one.

Deborah Millitello published her first story in 1989 in *Marion Zimmer Bradley's Fantasy Magazine*. Since then her stories have appeared in various magazines such as *Dragon Magazine; MZB's FM,* including the third-place Cauldron winner "Do Virgins Taste Better?"; *Science Fiction Age*; and anthologies such as *Aladdin, Master of the Lamp; Sword and Sorceress; Tales of Talislanta*; and *Bruce Coville's Book of Nightmares*. Her novels include *Thief's Luck* and *The Water Girl*. Her collection, *Do Virgins Taste Better? and Other Strange Tales* came out in 2015 Word Posse. She spends her free time baking, making jams and marmalades, knitting & crocheting, and gardening. A member of the Alternate Historians writers group, she lives in southern Illinois with her husband Carl, has three children, eight grandchildren, and a great-grandchild. She works at a doctor's answering service as her day job.

The Thendara kitchen was in frantic chaos when Telana walked in, still yawning in the chilly early morning. All the kitchen staff from the head cook down to the vegetable gardeners were chatting excitedly.

"What's going on?" Telana asked, rubbing her eyes and looking around for a cup of hot *jaco*.

"The Terrans!" Mila said, pulling her apron over her gray uniform. "The Terrans are coming to a banquet!"

Telana stopped dead still and stared at her friend and fellow pastry chef. "Terrans? Here? When?"

"In ten days!" Mila's thin face was flushed, and her eyes were wide with excitement. "Daylynn told Merit who told Sarren who told Beal who told Jinny that she overheard one of the lords speaking to the chief steward. The lord said the Comyn were giving a banquet to welcome the Terrans to Thendara."

"To welcome them? But they've been on Darkover for years."

"But they've never been invited to a banquet here." Mila paused and leaned closer. "The Comyn are trying to make a new treaty with the Terrans so the lord said it was imperative we impress the Terrans. And we only have ten days to prepare!"

Ten days! Telana thought as she grabbed her own apron. *So little time!* "But I heard their machines make their food. What can we possibly make for them?"

"I don't know, but we might be able to replicate some of their foods with our ingredients. Head matron is speaking with the chief steward right now. She should be back any moment."

Cleery, the head matron of the kitchen, hurried through the kitchen door, her round face frowning with thought. She smoothed a few strands of grey hair from her forehead. "We must prepare the most elaborate feast, including some Terran delicacies. They have graciously agreed to try some of our own food. It is imperative we impress the Terrans so they will sign the treaty with our lord."

"But how will we be able to make Terran foods?" Telana asked.

"I will try to find Terran recipes," Cleery said with a sigh.

"How many do we have to prepare for?"

"Possibly one hundred. Or more. Now let's get started."

Mila rested her fists on her thin waist. "I'll make goldflower cakes with wild jooliberry filling and decorated with candied goldflower blossoms," she said, "and apple tarts, too."

"I'll make nut-coated honey cakes and jooliberry pies. But we need something special," Telana said, her grey eyes glancing around the massive kitchen for an idea, "something different, something completely Terran. I hope head matron can find a good Terran recipe that we can make."

"I hope we can get enough jooliberries and goldflowers," Mila said, tying her apron strings in a bow. "It's nearing the end of the season."

For the next five days cartloads of fruit and vegetables, flour and other baking ingredients, cages of fowl, haunches of meat, and barrels of beer and wine arrived at the kitchen door almost hourly. Just storing the deliveries in the pantries and cellars took most of the staff.

By the sixth day the menu was set except for the special Terran dessert.

Cleery looked troubled as she spoke to Telana and Mila. "I found several recipes for the meat course, but I haven't been able to find dessert recipes that we can make for the Terrans other than the same type of cakes we make. Terrans don't let us have access to their machines. Our own desserts will have to suffice."

Telana watched as Cleery walked away. "There has to be something extra special we can make, some recipe we have the ingredients for." She tapped her cheek thoughtfully and scrunched up her mouth. "Wait," she said suddenly, turning to Mila. "I can ask my cousin, Fairen! He's worked for the main ambassador in the Terran zone for months. Maybe he can suggest something."

"I hope so."

After the evening meal was served at the castle, Telana walked toward her cousin's house on the south side of the city. The air was cool and filled with the fragrance of midsummer flowers. The streets were nearly deserted since most people were at home for the evening meal.

Her cousin Fairen was a metal smith who worked in the Terran sector to learn more skills and had an amiable relationship with the Terrans. Telana hoped he could suggest something exceptional that she could make for the banquet, something so exceptional, the Terrans would instantly sign the treaty.

She knocked on the heavy wooden door of the narrow two-story house. Soon she heard footsteps coming from inside.

Fairen opened the door and grinned widely. "Telana!" he said in a booming voice. He wrapped his muscled arms around her, lifted her off the ground, then set her back on her feet. "It's been too long since you've come to see us. Morene will be delighted. She made some honey cakes, and I know you love her honey cakes. Come in, come in!"

He stood aside while Telana squeezed past him.

Five children sat at the wooden table, munching on little square cakes coated with honey and ground nuts. Morene poured juice in mugs for them all. When she saw Telana, Morene gave a shriek of delight.

"How are you?" she said, hurrying over to give Telana a hug. "And I just made honey cakes for tonight. Did the aroma draw you down from the castle?"

"Of course," Telana said. "Like a magnet draws steel."

"Sit down and help yourself," she said. "Raul, move over so Telana can sit down."

A blond-haired boy popped a honey cake in his mouth, then scooted over to make room on the bench for Telana. She sat down and took one of the still warm cakes and took a bite. "I make good honey cakes," she said, savoring the sweet, nutty dessert, "but not as good as yours. You should be working at the castle."

Morene laughed. "With this gang of ruffians?" She motioned at the children. "No. Someone has to keep them out of trouble."

"I heard the Terrans are coming to Thendara Castle," Fairen said. "Must be busy in the kitchen,"

"Extremely," Telana said. "Actually, that's one of the reasons I came. You spend time in the Terran sector. I need your help."

Fairen raised his eyebrows and tilted his head. "My help? How?"

"I have to make a Terran dessert, but I don't have a recipe or even an idea of what they like. Even head matron couldn't find out what we could make. Does their food really come from machines?"

"Most of it does," Fairen said, "but they have some gardens and they buy some food from the city markets."

"But is there a dessert, something that's completely Terran that I could make for them?"

Fairen chewed on the side of his lower lip for a few moments, then his dark eye twinkled. "There is one, and it's the ambassador's favorite."

Telana nearly ran back to the castle, excitement warming her against the chilly evening. She hurried to the servants' quarters and knocked on Mila's door.

Mila was in her night dress and yawning as she opened the door. She blinked several times as she stared at Telana. "Do you need something?" she asked sleepily.

"I've got it," Telana said. "A Terran recipe. It's one of their favorites."

Mila's jaw dropped open. "You did? What is it? Is it hard to make? Can we get it made in time?"

Telana laughed. "My cousin had the information. He said he'd tried it once and it was good. We can get everything we need — well, most of what we need. We might have to substitute a few things, but it should be fairly easy. We can make a sample batch tomorrow and see if head matron approves."

Mila grinned. "You are amazing!"

"See you in the morning."

The sun was still sleeping behind the mountains when Telana walked into the kitchen. Cleery was there, supervising three new maids on making porridge and breakfast cakes.

"Head matron," Telana said, "I have a Terran recipe."

Cleery whirled around toward her. "How did you find one?"

Telana explained about her cousin and the recipe. "I'd like to make a batch today. That way we can taste it and see if it's acceptable."

"Yes!" Cleery said. "Let me know when it is finished."

Mila arrived minutes later. She and Telana began gathering the ingredients: eggs, cream, milk, honey, jooliberries, toasted nuts. Mila crushed the jooliberries and mixed in the toasted nuts while Telana beat the eggs and added the honey, then slowly added the cream and milk. Mila mixed in the berry-nut mixture, then Telana poured it all into a metal tin and put on its tight-fitting lid. They placed the tin inside a larger tin and added ice chips and salt, then set it in the root cellar and covered it with a thick blanket.

"We can check it after breakfast," Telana said.

After breakfast was served, Telana and Mila hurried to the cellar, carrying a large spoon. Removing the blanket and the lid, Telana stirred the nearly frozen mixture with the spoon.

"A little longer," Telana said. "We'll check back before midday, and we'll bring head matron, too."

Telana made tiny nut tarts and stewed cone-apples for the midday meal, but her thoughts were in the cellar with the Terran dessert. As soon as the tarts were out of the oven, she called to Mila, grabbed a spoon, and the two of them went to find Cleery.

"We think it's ready," Telana said, glancing at Mila. "We'd like your opinion."

Cleery nodded and followed them to the cellar.

Removing the blanket and the lid, Telana took a spoonful of the frozen mixture and offered it to Cleery. She tasted it, rolled it around on her tongue, then licked her lips and smiled. "Good, but it needs to be sweeter, I think. This will do nicely, but we'll need much more than one tin full."

"Yes, head matron," Telana said, her heart beating quickly with satisfaction.

When Cleery left, Telana and Mila grasped each other's forearms and gave a quiet shout.

"We'll have to start early in the morning of the banquet to make enough dessert," Mila said. "At least ten tins full."

Telana looked around the cellar. "There won't be room enough for that many in this cellar. And we can't keep them in the kitchen. It will be too hot in there."

"What about the ice cave behind the castle?"

"That would be perfect! We can bring one tin down at a time so the dessert won't melt. But we'll need a lot of kitchen help to accomplish it."

Mila nodded. "Let's take this tin up and share it with the kitchen staff."

Grinning, Telana said, "Yes, let's."

The morning of the banquet, all the kitchen staff was up before the sun. Meat and fowl were spitted and set to roast. Root vegetables were peel or scraped; other vegetables were sliced and marinated in vinegar and nut oil. Soups were set in kettles to simmer. Bowls of fruit were assembled, and loaves of bread were set to rise for baking. The kitchen began heating up to a nearly uncomfortable temperature.

Telana and Mila were relieved when a cartload of clear, green jooliberries arrived at the kitchen door along with a crate of goldflowers. Not long afterwards, another cart bearing large tin cans of milk and cream arrived.

"We can mix the Terran dessert first," Telana told Mila, "a couple of batches at a time since it's too much to do all at once. After we set the tins in the ice cave, we can bake our other desserts."

In a large bowl, Telana beat the eggs, then poured in the cream and milk. Mila crushed the jooliberries and ground nuts, added honey until it tasted sweet enough, then poured it into the egg-and-cream mixture.

Telana dipped her finger into the liquid and licked it off. "Just right" she said. "I could use a cup of jaco. How about you?"

Mila wiped her forehead on her sleeve. "Me, too."

Telana motioned to one of the young girls helping in the kitchen. "I need two cups of *jaco*."

The girl nodded and sped away.

"We need some boys to carry the small and large tins up to the ice cave and chip lots of ice," Telana said. "And bring salt. And blankets."

"Here's the *jaco*," the serving girl said and poured the steaming liquid into the milk mixture.

Telana and Mila gasped simultaneously and stared at the bowl.

"No!" Telana said. "It was for us to drink, not put in the bowl! This was supposed to be the special treat for the Terrans, and now it's ruined!"

The girl looked up at Telana, and tears started down her young face. "I'm sorry," the girl whimpered. "I'm sorry. I'm sorry."

Telana clenched her fists and trembled with anger as she glared at the girl. The child looked so upset, Telana gradually calmed down and slowly patted her on the shoulder, trying to keep her voice even. "It's all right. It's all right. Go on. Help the other cooks."

The girl hurried away, wiping her eyes.

"It *is* ruined!" Mila said, distraught. "This was enough to make two or three tins! And there's not enough time to get more ingredients. What can we do?"

Telana sighed, then took a spoon and tasted the mixture. It actually tasted good! Slightly spicy, more flavorful than the original. She let Mila taste it, too. Mila's eyes widened, and she slowly nodded her head.

"We can add *jaco* to all the tins," Telana said, smiling.

The banquet was well underway when Telana sent two kitchen boys to bring the first of the tins to the kitchen. She and Mila scooped the frozen dessert into small bowls and set them on trays along with the cakes, pies, and tarts. The serving men kept carrying the trays out to the banquet hall until all the guests were served. There was still one tin of dessert left.

"Can the kitchen and serving staff have the rest?" Telana asked Cleery.

"Yes," Cleery said, her wrinkled face wrinkling even more as she smiled.

"And could Mila and I take a peek at the banquet, just to see if the Terrans liked the dessert?"

Cleery glanced around the kitchen. "Everything is in hand, only the clean-up to do. Certainly. You can watch from the upper balcony, but don't be seen."

The two hurried from the kitchen, up the back stairs, to the long balcony that looked down on the great banquet hall. They knelt down and stared between the posts of the railing. Finely dressed Comyn lords and ladies intermixed with Terrans, dressed in heavy clothes. They all sat at the oblong tables and tasted the frozen dessert. There was silence for a few moments, then the Terran ambassador, a man with short, thick, white hair stood up and raised his glass of wine.

"We want to make trade agreements with someone who knows how to treat foreign guests. Your hospitality has convinced us that we should sign the treaty with you. This feast is indeed marvelous, but this last course," he paused and smiled, "this is the best. It has been many years since I tasted truly homemade ice cream. Thank you!"

"Hear, hear!" the other Terrans said, clapping their hands.

The Comyn lords and ladies raised their glasses to the Terran, and everyone drank a toast.

Telana and Mila looked at each other and grinned. "That's kitchen diplomacy," Telana said.

About the Editor

Deborah J. Ross is an award-nominated author of fantasy and science fiction. She's written a dozen traditionally published novels and somewhere around six dozen pieces of short fiction. After her first sale in 1983 to Marion Zimmer Bradley's *Sword & Sorceress*, her short fiction has appeared in *The Magazine of Fantasy and Science Fiction, Asimov's, Star Wars: Tales from Jabba's Palace, Realms of Fantasy, Sisters of the Night, MZB's Fantasy Magazine*, and many other anthologies and magazines. Her recent books include Darkover novels *Thunderlord* and *The Children of Kings* (with Marion Zimmer Bradley); *Collaborators*, a Lambda Literary Award Finalist/James Tiptree, Jr. Award recommended list (as Deborah Wheeler); and *The Seven-Petaled Shield*, an epic fantasy trilogy based on her "Azkhantian Tales" in the *Sword and Sorceress* series. Deborah made her editorial debut in 2008 with *Lace and Blade*, followed by *Lace and Blade 2, Stars of Darkover* (with Elisabeth Waters), *Gifts of Darkover, Realms of Darkover*, and a number of other anthologies.

The Darkover® Anthologies

THE KEEPER'S PRICE, 1980
SWORD OF CHAOS, 1982
FREE AMAZONS OF DARKOVER, 1985
OTHER SIDE OF THE MIRROR, 1987
RED SUN OF DARKOVER, 1987
FOUR MOONS OF DARKOVER, 1988
DOMAINS OF DARKOVER, 1990
RENUNCIATES OF DARKOVER, 1991
LERONI OF DARKOVER, 1991
TOWERS OF DARKOVER, 1993
MARION ZIMMER BRADLEY'S DARKOVER, 1993
SNOWS OF DARKOVER, 1994
MUSIC OF DARKOVER, 2013
STARS OF DARKOVER, 2014
GIFTS OF DARKOVER, 2015
REALMS OF DARKOVER, 2016
MASQUES OF DARKOVER, 2017
CROSSROADS OF DARKOVER, 2018

The Marion Zimmer Bradley Literary Works Trust publishes a quarterly newsletter with news of Darkover and the Trust's other projects. To subscribe, go to *www.mzbworks.com*.

91870527R00165

Made in the USA
Lexington, KY
26 June 2018